THE BAND 4

The Air We Breathe

BY MARGUERITE NARDONE GRUEN

 FriesenPress

Suite 300 - 990 Fort St
Victoria, BC, V8V 3K2
Canada

www.friesenpress.com

ISBN
978-1-4602-8353-0 (Hardcover)
978-1-4602-8354-7 (Paperback)
978-1-4602-8355-4 (eBook)

1. Fiction, Romance

Distributed to the trade by The Ingram Book Company

I would like to dedicate this book to:

My sister Jeanine for encouraging me to publish this.

My brother Frank for always just agreeing with anything I want to do.

My brother Joe for continuously telling me how proud of me he is for writing this book.

I would like to dedicate this book to:

My nephew Patrick who told me never to give up.

My friend Lisa S for all of her encouraging words while I was writing this.

The Awakening

Rain! Rain again! Marguerite thought, as she woke up in her hotel room in London. She didn't even have to look, because she could hear the heavy drops pinging on the windows. What was she going to do all day with it pouring like that again? All the plans to take tours around the city were on hold for yet another day. Day two in London of the personal holiday she was taking for herself and all she could think of was how she would be held hostage for another day—by rain!

Being a hostage was something she was used to though. At 27, she felt she had been held hostage her whole life by her parents—her strict Italian father and her mother, who always cowered to his old fashioned ways. She had lived under a rock her whole life, but not anymore. No more being terrified of her parents or anything else.

She remembered getting the phone call from the police saying there had been an accident on a country road back in Pennsylvania. Both her parents had been killed immediately when they swerved to avoid hitting a deer. At first she'd felt sorrow and shock. Then she stopped feeling bad and realized that she was finally out of prison. She didn't feel bad; she felt relief. At 27, she could finally control her own life and do things she'd always dreamed of. What Marguerite did feel bad about was not feeling bad about it anymore.

The day was already dreary and she didn't want to make it worse by thinking about a life she wanted to put behind her. She had just woken up from a long nightmare. She had finally been born. Now she just had to decide what to do with the rest of her life to make it something worth living for.

∞

Rain again! Chase thought as he looked out the window of the recording studio. His band mates were there with him, but he felt very alone. *Ten straight days of rain and gray.* He was stressed enough. Why couldn't the sun come out even for a little while to help lessen this pain and anxiety? He had something terrible he was thinking of doing. It would kill his three best friends. No, not friends; brothers. To call them friends, even best friends, would be an insult. The weight of that decision was killing him too. How could he tell them he didn't want to record anymore? How could he tell his brothers that he couldn't go on the road, not even one more time?

He knew they knew. Anyone who saw him knew. The deep circles under his eyes gave him away. Everyone knew he wasn't sleeping or eating. He couldn't look at any of them in the face. Not Blake, who was his oldest brother at 24; not Drew, who was the same age as Chase at 23; and not Quinn, who was only 21 but acted like he was 51.

His brothers were all just waiting for him to say it out loud and praying for some kind of miracle.

∞

Marguerite shook her head. *I am not spending another day in my room or roaming around this hotel, no matter how beautiful it is.* She felt like royalty in her suite, decorated with lavish window treatments and Queen Ann furniture. She had the bell captain get her a cab to take her shopping at some popular department stores. Since gaining her freedom, she always bought some personal things for herself from wherever she visited, as a reminder—no, a *fond* reminder—of where she'd traveled and how happy she finally was. When she was done and got back to the hotel, she stumbled past the bell captain, waving him off, and clumsily carted all her packages to her room herself.

She tried on everything again and decided that yes, she really did like all of her purchases. She was still on the fence with the black pumps though. Heels! She hated heels and didn't know if she could even walk in them. The sales person had talked her into them when she bought the pretty little black dress. *Hmm.* It was hanging up and seemed to be speaking to her, saying, "Put me on for dinner tonight." So maybe she just would!

She showered and got ready, pulling her long brown hair back into a thick braid, which she coiled into a bun. She put on makeup. She wasn't fond of that either, but she wanted to highlight her light brown eyes. When she was satisfied with her facial artwork, she slipped into the dress. Now she was ready to go to dinner in the formal dining room at the hotel.

When she got off the elevator, she thought she saw heads turning, but quickly dismissed the idea. *Why would I turn heads?* She couldn't really look anyway, because she was still trying to maneuver in the heels. Oh, how she hated heels!

During her shopping excursion, she had seen a coffee shop a few buildings away from the hotel. After dinner, she thought she would change into something more comfortable, grab her book and head there to spend the evening reading and just being around people. Luckily, it finally stopped raining, so she could walk there without getting wet.

At the coffee shop, Marguerite had gotten comfortable, sitting at a table near a beautiful fireplace reading her book, when she was interrupted by a strange feeling, like someone in distress. She felt butterflies, and then her stomach flipped. *Where is this coming from?* She didn't know anyone in London, let alone in the coffee shop. Even if she did, why would she be feeling their distress? She tried to dismiss it and concentrate on her book, but found herself reading the same page over and over again and still not knowing what it said.

Finally, she put her book down and looked around, noticing someone sitting by himself wearing a hoodie. He was looking down at the table, staring at it with a blank look on his face. Somehow, she knew it was him stopping her from reading. She felt anxiety dripping off him, and it scared her. *How could I be feeling his feelings?*

She just wanted it to stop. Making up her mind, Marguerite walked up to the clerk behind the counter and pointed over at the man. "What is that person drinking? And can you make another of the same but decaffeinated?"

∞

Uh oh, Chase thought, seeing a woman standing over him in the coffee shop, just staring at him. *I've been recognized.* He was in no mood to speak to a fan, and took a deep breath in preparation. Then she did something completely unexpected. She took his coffee away from him. Right from his hands! That threw him a bit. He took a closer look at her and kept staring. Once their eyes met, he couldn't look away. Her beautiful brown eyes are so filled with life, and swimming with emotion.

"I *feel* your anxiety six tables away," she said, sympathetically. "You should try to stay away from caffeine." Slowly, she placed another coffee on the table and slid it in front of him. It said *decaf* in white chalk on the side. She gave him a kind smile before walking back to her table... and it left him wanting more.

She walked back to her table, realizing that he probably thought she was crazy. *I can't believe I just approached him like that! Someone I don't even know.* Flustered, and now completely incapable of concentrating on her book, she sank down in her seat and let out a big sigh. Then she felt him again and looked up. He was standing in front of her table.

She felt immediately drawn to him, and somehow knew the feeling was mutual. Again, she *felt* it. She didn't realize who he was until he introduced himself.

"Hello, I'm Chase Martin."

Marguerite gave him a look that seemed to ask, "*Okay, and I should know that name... why?*

Chase continued. "*The Band 4.*"

Then it hit her. *Oh!* Then she thought about that rock she had lived under for twenty-seven years. *Okay, even I know who he is now.*

She hadn't recognized him with the scruffy blond beard he was sporting. Marguerite invited Chase to sit down because he was just standing there and it didn't look like he wanted to leave. Truthfully, she didn't want him to leave either. His hair was blond and wavy and framed his face, but she was looking directly into the biggest blue eyes she had ever seen. *How beautiful!* Yet, how sad he looked at the same time. She wondered what could be so bad that it made him look like that, and her heart started to ache for him. She didn't even know him, but her heart ached.

They sat and talked like they had known each other their whole lives, and didn't even realize they had been sitting there for hours until the clerk came over to say that the coffee shop was getting ready to close. Thinking they would have to leave each other at that point, they both doubled over, as though the wind had been knocked out of their lungs. The blood drained from both their faces. When their eyes met, there was something there. They both felt it. Some kind of emotion. Something they were both feeling but silently dismissed because they just didn't know what to think about it.

Chase looked at Marguerite. "Can we just walk? I really don't want to leave you yet." Marguerite didn't want to leave him yet either. She gave him another warm smile. They were both wondering the same thing: *How could they feel so drawn to each other?* He took her hand and put it through his arm as they walked, as if to lead her around town, and that somehow soothed them both. Chase felt that he needed to touch her and Marguerite felt the same about him. After hours of talking and walking, they wound up at his house. He knew that she was staying at a hotel not far from the coffee shop, but she hadn't even paid attention to where they were walking.

Marguerite checked her watch and saw that it was around three in the morning. *Where did those hours go?* They had been walking all night. She hadn't even noticed that a bodyguard was following close behind them, tasked with keeping Chase safe.

"Please stay with me," Chase said. "It's so late already."

She nodded, and noticed his eyes light up. He smiled affectionately at her.

As they entered the house, she looked at him, suddenly nervous about her decision to stay, but when he took her by the hand, she felt safe. He led her up to his bedroom. Marguerite froze just inside the door, looking at the large bed and then back at him. He immediately noticed her concern. "I won't bother you. Please don't worry." He went to the closet and gave her one of his t-shirts to wear to bed.

She felt his sadness and wanted to help him. Why did she feel so connected to him? "Somehow," she said, "I feel you need me." She noticed the dark circles under his tired eyes. He looked weary, like he hadn't slept in weeks.

He nodded quietly, somehow knowing that she wasn't referring to sex and being perfectly okay with that—for now. He turned his back so that she could change into the t-shirt, which was so big he knew she would be swimming in it. When he turned back, he saw that he was right, and that she had gotten into his bed. She was holding out her arms to him. He gravitated towards her, climbing under the covers and just holding her for a few long, wonderful moments.

Marguerite savored the feeling of his arms around her for as long as she trusted herself to do so, and then gestured for him to roll over so they could get some sleep.

Laying the back of his body to the front of hers, Chase felt her comforting arms wrap around him, holding him close as she gently caressed his face and hair. He felt the warmth of her embrace, along with the connection he felt toward her, and it gave him peace. After being awake for days on end, he finally felt that he was going to get some sleep.

When Chase woke up the next day, he felt like he was starting to come back to life. Then he rolled over and Marguerite was gone. The t-shirt he gave her to wear was folded neatly on the couch in front of the fireplace in his bedroom. He panicked. Then he heard her downstairs in the kitchen and started to relax.

When he got downstairs, he saw that Marguerite was looking for something. He smiled, watching her for a moment, and then asked, "What are you looking for?"

"Coffee, but you don't have any. No silverware, no dishes, no pots, and nothing in the refrigerator. You do live here right?" He nodded. He couldn't get the smile off his face. He was happy. "Well," she said, "since you have nothing in the house for me to make you breakfast, I should head back to the hotel." As soon as she said it, Chase and Marguerite both doubled over once again, like the wind was knocked out of them. Then they slowly stood up and stared at each other. There was that feeling again. They had both felt it in the coffee shop, and now here it was again. At that moment, they didn't know whether they should talk about it or run away from each other screaming.

Don't let her go, Chase thought. *She's bringing you back to life. You're happy!*

Chase shook his head. "No, please don't leave." There was desperation and panic in his voice. "Stay here with me while you are in London. Don't leave!"

Rooting through some kitchen drawers, opening and closing them like a maniac, he finally pulled out a key and held it out to her. "I have to get to work at the studio. My mates are already wondering where I am by now. I know you have to go to your hotel, all your things are there, but will you come back and stay with me?"

Her eyes were glued to the key he was holding out in one shaking hand. She could hear the panic in his voice. *Why is my heart breaking for him?*

In that moment, Marguerite made up her mind and answered quietly. "Yes, I'll stay with you." *What is happening here?*

He handed her the key and wrapped his arms around her. *How can I do this?*

He immediately calmed down and she felt him start to relax. *Why do I feel him!?*

He was in the shower getting ready to go and she was in the kitchen making a list of things she needed to pick up: groceries, dishes, and pots to start. Definitely coffee! The list would be long. Then she noticed the rest of the house. Her heart almost stopped as she walked around the other rooms. It was like no one lived there. *No wonder he feels lost.* The house was cold and colorless. There were no paintings or pictures on the walls and hardly any furniture. Almost ready to go, Chase came back downstairs and saw her looking around. He knew how his house looked. He wondered if she realized that she was saving him, or if that knowledge would make her want to run away. He sighed happily. He had to tell her. From the moment they met, he had felt a light in his heart again, one that had been nearly extinguished.

All his mates' girlfriends had tried to introduce him to girls they thought he would like, thinking they were helping him, but he never wanted to connect with any of them and always found it annoying. He had thought, *I can get my own dates!* But now? This was something different. It scared him, but in a good way. It woke him up.

Marguerite showed Chase the list of things she needed and asked about the little store around the corner from his house. She wasn't surprised when he said he had never been there. It was close, so she was going there to pick up the things they needed. He gave her a check and told her to get whatever she wanted. She felt funny taking it, but he insisted. He knew he needed a lot of things. He had just never had the energy or the will to get them before. Chase was happy and told her he was going to stop on his way to the studio to get himself a coffee.

"You can't just get coffee for yourself. Bring one for all of your friends too."

He looked at her and realized she was right. "Thanks for reminding me." They walked towards each other and embraced. The affection and attraction between them was tangible. He bent down to give her the sweet-est kiss ever. It lingered. Then they looked at each other and smiled. Neither one wanted to let go of the other.

"I promise," Marguerite said, "I'll be here when you get home tonight." Somehow, she knew he was waiting to hear this, and that it was the only way Chase would be able to leave her.

When Chase got to the studio with the coffee, and in a great mood, the boys just looked at him. Then at the coffee. Then back to him. He was smiling. They had thought he was coming in to quit, and instead he brought everyone coffee and looked like a different person altogether.

Blake had tried to prepare their manager, Peter, the night before, telling him that they all thought Chase would arrive at the studio any day now to quit. But things changed overnight. They finished a song they were working on and started another one for their new album.

Back at Chase's, Marguerite walked down the street to the grocers. It started to mist. *Please, not again! No more rain!* As she entered, she heard a man and woman, whom she just assumed were the owners, talking in Italian about it raining again. Marguerite didn't mean to join in their con-versation but said to them, in Italian, "Non posso prendere questo più o pioggia." I can't take this rain anymore either. Then she caught herself. "I am so sorry. I didn't mean to be eavesdropping on your conversation."

They were happy she did. They came over and introduced themselves to her. Their names were Franco and Anna, and they continued speaking to her in Italian, asking who she was and if she lived nearby, because they had never seen her before.

"I'm staying with a friend who lives right around the corner. We need a lot of things."

With that, she got out her list and walked around the store. It reminded her of a store she had seen in Italy just a few weeks before, when she was vacationing there. It made her feel like she was still there after speaking to Franco and Anna in Italian. She loved all of the different smells in the store. There were fresh-cut flowers in containers in front of the shop. She smelled the cheeses and the fresh fruits and vegetables. She saw some beautiful dishes she loved and knew they would be something Chase would pick out for himself. They had vibrant blues and yellows in an abstract pattern. She didn't know how she knew it but she did. After she picked out an unbelievable amount of stuff, from food to pots, she looked at the grocer and panicked.

"How am I going to get this all home?"

Franco said, "I will have my son Joseph help you take it where you are going." She thanked Franco and Anna, and smiling at them both, told them they would probably be seeing her a lot in the next few days and that her friend had nothing in the house to cook with. She liked them so much that she knew she would go back just to buy a candy bar so she could see them again.

After she put all the groceries away, she thought that she would straighten out the house a little. It wasn't dirty but it needed a woman's touch, and she wanted it to be *her* touch. She washed the sheets, cleaned the kitchen, and got ready for dinner. It was still damp outside, so she made some soup to warm them both up. She also felt like baking, so she made some chocolate chip cookies. She had already bought the milk to go with them. In truth, she didn't know where all that energy had come from all of a sudden. She couldn't wait for Chase to come home.

It was finally the end of the day, and when Chase called home to tell Marguerite he was on his way, she told him that supper would be ready whenever he got there. He didn't ask what it was; he was just happy she was still there.

As he came into the pantry, he yelled out that he was home.

"Shoes off!" she called to him.

He stopped, kicked his shoes off, and smelled soup cooking along with something else. Chocolate chip cookies?

"I scrubbed down the kitchen," she said as she stood before him with her arms folded, as though she were going to scold him. "It needed some work."

"Sorry," he shrugged. "I don't think about those things." They were both smiling at each other. She opened her arms to hug him, and he went over to her, melting right into the embrace and happily looking over her shoulder to see what was on the stove.

Drew said to Blake and Quinn, "Let's go see what's going on over at his house! Something is happening there, because he was actually happy to be going home! Not to mention the good mood he was in today."

Quinn wasn't sure. "Do you think we should? I mean, following him to his house to see what's going on?" They all looked at one another and then nodded. They had to see what was going on with their brother.

When they arrived through the pantry door, they heard Chase's voice. "Shoes off."

It made Marguerite laugh to see how easy it had been to train him. She already had four dishes waiting because she'd figured they would all follow him home. Somehow, she had just known.

When Chase saw the dishes she bought, he stopped dead. "Where did you get these?"

"At the shop around the corner," she said. "When I saw them, I loved them, and thought they looked like something you would pick out for yourself."

He had looked at those same dishes. He loved them! He'd just never gotten around to actually buying them.

The three brothers were all standing there looking at Marguerite. Chase introduced them to her one at a time, from the oldest to the youngest. First, Blake Thomas. Striking, he had black hair that was buzzed on the sides and long on top, and piercing golden eyes that almost shined. He was taller than the rest but not by much. Next, he introduced her to Drew Bishop, who was the same age as Chase. His hair was brown and curly and he had pale blue eyes. She could tell he was the character of the group just by his mannerisms, which seemed full of life. Last came Quinn Howard. The youngest of the brothers, he had a peacefulness about him, but she couldn't put her finger on what gave her that impression. He was just adorable. He had blond hair and blue eyes and was only about 5'6". They were all thin. *Probably from working so much, what with the schedule they have.* The thought made her worry.

She told them how happy she was to meet them and invited them all for dinner, which only made sense as she had already set the four bowls of soup out on the snack bar. She poured four glasses of milk, because you have to have milk with chocolate chip cookies for dessert, and made them all sit down to eat.

"How long will you be staying in London?" Blake asked.

Both Chase and Marguerite doubled over like they had been gut punched. There was no getting around it. They were connected somehow. The incident in the coffee house where she had felt him, their discomfort whenever they thought about parting ways, the dishes... It scared them to feel so connected to each other without really knowing one another. They looked into each other's eyes, and there was no denying their feelings, which were very noticeable to the brothers.

The brothers stayed for hours, talking to her and telling her all about Chase, which of course embarrassed him. When they had all met, Quinn was 16, Drew and Chase were 18, and Blake was 19 years old. They had been together for five years now and spent those years mostly on the road or in the studio recording. They told her how tiring it was and admitted that they didn't know how their girlfriends put up with them being gone all the time. It seemed to Marguerite they were grateful to the girls for sticking with them for so long. Most of them had been in the same relationships for over two or three years. Of course, they asked about her also. She told them that her mother and father had recently passed away in a car accident and that she didn't have much family. There were just two cousins, Donna and Sue, back in her home state of Pennsylvania. She told them how beautiful it was there and how she loved the mountains and scenery during the changing seasons. She told them all about her job working for a famous brand of snacks in the United States, and how much she loved it. She told them about the holiday she was taking, traveling for a few months around Europe, because it was something she had always dreamed of.

As everyone was leaving, they each kissed and hugged her, and said thank you. But she felt, for some reason, that they weren't saying thank you for dinner; they were saying thank you for something else. At the time, she just couldn't understand what. The smiles they had on their faces when they hugged Chase warmed her heart.

Everyone left and they were both tired, so they went upstairs to bed. They talked for hours about their days. As they got in bed, she opened her arms for him again, wrapping them around him, holding him tightly, still trying to take away what was left of his anxiety.

"What's different about these sheets tonight?" Chase asked.

"I washed them."

"Do I have a washing machine?"

Marguerite laughed. "Yes, and a dryer too!"

They both cracked up laughing as they tried to get some sleep.

2

Curiosity

This time, as Chase prepared to go to work, coffee was made.

"I am going to make pasta for supper tonight," Marguerite said. "Do you want to invite your friends again, and their girlfriends this time?" She felt she knew the girls already after hearing the guys gushing about them the night before. Chase smiled and immediately texted his brothers with the invite. They all responded happily and accepted. They wanted her phone number though, so the girls could call her to see if she needed anything. He cleared it with her before giving it to them.

Before he left for the studio, they shared another warm embrace and an even warmer kiss. This time the embrace was longer. He was smiling and relaxed as he wrapped his arms around Marguerite. He kept looking at her, as though he wanted to say something. She had a big grin on her face and playfully slapped his butt. "Go get to work!"

He left, laughing as he got in the car.

Marguerite realized that the rest of the house needed the same TLC she had given the kitchen the day before, even though there was no furniture in most of the rooms. The family room was huge, with a big fireplace. There was a formal dining room, which she thought was such a waste for Chase. She wondered if he would ever use it. The kitchen was huge also. It was her favorite room. The cabinets were white with black quartz counter-tops. There was a huge island in the middle with a sink in it, and it overlooked a big table that could seat twelve people easily. There were French doors that led to a patio that would be perfect for dinners and cooking out. Beyond the patio was a big yard.

She was so busy buzzing around the house that, before she knew it, it was time for lunch. While taking out the leftover soup, the doorbell rang. She called Chase immediately and he told her it was his manager, Peter. He had called Chase to tell him he was going to see what was going on there. She could let him in. He wasn't surprised that he wanted to see Marguerite, but knowing he was coming to check her out made her nervous.

Marguerite introduced herself and was gracious towards Peter, noticing how tall he was, with short blond hair and blue eyes. He walked with confidence and looked very business-like. She led him to the kitchen, where she set out two bowls for soup and invited him to have lunch with her.

He asked her directly, "What is your angle with Chase?"

"I have no angle. I just met him and felt his anxiety."

After she told him how they met, Peter asked, "Are you sleeping with him?"

She looked at him, her face flushed—anger, not embarrassment. "It's none of your business, but no. I don't sleep with men I just met!" She took a deep breath and let it out. "Look, I don't have a problem with you checking me out either. I don't need Chase's money or anything else from him. I have my own money."

Peter could see he hit a nerve, so he backed down and let it go. He knew he should really be thanking her for waking Chase up again, but didn't say more. He was still going to keep an eye on things. After all was said and done, it *was* his business, and so much was at stake.

All the girlfriends called one at a time to see if there was anything they could bring to dinner. She let them so they would feel included.

Cara Goodwin, who was Drew Bishop's girlfriend, would bring Italian bread; Jeanine Mercer, who was Quinn Howard's girlfriend, would bring dessert; and Abbey Adams, who was Blake Thomas' girlfriend, would bring the wine.

They were all so nice and they got along famously on the phone. It was like they had known each other all along.

Chase arrived home from the studio and saw that the table was all set. He noticed how beautiful it looked, and smelled the spaghetti sauce cooking on the stove. It made him hungrier than he thought. The house felt so alive and inviting. He took notice and it made him feel good inside. He walked over to Marguerite, who was holding a wooden spoon with some sauce on it for him to taste. He was smiling as he tasted it, nodding his head with approval, and gave her the warmest hug she'd ever felt. Their bodies just melted into each other. She was starting to love the feeling of Chase's arms wrapped around her.

She wondered what it would be like when they finally gave in to the pull of attraction between them. They had talked at length about their thoughts on love and sex and marriage, and they were firmly on the same page. They wanted to wait. It was strange. She couldn't remember ever being as attracted to anyone as she was to Chase, and she could somehow sense that he felt the same way about her, but the urgency they both felt to consummate their relationship was being overpowered by the desire to do things right. They were both savoring the suspense, drawing it out without any doubt that they would get there when the time was right. Somehow, it felt like they would have their whole lives to enjoy that side of things, and were enjoying just getting to know each other. She had to keep reminding herself that she had just met him. No matter how many times she reminded herself though, she just couldn't make herself believe it.

Eventually everyone arrived, one couple at a time. Quinn and Jeanine arrived with an enormous cake for dessert.

Marguerite grinned. "I might skip the pasta and go right for the cake."

It made Jeanine feel better, because she had been unsure of her choice of dessert. When Marguerite first saw Jeanine, she thought, *they are the perfect couple.* She was just as adorable as he was with her long black hair and big brown eyes.

Then Drew and Cara arrived with the Italian bread. "This will be perfect," she told them, "to have with the pasta I'm cooking." That made Cara feel better, because she had been worried it wasn't the right bread. Marguerite thought that she and Drew also looked good together. She had brown curly hair with big blue eyes, just like he did. *They could be related!* She quickly wiped that thought from her mind because it was so wrong!

Blake and Abbey were next with the wine. Chase looked at all the bottles and laughed. "I see you brought enough for a few rounds tonight. Thank you, brother!" They had gone totally overboard, buying more than they could possibly drink. They all laughed about it. Abbey was only about 5′2″, with long brown hair and deep blue eyes. They also looked like they belonged together.

She was glad to have a visual of them all now to put with the stories she had heard.

Surprising Marguerite, they all hugged each other as they arrived, and seemed genuinely happy to meet her and see Chase. Marguerite was relieved at how down to earth they all were. Watching Chase, she could see that he looked happy and at ease. Everyone noticed it as he poured the wine, and also noticed that, yes, he now had glasses to drink out of. He was being the perfect host and was truly enjoying all the company.

The girls all watched her and Chase interacting. None of them had seen him look so good in months, no matter what they did to try to help him. The dinner went on for hours, with everyone sitting around the table, talking and laughing until they cried. The stories were amazing. Everything from when they first met to the present.

Marguerite could see that the bond between them was strong, heart-warming, genuine, and real. *No wonder they were all so upset about him wanting to leave the band. It's a brotherhood, and the girlfriends are all sisters to them and to each other.*

Everyone helped clean up before they left. As expected, the boys knew nothing about a dishwasher or how to use it. It made everyone laugh. They got a quick lesson, and once they caught on, they started loading up their dishes like Marguerite had showed them. Chase told everyone he had just found out he had a washer and dryer. That made them laugh even harder!

Everyone hugged and kissed each other as they left. The embraces really got to Marguerite. When they hugged her, it was like they didn't want to let her go. She felt like she wanted to cry and had to try to control the tears. They made her feel like they loved her already, and she felt it. She knew they were worried about what would happen when it was time for her to leave. No one asked because they were afraid to.

As they headed upstairs to go to bed, Chase finally asked, "What did Peter want?" She told him that she knew he was checking her out. He wanted to know if she had slept with him. Chase was extremely upset with that question, but she quickly countered. "Can you blame him? You are one quarter of the biggest show on earth, and he's your manager. He has every right to know what's going on. I was upset he asked, but I knew he had to. I also told Peter I wasn't after your money. I have my own."

She was getting annoyed all over again, thinking about that conversation with Peter, so she decided to change the subject. "Can we go out to dinner tomorrow night? I saw some restaurants around the corner, near the grocers, and maybe we could go to one of them."

He was hesitant. "I can rarely go out without a scene."

"What if I talk to Franco and Anna, the grocers, and find out where we can go unnoticed and private. I'll see what we can come up with tomorrow." He felt better and agreed. If they could find a place, he would gladly take her to dinner. *Wow,* Chase thought to himself, *a date. A real date!* He was so happy they had found each other.

Lying in bed, she asked him, "So did you ever run your dishwasher before tonight?" She answered her own question before he had the chance. "Oh that's right, you had no dishes."

He laughed as he pulled her in for a tighter hug.

Fate and Faith 3

During the day, Marguerite walked to the grocers for some food for the house and spoke to Franco and Anna, who always seemed happy to see her. They loved when she spoke Italian to them. She told them that she and her friend wanted to go out to dinner but couldn't be seen, for obvious reasons, so as not to cause a commotion in the restaurant (or outside it) once people knew they were there. Franco knew immediately what she was talking about, because he knew where she was staying. They called his friend Rocco, who had a restaurant down the street, and discussed it. The owner told them to come in through the kitchen; he had a private room available for small parties. Marguerite said that she thought it would just be two of them but asked if he could be prepared for eight. She had a suspicion that she and Chase would only rarely be eating alone. After the arrangements were made, she thanked Franco and felt sad to think that she would be leaving soon and wouldn't see him after that. Then she texted Chase to say that they had a reservation, and told him all that had happened. They would enter through the kitchen and go right to the private room. Chase was thrilled and seemed surprised that Marguerite was able to pull it off.

It was getting late, so she started getting dressed just as he arrived home. He'd had a great day and she could see it on his face. She was standing in her black bra and panties putting on makeup in the bathroom when he came in. His eyes widened as he looked at her for a brief moment, before looking quickly away. She smiled at his reaction.

"Wow," he said. "You look..." He couldn't seem to find the words to complete the thought. So instead, he turned and quickly turned on the shower. "Hope we have lots of cold water," he said, pulling his t-shirt off over his head.

She laughed. "Sorry, the lighting in your bedroom was no good for putting on makeup. But I'm done now." She leaned in and gave him a quick kiss, trying to ignore his bare chest close enough to touch.

She turned to leave the bathroom, and then hesitated, turning back towards him. "I have a favor to ask."

He looked at her again, and knew he would do anything she asked. He had thought she was beautiful before, with her light brown eyes that shone when she smiled, and her long brown hair. But looking at her now, he could hardly tear his eyes away. What put him over the top was that he knew she was beautiful on the outside *and* in her heart. That much, he was sure of.

"Name it," he said, trying hard not to stare.

"Can you please shave?" Even though his hair was blond, his beard grew thick. He looked at her and raised an eyebrow. She smiled at him, and shrugged cutely. "I love your beard, but you are even better looking without it!" Her face turned bright red and she laughed. "I can't believe I just said that. I am so sorry!"

Chase laughed. "I don't mind. Being that this is an official date, I was going to shave anyway." He kept smiling as he was speaking. "Now I better get in that shower before it's too late and we don't even make it outside of this room."

That little black dress she put on made him stop dead in his tracks. She was thrilled she'd bought it and was surprisingly happy about the heels too!

"You look so beautiful," he said. She smiled, because for the first time in her life, she believed it.

She had on makeup again, which she really only wore rarely. She finally felt good about herself, and something else was happening. The physical attraction between them was becoming more obvious. They had felt it all along, but there were too many other emotions going on at the same time. Chase was distressed and Marguerite was trying to find herself, so none of those feelings came into play. It was almost like they were on the back burner. They were so comfortable with each other, and now they were emotionally in the clear to let it happen... when the time was right. Marguerite was happy nothing was happening yet in that area. She wasn't ready and was still trying to sort out her feelings for him. Or maybe she just wasn't ready to admit them to herself.

Chase drove them to the restaurant and Marguerite still didn't notice that bodyguards were following them. When they arrived, they were greeted in the kitchen by the owner, Rocco, who was waiting for them and happy to see them. He was a nice man, and he seated them in the private dining room. He suggested some wine before dinner and they accepted. Before he could say another word, one by one the others showed up. They looked at each other and started laughing. They came in through the kitchen because Chase had shared his plans with them. Quinn and Jeanine were first. They both looked good all dressed up. They hugged and kissed both Marguerite and Chase. Then Blake and Abbey arrived and hugged and kissed everyone. They looked sharp too. Drew and Cara were next, and apologized for being late.

"Drew couldn't decide on what he was going to wear," Cara said, which made them all laugh. There was room for everyone because of her premonition that they would all show up. They sat for hours again, talking and laughing. No one knew they were there. They were able to go out to dinner just like normal couples, and they loved it. Chase picked up the bill, which was funny to all of them. Then Abbey innocently asked how long she would be in London. Again, they both almost doubled over, gasping, but recovered quickly. They didn't want the others to see their distress. But they did notice it, and they were all worried.

To change the subject, Marguerite said, "Tomorrow night, I want you all to come over. We are going to make pizza." They all looked happily at each other. "Someone has to bring the beer."

They shared hugs again, vowing to try to eat out like that more often. After thanking Rocco while leaving through the kitchen, they headed home with the biggest smiles on their faces.

As they got in the house, Marguerite started to hyperventilate. Remembering that she was going to leave soon, she couldn't breathe. "Chase, I left my purse in the car. Could you go get it?"

As he did, she flew upstairs and stripped out of her dress. She headed into the shower, because she didn't want him to hear her sobbing uncontrollably. *I can't leave him!*

But he *felt* her. He finally *felt* her the way she *felt* him. He knew immediately that he couldn't let her go. He went into the bathroom and saw her sitting on the floor of the shower, crying as the water cascaded down on her. He grabbed a towel and turned off the taps, stepping into the shower to get her. He pulled her to her feet, held the towel out for her, and wrapped it around her. She was shaking, and so was he.

They said nothing as his tears joined hers. He knew what she was feeling, because he felt it too. The feeling was overwhelming as he sat her in front of the mirror, took out the dryer, and tenderly dried her hair, stroking and brushing it. Then he got a t-shirt and a pair of his briefs. He helped her step into the shorts, and then said, "Arms up." He slipped the t-shirt on over her head, then removed the towel he had her wrapped in, picking her up and carrying her to bed. When she was lying down beneath the covers, Chase pulled a chair over to speak to her, and took her hand.

"You can't leave me," he was looking down, as if he was afraid to meet her eyes. "I *felt* you, the way you said you felt me. I know what you mean now. I *feel* your distress and your confusion."

All she could get out of her mouth were two words: "I know."

"My heart feels like it wants to explode."

Marguerite nodded, acknowledging that she felt the same. "I'm so scared of the feelings I have, Chase. This connection to you is something I've never even heard of before. I don't even know you!" She cried and hid her face in the pillow.

He put his head down closer to hers. "You're right, but I can't let you go. I can't breathe without you. That is the one thing I know."

Marguerite realized that was exactly the way she felt. She couldn't breathe without him either.

He looked closely at her, seeming to study her features, her skin. "Did God send you to me? Are you my angel?"

Shocked, Marguerite shook her head and whispered, "I thought you were mine."

"No," he said, more serious than she had ever seen him. "You were sent to save me. I don't think I was supposed to save you."

After pausing to gather her thoughts, she said, "Then we were meant to save each other."

He held her hand tightly. "I am so in love with you. You *cannot* leave me. Marry me. *Please* marry me. I will always take care of you. I will always keep you safe. I will always love you. I know you have a life back in the States, but please agree to marry me. We can look at my schedule tomorrow and plan around it, but for tonight, please say you'll marry me. Please, say you love me too."

All of those emotions she was trying to figure out? She knew exactly what they were now. "Yes, I do love you," she whispered. "And yes, I will marry you." She knew she couldn't say no.

They were overwhelmed by what had just happened. Chase grabbed her hands and kissed them, then gave Marguerite the warmest, softest kisses, while they both had tears streaming down their faces. Chase always wore his heart out on his sleeve. Marguerite loved how sensitive he was.

He took off his shirt and pants and crawled in beside her under the covers, wrapping his arms around her for a change to comfort her, holding her tightly and burying his face in her hair.

"I want to wait until you marry me before making love to you. It's going to be hard though. I want you *so badly* right now." He kissed her hair. "I am so happy, and I never thought I could be."

She was amazed at what he said, and she agreed.

After they were both calm, and lying in bed holding each other, she said, "Did you just lay your wet clothes at the bottom of my bed?"

"And so it begins," he said.

They both cracked up laughing.

Plans

It was midnight. Marguerite felt like she'd just fallen asleep when she heard her phone go off next to the bed. She checked and it was her boss, Joe. She looked over her shoulder and Chase was still sound asleep. She slid out of bed and went downstairs to take the call. Joe apologized for calling so late where she was—it was still early in Pennsylvania. There was an issue that he needed her help on, so she got her laptop and logged into the system. They worked together for about an hour, learning what the problem was and determining a solution.

In the meantime, when he didn't feel her in his arms anymore, Chase got up. He immediately panicked, thinking he might have scared her away with the heavy conversation they'd had only two hours before. As he got closer to the kitchen, where she was working, he stopped to listen. She had someone on speaker and he got to hear them both brainstorming to correct some issue that was going on.

Then Joe asked her, "When are you coming home? We need you here."

She doubled over again. Chase wrapped his arms around her and just stood there hugging her. She hadn't seen him come up behind her, because she'd been deep in thought over the issue they were discussing. She leaned back into him to feel his whole body against hers.

Immediately, she knew what to say to Joe. "I'm getting married." The phone line was dead silent. Joe did not know what to say to her. He knew she'd had no boyfriend when she left on her journey a little over a month before. Finally, he broke the silence. "Congratulations. To whom?"

She said that she couldn't tell him right then. They were just making plans and would let him know. "Will you walk me down the aisle?"

Joe was blown away. She went on to tell him that the wedding would be in London, but she didn't know when yet. It was a lot for him to take in. She told him she would talk to him more the next day, as it was late. He seemed eager to hear more, but they ended the conversation. She shut down her computer and turned to Chase.

When their eyes met, it was as if their legs turned to jelly. Their knees got weak. They said nothing, but went back to bed hand in hand.

"I will get my schedule tomorrow first thing," he said, "and we'll make plans."

The next morning they both were happy and radiant. They wanted to get married. They knew it was the right thing to do. They wondered, and discussed, how much love would be left for them for the rest of their lives, what with experiencing this much in only a few days. It seemed as though saying 'I love you' was insufficient to describe the feelings they had. The connection to each other was overwhelming to them, as were their feelings of contentedness and happiness. 'I love you' just wasn't strong enough to express those feelings.

He turned towards her suddenly. "You are the very air I breathe." And there it was. That was the 'more than I love you' they were looking for. She was floored when he said it. That was it exactly. Because every time they thought about her leaving London—leaving him—it knocked the air out of their lungs. She stopped and walked towards him. His arms were already open for an embrace.

Now all the plans had to start. She nearly dropped when he said he wanted to get married in two weeks. There was too much to do. Too many people to tell. And boy, were they going to be upset! Like her family. She only had two cousins but knew they would not be happy. Chase got his schedule and they looked and planned.

They discussed her job as well. She looked at his schedule, and he was going to be gone for months. At first, she thought she could keep working too, but then reality kicked in. Chase told her she would need a bodyguard once it got out that he was married. Chase had told her about his body-guard, Alex, and how he had been following them all along. Marguerite was stunned. She had not even noticed him.

Chase wanted her to travel with him as much as she could. He didn't want to leave her, but they talked about that and agreed it would be best for her not to tag along everywhere with him. It wouldn't be right or fair to the rest of his band-mates.

There was tons of stuff for her to do with the house. It wasn't painted and it needed furniture and some pictures hung. It was going to take some time to make that cold, hollow building into a home. She thought she would do it when he was gone, and continue to work as well. She knew in her heart that she had to leave her job. It could no longer be a part of her life. Her new life would be so different, and she was only just realizing how drastically it would be changed. *Bodyguard?* She had never thought about that. Sneaking into restaurants for lunches and dinners through kitchens! *Really different.* She would get through it. She had to. She couldn't leave him.

How and what would she tell her family? She wanted them to come and help her pick out a wedding dress. What about his mother? She was his only family outside of his band of brothers. Holy crap! Everyone was going to flip! She wondered if they should just run away and get married somewhere, but she knew she wanted to do it right. A chance like this only came along once in a lifetime.

With so many thoughts going through her mind, she jumped from one conversation with Chase to another. She was getting so flustered that they made a list of everyone they had to tell first, and then of what had to be done. The key was to swear everyone to secrecy. Word could not get out or the whole wedding would turn out to be a circus. Cameras, people everywhere, and no privacy.

They went to tell his mom, Jessica, first. If looks could kill, Marguerite would have been shot with a hundred daggers at the moment they told her. But Marguerite kept her cool and his mother noticed a big difference in Chase, so she relaxed a bit and they sat down and told her the date they were planning for. She agreed that it wasn't enough time, but with his schedule, it had to work. They would get married two weeks from Tuesday, because on Friday he had to be back in London for concerts at the o2 Arena. Then he would have another few days off and be back on the road again. They told his mother that they really needed her help, and she said she'd do whatever she could for them. She also agreed not to tell a soul about the wedding. They really didn't have to tell her. Jess figured that out herself.

Next they called her cousins, Donna and Sue, back in Pennsylvania. That was difficult. They were livid and wanted to know what she was doing or thinking. She tried to explain, but they would not listen. When she said she couldn't tell them whom she was marrying, it got even worse. She tried to explain that for safety reasons they couldn't know until they came to London for the ceremony and to help her out. She asked if they would come as early as possible, to help her pick out a gown and arrange the wedding dinner. They immediately said that they were coming to London as soon as possible but not for the reason she was expecting. They were coming to see what was going on. When she told them she would send a plane for them, they stopped talking. Then Donna asked, "What do you mean you are sending a plane? Are you going through all of your inheritance?"

"The money is his, not mine. He doesn't need my money." Then it started to make sense to them. And they agreed they would come as soon as the plane could pick them up.

The boys and their girlfriends were all at the house, making their pizzas, when Chase just blurted out, "Marguerite and I are getting married!"

Everyone just stopped and looked at them. They were stunned but then quickly thought, *Thank God.* Was she the miracle they were praying for? He had been in such a good place since he met her. Every day she was with him, they saw him come back to life.

They all erupted with cheers, hugs, and good wishes. Finally, people who were actually happy about it!

On Board

Donna and Sue arrived with their husbands, Mark and Jack, and the kids, Ashley, Marie, and Kristen. They were lodging in a local hotel because Chase's house still had no furniture in it for visitors. When they finally met him, they were blown away. They didn't really know how to react to the whole situation. They didn't have to worry about him wanting her money. That much was true and a relief, but they thought Marguerite was completely crazy for getting involved with him and the circus that followed him and his band-mates.

"Have you lost your mind?" Donna said to her. "Every move you make will be recorded, photographed, and scrutinized. Every friend you have will be questioned and followed for information on you. Every guy you ever knew or slept with will be hunted down for information. And many will give it all willingly for the right amount!"

Marguerite was aware of what could happen. Chase's manager and security team had already told her just as much, but there was nothing she could do about it. This was a definite. She was marrying him no matter what.

While in the bridal salon, she tried on many gowns. They all looked nice, but none of them caught her eye. It could have been because her mother-in-law and her cousins were no help at all, and only did what they could to make her life miserable. The bickering back and forth made her seriously nervous and upset. She was overwhelmed. When she finally couldn't take it anymore, she let them all have it. She told her cousins, "If you can't be happy for me, then go home." She would do everything herself. She looked at her future mother-in-law. "I will always take care of Chase. He will always come first, even before me. But I need a mother right now." She looked into her eyes. "I will never let you down, Jessica. I need a mother. I want you to be it. I want to be your daughter. Will you have me?" Donna, Sue, and Jess just look at her, stunned. They had pushed all of her buttons and now felt terrible about it. As Marguerite turned and walked away, Jess followed her into the dressing room and broke down. Yes, she would be her mother. "I am so sorry! I know I treated you so badly and I will do everything I can to support you. And more importantly, I will love you like a daughter."

They were embracing, in tears, when they saw it. The perfect dress. She tried it on but didn't come out in it. It was the one. So elegant and classic. Off the shoulder, with a lace top and chiffon bottom, and a veil that would fall from a pearl tiara, where some of her hair would be pulled back and curled. The veil was the most elegant thing she had ever seen, and it would also act as her train. Amazing!

All the arrangements were made. The flowers, cocktail hour, dinner, and the cake. Chase had an idea about the entertainment for the evening. It would be a surprise. His band-mate Quinn, who was very spiritual and more than a bit religious, got his parish priest, Father Cummings, to agree to perform the ceremony, so that was taken care of. Next would be to get the license, which they couldn't do until the last minute so no one would see it. Everyone understood the secrecy of the entire day. They even registered at the hotel, for the event and rooms, under false names so that no one would guess. They blocked off the entire penthouse floor and the floor below. Marguerite would stay there the night before.

As expected, a bodyguard was hired to protect her immediately. His name was Mike, and Chase brought him home for dinner the night before meeting the family, along with his bodyguard, Alex. She liked him, but everything was so new to her that she felt uncomfortable. They explained everything to her. She would not be allowed to drive anymore, but she really hadn't been driving in London yet anyway. She was hoping they didn't mean back home in Pennsylvania too, but as she later found out that *was* what it meant. Her bodyguard would accompany her in the car wherever she had to go, and she would not be allowed to exit the car without him opening the door and sheltering her. She had a driver now as well, named Nick.

Peter, the group's manager, took care of a lot of things, like swearing everyone involved to secrecy—the hotel staff, the bridal salon staff, the tuxedo place staff, as well as all invited guests. It was important that everyone knew how devastating the whole event could turn out if the word got out. Peter also arranged for two magazines—*Greetings* in London and *Citizens* in the States—to cover the wedding. They would have exclusive rights to the photos, and all the money they would pay for the right to cover the wedding would go to the bride and groom's favorite charities. In Marguerite's case, it would go to a children's hospital in Pennsylvania, and his would go to a children's hospital in London. Of course, it was made very clear that the deals would be off if word got out before the big event was over.

With everything planned, they waited and waited for the day to arrive. It seemed like forever, even though they were both incredibly busy. It couldn't come fast enough.

As they lay in bed in the days leading up to the wedding, they often talked about her name change. Her new name would be Marguerite Angeli-Martin—MAM.

"MAM," he repeated. That was what he wanted to call her. MAM. It came to him so easily. It rolled off the tongue, sounding sweet and polite at the same time. Would she mind? She said she wouldn't mind at all. She loved that he was going to call her "Mam". Mam and Chase Martin. That is who they would be in just a few days.

Surprise

Chase started working on Marguerite's surprise for the wedding. He'd said that he would take care of the entertainment and knew exactly where to go. He called his close friend, Ed Mehan. A musician who wrote the most amazing love songs anyone had ever heard. Ed's concerts sold out stadiums, just like the Band 4's did. He had also won six Grammy awards for his work. Chase told him he needed to speak to him. Ed thought he was coming to tell him that he was leaving the band, so he told Chase to come over immediately so they could hang out for the rest of the day. When Ed opened the door and saw Chase standing there, he couldn't believe how good he looked. He was so relaxed and yet excited at the same time. It was confusing. Chase had spoken to him in the past about how unhappy he was touring and having people following him everywhere.

Ed did not waste any time asking him what was going on.

"I'm getting married in a few days and need a favor."

On top of being invited to the wedding, he was asked to sing a few songs for them. Ed was floored. He could not have ever imagined he would be having this conversation with Chase.

"Are you going to be a dad?"

Chase just laughed. He didn't get offended. They hadn't even had sex yet. He told Ed that, and Ed had to sit down. Now he was really confused.

Chase explained the whole story to Ed, and his friend admitted it was mesmerizing. He couldn't believe what had happened. He had so many questions. What do his mates think of her? What about his mom? Did she freak out? The questions flew at Chase. He felt like he was in an interview. It made him laugh. Ed saw how happy Chase was and it made him happy for his close friend.

"Absolutely, I will sing at your wedding," Ed said.

"No one can know," Chase reminded him. "If it ever got out, the wedding would be a zoo."

Ed understood, because his life was just as hectic as Chase's.

To celebrate, they went to a local pub that Ed often frequented and where no one would notice them. They were there for hours, doing shots and drinking beer. They had a lot of fun.

"Why don't we do this more often?" Ed asked him.

Chase told Ed about everyone going out to dinner recently and how he had thought the same thing. Why don't they try to get out more? "We should all try being more normal, rather than living in a bubble and staying closed off." The problem was that they had to find places that would shield them from the public. It would be tough, but they vowed to try to find more places and get out together more.

Chase called Marguerite to tell her where he was and that he was with a friend he wanted to invite to the wedding. She could tell how relaxed he was and that he was having a good time. She told him to stay out if he wanted. She was busy too and would see him when he was done. After all, she knew she didn't have to worry about him driving. Like her, he had a driver and bodyguard with him. As did Ed.

Marguerite took the time to pamper herself. She took a long hot bath, did some body maintenance, and conditioned her hair while soaking and relaxing in his tub, which was so big it was more like a swimming pool. She looked around. *Would this ever feel like her bathroom? Like her house and her things?* Thinking about living there with Chase made her feel warm inside, and completely in love with him.

Afterwards she went to the kitchen and opened her laptop to review some emails. When she eventually looked at the clock, she realized she had been online for two hours, doing work and reading about Chase and his band-mates. It was entertaining, all the sites that had *exclusive* information on them. It made her laugh.

Then Marguerite heard the door open and Chase saying, "Shoes off." She wondered who he was addressing, and laughed again at how quickly he had been trained to do that.

Then she realized she was standing in her nightgown. She hadn't thought about him bringing anyone home. She looked down at herself. *Well, too late to do anything about it now.* She was happy she had picked a nightgown that was double layered so nothing was showing through.

Chase entered the kitchen, with Ed right behind him, and stopped dead in his tracks. He started stuttering, trying to say something about not giving her notice, but she just laughed. "Sorry. I didn't think you would be bringing someone home. I'll go change."

"I think you better," he says, "because I won't last long standing over here with you looking like that over there." They all laughed at that. Gathering his wits about him, Chase remembered that they hadn't met and moved to remedy that. "Ed, this is my wife-to-be, Mam."

Ed was just standing there grinning from ear to ear; his face flushed bright red to match his hair. The color of his face highlighted his light blue eyes, which now stood out making him look adorable.

"Mam, this is a good friend of mine, Ed Mehan."

"I know who you are," she smiled at him. "I like your music."

He grinned back. "Thanks. I like your nightgown."

She excused herself and left to change. Chase looked at Ed. "How long till the wedding night again?"

Ed laughed. "I wouldn't have waited."

Marguerite came back down dressed in a t-shirt and shorts and made them sit down at the counter to eat. She knew he would be hungry after drinking all evening. She fixed them a snack, was pleased that they actually ate, and enjoyed laughing at the two drunken idiots.

Eventually Marguerite said she was going up to bed. Getting up to leave the two friends to their talking and laughing, she kissed Chase goodnight and then went to Ed and kissed him also. "I'm so happy to have met you and hope you can make it to the wedding."

Once she had gone upstairs, Ed told Chase, "I am so happy for you. I can see the connection between you two. Now I understand a lot of things you said to me."

Marguerite woke up with Chase's arms around her but felt crowded somehow. She raised her head and looked across the bed over Chase's back. There was Ed. Both of them are passed out cold. She stifled a laugh as she got out of bed. *Wow, I slept with Chase Martin and Ed Mehan—at the same time! In my whole life, who would have believed that?* She headed downstairs to make a pot of extremely strong coffee.

Sworn to Secrecy

The day before the wedding, she sent a plane to Pennsylvania to retrieve her friends. All she could tell them was that she was getting married, and that they wanted no gifts. They were all intrigued and couldn't wait to see what was going on. Marguerite had rooms for everyone at the hotel where the ceremony would take place, and picked up the tab so as not to constrain any of her friends.

Joe and his wife, Mary, who were her closest friends, were the only two on the plane who knew who she was marrying. He had agreed to walk her down the aisle, and his wife happily agreed to be her matron of honor. Joe and Mary were in their late fifties, and he was the vice president of the company she worked for. Joe and Mary had always taken to Marguerite. They had no children of their own and so she had filled that role for them. They had always cared deeply for her.

Before she could tell her friends whom she was marrying, she swore them all to secrecy. "Word cannot get out about whom I am marrying tomorrow. You cannot take pictures with your phones or cameras and you cannot discuss it with anyone." Confused and wondering what was going on, they all looked at her like she had two heads.

Then she told them. When she said his name, it was like he miraculously appeared, along with all his band-mates. Everyone looked astounded. Eyes got wide, jaws dropped open. Chase came over and hugged her and gave her the softest kiss. All the brothers, Blake, Drew, and Quinn, came with him and did the same. They were all smiling from ear to ear, excited and happy for their brother. As they turned to look at all of her friends, the place erupted in chatter. The boys went and introduced themselves to every person who had flown in for the wedding, and Marguerite and Chase hugged and cried with all of her friends. Joe and Mary were especially thrilled to meet him and his mates. It was the best afternoon ever for Marguerite, who loved being with all of her family and friends. Now they understood what she meant when she'd said absolutely no one could know about the wedding. They all vowed to not say a word—not even when they were pressured by their family and friends from home. After the reception, they could tell whomever they wanted.

There was a rehearsal that night with everyone who was involved in the wedding and a dinner afterwards. She'd felt nervous during the rehearsal and felt that Chase was also. When they had ten seconds alone, she asked him, "Are you sure you want to do this?"

"I have never been surer of anything in my entire life than I am about marrying you." He took her hand and kissed it, which made her relax a bit. She wondered if she would sleep at all that night.

Ed was in charge of the rings, which were plain platinum bands. She had Chase's name engraved across the top of hers. Marguerite's name was engraved across the top of his.

It killed them to have to say goodnight to each other. They lingered as long as they could, but the brothers pried them away from each other and took him home. Their girlfriends, Abbey, Cara, and Jeanine, said they would stay with her in her suite, because it was obvious that she didn't want to be left alone and they didn't want to leave her.

As expected, she couldn't sleep. There was girl talk for hours before they finally convinced her to try to close her eyes and get some sleep. She was really enjoying being around the other three girlfriends. She told them how happy she was to have them as family, and that she would always consider them sisters. They all cried and hugged and then forced her to go to bed.

Marguerite was lying in her bed, surrounded by the sleeping girls. Chase was lying in his bed, surrounded by his brothers, who were also sleeping. She was thinking of him when she started to *feel* him, as though he was sending her a message. He started feeling her the same way. At the same time, almost on cue, they said out loud, "You are the very air I breathe." Somehow, they could tell that they had not spoken alone, and it sent a shiver down their spines.

Wedding Day

The day had finally arrived. The hotel brought up breakfast and set it up in her suite, which had its own dining room. Everyone on her floor had their doors jammed open and were all walking in and out of each other's rooms. The excitement and electricity in the air was amazing. Marguerite tried to take it all in, but after a while, it became a blur.

The photographers and camera crews were arriving from the magazines to start taking pictures. It was time to get ready. She headed into the bathroom, which was huge, and got started on her hair. Vita, the stylist for the band, had volunteered to come and help and she arrived a few minutes later. They had met once before when Marguerite had gone to the studio to bring the boys lunch. Chase had introduced her to everyone and they'd all loved her.

She showed Vita her veil and told her what she'd thought about doing. Jess and Mary, who were like substitute moms, came in to help, heard her thoughts, and agreed with her. She asked Vita what she thought, and she also agreed that it would be just perfect. It would be classic, with soft curls in the back cascading from the tiara. So the process began. She pulled her hair back from the sides of her face and the top and fastened it with a clip. Then she styled soft curls all down her back. She sprayed them so they wouldn't fall with the long day ahead of her. Vita attached the tiara but not the veil yet. Marguerite still had to get her gown on first.

It was an off-the shoulder gown, so the bridal shop had supplied under-garments that would work with the style. It looked sexy, even though it was very comfortable. Pantyhose were supposed to be the finishing touch, but she hated it and wouldn't put it on. Not everyone was happy about that, but she stood her ground. As was customary, the groomsmen had purchased a garter for her. She was impressed with their selection, which was a beautiful pale blue.

Then it was finally time for the gown. She couldn't wait to put it on. It was like a dream to her, and now it was becoming reality. The top was lace with pearl beading, and left her shoulders bare. It was the purest white imaginable. The bottom was chiffon, with even more elaborate beading. It was elegant, with just enough bling and softness to make it extraordinary. It flowed when she walked. She wanted to cry when they put it on over her head, but Jess and Mary were right there calming her down.

Then they had to do it up. Oh those buttons! There were one hundred twenty satin buttons that needed to be closed with a knitting needle.

"How is Chase ever going to get you out of this?" Jess asked. Marguerite laughed, and then everyone joined in. It relaxed her.

Okay so, the gown is on, my hair is done, my shoes are on... She looked up with a big grin on her face. It was time to connect the veil. She stopped, looked in the large mirror, and then turned towards her two moms. There wasn't a dry eye in the room.

"Careful," Jess said. "You're going to spoil your makeup."

In the meantime, back at Chase's house, the groomsmen and Ed, the best man, were all getting ready. You could tell Chase wanted to get there and be married already. They had a hard time keeping him calm. After they put on their tuxes, they headed for the hotel. They had rooms there too, where they would be holed up until it was time.

Abbey arrived with a gift from Marguerite, just as Chase sent Blake off with a gift for her. He opened his gift. It was a four-sided pendant to wear when he was on tour. It had no center but the four sides had room for engraving. On the top was his name and on the bottom was hers. The two sides were blank. There was a note in the box, which he carefully unfolded and read.

"Chase, we are the beginning of a family. Once our children are born, we will fill the sides of the square with their names. Then, when you are on tour or even just at the studio, we will always be with you."

He wept openly as he read it. He showed his brothers, and Ed. They were blown away. He would cherish it until the end of time, and always wear it when they were apart.

Blake arrived at Marguerite's room with a present from Chase. When he looked at her, he was stopped dead in his tracks by how beautiful she looked. Wordlessly, he handed it to her, and she thanked him. "Please tell Chase that I can hardly wait another minute to marry him." Then she kissed him and gave him a huge hug. He headed back to Chase's room as she opened the small box. Inside it was a sapphire ring with little diamonds going down the sides of the platinum band. It matched her wedding band. It was a square stone, about three carets. The setting was elegant and simple, and one she would have chosen for herself. How did he know exactly what to buy? And he knew sapphire was her birthstone? She put it on her right hand and it fit perfectly. Everyone gathered around her and cried. Again, she had to try to stop the tears.

It was time for everyone to head down to the chapel at the hotel. Joe came in to escort her down to the ceremony. She needed him too, as she was shaking like a leaf.

He kissed her on the cheek. "You look so beautiful. It will be an honor to escort you down the aisle." They had guards everywhere so that no one could get by or see them.

The wedding planner at the hotel, along with Vita, stayed back to help her get ready for her walk down the aisle. The little bridesmaids went first, followed by Mary. Then the doors to the chapel closed. They adjusted her gown and her veil so that it would flow behind her as she walked. The doors opened and everyone was standing and looking back at her.

She was holding so tightly onto Joe's arm that he turned and whispered something that only she could hear, trying to calm her down. She smiled at whatever he said and relaxed a little. Then she looked up and saw Chase. Tears were streaming down his face, and were mirrored on the faces of his groomsmen and many of the guests. She felt just the way she always thought she should feel when she got married. He looked so handsome that she couldn't take her eyes off him. He thought she was an angel and couldn't take his eyes off her either. Everyone was beaming.

She arrived at the altar, where Father Cummings stood waiting for her. Joe stood by her side, in between her and Chase, as Mary fixed her train and veil behind her.

"Who gives this woman to be married to this man?" asked the priest.

"My wife Mary and I," Joe said. Then he turned and kissed her on the cheek, and whispered something in her ear that made her smile widely. He took the hand that rested on his arm and handed it to Chase, who couldn't wait to hold it. Then Joe took his seat in the front row.

Chase took her hand, kissing her palm, and held it to his face. Neither of them could stop smiling.

The vows were taken, and both said the words that would shape the rest of their lives, pledging to love each other in sickness and in health, until death parted them.

They exchanged rings as the audience held its collective breath, waiting for Father Cummings to say the words they were all so anxious to hear.

"I now pronounce you husband and wife" He turned to Chase. "You may kiss your bride."

He barely got the words out before Chase's lips were pressed to hers. There they stayed until the chapel erupted in loud applause, cheers, and whistles at Father Cummings next words: "May I present to you, Mr. and Mrs. Chase Martin!"

The celebration only got louder and more enthusiastic as they broke their kiss, laughing with joy, and marched down the aisle to the back of the chapel. Because of security, they were rushed to a separate room to have more pictures taken with everyone who had been involved in the wedding. After about an hour, the wedding party joined the reception, being announced one at a time by the best man, whose enthusiasm level only grew as he introduced the couple of the hour: "And now everyone, please put your hands together for Mr. and Mrs. Chase Martin!"

As they came through the doors, Marguerite was amazed by the electricity in the room. If they could, she thought people would actually be jumping up and down for them. That was how excited and happy for them everyone seemed.

Before they even got to sit down, they were ushered out to the dance floor for their first dance and the surprise Chase had planned for her. As the music started, she recognized the opening refrains of "Thinking of You". Written by Ed Mehan, it was her favorite song, and when she realized that he was actually going to sing it to them, she was over the moon. It was so fitting for the occasion, like he had written it just for them. They held each other tightly on the dance floor, looking into each other's eyes and feeling as if nothing else existed.

"You look so beautiful," Chase said quietly. "I feel so lucky today. The gift you sent me put me over the edge, especially after I read your note."

"Thank you for the beautiful ring." She shows him her hand, where it sat perfectly nestled alongside her wedding band. "It is exactly what I would have chosen for myself." She looked away from the ring for a moment, and saw his lips. Before either one could think, they were kissing again. It was soft and full of love.

Before the end of the song, all his band-mates rushed onto the floor, unable to contain themselves any longer, and wrapped their arms around them. Laughing, they continued the dance with all of them hugging each other. It was an amazing scene. The audience kept applauding and yelling in appreciation. The song ended, and Chase and Marguerite hugged and kissed everyone, then went to Ed and hugged him tightly, thanking him for making their day so special. Ed was beaming.

They got through dinner and the cutting of the cake, then the party got started. Ed sang some more, and everyone danced along. Over the next few hours, the couple walked the whole room and spent time with everyone— never letting go of each other—thanking them for spending their evening with them. Before Marguerite knew what was happening, Chase swept her up in his arms and carried her out of the banquet room, heading to their suite on the top floor. Everyone applauded and whistled and screamed. Then, in a flash, they were gone.

Security got them to the elevator and they made it to the suite without anyone seeing. They barricaded themselves in the room so that no one would come in. They thought it was better to be safe than sorry, just in case someone wanted to play a prank on them. Then they just stood there, looking at each other. They were overflowing with the love they felt for each other. He walked slowly towards her and then kissed her and hugged her tight.

She undid his tie and took off his jacket. Trying to keep herself from just kissing him wildly, she unbuttoned his shirt, but did not take it off him yet. Instead, she turned and asked him to help her out of her dress.

When he saw the buttons, he freaked out. "How many buttons are here?"

"One hundred and twenty." She was trying not to laugh as he struggled behind her.

"It just took me three minutes to unbutton one. At this rate, it's going to take three hours to get you out of this dress." She laughed. She couldn't help herself. She handed him a pair of small scissors from a nearby dresser. Vita had given them to her. *"Just let him struggle for a bit first, okay?"* Marguerite could still see the mischievous gleam in her eye when she'd said that.

"Here. Just cut the loops. We'll get them fixed later."

"Thank God," he laughed, sounding relieved. He kissed the back of her shoulder, sending chills through her, and then cut just enough loops to let her step out of the dress. Then he saw the corset she had on. She looked very sexy in it and he approved—wholeheartedly. She turned and removed his shirt, and then unbuttoned his pants and told him to step out of them.

There they were. Finally, they were ready to make love for the very first time. The lights were low and they trembled as they touched each other. They kissed and kissed, trying to prolong each moment indefinitely, until finally holding back became impossible. He scooped her up in his arms and brought her over to the bed, while his mouth devoured hers. She responded with sighs and gasps of approval. Their breathing was heavy and rapid. Falling together into bed and wrapping themselves around each other, the passion they shared was like nothing they had experienced, seeming to echo and reverberate through the bond they shared, and allowing them to feel each other in ways they never thought possible. There was no more "him" or "her". No more Chase or Marguerite. They became one, both physically and spiritually. It was everything they had waited for and more.

They made love all night, and by morning, the closeness they'd been feeling since they first met, and the bond they had shared, was nothing but a pale shadow in comparison to their new love and awareness of each other.

They held each other as the sun came up, whispering amid soft tangles of expensive bedding, and expressing how glad they were that they had waited until their wedding night to make love. It was truly a night they would never forget.

Chase kissed her forehead, breathing in the soft fragrance of her hair. "You are the very air I breathe."

She smiled softly and snuggled closer, resting her head against his chest and settling in for sleep. "And you are mine."

Frozen

When they woke up, they found they really hadn't been asleep for long. Marguerite said that it was because they still had so much to talk about—and so much more sex to have. It made them laugh. They were so happy and relaxed, lying next to each other with their arms and legs intertwined. They started talking first, going over everything that had happened the day before and remembered how nervous they had been, and completely oblivious to the thousands of things going on around them.

"I wore out the tile at the house," Chase said, "because all I could do was pace back and forth. The next time we get married, we are doing it at seven in the morning instead of five o'clock at night. That was too long to wait." That cracked them up, but she agreed. The brothers hadn't known what to do for him, and then when he'd gotten the gift from her, he had completely lost it.

She had to admit that Vita had given her the idea and another one that she knew he had appreciated. "When Vita looked at those 120 satin buttons on the back of my gown, she just froze. It took *so* long to button up. We were all laughing and crying at the same time, because all we could think of was how you were going to get those undone. Finally she gave me her hair scissors and said you had better use them or it would be a very long night." Thinking about it made her laugh again. Shortly thereafter, the photographers showed up and it was suddenly very real. "They snapped so many pictures, I didn't think I could even smile that much." It had been easy, really. She couldn't have gotten the smile off her face if she'd tried. She was too happy.

Marguerite told Chase about how much she had been shaking, and how tightly she'd been clinging to Joe's arm.

"I saw him say something to you as you were walking towards me," Chase said. "You smiled but I couldn't imagine what he was saying."

"Yeah," she smiled again, remembering. "He said, 'If you don't loosen your grip on my arm, I am going to give you a terrible work review the next chance I get.' That broke the ice and I relaxed. The trick was not starting to laugh." She sighed happily, savoring every moment of the memory, and knowing she would be doing so for the rest of her life. "That's when I looked up and saw you standing there, looking so good that I just wanted to sprint down the aisle to you."

Chase nodded. "When I saw you, it was like you were moving in slow motion and would never get to me. What did Joe whisper to you when he kissed you and gave your hand to me?"

"He told me that he and Mary would always be there for us—no matter what, no matter where, no matter when—and that I was a daughter to them." As she repeated Joe's words, they brought tears to her eyes. Chase was also moved by what Joe had said, and at that moment, he realized that they were Marguerite's family.

They looked at the clock then and found that it was almost time to meet everyone for brunch, which would be followed by their departure for a short honeymoon. It had been carefully planned and they couldn't be late, but Chase grabbed Marguerite anyway, wanting to show her how much he loved her one more time.

Down in the banquet room, the guests started taking bets as to whether or not they would even make it down to the brunch.

Eventually, there was a knock on their door. It was Joe and Mary, who were very happy to see them and hugged and kissed them like proud parents hugging their children. At that moment, Marguerite and Chase felt like that was exactly who they were. *Here is my family,* Marguerite thought. They all went down for the brunch together.

As they walked in, everyone stood and applauded and cheered. Marguerite's face turned three shades of red as the brothers and their girlfriends all ran over to embrace them. She was getting used to the group hugs and decided that she loved them. They sat with everyone again and talked about everything that had happened yesterday. The entire wedding party laughed so hard they could hardly breathe when the brothers told the story of Chase getting so impatient for the wedding to start that they had considered tying him down.

The band's manager, Peter, came over and sat with them for a while and had to admit that he had never seen Chase so happy and relaxed. He gave Marguerite his nod of approval afterwards.

It was time for them to go. They were packed and ready to leave. Security was very tight; only Peter, security, and the driver knew where they were going. It turned out that Marguerite had a reservation in Scotland, which was where she had been headed before she'd been sidetracked in London. Peter and the security detail went on ahead to St. Andrews to alert the hotel that they were coming and tell them to keep everything private or the place would become a circus. The hotel agreed and made all the arrangements necessary to let them have their privacy. *Another headache over,* Peter thought. But the worst was still to come. He had to alert the media and fans that Chase had gotten married before the news got out through some other channel. As soon as they left, he issued a formal statement:

Chase Martin of the Band 4 married Marguerite Angeli of the United States in a private ceremony on Tuesday, August 21st. They were surrounded by family and close friends for the ceremony, which lasted twenty minutes and was followed by a reception at a private location. They presented each other with platinum wedding bands engraved with each other's names. After a brief honeymoon, Chase will return to work and prepare for their concert series at the O2 Arena in London, the first stop of their upcoming tour. Citizens magazine of the USA and Greetings magazine of London shared access to the event, and photographs will be forthcoming.

The Internet blew up. Servers were overloaded and people were frozen online. One could not get anywhere on social media. All hell had broken loose! Everyone wanted to find out more.

Chase and Marguerite were having dinner in their room when the brothers texted them to tell them what was going on. They just looked at each other, shocked. They didn't know if they should do something or stay hidden, so they sent a message to Peter to see if they should make an appearance somewhere or send a picture of themselves on their honeymoon. Then they waited for his reply.

10

First Concert

The couple had been so blinded by wanting to get married and to have a somewhat normal life together that they did not think of all the consequences. Marguerite knew that the band's fans were amazing and numerous, but she had never imagined this happening. Freezing the Internet! Chase admitted that he had not realized that would happen either. In a way, it scared them both. It made them wonder how they could have possibly not realized what would happen. Peter had told them it would get rough, but they'd never imagined this.

They tried to enjoy the short time they had scheduled for their honeymoon, but what happened was always in the back of their minds. They felt like they just wanted to get home and start being a married couple and have some normality. But normal would never be in their vocabulary.

Peter got back to them, saying that he thought it might be a good idea to release some honeymoon pictures, but not until the two magazines covering the wedding published theirs first. They had someone take pictures of them in Scotland and saved them for later.

When they finally got home, they were surprised that everything was so quiet. They had not known what to expect, but Peter had pleaded with the police to help keep the area where Chase lived safe and private for them. It must have worked, because no one was around. At least for now. They unpacked and made plans for her to go to Pennsylvania while he was gone on tour, to pack up all her stuff and ship it to their new home. He insisted that they hire a packing and shipping company, so as not to stress her out. Whomever they hired would have to sign waivers, of course, stating that they would not disclose anything about her or her things. That would become the normal for them.

She wanted to scream, *Waivers for everyone!*

She could no longer walk to the grocers, so her driver, Nick, took her there, along with Mike, her bodyguard. Chase wanted to go with her too the first time. He wanted to thank Franco for everything. When they walked in, Franco and Anna's eyes lit up. They were so happy to see them and hugged and kissed them enthusiastically. The couple wouldn't accept a wedding gift from anyone, but the grocer already had a box of goods ready for her. Marguerite and Chase were blown away and told them that they didn't have to do that, but took the box, as it was a gift. Marguerite then picked up some other things she would need, paid for them, and then they left without anyone noticing. They made another quick stop to the jeweler, because (as it turns out) that was where they had both purchased their wedding gifts to each other. The jeweler was also thrilled to see them. It was just a quick in and out visit—hugs and heart-felt thank you.

Back home, the brothers and their girlfriends (whom Marguerite had started thinking of as "the sisters") came over once they heard that they were back and settled in. Marguerite whipped up something for dinner and the sisters brought some food with them as well. They were all stunned about what had happened on the Internet, and concern was plain on all of their faces. They all decided that they would try to go about their lives as they were, and try to live as normally as possible.

After seeing that Chase and Marguerite could actually pull off a beautiful wedding, in spite of his fame, they had also all started talking about getting engaged themselves, and soon. They didn't want to waste any more time. Right then, Marguerite knew the girls were truly going to be her sisters, and was extremely happy about it.

The next day, Chase had to go to the o2 Arena to prepare for the concert that was coming up. He wanted Marguerite to go too, so that she could see what went on—how everything worked—and watch them rehearse. She did, and was blown completely away by it all. She'd had no idea how much went into preparing a show like theirs, both before they went on stage and while they were performing. It took so much energy! She didn't know how they could survive the whole concert. She couldn't imagine how their voices withstood all the singing. She met everyone associated with the band again. They had all been at their wedding. Everyone was pleased to see her and took her around to show her everything there was to see, explaining everything that went on behind the scenes.

There was the clothing stylist, Lisa, who helped Chase pick out what he wanted to wear that night. Vita, who had done her hair for the wedding, was going over what she was going to do with Chase's hair. That made Marguerite laugh. Quinn, the youngest band member at 21, came in to get his hair cut but was so wired that he couldn't sit still and started driving Vita crazy. Marguerite looked at him with disapproval and folded her arms, as if to scold him. He stopped dead and sat still for Vita. Vita and Marguerite looked at each other and smiled. Vita mouthed a big 'thank you' to her. Even Marguerite was surprised that he had quieted down for her.

The couple was able to go home for about four hours before they would have to head back to O2 for the concert.

At home, Chase tried to get some rest while his wife puttered around the kitchen, preparing something light for dinner. He came downstairs to find her.

"Can you lie down with me for a while?" He thought he would relax more easily if she was next to him. She joined him in bed and he fell right to sleep. She got him up just in time for a shower and some food, and then it was time to go. She asked him if he got nervous before his shows.

"Yes, but I am not as nervous this time as usual. I think it's because I know you'll be at my side."

At O2, they went directly for his clothes. He got dressed and then went to Vita for hair-styling. One by one, they all followed the same procedure. The sisters were there too and Marguerite enjoyed being with them. It made her feel more comfortable. When they were done getting ready, they all just chilled out in a waiting room that was big and comfortable, filled with couches and chairs, and stocked with drinks and food. They talked about the concert and practiced some songs *a capella*. Their voices were strong and clear.

Peter was there and pulled Chase aside to talk to him. Marguerite didn't know what that was about but saw Chase nodding as Peter talked to him. Then he called the rest of the band over to talk to them and she could hear them agreeing on something. "Yes, good idea. No problems here." She assumed it was something about their performance.

Vita came over to give her a tip about what happened after the shows were over. "They are drenched when they come off stage." She gave her a t-shirt for Chase to change into. She told her that they would only have about ten seconds to change when they came off stage, because they would have to rush into the cars that were waiting to take them away from the arena before traffic got jammed up or anyone saw them. If they missed that window, their vehicles would be mobbed.

Marguerite told Vita that she was thinking of having a cold towel ready for him also, which she thought would cool him down. Vita thought that was an excellent idea and was surprised that Marguerite had given it any thought at all. She shouldn't have been surprised though. She saw how concerned Marguerite was about Chase, and it made her feel good. She had been with the group as their stylist since they'd first gotten together, and really cared about them.

It was time for the show and they all began the walk to the stage, which was quite a distance from the waiting room, the band members each holding the hand of their respective partner. Chase was holding onto hers like he was afraid he was going to lose her. She was feeling tremendously excited and nervous for him. They all laughed and joked around while walking to the stage area. Then they arrived and the band-mates had to leave them behind.

Chase gave her a big hug and a soft kiss, and she wished him good luck. They touched foreheads as he whispered, "You are the very air I breathe." She responded in kind. "You are the very air I breathe." When they looked at each other, two of the biggest smiles imaginable were plastered across their faces. The brothers pried him away from her, which made everyone laugh. In a good mood and laughing, they climbed onto the platform that would pop up onto the stage with them on it.

Chase's smile wasn't going away, or fading in the slightest, and the brothers all started gawking at him. "Why are you smiling so much?"

"My wife is here."

They patted him on the back and then all put their arms around each other as the platform lifted them up to the stage. They knew tonight's concert would be sick!

11

Meet the Fans

When they arrived on stage amidst smoke and fireworks, the fans were screaming so loudly the band could hardly hear themselves. They put in their ear pieces. In one ear, they heard each other, and in the other, they heard the band. It drowned out some of the screams, but not by much. The girls, including Marguerite, had seats on the side behind the stage, but they could see everything that was going on.

When the music started and the boys started singing their first song, it almost brought Marguerite to tears. She felt so proud of him—of all of them. They were completely amazing. All she could think of was that he was *all hers!* His voice was so different and strong. He looked so happy out there. They were all jumping around the stage, going from the front of the stage to the sides, making sure they acknowledged all of their fans. The place was packed to the rafters with about 80,000 people—most of them screaming.

Between songs throughout the show, the band-mates would take turns walking to the end of the runway to speak to the fans. They would talk to them for a moment, and then introduce the next song, which would feature the one speaking. Finally, it came time for Chase to speak to everyone.

He made his way down the center of the stage, waving to everyone in all corners of the arena, careful not to exclude anyone. As he started to speak, Marguerite found that she couldn't stop smiling. *That's my husband!*

"Thank you all for coming to hear us tonight," he called out. Everyone was screaming!

"Is everyone okay?" More screaming!

"I think you've all noticed that I'm wearing a new piece of jewelry on my hand!" He spoke louder, struggling to be heard over the fans. "Well, my wife is here tonight! Would you like to meet her?" Screams, screams, screams!

Marguerite nearly passed out. She turned white and all the girls' jaws dropped. They looked at her, saw that she was white as a sheet, and started asking her if she was all right. She nodded, but couldn't speak. She was shaking.

Abbey said, "You have to go say hello or they will never forgive you."

From the stage, she could hear Chase. "Marguerite? Come out and meet everyone!"

The tour manager, Jack, who was running the show, had been warned that Chase was going to do this, so he was ready for her. He went and got her, taking her by the hand and leading her to the platform, where she would be lifted up to the stage. Her legs were jelly. She didn't know if she could even move to her place on the platform. Jack saw that she was shaken and started talking to her. Slowly, the color came back to her face. She nodded then, and told him that she knew she had to go out there, and she was ready. She took a few deep breaths and looked back at the girls, who were laughing, enjoying every nerve-wracking moment of Marguerite's grand unveiling. Jack asked her again if she was ready, and when she nodded, up she went. As the platform started raising her up, all she could think of was thank God she chose a beautiful white lace tank top to go with navy Bermuda dress shorts and navy flats where ribbon laced around her ankles and tied in a bow to wear. She felt she looked special enough for meeting the fans for the first time. Before she knew it, she was on stage.

Everyone started screaming once they saw her. She started walking forward, amazed and overwhelmed by the spectacle she was now a part of. She saw the brothers first. They were waiting for her, and kissed her one at a time, which helped her calm down. Then she was in the middle of the stage. *I can't ignore the people on the left and right.* She started to the left and took a deep bow and waved to everyone—the people up under the rafters, and those within arm's reach of the stage. Then she turned to the right and repeated the gestures. She started searching for Chase on the huge stage, and then she finally saw him, standing there waiting for her. She ran to him and jumped into his arms. He could feel her shaking but once he wrapped his arms around her, she settled down.

She felt calmer in his arms, but the crowd went wild. After a long moment, she left his embrace, feeling like she was ignoring the people facing center stage. She walked to the end and took a deep bow and waved to them as well—the specks of people so far away they could barely see her, and those close enough to see her joyful tears. Chase came over and grabbed her hand, kissing the backs of her fingers where her wedding ring sat. Then he kissed her softly on her lips. She was afraid people in the audience were going to pass out from screaming.

She asked Chase if she could say something to the crowd, and he gave her the microphone, looking perplexed.

Facing and pointing to the fans in the middle seats, top and bottom, she said, "I need a favor from you all." Slowly a hush fell over the arena. When she had their attention, she went on. "Will you take care of Chase for me when I can't be with him on the road?" The crowd went nuts, screaming like they were all having coronaries.

"Yes! Yes! Yes!"

Then she moved back toward the left side of the arena and asked the same thing. High and low, close and far away, everyone went wild, screaming "Yes! Yes! Yes!"

She completed the circuit, questioning the people to the right of the stage, who echoed the sentiment of the rest. Thunderous screaming and chanting answered her. "Yes! Yes! Yes!"

She thanked them in a sincere voice that broke with emotion and failed to reach most of the people in the arena. But they all understood. They started chanting her name. "Marguerite! Marguerite! Marguerite!"

That was that; she had won them over. Before she turned to say goodbye, she put the icing on the cake, addressing all the people in the arena. "Now I'll believe it when Chase tells me that they have the best fans in the world. I love you all already! Thank you very much for being so kind to me!"

With that, she kissed Chase one last time and then patted him on the shoulder. "Now get back to work." They both laughed, as she ran up the runway back to the platform. Then she turned and gave one last wave before the platform lowered her back down out of sight.

Peter was waiting for her. He grabbed and hugged her. "Very well done! You just saved your husband!"

He thought it would be touch and go, but with what she had just done, she had sealed the deal with all of the fans. They loved her already, and what she had done would be all over the world by tomorrow. Peter asked her if she'd had any of that planned, but she said no. It had come to her when she was out there. She thought the fans would be upset thinking they had lost Chase now that he was married, and she wanted them to know that he still needed them. Peter told her she was brilliant. He knew it would be all over social media in moments, so many of them were recording her on stage. She had won them over.

The girls were waiting for her to be done talking to Peter. They also knew she'd been amazing out there. When she was done, they all flocked around her. She was spent. She had never expected that and was utterly drained. They got her some water and then they all sat back down to watch the rest of the concert. She was trembling and didn't want Chase to see her like that, so she just tried to enjoy the girls' company and the music.

As the concert ended, she was anxiously waiting for Chase to come off the stage. She had a clean shirt for him and a cold towel, which she had kept in the refrigerator. He found her immediately, and as she gave him the shirt, he nodded his thanks. "How did you know?"

"Vita told me what to expect." Then she held up the cold towel and he was amazed. She wiped his face and then put it around the back of his neck, which felt wonderful. "The cold towel was my idea."

He kissed her and told her how proud he was of her for what she had done. He was amazed at how well she had handled herself. Then they were both ushered out of the building by their bodyguards, who hurried them out the door as though the place was on fire.

First concert. First success.

12

New Life Realities

The other two concerts at O2 went the same as the first. Each night she cried when he first went out on stage and started to sing. She just couldn't help all the love she felt for him and how proud of him she was. The boys seemed to have a blast on stage, with the fans and with themselves. Everyone backstage commented on how well everything was going. They thought these were the best concerts the band had had to date. The buzz in the air for the three nights was electrifying. Ed even came to the last concert and sat with Marguerite and the girls. He was truly a good friend to both of them now.

Chase only had one day off before leaving for the tour. There was so much to do in a single day. They went to the bank and opened a joint checking account, from which they would pay the household bills. She transferred money from her own account back in Pennsylvania into their new account, which upset him. He wanted to pay the bills himself. He could afford it, and he'd meant it when he said that he would always take care of her. He had meant financially too. But she insisted. They had their financial advisor Marion with them, because she was the person who would be handling all of the bills and whatever else needed to be paid. She would get them ready and then Marguerite would sign the checks. Chase had never done this before, but Marguerite wanted to see what was going out and to whom.

Marguerite now had an assistant named Gail. She nearly fell over when Chase brought her to their office to meet her. She hadn't even realized they had an office before this. Gail was the one who arranged all of the transportation for her and Chase. She kept their schedules and kept them on time for everything. If anything needed to be done, she was the person to do it. She was also the one who worked with the driver and security team. The brothers had the same kind of people to handle their affairs, and they were all in the same group of offices. This just made sense, because they needed to coordinate events and trips together. It never occurred to her that Chase was actually a corporation. And now *they* were a corporation. She would have to be good friends with all of these people. Every plane ride, doctor visit, luncheon, and shopping trip had to be arranged and approved by someone, and Gail would likely accompany her almost everywhere she went.

Chase told her to decorate the house however she wanted while he was gone. Knowing how connected they were, he knew that he would love whatever she did. She put that second on her to-do list. First, she had to go home to Pennsylvania and resign from her job. While there, she would get her house packed up and her belongings shipped out. Even thinking about going back to the house she grew up in struck a nerve. Chase felt it immediately, because she started stressing out.

He knew the conversation had to take place, so when they were home alone, he asked her about it. He knew her parents had been horrible to her but not to what extent. When she started to tell him things they had done and said to her, he was stunned that any parent would do that to their child. They had told her constantly that she was ugly, when that was so far from the truth. She was beautiful. But according to them, no one would ever want her because of how she looked. Intellectually, Marguerite always knew that it wasn't true, but it was still always there in the back of her mind. If you say something to someone enough times, they start to believe it. That is why, until only recently, she had never felt beautiful or thought anyone would think she was. They had instilled too much fear in her, and that was why she loved work so much. It was the only way to get away from her parents. It was also probably why she was so good at her job. She threw herself into it wholly. Her parents took most of the money she made and kept her on a shoestring budget. Everyone, even the cousins, knew how terrible they were. No one could understand why she had stayed in the same house with them, even after she'd grown up, but every time she had tried to leave, it wound up being a nightmare. Her mom or dad would wind up in the hospital. She always believed that they were faking illnesses to get her to stay. In the end, she had simply thought, *they're my parents.* Even though she did not like them, they were her parents.

When they had died tragically in a car accident, it had stunned her. Her first feeling, of course, was sorrow, then relief that she was finally free of the nightmare they had made out of her life. Marguerite felt guilty feeling relieved that they were gone, and then felt even more guilty because it turned out that they had saved every dime they'd taken from her and more, investing it for her and turning it into a fortune. In the end, they had given her peace of mind and three million dollars. Three million dollars! She had been shocked and stunned for days after the funeral.

That is when she decided to take a leave of absence from work and travel around the world. She had been cloistered for twenty-seven years of her life, and now she needed to get out.

She had spent a month in Naples, Italy. That was where her family had originally come from. There were so many Angelis in the phone book that she couldn't begin to guess which ones she would be related to. The cousins, Donna and Sue, didn't know either. They couldn't believe that she was venturing out on her own like that. They had been worried for her, traveling on her own, but she had made up her mind.

After the month she spent in Italy, which she had loved, she headed to London. The rest was history.

Chase listened raptly to every word she said. He watched every expression form on her face and felt her sadness, frustration, disappointment, hurt, and anger. He thought that maybe he *was* supposed to save her. He had always felt like she was his angel of mercy, and now he felt that maybe he could be hers as well.

Chase held out his arms. She melted into them and he held onto her tightly as she started to weep. He guessed that this was the first time she had ever wept for her parents, and it was long overdue. She wept and wept until her breathing was choppy. He wanted to help her cope with the tragedy and loss. He was her husband, and that's what husbands do for the person they love. That's what they do for their wives.

He smiled sadly, wishing he could take away her pain, but still amazed that she was his wife.

There was still more to discuss in the short time they had before leaving. She had wanted to give two weeks' notice at work, but that was obviously a big no. She couldn't go back. Everyone on earth would be waiting for her.

Chase reminded her that Joe would understand why she couldn't go back, and how impossible it would be.

In any case, Gail had arranged a trip over to the States for Marguerite, Mike, Nick, and herself. Marguerite found it upsetting that all their lives would be interrupted just because she had to go overseas, but Chase explained that this sort of thing happened; it was part of their jobs, and they expected and accepted it.

Everything was set. She pulled herself together and helped him pack for the two weeks he would be traveling. After those weeks, he would come home for three days before hitting the road again. She was packing her things for her trip also. They were both leaving the next day but at different times. He would be gone first. They were both worried about how they could ever leave each other, and so was everyone else. The brothers were worried; you could see it on their faces and hear it in their voices. During the concert series at the arena, they kept asking Chase and Marguerite if everything was on schedule and if they would be ready to leave when the time came. Now the time had almost arrived and they were picking him up tomorrow at ten. Marguerite felt that she needed to make sure he left with them and was relaxed about it. The sisters would come over later and stay with her until it was time for her to catch her flight.

Marguerite and Chase were lying in each other's arms, talking about how hectic the last few days had been, what with the concerts and then getting themselves organized for what would come next. They talked about how much they loved each other. He was worried about her going to Pennsylvania, but she would have her posse with her, so she knew he shouldn't be too worried. He said that she had to remember that people would be looking for her everywhere. She had to be careful. She knew that would be hard to do, but would rely on Gail a lot for help with anything she couldn't manage on her own. She asked Chase if he had packed his pendant and he told her that it was the first thing he'd put in his suitcase. He kissed her forehead then and buried his face in her hair. Then he looked down at her. "You are the very air I breathe."

She nodded, trying not to cry. "You are the very air I breathe."

With that, they settled down beneath the covers, taking comfort in each other's warmth, and fell asleep as they usually did, with their arms and legs wrapped around each other.

13
Going Home

They were both a little nervous the next morning when he was preparing to leave. She tried to keep a brave face on. She knew she had to. She couldn't waver because too much depended on it. She tried to make jokes about his trip, saying that she was planning a shopping trip to the furniture store, so he had better get out there and make some more money. He smiled from ear to ear, very much wanting her to spend his money.

Then the brothers all came in, wanting to say goodbye to her. She was now a sister to them. One by one, they hugged her tightly and kissed her. They told her they would take care of Chase for her. Then each one shocked her in turn, telling her that they loved her. She happily told them that she loved them too, and to be safe. She really felt like their sister telling them that. She was worried about all of them. Next it came time for her and Chase to say goodbye. They grabbed each other as though they were never going to see each other again.

"Please don't make me cry," she said. "It will only make this harder."

He kissed her and hugged her tightly. "I will call you once I'm on the plane and during every step of the trip. From the hotel, at the shows... I'll tell you everything I'm going to do just as if you were right there with me."

She would do the same. "You are the very air I breathe." She said it first this time.

"And you are the very air I breathe." He kissed her one more time and then turned and left, opening the door of the shuttle van and climbing inside, followed by all the security guards and his three brothers.

She waved and smiled brightly because that was the last thing she wanted him to see. They drove off, and she closed the door and collapsed. She knew he would feel her distress, but she just couldn't control her emotions at that moment. The sisters knew she would be a mess, so they showed up almost immediately to comfort her. They were all just as upset though, so they all cried together.

Eventually it was time for her to catch her plane back to the States. Gail came with Mike and Nick to retrieve her and get to the airport. Gail had made all of the arrangements and Marguerite didn't even look at her tickets. She had surrendered her passport to Gail for safekeeping the day before, at her insistence. Once at the airport, they headed off somewhere strange—to where the small puddle jumpers were parked. She thought it odd that they wouldn't be on a big jet back to the States. It was a long flight after all. Then she saw it; a private jet. She started to cry. Gail got worried that something was wrong. Mike was all over her, trying to shelter her from whatever the problem was. "Please don't tell me we're going on a private jet." They all just looked at her. They didn't realize that Chase hadn't told her that was how she'd be flying from now on.

"Yes," Gail said, "that's the only way you'll be able to travel safely."

Marguerite just stood there. She couldn't get her legs to move. They eventually managed to get her on the plane, and a very nice flight attendant and the pilot welcomed them. She shook both their hands to be polite, and because she didn't want them to see she was flustered. They guided her to her seat, and Gail asked the attendant to bring her a brandy. She took slow sips and tried to regroup. The jet was beautiful. Very sleek and elegant, decorated in earth tones. It had big leather seats that reclined and could actually fold out into single beds. The leather was so soft it felt like butter. She sat very still, trying to take everything in. Once she had calmed down, she went to Gail and Mike and apologized for being so upset. She had never expected a private jet. She'd thought they might have booked them in first class, but never a private jet. They smiled and were not bothered by it. Gail apologized also, and told her that the next time they would go over the whole game plan up front so that she wasn't caught off guard. Marguerite felt better then.

Chase had already texted her multiple times before she even boarded her flight. She texted him back and told him she was on a private jet, and that it had caught her completely off guard. She told him how she'd reacted and he got concerned. She reassured him that she was fine now and there was nothing to worry about. She just felt stupid about her outburst. He apologized for not going over everything with her, but said that with so much going on he hadn't thought twice about it. She told him never to hold back on her just because he thought she couldn't handle something. He agreed and apologized again. By then the plane was ready to take off and they said their goodbyes and both said, "I love you." She took a deep breath. This was all going to be so new to her. She knew she would need to rely on Gail for her help with it all.

The flight went smoothly. They had dinner on board and it was surprisingly very good. She didn't know why she should be surprised. Of course it was good. She supposed she would have to get used to everything being very good.

Right before they landed at the Scranton/Wilkes Bare airport in Pennsylvania, Gail came and sat with her, going over what they thought would happen next: Once they landed, they would stay on the plane until Nick went and got the car. Then he would pick them up at the hanger, where the plane would stay until she was ready to go back to London. There was a good chance that the press would be at the hanger, because somehow they had found out she was coming. Mike and Nick would shield her as much as possible and, Gail reassured her, she would be right there the whole time.

"Now," she said, "if you felt the need to say anything to the press, what do you think you might want to say?"

She thought for a moment before responding. "That I'm thrilled to be back in my home state of Pennsylvania for a few days?"

"That's perfect. What if they asked what you're doing here."

"I am going to see my family and settle some things before going back to my new home in London." It seemed perfectly obvious to Marguerite, but Gail seemed pleased with the response.

"Excellent. Now, what if they ask about the wedding or married life with Chase?"

"Well," Marguerite paused for a moment to think. "I will say that I am extremely happy and look forward to spending the rest of my life with him."

Gail was blown away. Clearly, she did not need any coaching. She did tell her to stop there though. That would be enough questions.

Marguerite told Gail that she loved her home town, and wouldn't want to offend anyone in her home state. Gail took that into consideration and decided that, if the press were there, she should stop to speak to them, but only a few questions. She conveyed that reasoning to Mike and Nick, who agreed and understood.

The local press were there in abundance at the hanger.

When she got off the plane, she shook the pilot's hand and thanked him for the smooth ride. The local stations got it all on tape. She had meant it though, and hadn't just said it for the press. Then she stopped and took a few questions, ending up with pretty much the same questions she had rehearsed. Once those had been answered, she excused herself, saying that she was extremely tired from the trip and needed to get on the road because her family was waiting for her. Mike ushered her to the car, where Nick was waiting, and Gail was right behind her.

Marguerite called Chase when they got in the car. She told him what had happened and that she was fine. Gail said that she had done better than fine. She was great! Chase already knew that though, because Gail had texted him to tell him how lovely and smart his wife was, and that she hadn't felt the need to coach her at all when she talked to the press tonight. She'd nailed it. The stations were pleased and everything had gone smoothly. Chase told Marguerite how proud he was of her, and that he was going to see if he could see the footage of her arrival online. It was late for both of them, so they said goodnight and reminded each other exactly how they were feeling. "You are the very air I breathe."

Bad Memories

Marguerite really did not want to stay in her parents' house when she got back home. Too many bad memories. So her cousin Donna had made room for everyone to stay with her. She was happy to see her and her little cousins, Ashely, Marie, and Kristen. The next day, they would go to the house and start packing it up.

Donna asked, "Do you think you will take many things with you?"

She thought about it. "No. I really don't want many reminders of the prison I was in for twenty-seven years. I'm thinking of bulldozing the house and just keeping the lot."

Donna was not shocked she felt that way. She had seen what happened to her cousin there and certainly couldn't blame her.

When they were alone, Donna asked, "Are you happy?"

The smile on her face said it all. "Yes, more than I could ever imagine. But things are going to be so different. I have to choose every word I say from now on. I have to watch the way I dress and look. I won't be able to just go anywhere I want, especially without clearing it with Gail or without Mike tagging along."

She wanted to arrange a lunch with her friends while she was in town and Gail had to make all the arrangements for her. She couldn't just say to her friends, "Meet me at Arcaro and Genell's for lunch." Everything had to be cleared first for safety reasons. She told Donna to watch what she said about her, Chase, or the brothers. The walls had ears and she didn't want anything she said taken out of context or repeated incorrectly. Donna acknowledged that she understood what would happen, and so did her other cousin, Sue. They would be careful in their comments if anyone asked about her.

She had already spoken to Joe and Mary and was having dinner at their house the next night, which she was excited about. She felt like they were her parents. Gail had cleared it and they were all set. She prepared herself for a long day of packing and trashing everything she did not want or couldn't donate. That was another thing. The donations had to be made anonymously to avoid creating chaos.

The packers were at the house. She expected that she would only end up taking her own things back with her. There weren't many. Gail made arrangements for the Salvation Army to come and take everything else. Anything they couldn't take would be auctioned off and any money collected would go to charity.

Marguerite spoke to Chase many times during that day. He called first thing to say good morning and said that he hoped she would have a good day. He knew her trip back to her house was going to be difficult and had started wondering if he should have stopped her from going home until he could have gone with her. Everything was just happening so fast at the time and he'd thought about it too late. He tried to keep his mind open so he could feel it if she was in distress or upset, but so far, nothing. It amazed him that she was so strong. He knew she could hold her own but didn't realize she was this strong, and it made him extremely proud of her.

Marguerite tried to visit everyone she could because she didn't know when she would be back again. She snuck through kitchens to have lunches and dinners at her favorite restaurants, and everything went well there. Only once did she get caught, coming out of Ghigiarelli's with her friends, whom she had met for pizza. The camera flashes did not take her by surprise, but her comfort level surprised her. Her friends were concerned for her, wondering how she was going to be able to stand living like that for years to come.

"This is my life now. I have to get used to it."

They all hugged her and said goodbye, realizing that it would be difficult to keep in touch with her. But they all promised they would try.

As things were cleaned up at the house, Marguerite thought about how much she wanted to get back to London. She felt that being there would make her feel closer to Chase. She wanted to be in their house, around his things. She had plenty of things to do in that house too. She made a list of what she wanted done to keep her mind off being without him.

After ten days of packing and cleaning up, she decided it was time to go. She had done everything she wanted to do, seen everyone she wanted to see, and now she wanted to go. Gail made all the arrangements. They would be ready to leave first thing in the morning.

She had one last dinner with her cousins before she left. It was bittersweet. She had decided that she was going to knock down her parents' house. They understood and agreed with her. They would take care of it with Gail's help. Of course, she needed to talk it over with Chase first, and then they could finalize everything. She was sad leaving her cousins, and they were upset because they didn't know how often they would get to see her. She told them that she was going to try to go on the road with Chase when he had days off in his schedule. Otherwise it made no sense, since he would be working every day and would have no time for her.

The next day she left bright and early. The cousins were there to say goodbye and they all hugged and cried together. They told her they loved her and she told them the same. Then off she went, not knowing when she would see them again.

On the plane, she called Chase and they talked about her trip and how bittersweet it was. She had been so happy to see her family and all of her friends and Joe and Mary. When she told him that she wanted to knock down her parents' house and just keep the empty lot, he asked if she was sure she wanted to do that. She was positive, but he asked her to wait a few months before deciding. Right now, she felt like she wanted to knock it down, but maybe down the road she might change her mind. She thought about it and agreed to table it for a few months.

Marguerite told him she couldn't wait to get back to London to their home. That blew him away. She thought that she would feel closer to him if she was in their house and around his things. It almost made him cry it was so sweet.

They were just about ready to hang up when she said, "I keep meaning to ask you something."

"What's that?"

"The night before we got married, when I was lying in bed at the hotel, I couldn't sleep. I thought I heard you say, 'You are the very air I breathe.' So I closed my eyes and said it back to you."

The phone went silent for a long moment. When he finally spoke, his voice was very quiet and thoughtful. "While I was lying in bed, I couldn't sleep either. So I closed my eyes and thought about sending you a message: You are the very air I breathe."

Chills went down both their spines. "I heard you say it," she said, "or felt it at least. So I sent you the same message back."

"I heard you too, or sensed it maybe."

They didn't know what to say to each other at that moment. If he had been with her, he would have grabbed her and held on to her for dear life. Once again, something had happened that confirmed their connection to each other. Marguerite slept through the flight home and Chase finally fell asleep at the hotel where he was staying.

Overwhelming

Marguerite had so many things to do to
make their house into a home that she started to panic. To combat the
stress, she decided she would just work on one room at a time. They already
had bedroom furniture, so she put that room on the back burner. As far as
the bathrooms were concerned, they just needed towels and decorations,
which was an easy fix. She chose to concentrate on the living room. She
wanted it to be comfortable, because it would be a family room as well.
Right now there was only a fireplace, bare walls, and all sorts of awards
that Chase had left lying around on the floor. At first, she thought that some
of them could be hung on the walls in the living room, but then decided
to make an office out of one of the empty rooms and display them there.
It would have book shelves and desks, so they would both have a place
to review paperwork and appointments. There needed to be a designated
place for stuff like that, so everything wasn't lying all around the house.
Marguerite hated clutter. Everything had to be in its place.

She had a game plan, for the office and the living room, and called Gail to
tell her where she wanted to go. Gail made all of the arrangements for her
with both a furniture and department store.

Marguerite called the sisters to see if any of them wanted to join her,
and they said they would meet her there. Mike and Nick escorted her to the
furniture store, where Gail and the sisters were waiting for her. She circled
the store three or four times, talking everything over with the girls before
starting to make decisions on what to purchase. The couches had to be

comfortable and the bookshelves should have pieces she could add to later. She picked out the lamps, the end tables, and a huge coffee table. The desks she purchased were ornate and beautiful, and would make her want to sit there to get all of her business done.

Once done at the furniture store, they all headed to a department store to purchase some bedding, towels, and shower curtains for the bathrooms, as well as little decorations. Marguerite had a list of what exactly she needed, and it was lots of fun picking everything out. The sisters were a huge help. She had so many packages that they all had to take some stuff in their cars.

They realized they were starving, so they stopped at a restaurant they knew that had a private dining room and went in through the kitchen, where they caught the owner, Rocco, off guard. He was happy to see them though, and sat them in the private area so no one would see them. They joked and laughed all through dinner. Marguerite couldn't wait to get home to start putting out all the things she'd bought.

Chase had been trying to reach her and couldn't because her phone was dead. When she got home and plugged it in, she saw that there were multiple messages from him. She called him immediately and could tell that he was a little miffed. She told him that he should have just called Mike or Gail. They were always with her. He admitted that he hadn't even thought of that. Then he settled down and was himself again. She told him all about her shopping trip and what she'd bought. He was pleased that she was fixing up the house the way she wanted it. He wanted her to feel that it was her house too.

Then he hit her with something unexpected. "Did you find anything for a nursery when you were shopping?"

She just froze. "No. I didn't really think about a nursery."

That's when he blew her out of the water. "Mam, I want us to fill the house up with lots of children." They had never talked about when or how many, but they knew they both wanted children. She was completely taken back by his honesty, and the gentleness in his voice. It brought a tear to her eyes.

Then she regrouped. "We can't really start a family with you being 1200 miles away." She smiled teasingly at him, and hoped he could hear it in her voice. "To make that happen would require lots and lots of sex."

"Turn around."

She frowned slightly, confused, and then comprehension dawned. After freezing in place for a moment, she did as she was told. He was standing in the doorway. She hadn't expected him for two more days, but he was right there. She ran to him and he picked her up in his arms, hugging and kissing her. She started to cry, which made him emotional also. After a long heartfelt embrace, she squirmed to be put down and then grabbed his hand, pulling him to their bedroom where they stayed until sometime the next day.

He had two days at home. They tried to accomplish everything they could in that time. She forced him to help her paint the living room, because the furniture was coming in another day. He wanted to hire someone, but she insisted that they should do it together. When they were done, it looked just the way she wanted it to. He was pleased that they'd painted it themselves. They'd enjoyed doing it together. It had been a lot of work but fun, and he had never done anything like it before.

"Once is enough though," he said with a smile. "Make sure you hire someone to paint the rest of the rooms."

Before he left, they talked again about having a baby. They had only been married three weeks. "Why are you in such a hurry?" she asked.

He said he wasn't, but he knew that they were both old souls and assumed she would feel the same way about it, which she did. He'd always wanted to be married and have a family and so did Marguerite. But until they'd met each other, that dream had always seemed far off in some uncertain future. She loved Chase so much. She'd felt right from the beginning that she wanted a baby with him, but hadn't known how to approach him. On the surface, it always seemed like they hardly knew each other, but down deep, they were so connected that they might as well have known each other their whole lives.

It was difficult for him to leave her, but he knew he had no choice. He didn't want to start making it difficult for her to see him off. This was his job and they just had to cope with his schedule, so he hugged and kissed her enough to last them until they could be together again. He was going to check with the tour manager, Jack, to see if he had any days off where she could meet him on the road, and promised to let her know.

"So," Chase said to his wife, "do you think we had enough sex to make a baby?"

She just laughed. "We shall see in about four weeks."

"Four weeks? We have to wait that long?"

"Yes. It will take a little time to find out."

16

New Friend

Chase was gone for weeks, and every other day he asked her how she was feeling. She knew what he was waiting for. "Chase, if I'm pregnant, you will be the first to know besides me."

The four weeks passed by and no pregnancy. She was a little upset when she had to call and tell him that she got her period. She was not pregnant.

He knew she was upset and did everything he could to make her feel better about it. He said that it would happen eventually, at the time when it was meant to be. It was only September, and he would be on the road until at least November. Then he would be home until late January.

Almost three months together! She was counting the days until the next time he walked through the door. Thanksgiving, Christmas, and New Year's Eve were the perfect time for him to be home. She didn't even know if they celebrated Thanksgiving in the UK. She had to look it up, because if they didn't, she would still celebrate with all the brothers and sisters. It would become their new family tradition.

The fourth week Chase was gone, when she found out she wasn't pregnant, hit her hard, and he felt her distress. He called to say that he had three days off in Paris before their concert, and he wanted her to meet him there. She was packed before they even hung up and couldn't wait to see him. Gail made all of her arrangements but couldn't make the trip, and Nick was not needed this time around, so it was just her and Mike. This time she was on a regular flight and not a private jet, which pleased her. She'd felt guilty traveling on a private jet, as though she were inconveniencing everyone involved.

Chase was waiting for her when she got to the hotel. It was late, so they really couldn't go anywhere when she arrived. Instead, they ate in their suite and got caught up on what was going on with everyone, as well as how far she had gotten with the house. Even though she told him every day what was happening, it felt better saying it to him in person. He also told her about all of his concerts. The thing that amazed him the most was how kind people were being to him when he got to the venues. Everyone congratulated him on his marriage and some even gave him gifts. He had them stored and shipped to the house so they could open them together. He had wanted to tell her that detail in person. He was very grateful to everyone.

Chase asked her how she was feeling about demolishing her parents' home. Had she changed her mind? Her reply was still the same. In the spring, she would have it torn down. She was considering building a different house there. She asked him if it could be their home in the US, because she loved Pennsylvania. She felt they could make it their home for all the time they spent in the US, touring and recording. Recording generally happened in Los Angeles though, not Pennsylvania, so he still wouldn't be able to be with her if he was in LA working.

He saw how disappointed she was by this reasoning, so he encouraged her to go ahead with the plan to demolish the house in the spring and find plans for a new home on the lot. They could make it their home in the US. They'd find a way to make it work. She was thrilled that she would be near Donna and Sue, who were like sisters to her. She figured that she could go home more often if she had her own home to go to. Chase agreed and was happy with the plans. Especially seeing how happy it made her.

When they went out in Paris, they literally had to sneak around. They tried everything to look inconspicuous and hide their identities. Sunglasses and coats with hoods, to hide who they were, became the common fashion. It was a good thing it was cold in October there, because they pulled off most of their excursions without being noticed. Chase was thrilled, because it had never worked before. Probably because the four brothers would go out together, and everyone recognized them in that context. Just the two of them worked much better. Abbey and Cara were already there, but Jeanine could not make it that time, so poor Quinn became the third wheel to various couples, which no one seemed to mind. He mostly went out with Chase and Marguerite. For some reason, he clung to them more.

It was fashion week in Paris, and they got to meet some important people. Peter insisted that they go to some of the fashion shows and be seen. Marguerite almost stuttered when she met Victoria and David Baker. Victoria had her own fashion house and David was a tremendous hockey player. Victoria was absolutely beautiful in person. *Please do not take our picture together,* Marguerite thought, because she felt so inferior in comparison. But the cameras started flashing away, especially once they recognized Chase. Victoria told her that she thought Marguerite had looked beautiful on her wedding day. She had seen all of the pictures, which surprised her. They sat and talked for over an hour, while the men went off and did something else. Before Victoria left, she gave Marguerite her phone number, and vice versa, and told her to call her once she got back home. Marguerite volunteered to babysit her daughter, Holly, anytime she needed someone, assuming she was available. Victoria was surprised that she suggested it, and that was when a truly deep friendship was born. When they parted, they hugged, which took both David and Chase by surprise. Both were beaming when they saw it. And all the cameras loved it too, because the flashes were going off like fireworks. Chase commented that it seemed like a really nice moment between the two of them, and she had to admit it was. She felt comfortable talking to Victoria and thought they had formed a friendship. Chase knew how busy the Bakers were and told her not to be upset if they did not hear from them. She understood completely what he was saying, but felt that he was wrong. She kept that to herself, of course.

The day after the fashion show and meeting the Bakers, her phone went off around noon. She did not recognize the number, so when she answered, she was shocked by who was calling. After a brief discussion, she hung up.

"What was that about?" Chase asked.

"It was Victoria. She was heading home to London and wanted to say how nice it was to meet us. Then she invited me to lunch next week. She's going to call me to confirm which day would be good for us both."

Chase just stood there looking at her as if she had two heads. "I can't believe it. I never thought she would call, just because of how busy she is with her fashion line and Holly." He was amazed and pleased for Marguerite. *Her first new friend aside from the sisters and people on the payroll.* He smiled. *Why did I ever doubt her when she said she thought they would be friends?*

17

Getting Ready

What had Marguerite been thinking when she thought there might be a Thanksgiving holiday in the UK? That rock she crawled out from under had just gotten a little bigger. She went online to see what holidays they actually did celebrate in her new country and familiarized herself with them. She also noted them on the calendar so she wouldn't forget and would know what to expect. There were a lot of bank holidays too.

Before she knew it, Chase was home for his three-month break. He did still go to the studio with his brothers to write and go over plans for the continued tour, which would start back up in February, but he was at least home.

Marguerite told him about having a dinner on the day Thanksgiving was celebrated in the US. She did not want to lose her traditions. He agreed that she should feel free to celebrate any holiday she wished—well, except for the Fourth of July. They laughed when she mentioned that one.

She called Joe and Mary to invite them and they said that they would love to come over for the holiday. Chase's mom, Jess, and all the brothers and sisters would be there also. The cousins could not make it but said that maybe they could come for Christmas, which pleased Marguerite. Ed was in the US at that time and was bummed that he couldn't make it. David and Victoria said they would have loved to attend but they would be in the US at that time as well. They took a rain check, which pleased Marguerite to no end. Victoria had become a true friend to her since their meeting in Paris.

Joe and Mary would be staying with Marguerite and Chase, which meant that she needed to get another room completed. If the cousins were coming for Christmas, that meant all the bedrooms had to be completed by then, so she ventured off with Chase one morning to pick out more furniture. They found many wonderful pieces in the furniture stores around London. They did one bedroom in Victorian style, choosing vintage pieces they found in an antique shop. The pieces were rich, dark, chunky wood with carvings in the bed posts and matching pieces. Another bedroom was very traditional, with a lighter, rich oak bed and matching dressers and nightstands. The last room they thought about had twin beds for children. It amazed both Chase and Marguerite how alike their tastes were in just about everything.

They hired someone to paint the rooms in neutral colors and then set them up when the furniture arrived. Marguerite and the sisters went shopping for the bedding and decorations for the rooms. It seemed never-ending and exhausting, but so much fun. She always thought, *Thank God for the sisters*. Without them, she would never have gotten every-thing accomplished.

The week of the holiday dinner, Marguerite began feeling sick in the mornings. She didn't think much about it, because she was so distracted and excited about company coming and staying with them. So was Chase. The house, or what was completed so far, looked beautiful, warm, and cozy. Chase loved being home. Especially with her.

She was all ready to cook up a storm on Thursday—their new Thanksgiving holiday in the UK. Everyone else was excited too. The sisters were all buzzing, asking what they could bring, and she included them in the dinner preparations. They were to all bring side dishes to go with the turkey and stuffing. Joe and Mary would arrive on Wednesday and Chase would pick them up at the airport. Gail insisted that they send a plane for them and this time Marguerite didn't object. Mary was going to make the pumpkin pies when she arrived and couldn't wait to work in the kitchen with her daughter. Marguerite ordered a big turkey from Franco and Anna, and told them all about her dinner coming up. The three had become good friends. She felt they were like extended family, because she was Italian too and they were able to converse in their language.

Again Joe and Mary made them feel like they were their children by the warmness in their voices and the affection in their actions. It made them feel good.

Chase felt as though Mary and Marguerite were in the kitchen all night making desserts. He saw how happy Marguerite was. Mary was beaming helping her get ready for the dinner. She was learning that making lists would save her from forgetting something important.

They set the table the night before so it would be one thing off Marguerite's list. The formal setting looked like it was out of a magazine, which was exactly the way she wanted it to look. The dishes were strategically placed on the table with the bread plates to the top left. The silverware shined where she placed it on either side of the plates. The water and wine glasses stood like soldiers, all in perfect alignment next to each place setting. Each napkin was folded like a tent and placed in the middle of each plate. Chase surprised her by buying a beautiful cornucopia filled with fresh flowers for the middle of her table. The smell throughout the house was amazing from all the baking, as though pumpkin candles were lit all over the house. She couldn't wait to add the turkey smell the next day. That would put Chase over the top for sure.

One of the conditions of Joe accepting the Thanksgiving invitation was that Marguerite could get all the football games on the TV. Marguerite was also a big football fan, so Chase had a system set up where they could get all the games—college and professional—on their big-screen TV in the family room.

Joe laughed his ass off when Marguerite told him she had made Chase paint the living room with her. He said he would have loved to see that. Then they all laughed when they heard about Chase telling her she would have to hire someone to do the rest of the house. Once was enough.

Chase understood why Marguerite had wanted him to do it. He was used to being sheltered from doing anything, because he was always on the road and didn't have the time or know how to do anything around the house. Chase was 23 and had spent the last five years on the road, which meant that his normal life had ended at 18.

When Joe and Mary thought about it, they thought it was no wonder he had been considering quitting the band. They were glad he had changed his mind.

"Since the day I met Mam," Chase said, "my whole life seemed to get easier." The smile on his face, when he said it, pleased Joe and Mary a great deal.

Turkey Day! Mary and Marguerite got up at six in the morning to prepare the turkey and stuffing for the oven. Once that was done, they were both able to get back to bed. Chase was waiting for her. He wanted to make love to her and never wanted her to leave his side again. She just laughed when he said that, but inside her heart was exploding with joy. She was over the moon. Chase was the love of her life and their families would all be coming over for their new holiday. She thought life couldn't get any better. And then it hit. She turned green lying in bed with Chase. He actually saw her color turn.

He immediately jumped up. "Do you want me to get Mary?"

"No, it will pass."

And it did. She was just so excited and exhausted from everything she was doing that her stomach had flipped. It was in that moment that she realized she might be pregnant. She kept it to herself. Chase came back to bed, and they held and kissed each other, and made love like they always did, with the passion generally reserved for the greatest loves of all time.

"So how long does that turkey actually have to cook?" Chase asked later on, as they were catching their breath. "I want to know how long I can keep you here in bed."

"Seven hours, because it's so big. We could barely get it in the oven."

"I have an oven?"

They started laughing almost instantly at the now-familiar joke. "Oh definitely. You have lots of things. You do know you have a back yard, right?"

"No!"

"Yes." Having too much fun, she went on from there, listing the various items he possessed while Chase laughed. Eventually as she was starting to run out of things to mention, she circled back to the back-yard theme. "... and a garden shed, and a rake... and I think you even have a Weed Wacker!" That last one was too much for Chase, who was near hysterical by that point.

In the next room, Joe and Mary heard them laughing and it made them start too. They thought about how happy they were for them and said a silent prayer that they would be that happy for the rest of their lives.

18

Turkey Coma

Everyone started coming to dinner around three. Marguerite told them all to come early so they could watch some football games and spend the day together. Quinn was the first to arrive with his girlfriend, Jeanine. They were the cutest couple. Chase always felt like Quinn was a little brother to him. They actually looked alike. They both had blond hair and blue eyes. Maybe that was why Quinn always wanted to hang out with them. He came over to the house a lot, sometimes by himself and sometimes with Jeanine. Those two arriving first did not surprise Marguerite. She corralled Jeanine, along with Mary and Jess, to help her in the kitchen. One by one, the rest arrived and it was lots of fun. The smell of the cooking turkey was amazing. Everyone wanted to eat as soon as they arrived, but Tom wasn't ready to be carved yet.

Joe teased Chase, saying that he would teach him how to carve a turkey.

"It might not be a good thing," Marguerite said, "putting a sharp utensil in Chase's hand."

Everyone got a kick out of that and they all said they wanted to watch.

"All you guys are going to watch and learn, because you should take turns carving it every year."

That was when they all really started laughing. No one could even picture it without seeing someone cutting themselves and winding up in the emergency room.

"Can you just hear them," Jeanine said, "trying to explain to the doctor how they managed to carve *themselves?*"

Marguerite smiled. The fun they were all having together was exactly what she had been hoping would happen.

As expected, all the women were in the kitchen and all the men were in the family room, hollering at the TV while watching the game. Rounds of beer were delivered to the men, who were sprawled out everywhere—on the couches, chairs, and even on the floor—to keep them occupied until the dinner was ready.

Finally, Marguerite and Jess checked the turkey and decided it was time. They took it out of the oven to let it rest for a while, because that was what was suggested online before beginning the carving lesson. Marguerite had everything ready for the veggies and Mary was mashing the potatoes.

Then she called to the men to come carve the turkey. The ladies in the kitchen couldn't stop laughing. They got to sit and take a break while the carving was going on. Chase had no idea how to even turn on the electric knife. When Joe showed him, he didn't expect the vibration and the knife started skipping all over the turkey. The ladies weren't even drinking and they were laughing so hard they couldn't stop. With Joe's instructions, Chase eventually got the hang of it.

Then the other guys said they wanted to try, which really sent the ladies over the edge. Mary and Jess laughed and laughed, shaking their heads in amusement.

Everything was ready now—with no injuries to report—and the food was on the table. Quinn happily said grace and people started passing around the food. Chase sat at the head of the table and Joe sat at the foot. *Like father and son,* Marguerite thought. It looked perfect. The whole week had been perfect.

After dinner, they all cleaned up. Mary was stunned when all the guys took their plates and loaded them into the dishwasher.

She asked Marguerite, "How did you get them to do that?"

Marguerite told them they had never even seen a dishwasher before they started coming into her home to eat, so she had showed them how to load it, and they had been doing it ever since.

When she told her about them all kicking off their shoes automatically now when they came into the house, they started laughing again.

They all ate so much that they decided to watch the rest of the game and have pie and coffee later. No one was in a hurry to go home, so they had lots of time left in the day. Marguerite also thought some of them might not make it home that night and was pleased that she now had bedrooms ready for more company.

The game was over and it was time for the pie and coffee. What is it about men and food? You didn't have to tell them twice that food was ready. They were at the table so fast it was like there was a fire in the family room and they had to get out quickly. It stunned Mary that they all loved coffee so much. She thought that young adults usually drank soda, even for breakfast, but the boys all loved coffee and so did their girls.

The pies that Mary made with Marguerite were amazing. She let Mary take the credit for them because she totally deserved it. That is when they all admitted they were beached. They could not eat another thing. They all felt like the stuffed turkey they had consumed.

They went back to the family room and watched the next game, or tried to, because in ten minutes the men were all asleep. Sprawled out on the floor, on the couches—there were bodies everywhere. "How can they just sleep on the floor like that?" Mary asked.

"At least they have pillows," Marguerite said. "When they travel, and are held up in airports at all hours of the night, they just sit or lay down anywhere and most of the time it's just on the floor with their luggage or coats as pillows." She showed her pictures of all of them passed out at an airport. Mary had just started to realize how difficult it must be to be on the road all the time.

Mary got concerned for Marguerite, and if she would be safe enough when she traveled with Chase. "Gail is with me most of the time and Mike is with me all of the time," she reassured Mary, "and I try to always be careful." She promised Mary that she'd do everything she could to stay safe when traveling. Mary was still concerned but didn't let it show.

It was midnight and everyone was just getting up from the turkey coma they had fallen into. Jess had gone home earlier, but everyone else was still there. Marguerite and Chase had two extra furnished bedrooms, so Blake and Abby took the bedroom with the queen-sized bed—because he was the oldest—while Drew and Cara and Quinn and Jeanine each took one of the twin beds in the other room. No one seemed to mind at all. No one wanted to leave and were happy they could stay the night. In fact, they all seemed strangely prepared to do just that.

"Can you believe they all had a bag packed?" Chase and Marguerite were in bed, talking about the day. "I know, right?"

Chase told her he thought the brothers felt that their house was like base camp, where they expected to spend holidays and share all kinds of celebrations. They loved coming over and that was why they visited so much. Chase had never told her that before. The tears started streaming down her face. She was thrilled that they felt that way and had never minded them being there all the time. Chase admitted that he was thrilled they considered their house a home base. He'd never thought in a million years that he would be so happy. He told her how proud he was of her and how she had saved him.

"You are the very air I breathe," he said.

"And you are mine." Then they slipped happily back into their turkey comas before they'd even kissed goodnight.

Parents

In the middle of the night, Marguerite felt boxed in again. She knew Ed wasn't there this time. The memory of finding him passed out in their bed with them made her chuckle quietly as she picked up her head to look across her sleeping husband. Sure enough, there were people in bed with them again. This time it was Quinn and Jeanine spooning right next to Chase and her. She sighed fondly, baffled by this odd new trend. She guessed the twin beds must have been too small to fit them.

She got up to see how Drew and Cara were doing and found that they were still asleep in the other twin bed. They certainly seemed to fit well enough. She quietly crept back to her own bed. *Maybe they had just wanted company?* She would see what was going on later, when they all were a little more coherent. In the meantime, she was just glad she and Chase weren't in the habit of sleeping naked.

At about eight the next morning, it seemed to Marguerite that everyone was still sleeping. She got up to go downstairs and start the coffee. Halfway down, her stomach turned, and then it hit her again that she might be pregnant. Could it be? Chase had told her it would happen at the right time! Was it time now?

In the kitchen, she found that Mary was up as well and already making the coffee. She took one look at Marguerite and asked if she was all right. Her color looked off.

"If I look green, then yes my color is off." They both smiled and just stood for a moment looking at each other.

"Are you pregnant?"

Marguerite said that she didn't know yet and didn't want anyone to know until she was sure. It had just really occurred to her. She had been sick in the mornings lately but had thought it was just because she was doing too much: fixing up the house, shopping for bedding and furniture, and trying to get ready for the holidays.

Mary and Joe had no children. Marguerite and Chase were the closest thing to children they'd ever had. Mary was incredibly excited, while being worried and concerned at the same time because they had only just gotten married. Marguerite and Mary talked it over, and she explained that she and Chase wanted a big family. They wanted to fill up all the bedrooms, which Mary thought was a good plan but not so soon. They talked and talked about it, and after all was said and done, Mary felt somewhat better about it. She asked Mary not to say anything though, because Chase had to be the first person she told. If it were true, she wanted it to be his Christmas present.

"You are like our children to us," Mary said. "We worry for you both with the way you have to live your life. Our concern for your safety and well-being is always on our minds."

Marguerite started to cry. She'd had parents who never even asked her how she was, let alone told her that they were worried about her. They'd never said they loved her and always treated her like she was an inconvenience to them.

Mary had blown Marguerite away with her sentiments, and the water works were turned on. She couldn't stop crying. Then Chase came into the kitchen and saw her and panicked immediately.

"We were just having a conversation," Mary quickly reassured him, "about how much Joe and I love you two. You're like the son and daughter we never had."

Being just as sentimental as Marguerite, Chase started the water works too. He walked over to embrace his wife and Mary together. "You will be parents to us always. I promise that we will see you as much as we can, and will always stay in close contact with you. All the time!"

Joe came into the kitchen and saw the tear-fest going on, so Mary had to fill him in on all that was happening.

Joe nodded his agreement. "We would be honored if you called us Mom and Dad."

Now there were four people in the kitchen bawling their eyes out. Chase was amazed that they felt this way about him. His father had died when he was four, so he'd never really had one.

What a turn of events. Everyone came down for breakfast then, which Mary insisted on cooking. While they were sitting around the table, Chase told the brothers and sisters what had happened with Mary and Joe. They were all thrilled. They said that they'd always felt as though Mary and Joe were Marguerite's parents anyway. The boys, being boys, naturally jumped on the bandwagon and started calling them Mom and Dad too. Everyone laughed, but it came out of their mouths so naturally that it stuck. So now Marguerite had parents and Chase got an extra mom to go with the father he'd never had.

Around noon, the brothers and sisters left, hugging and kissing goodbye, telling them what a great time they'd had, and saying that they would like to keep and celebrate that holiday again every year. They all agreed and just like that, it was etched in stone.

That day Chase spent some time in the office making calls. Although it was Black Friday, that wasn't a holiday in the UK, so everyone he needed to speak to was still around. First, he had Mary and Joe added to his list of people to contact in case of emergency. Then he asked Gail to make sure that Marguerite's schedule and his own were forwarded to them daily, so that they would know exactly where they were at all times. That same list had always been sent to his mom and now he wanted it sent to these parents too. Gail understood completely and agreed to start immediately.

He had something else on his mind though. He wanted to give them a check to compensate them for trip expenses, but didn't want to insult them. He called in Marguerite and asked her what she thought. She had no idea. Joe made a lot of money as the vice president of the company she'd worked for, so money was not an issue for them. She suggested that, for now, they should just offer to pay for their trips to London, until the opportunity came up to feel them out about financial issues. Chase agreed. Then they called in Mary and Joe to tell them about all the arrangements Chase had just made for them with Gail. They were blown away. They were especially happy about getting their schedules, because they worried so much about them all the time. There was one more thing to discuss with them, but Chase decided to wait until it arrived.

Marguerite and Chase were lying in each other's arms when she remembered waking up that morning and seeing Quinn and Jeanine in bed with them. She asked Chase if he knew what was going on. Chase shrugged. He had woken up, saw that she was gone, and noticed the two of them in bed with him. They were snoring away, so he'd decided not to wake them. He didn't know what to make of it either. As the morning had gone on, he'd never gotten a chance to ask them about it in private.

They both decided to just let it go and hoped that, someday, they would tell them why they'd ended up in their bed.

20

Afterwards

The day Mom and Dad left to go back to the US, the package Chase was waiting for arrived—just in time. It contained a phone for each of them, with the phone numbers of fourteen people programmed in: Marguerite, Chase, Blake and Abbey, Drew and Cara, Quinn and Jeanine, Jess, Peter, Marguerite's bodyguard Mike, Chase's bodyguard Alex, Gail, and Nick. If they couldn't get in touch with either of them and were worried, they could try any of those numbers. Mom and Dad were blown away. Gail had seen to it that they had secure phones to take home with them. Chase told them to never give those numbers out to anyone, and to only call them with those phones. That way they could be sure of having safe and secure conversations. All the people whose numbers had been programmed in also had Joe and Mary's numbers added to their own phones, in case any one of them needed to get in touch with them in the States.

If they hadn't felt like their parents before, they truly did now. Nick chose that moment to arrive, ready to take them to the airport. Mike would accompany them as well to make sure they escaped without any issues. It was so sad to see them leave. They couldn't be back for Christmas, but Joe would see if they could return for New Year's. That thrilled Marguerite and Chase to no end. Smiling hugely, they both thought, *this is how it's going to be. Our parents trying to spend holidays with us.*

"I can't tell you how proud I am of you," Joe said to Chase. "For all you've accomplished in your short life, and for being such a good husband to Marguerite."

Chase and he hugged like they would never see each other again. *I have a dad,* Chase thought, *and he's proud of me!* He had always imagined hearing his father say those words to him.

Marguerite hugged her mom and cried, making her promise to call as soon as they arrived home, no matter what the hour was, so she wouldn't worry.

After the events of the entire week, Marguerite was exhausted. She told Chase she was going to lie down and get some rest. He went with her and they both fell asleep until midnight, when Mom called to say they were home. Right on cue. Chase took the call and let Marguerite sleep. He knew she had worked her tail off all week and thought she needed the rest.

It was mid-morning when they finally woke up. Chase loved his sleep and sometimes it was hard to get him up. Marguerite got up first, which was good because her stomach was upset again. She felt sick but didn't throw up, which she was thrilled about. She would take an upset stomach over vomiting any day. She decided that the next time Chase went to the recording studio, she would go to the drugstore for a pregnancy test.

All of a sudden, she was famished. She was so hungry, she felt like she could eat everything in the refrigerator. She got Chase up and said she was making breakfast. He was still groggy. "Breakfast? Morning already?"

"Yes, lazy bones. Get out of bed."

He did, almost dragging himself to the bathroom to brush his teeth and wake up. Then he stopped. "Why are we not in bed making love now?"

She just laughed. "If you can catch me, you can have me." Then she took off running. After a few trips around the table in the kitchen, he caught her, threw her over his back, and carried her back up to bed to make good on her challenge.

When they were done, he heard her stomach growling and released her from his grip so they could go get something to eat. He sat in the kitchen as she whipped up some eggs, ham, toast, and of course, coffee. He watched her move around the kitchen with ease. She had made the kitchen her own, which pleased him to no end. She noticed him watching her. "What are you looking at?"

"Just enjoying how beautiful you are. And thinking, 'Wow, you are mine.'"

It was such a nice moment between them. Marguerite could only smile from ear to ear. She was glowing, and he noticed. They were rarely alone. Someone was always with them, whether it was security or one of the brothers, but they never minded. At that moment, they were happy to be alone.

Around noon, Blake called to see if they were going to be watching any games. They said that they were and that he could come on over if he wanted. Of course, once everyone found out that Blake was coming over, they would all do the same. There went their peace and quiet.

They were amazing, the four of them. They were so connected, just like brothers, but even closer in some ways. They seemed to move together and each of them could predict where the others would be at any time, especially on stage. There was never any jockeying for position, or pre-planned choreography. When they went on shows to do interviews, they made room on the couches for each other without ever seeming to try. No confusion or bumping into each other. It was like a puzzle that went together effortlessly. It was truly amazing. It warmed her heart to see it. She thought back to when he had been thinking of leaving the group. They must have been devastated, sensing his anxiety and depression and imagining going on without him. He was one quarter of them, and she didn't mean one quarter of the group. Each of them was one quarter of every other one of them. She knew Chase felt that too, which was why he had been having such a hard time understanding and coming to terms with his desperate need to go his own way.

There was a rule in the house for college football: They watched Penn State first. If they were clearly going to get stomped, then they could change the channel. But college football was almost over except for the playoff games, and then the finals in January.

They moved on to professional football. There was a rule for professional football too: They watched the Steelers, Giants, Eagles and Saints first. Same scenario. If they were getting trounced, then they could change the channel. Marguerite was adamant about this. The sisters loved football just as much as she did, which was a great thing to have in common. Football Sundays were the norm in the Martin household. Everyone knew where they would be on a Sunday afternoon or evening. Even Peter knew where they all were on Sundays. Sometimes he would show up with pizza and beer.

Marguerite and Chase never minded everyone being there. They were happy that everyone considered their house their home as well.

Chase knew his wife was holding something back from him. Lately she seemed to have forgotten how clearly they could *feel* each other. Every morning he felt her sickness, but he waited for her to say something. He did not want to jinx it if she was pregnant, and he wanted her to tell him when she was ready to do so. *She could just be waiting to confirm it.*

So every night, before he kissed her goodnight, he whispered, "You are the very air I breathe."

"And you are mine."

Waiting

Chase went to the studio and Marguerite headed straight out to the drugstore to get the pregnancy test. She read and followed the instructions and then waited for the results. The wait seemed to take forever, but then she saw it: inconclusive. She was devastated. Maybe it was just too early, which is something the instructions warned of. *Dummy me,* she thought. Why hadn't she gotten more than one test? Before she knew it, she was crying inconsolably, and wasn't even sure why.

Chase and the brothers were talking at the studio when he felt her becoming upset. He was shaken, because he figured she had gotten her period and wasn't pregnant. He turned white as a sheet. The boys all saw it. They became concerned, but he said it was nothing and tried to brush it off so that they wouldn't ask more questions. He didn't know how he was going to go home and try to pretend he didn't know what was happening.

He stopped at the grocers on the way and picked up a huge bouquet of flowers. He knew Marguerite loved flowers. She always had them in a vase in the kitchen. Franco could also see on Chase's face that something was wrong. He couldn't hide it, but he had to.

"Is everything all right?"

"Yes, it's perfect," Chase said. "I just wanted to give Marguerite something to brighten up her day after working so hard on the house lately." He told Franco that the turkey had been fantastic and that everyone had enjoyed themselves but had eaten entirely too much. Chase's face lit up when he talked about the dinner. He told Franco about Joe and Mary, and how they thought of them as their own children. It had been a great week. He took the flowers and headed home, and as he looked back, he saw the biggest smile on Franco's face. It made him smile too, if only for a moment.

Marguerite felt him on his way home, so she tried to pull herself together. Then, before she knew it, he was home with the biggest bouquet of flowers she had ever seen. She lost it completely when she saw him.

"I felt you all those mornings being sick," he confessed, "and felt how upset you were today. Please don't hold back. Just tell me what's wrong."

She was sobbing so much that she couldn't get any words out, so she just sank to the floor. Chase ran to her, and held her in his arms, rocking her back and forth like a child. *This is my wife. How can I help her?*

He stroked her hair, saying small things like, "I'm here. Let me help you. Just tell me what's wrong. It will be all right." When it seemed like she was strong enough, he added, "I can't live without you though, so if you're going to die, then don't tell me that. *That* you can hold back from me!"

That made her stop and chuckle, and so did he. He brushed her hair from her face, but she wouldn't—couldn't—look at him.

"Chase, I love you so much." She could barely choke out the words.

"I love you too! Just tell me what's wrong," he said, pleading with her.

They sat on the floor for almost an hour. She fell asleep there, in Chase's arms, and he wondered how he was going to get her up and to bed. She still had not told him what was wrong. As soon as he started to move, she woke up. She was much more composed now, but when she looked at him, she lost it again.

He grabbed her and made her look at him. When their eyes met, his had tears in them. Finally, he couldn't wait any longer.

"Are you not pregnant? Is that why you are so upset?"

"No, I took the test and it was inconclusive."

Chase was hugely relieved, but confused. If it was only inconclusive, why was she so upset? He got her up to her feet, and she finally pulled herself together enough to explain. "I have been sick every morning and felt sure I was pregnant, but when the test didn't register, I just sort of lost it. I guess I was so certain, and I wanted to tell you good news so badly, and everything caught up with me. I'm so sorry, Chase."

He kissed her softly and assured her that there was nothing to be sorry for. He just wished she had told him so she wouldn't have had to carry everything all alone. "Whatever we go through, we need to do it together.

We're *so* much stronger when we're together." She nodded, and he kissed her cheek before continuing.

She nodded again, and wrapped her arms around his waist, giving him a squeeze and pressing her head against his chest. "Thank you."

He pressed his lips against the top of her head and then gave her a little shake. "Okay, let's see what's what."

They got the test box, read all the directions again, and decided it was probably still too early to tell.

"Let's wait another week and take the test again," he said. "But next time, you'll take the test when I'm home with you. I don't want you to be alone." At that moment, she didn't think she could ever love him more than she did right then. He was amazing.

The water works started again, and she sank down onto the recliner in the living room, holding her face in her hands. Taking a few deep breaths to calm himself, he knelt quietly in front of her, placed his hands on her knees, and insisted that she just tell him everything that was bothering her.

She tried to explain. "I don't want to disappoint you, Chase. I feel so much pressure, trying to get pregnant. I want to so badly just for myself, but knowing that you want it so badly too...? I don't want to let you down."

Chase had a look of sorrow and amazement on his face. "You could never let me down. I'm in constant awe of you." He reached out and took her chin in his hand, gently raising her head to look into her eyes. "Don't you know that? You could never disappoint me. Even if we were never able to have children of our own, we could adopt as many as you want. But as long as we are together, and as long as you love me the way you do, I don't need anything else."

There was a long pause as she tried to absorb this. When it finally sunk in, he could feel her sense of reassurance through the bond they shared. He could feel her loving him, and being comforted by how much he loved her.

He pulled her to her feet, holding her for a long moment. Then, exhausted by all the drama, they headed wordlessly up to bed. Chase held Marguerite all night and they slept like babies.

Marguerite woke up still in the same position in which she'd fallen asleep: with Chase's arms wrapped tightly around her. The minute she moved, her stomach turned. *Okay, that's a good sign.*

Chase opened one eye. "I feel you getting sick. That's good, right?"

She kept forgetting how connected they were to each other. Of course he felt her. They both felt everything about each other. She just kissed him and smiled wide.

"Yes, that's very good."

22
Confirmation

Marguerite and Chase were anxious all week. It was like they were on speed. They laughed when she said that to him. They couldn't wait for the week to go by, so that she could take the pregnancy test again. She was still sick every morning and was happy to be sick. So was Chase. At the studio, the brothers knew something was up but didn't know what.

Blake suggested they try a new restaurant for dinner one night. He didn't realize what a welcome suggestion it was, as it kept Marguerite and Chase's minds off what was going on. When the waiter brought out some wine, she only took a few sips and didn't finish it. Being women, and noticing everything, the sisters just looked at her. She smiled and said nothing, because she had nothing to tell them. Yet.

The manager of the restaurant didn't do a good job of keeping everyone away from them. He actually kept bringing people over to meet them. They agreed they had to take that place off the list. It seemed that every time they took a mouthful of food, someone else would come over to meet them. It got taxing after a while. They were gracious to everyone who came over, of course. Marguerite was always amazed at how well they handled themselves. The women all followed their lead, saying that it was a pleasure meeting them and thanking them for stopping by to say hello. Mike and Alex were with them, as well as the bodyguards for the rest of the brothers, but they were told to just let the people come over. They didn't want to cause a scene.

After what seemed like forever, the end of the week arrived and it was time to take the test again. She had bought three different types of tests and followed all the instructions precisely. Chase was right there, reading the directions over her shoulder, which made her laugh. As stressful as the tests were, neither one of them could stop smiling. After setting a timer, they turned away, not wanting to look at the test until it was definitely time to do so. They waited the three to five minutes the directions called for. *How can five minutes seem like an hour?*

Marguerite was shaking. Chase had to hold her tight to keep her still. "No matter what they say. I will love you even more than I did five minutes ago."

She didn't want to cry, because she figured she would be crying soon enough if they turned out to be negative. Finally, the timer buzzed.

Test #1. Positive!

Test #2. Positive!

Test #3. Positive!

They looked at each other and then started jumping up and down like kids, all around the bathroom, and then the bedroom, and up on the bed, and down the hall... screaming and yelling and crying happy tears like children. They danced around the room and couldn't stop. They were so happy they thought they would jump out of their skins.

They called his mom first and told her. She cried and cried. Then they called Mary and Joe in Pennsylvania. They were both so happy and they all cried together. They told them they couldn't tell anyone else though. They wanted to wait until her first trimester was over. Then they would tell everyone. They agreed that she should wait until then.

Chase knew he had to tell the brothers, and Marguerite knew she had to tell the sisters. They were going to do it as a Christmas present, because they were all coming over to celebrate Christmas day with them. They figured they would give them all a gift with a tag that read: To my aunts and uncles from Baby Martin (to be named at a later date). The joy they both felt was surreal. They could not believe that they were actually happier than they had already been. There seemed to be no end to the smiling.

Marguerite called her cousins to see if they were still coming for Christmas, and they were. She would send a plane for them on the twenty-third, so they could all settle in before Christmas Eve and Christmas day celebrations. The brothers spent Christmas Eve with their families, but Christmas day was, and would always be, reserved for the band-mates and their partners to spend together. That was a pact they'd made on Thanksgiving that they promised they would always keep.

Marguerite and Chase were trying to fall asleep, but short of gluing them shut, they couldn't keep their eyes closed. Chase finally said to Marguerite, "Thank you."

"For what?"

"For saving me. I was lost until you found me. Even if we couldn't have any children, I will be forever thanking you. You are my life and the very air I breathe."

"You're the very air I breathe."

They just held tightly onto each other. Then they drifted off.

Family

Christmas week arrived and it was hectic, but in a good way. Marguerite had always loved Christmas but rarely enjoyed it with her mother and father. She barely got presents from them, which got easier as she grew older, but they did cook traditional Italian dishes for the holiday, which she loved—seven fishes on Christmas Eve and homemade pasta on Christmas day. Marguerite thought that once the cousins were in and settled, she would see if they'd like to help her make some cookies and the pasta. Anise and pepper cookies were her favorites. Of course, there were also chocolate chip cookies and cut-out sugar cookies. She had already started making those, but waited for Donna and Sue to help with the anise and pepper cookies. They were tricky. They either came out right or you threw them all away.

The day Marguerite made the cut-out cookies, she called Blake and Abbey, Drew and Cara, and Quinn and Jeanine over to help put the icing on them. They came right over, and of course, did a lot of taste testing, giving her the thumbs up on all of them. She was surprised there would be any left for the holiday.

While they were all there, Chase and the brothers went to pick out a Christmas tree. What a trip that must have been! Marguerite told Chase where she wanted to put up the tree and suggested that he measure how high the ceiling was and how wide it could be, so as not to take up the whole family room. It made all the sisters laugh when they thought about it.

They couldn't wait to see what they picked out and how they were going to get it in the stand.

She also reminded him to ask for help if he needed it. Someone there could always point them in the right direction. They took the measurements and then they all went off to the tree farm. None of the girls had much confidence that their wonderful but sheltered mates would have much success in this particular venture, but they were pleasantly surprised. They came home with one that fit perfectly in the family room. It was exactly the right height and width, and beautiful besides.

Marguerite asked everyone if they would like to stay and help decorate the tree and they were thrilled to do so. There was a great deal of laughter and fun had by all. That was one thing she noticed: When they were all together, they always had fun. They truly enjoyed being together. Chase's mom came over to help and everyone enjoyed her company too. Once the tree was up and decorated, Marguerite thought she had never seen a nicer tree in her life, but she was a little biased because it was hers.

Donna, Sue, and their families arrived as expected at around six in the evening on the twenty-third. Again, the time change was a killer. They all loved their rooms. They were short a bed but two of the little cousins wanted to sleep together in one of the twin beds anyway, so everyone was set. Each bedroom had its own bathroom, so it made it easy for everyone to get ready in the morning.

On the morning of the twenty-fourth, they went to the grocers and Marguerite reintroduced them to Franco and Anna, whom they had met at the wedding. They all spoke fluent Italian together, and enjoyed having the opportunity to do so. Franco had the fish all ready for them, so they had no real excuse to linger. They all wished they could spend more time there, but they had to go home and make cookies. Donna and Sue did not say anything to Marguerite about Nick driving them all around or Mike accompanying them. They just went with it.

They made the anise cookies first and then the pepper. They sat Ashley, Marie, and Kristen down and put them in charge of icing them. They turned out nice and didn't have to be thrown away.

Chase took Mark, Donna's husband, and Jack, Sue's husband, to the studio to show them how they recorded their songs. He had told the brothers that he would be giving them the tour, and they all showed up to see

Mark and Jack. The men had a great time, even having a celebratory shot together before leaving for home.

While they were gone, the women got a lot accomplished. Chase's mom came over to help too. They got the table set the way Marguerite liked it, and got the pasta made in no time at all. They had trays of it lying in the office to dry. The new pasta machine she bought worked really well. She was amazed at how much easier everything was with so many people there to help.

Everything was set, and now all they had to do was go get changed into their Christmas outfits. That was one tradition of theirs that Marguerite loved. They dressed for dinner in their holiday finest. The little girls were all in velvet, as were Donna and Sue. They matched their hostess, who had on a beautiful blue velvet dress with lace-trimmed sleeves. She glowed and everyone noticed.

The guys dressed up also. Chase looked so good she actually wished she could have him all to herself. He had on black dress pants and a gray knit pullover that hugged his body. Marguerite loved it. She thought he looked incredibly hot. She knew then that her hormones were kicking in and laughed at herself.

The dinner was great and seemed to last all night. There were hardly any leftovers, which was good since there was no room in the refrigerator. Chase's mom, Jess, enjoyed being around family on Christmas Eve. Chase commented that he saw her more now than he ever had, and in private, told her how grateful he was.

"I'm so happy that you're always here with us," he said. "Thank you for loving my wife and treating her as your daughter. It makes me so happy. And you know, I worry less when I'm on the road now, knowing that you're here with her."

Jess started crying. "Thank you for being a good son and a great husband. Your father would be so proud if he were here to see it. I can't tell you how happy I am that you both want me here."

They convinced the little cousins to go to bed around ten, because after all, Santa was going to come that night. With that thought, they all happily went to bed. Truthfully, they were exhausted from all the traveling and excitement. Once they were sleeping, Marguerite and Chase told them their news: They were going to have a baby. But, they explained, they couldn't tell anyone about it until she was through her first trimester. She hadn't even been to see a doctor yet.

Everyone exploded with happiness for them. Donna and Sue finally realized how committed Marguerite and Chase were to each other, and it made them extremely happy for them. They also told them that they were going to tell his brothers and the sisters on Christmas day as a surprise. Everyone had smiles on their faces as they went up to bed.

Marguerite told Chase how happy she was. "This is the best holiday in my whole life."

He knew what she meant. She had shared her terrible experiences living with her parents. He wanted this holiday to be special for her. So far, it was for them both. They exchanged gifts before they went to bed. It was their first Christmas together, so they wanted it to be more intimate than opening them in front of everyone. Chase gave Marguerite a beautiful pair of sapphire earrings to match the ring he'd gotten her for a wedding present. She loved them. They were gorgeous.

Marguerite gave Chase a set of diamond-studded earrings. He always had hoops in and she thought he might want to change them. They were not big, but they were beautiful. She also got him some new pullover shirts, like the one he'd had on that evening. He loved his presents.

She was tired, but not too tired to make love. He was afraid to touch her, but she assured him that every book she read said that sex was okay until the end of the pregnancy. The doctor would advise her when they should stop. Chase was relieved. He wanted to show her just how much he loved her. And he did, again and again...

Surprise for the Brothers

Christmas morning arrived and everyone was buzzing around the house. The little cousins had so many presents to open that they didn't know how they were going to get them all home. Marguerite, Donna, and Sue had decided they didn't want to exchange gifts. They had never done so in the past and had no idea what they could possibly get each other. No one was upset about it. They'd all decided to spoil the little cousins instead.

Early that afternoon, as if on cue, all the brothers and their mates started to arrive for dinner. It was as if they couldn't wait to get there. They were all dressed up in their holiday attire and looked fantastic. Chase's mom arrived and they all got ready for the dinner.

Out of the whole group of them, only Marguerite's family had ever eaten homemade pasta. Everyone else couldn't wait to try it. The cousins tried to explain that it was a little lighter than store bought because it was fresh and homemade.

Everyone sat down and automatically turned to Quinn to say grace. When he was done, they quickly dug into the meal. Donna made the best salad on earth and they started with that. As predicted, it was excellent. It was quickly gone.

Then Donna, Sue, and Marguerite went to boil the pasta. While they waited for it, they placed the meatballs and sausage in a fancy silver bowl and set it on the table. The guys really wanted to dive into it. The whole dinner would be a new experience for all of the Londoners. The pasta was finally ready, so they poured it in a huge bowl, put sauce on it, and served it up.

One by one, they commented on how much they loved it. They couldn't believe the difference the freshness made. That was a big relief to the Italian/Americans. They hadn't known if they would like it or not, but it was a success. They took a break before dessert and decided to let the rest of the family open their gifts.

Chase and Marguerite handed a small package to each of the brothers and sisters. They had to open them all at once. Marguerite signaled for them to wait, and once she had all of their attention, she gave them the go ahead.

"Go!"

Then they went wild. They unwrapped the packages to find vouchers for diaper-changing classes and tags saying that they were from Baby Martin, who would be named in about eight months. Everyone started crying. The brothers were slapping Chase on the back and grabbing him and hugging him. The sisters were crying and hugging Marguerite enthusiastically. The excitement was amazing. Then the brothers came and hugged Marguerite, and said they loved her and thanked her for being their sister. The girls went to Chase and told him they loved him and hugged and hugged him. No one could stop crying. Donna and Sue couldn't help noticing that they were like a big family. They loved each other openly and told each other often. It gave them a warm feeling.

Then Drew got a little nervous. "Wait, these aren't real classes, right?"

"Yes, they are," Chase said. "Mam is making me go too." Everyone started laughing. Everyone would have to know how to change diapers for when they babysat.

"We should think about recording it," Marguerite said. "It would be a comedy show."

They told everyone that they didn't want to say anything outside of the family until her first trimester was up. Then they could tell everyone. There was one more person they did want to tell though, and that was Ed. Once the brothers knew this, they dragged Marguerite and Chase to their office and called Ed to say Merry Christmas. They couldn't wait to tell him the news, and when it got blurted out, by several band-mates at once, Ed was thrilled.

"Can the baby call me Uncle?"

"Absolutely! Uncle Ed!"

No one wanted to go home after the wonderful news, but all the bedrooms were taken, so they all camped out in the living room for the night. They didn't care. They had brought pajamas to sleep in again, which blew Marguerite and Chase away.

When they were alone in the kitchen with Quinn and Jeanine, they finally asked them about Thanksgiving and finding them in bed with them. They didn't have a clear reason. All they could say was that they had gotten up and something had just made them want to go and see them. When they saw that they were sleeping, they'd just hopped into bed with them. It seemed to make sense at the time, but looking back, they agreed that it was an odd thing to have done.

Quinn shrugged. "Maybe it was all that turkey. It messed with our heads." They all chuckled at that, remembering the turkey coma they had all fallen into after dinner.

Jeanine said that they hoped they weren't upset.

"No, we weren't upset," Chase said. "We just wanted to know if anything was wrong."

Marguerite and Chase were going over the day's events and beaming about how well the holiday had turned out. After a few minutes, they both realized that they were waiting to fall asleep because they thought Quinn and Jeanine might be in to see them. Marguerite giggled at the thought, but right after they said it, there was a knock on the door. It was them. There was a big couch in Marguerite and Chase's bedroom and they told them that, if they didn't want to jump into bed with them, they could just sleep on the couch. Jeanine and Quinn just looked at each other and jumped into bed with them. They said that maybe they would take the couch later. They really just wanted to stay up and talk to them. Marguerite and Chase looked at each other, still unsure of why the couple liked being with them so much.

Scheming

January flew by. Chase was home and they spent as much time together as possible. He doted over her. Sometimes too much. It was always, "Don't lift that, eat more of this, go take a nap." He was careful to back off when he felt that he was annoying her. They ended up telling Gail, Mike, and Nick about the pregnancy, because they had to know in case she got sick or something happened. And they had to tell Peter. He agreed that they should wait to tell everyone after Marguerite was through her first trimester.

She wanted to go back home to Pennsylvania before the doctor told her she couldn't travel anymore, so they made arrangements to go in March. She wanted to talk to builders about constructing a new house where her parents' had been. Donna and Sue were thrilled that she would be home for a while so they could spend more time with her.

They felt that, after her parents died, she had left for a little excursion and just never came back. When she returned, they had thought they would finally be getting to spend time with her, but then she met Chase and the rest was history. They were happy for her, but missed her terribly.

Chase would be with her in Pennsylvania this time, because he would be on a break from touring. Marguerite was thrilled. He was going home with her.

Valentine's Day was approaching and the girls wanted to do something special for the boys. They went to lunch one afternoon at their favorite res-taurant, entering through the kitchen where Rocco was always so happy to see them. They tried thinking about something different with which to surprise them.

Marguerite had an idea. "They have a concert in Verona on Valentines' Day. Why don't we go there and surprise them?"

They loved the idea, but Cara took it one step further. "Let's surprise them on stage and sing one of their love songs to them."

Then all the wheels started turning. Before they got their hopes up, they called Peter and asked to see him. He told them to come right over to the studio. They did, and when they ran their idea by him, he didn't rule it out. He did say that he was worried that it might not be a good idea, though. He was in a love/hate relationship with it. He called Jack, the tour manager, while they were still in his office, and asked him to pop over to discuss something.

When Jack walked into Peter's office, and saw all of them there, he panicked for a moment, thinking something had to be wrong.

"The girls want to do something special for the guys at their concert on Valentine's Day in Verona," Peter said. "They want to sing one of their love songs to them, on stage. What do you think?"

Jack thought it was a great idea, and immediately knew which songs they should sing.

"Songs?" Marguerite said, getting more nervous by the moment. "We thought *song*—as in one. Singular."

Caught up in his vision for the moment, he ignored her. "There is a series of three songs where the guys stand in a row and just sing. I'll get Patrick, the choreographer, to work with you and see how it pans out!" His wheels were spinning double-time. He loved the idea, and really got carried away. "We can record it maybe, for something down the road, or release it online or even just record it for us to have and enjoy ourselves." He was rambling. He hadn't even asked any of them if they could sing. He figured that, as romantic a gesture as this was, it would only mean that much more to the boys, and their fans, if they sounded terrible but were willing to embarrass themselves for love.

So it was a go. "Until the guys go back on the road next week, we should listen to their songs and learn our respective parts. That way, when we start practicing, we'll at least have the singing part down and will just have to mimic their movements." Patrick wanted them to move and sing those songs just like the guys always did.

Peter had to tell Jack that Marguerite was pregnant, concerned that he would change his mind. His reaction was unexpected. His face lit up and he was very happy for her and Chase. He would make sure she would be safe and not work her too hard. Peter assured her that he wouldn't let Chase know Jack knew about the pregnancy, because he would wonder why he had been told. He didn't want to spoil the surprise in Verona. They told him that they were also waiting for Marguerite to get through her first trimester before they told everyone. Jack agreed not to let on that he knew.

Now that it was settled, the girls started to panic. Peter and Jack reassured them that the idea was awesome and that they couldn't wait.

"We will have to do a lot of practicing once the guys go back on the road," Jeanine said.

He gave them a list of the songs to practice and they got up to leave.

Before they got to the door, Peter asked Marguerite how far along she would be by Valentine's Day. With the help of the girls, she figured out that she would be about fourteen weeks along. Two weeks past her first trimester. She had a doctor's appointment the week before Chase headed back on the road. Peter told them that, after her appointment, they should release a statement saying that they were expecting a child. He would discuss it with Chase also, of course. It sounded like a good plan to her.

They were all excited and Marguerite told the ladies that she had to be careful. If she got too pumped up, Chase would feel it and start asking her what was going on. *Oh wait!* She was pregnant. "That's what I can say! My hormones are out of whack! The pregnancy is making me crazy!"

The girls laughed and agreed that that would work. After all, hormones had always been a mystery to guys, and always would be. They don't question them, they just back away slowly.

It was a fact that her hormones *were* working on her though. *Poor Chase!* When he came home from the studio the previous night, he had taken his shoes off in the pantry and started walking towards her in the kitchen. He was talking about something that seemed important or interesting to him, but before he could get out a single sentence, Marguerite grabbed him and started kissing him like there was no tomorrow. Then she started taking his shirt off and unbuttoning his pants. She had them off before he could even ask her what was going on. He had no complaints of course, and figured he would just go with the flow!

Never upset a pregnant lady, he had thought happily. They didn't make it to the bedroom but Marguerite hadn't cared. She had pulled him down on the floor in their office and it hadn't bothered either of them. They hardly noticed, in fact. He sensed the urgency of her kisses and responded enthusiastically. *Keep the pregnant woman happy!* It wasn't as if he wasn't enjoying himself after all. It was just quite different from their normal passionate but tender interludes. This wasn't about feelings or romance. There was simply a passion that needed to be quenched. It flowed back and forth through the bond they shared like an unstoppable tide. Sensations were doubled, shared between them from both perspectives and driving them both wild.

Finally, unable to bear the prickling pains he was feeling through the bond from his wife's delicate skin on the rough surface of the office floor, he scooped her up and carried her upstairs to bed. He wasn't going to disappoint her, or let any discomfort get in the way of her pleasure.

He didn't disappoint her. Not then, and not hours later when she finally agreed to take a break to eat and catch their breath. He was exhausted, but she couldn't get enough of him. Neither one of them had eaten dinner and she admitted that she was hungry too. Reluctantly, she went down to the kitchen with him and grabbed a quick bite to eat.

It wasn't quick enough though. By the time they were finished eating, the hormonal urges were gone. When he asked her if she wanted to go back to bed and she declined, saying that she actually felt like watching some TV, he said a silent prayer, thanking God that she was done for the night. He had savored every moment of their passion, and would flash back to it in happy recollections for years to come, but his masculine pride was incredibly relieved that she had run out of steam... before he had.

Chase and Marguerite were on the couch watching TV when she turned to him. "I am so sorry."

"For what?"

"I think I used you before." Embarrassed, she hid her face, trying not to laugh.

When he started laughing though, she quickly joined in.

"You can use me any time you want. Anywhere, any way, any time!"

He leaned in, kissed her cheek, and made a move to grab her.

"Hands off," she said, smacking his hand away with a smile. "We're done for tonight."

First Visit

It was time for Marguerite to have her first visit with a doctor, and of course, Chase was going with her. Gail helped her find a good OBGYN: Clair Robbins in London. Gail had gone to the office herself and explained who she was making the appointment for and how imperative it was that no information about it or Mrs. Martin left their office. The staff understood completely and Gail asked them all to sign waivers, saying that they would not discuss anything about Mrs. Martin, her pregnancy, or her husband. Not even the fact that she was there. Everyone in the office signed.

Gail also met briefly with the doctor to ask her if she understood what she was getting into by accepting Marguerite as a patient. She laid it all out for her: Once the baby arrived, the doctor would probably be holding press conferences, addressing people around the world. The doctor agreed and said that she didn't have an issue with it.

The next day was the initial appointment. Chase was right there and Marguerite was holding onto his hand so tightly that she stopped the blood from circulating through his fingers. His fingertips were white. When the nurse called her in, she was relieved because she just wanted to meet the doctor and get this first appointment over with. She wanted to hear that her baby was fine and everything was proceeding normally.

They checked her blood pressure and all her other vital signs. They asked her questions about her health and family history. They did a blood test and all the while Chase stayed at her side. Then Doctor Robbins came in and spoke to the both of them. She introduced herself and said that she was honored they had chosen her as their doctor. She promised that she would monitor her closely and that Marguerite could call her any day or time with any questions or issues she was having.

Marguerite confirmed that she wasn't having any real issues at the moment, aside from some morning sickness, but that she was not even throwing up. She just had some queasiness. Her appetite had increased and she was getting a little emotional, which she just assumed was her hormones changing due to her pregnancy. Doctor Robbins was impressed by what she already knew, and Marguerite confessed that she and Chase had started reading up on pregnancy and what to expect. The doctor asked if they had any questions before she examined her, and Marguerite said yes.

"It's kind of embarrassing, but what about sex? Will you tell us when we should stop?"

The doctor thought that was a great question and told them to continue as they normally would. She said that she usually tells couples to stop nearing the end of their eighth month. Chase and Marguerite started laughing, thinking about the romp on the office floor the previous week. Marguerite told her that she thought her hormones were affecting her sex drive, because she had nearly attacked Chase last week when he got home from work. They all laughed at that, and she told Marguerite that that was completely normal. Then she turned to Chase. "You should expect that even more down the line."

He just laughed. "Oh no!" he said teasingly. "Thank God I'm going back on the road."

They all got a kick out of that. Then the doctor asked Marguerite to get up on the table so she could examine her. Chase helped her up. She asked Chase if he was staying or leaving and he asked if he could stay.

She nodded. "Of course."

Then she got started with the exam, saying a bunch of medical terms that neither one of them understood. The nurse in the room wrote it all down. When the exam was over, she told Marguerite that she looked to be about twelve weeks along. She wanted her to go for an ultrasound the next day, and asked if she wanted to know the sex of the baby. Chase and Marguerite did not even think about that, but Marguerite looked at Chase anyway and said that she wanted to know.

The doctor gave her multiple prenatal prescriptions with tons of instructions on what to eat and what to stay away from. Then Marguerite froze. She forgot to ask about traveling.

"Doc, what about traveling? I'm going home to Pennsylvania in March and I like to travel with Chase when he's on the road."

The doctor said that she should go about her days as she usually did. There were no restrictions yet.

They would schedule appointments monthly until the last eight weeks and then would switch to weekly. Travel was not a problem until the end. Both Marguerite and Chase were relieved. It had pained him to think she couldn't be with him on the road, because he had a busy schedule coming up in April after the trip to Pennsylvania.

They left the doctor's office on cloud nine. Everyone was waiting to hear how she'd made out. They were all waiting at the house for them. They told them all about the appointment and how much they liked the doctor. After everyone was satisfied with everything they said, they all went home and left the two of them alone.

Marguerite and Chase were still discussing the doctor visit when they went to bed.

"Do you really want to know the sex of the baby?" he asked.

"Yes, but if you don't want to know, we could tell the doctor tomorrow during the ultrasound."

He said he wanted to know too, so he would know what color to paint the nursery. That made them both laugh because he'd already said his painting days were over after the living room job. One and done!

Everyone Knows

Chase went to the studio in the morning because Marguerite's appointment for the ultrasound was not until one. He had just been pacing back and forth so she told him to go. He was driving her insane. She was anxious already and it was worse with the both of them being around each other.

Around twelve thirty, Chase told the brothers that he had to go because Marguerite had an ultrasound at one. Drew asked him where it was and he told him the name of the hospital. The minute he left, the brothers called the girls to tell them what was happening.

Chase went to get Marguerite and she was ready and waiting for him. Nick drove and this time they had Mike and Alex with them too. When they got to the hospital, Mike and Alex ushered them into the hospital and knew exactly where to go because they had already mapped out a route to take them through without being seen. Marguerite forgot how efficient they were. So far, so good.

When they got to the waiting room, they were stunned. Blake and Abbey, Drew and Cara, and Quinn and Jeanine were already there waiting. They were blown away. The nurse at the window had kept asking them if they had appointments, and they'd kept telling her that they only had one, and she wasn't there yet. They laughed when the nurse came out to get them. Mike and Alex stood at the door to make sure no one came in and saw them.

They went into a dark room with low lighting. The doctor put a sheet over Marguerite so she wouldn't feel embarrassed. Chase was standing at her side and they were both shaking. The doctor sensed it and started talking to them to calm them down. She told them everything she was going to do and why. They started to ease up. She squirted a cold clear gel from a tub onto Marguerite's abdomen. Then she started going back and forth over it with a wand-type thing, pressing it against her skin and moving it around until she found what she was looking for. Of course, Chase and Marguerite had no idea what she was seeing so they just waited for her to say something. Then there it was. They saw it. The baby. They both started to cry. They were amazed. Chase practically jumped on Marguerite when he saw it. He kept kissing her head. The doctor was laughing. She explained everything they were looking at: the placental sack, the umbilical cord, the heartbeat...

"Before I go any further, did you want to know the sex of the baby?"

They both said yes. The doctor pointed to a specific spot on the screen and confirmed that it was what they thought it was.

It's a girl! They cried and cried. *A girl!* They were so thrilled, they couldn't contain themselves. The doctor also noted that she was actually about thirteen weeks along.

Marguerite looked at Chase. "Do you want the family waiting out in the room to come see?"

He kissed her. "You're reading my mind. Would you mind showing them?"

"No. I think they would be disappointed if we didn't include them."

Then they asked the doctor if it would be all right if his brothers and sisters came in to see, and would she show them everything like she had showed him and Marguerite? She admitted that it was an odd request but allowed it.

Chase went out to the waiting room and they could see that he'd been crying. They got nervous. Quinn was the first to speak up. "Was everything all right?"

Chase smiled. "We want you all to come in and see for yourselves."

So they all piled in the room and saw Marguerite on the table crying. They were still nervous until the doctor found the baby again and there it was on the screen. They all started crying, hugging Chase and each other.

"It's a girl," the doctor said. They almost raised the roof and nearly crushed Marguerite trying to hug her all at once. Now the doctor understood why they had wanted to include them. She saw how tight-knit they were. They were a family. Marguerite saw tears of joy in all of their eyes.

It made her cry even more. Chase stood beside her head and just kept kissing her.

"Okay," the doctor said, throwing the brothers and sisters out. "You can see them again in a few minutes."

"My manager Peter would like to release a statement to the press about the baby," Chase said. "Can you work with him on it and speak to him about the correct terminology?"

She agreed and they got Peter on the phone. He answered on the first ring because he knew where they were and had been waiting for the call. Chase told him it was a girl and Marguerite could hear how happy Peter was for them over the phone.

"Here is the doctor. She will give you all the information."

The doctor and Peter worked out a formal press release:

Chase Martin of the Band 4 and his wife, Marguerite, are extremely pleased to announce that they are expecting their first child in July. They would also like everyone to know that it's a girl! So far, the pregnancy is normal. Mrs. Martin is not experiencing any issues at this time and is past her first trimester at thirteen weeks. Chase will resume touring in February with his band-mates as planned. Mrs. Martin will be in the best of care while Chase is on the road. Abbey Adams, Cara Goodwin, and Jeanine Mercer—you all know who they are—will be with her, as well as Chase's mother, Jessica, and Mrs. Martin's mother, Mary.

The statement would be released at 5:00 pm, London time. This gave them time to get home and call the family. Without exception, the news was received with joyful tears and excitement. Jess promised Chase that she would keep an eye on Marguerite for him while he was on the road, and Mary offered to come to London to stay with her. Plans would be made to make that happen.

They told everyone that the statement would be released at 5:00 pm London time, so they would hear it in Pennsylvania at around eleven in the morning.

Marguerite asked Peter if he could release the information to the local news stations and newspapers back in Pennsylvania. It was her home and she thought she would like to keep that link with them. Peter thought that was an excellent idea. This way her home town would get the news at the same time as the people in London without it having to make its way through various social media first. That made her happy.

As expected, the Internet was buzzing the next day. It didn't freeze this time, but it certainly slowed down a bit.

Chase and Marguerite were lying in bed. He bent over and kissed her abdomen. "Goodnight, my beautiful daughter. I love you."

It was the sweetest thing she had ever seen or heard. Her eyes filled with tears.

Chase laid his head on her stomach and sang his wife and child to sleep.

Practice

It was so difficult for Chase to leave Marguerite, but their mothers were both there at the house to pick up the pieces when he left. She was doing better than he expected. She knew something he didn't. There were only two weeks left before Valentine's Day and their surprise. There was a lot of work to do.

Off went the men, and the practicing started. The two moms accompanied Marguerite to the warehouse where a mock stage had been assembled so that they could practice and get their footwork down. The stage was huge and intimidating.

Patrick, the choreographer, was busy working out all the details and the girls were stunned at how much preparation had already gone into what they were planning. Jack was away on the tour, so he couldn't be there, but he'd told Patrick what he wanted them to do.

They all knew their vocal parts, so first they just stood in a line on the stage, behind the microphones, and sang and sang and sang. Patrick blasted the music so that they could sing it with the background tracks. They got measured for their ear pieces—the same type the boys had. They practiced popping up onto the stage. Patrick asked Marguerite if she felt okay doing that in her condition, but it didn't bother her at all. Patrick had also decided that they would be stepping out through fog on the way to their microphones.

They kept practicing until their throats were raw—popping up on stage, waiting for all the screams from the arena to die down, marching through the smoke and up to the microphones, and then singing their hearts out. They did it over and over again, day after day for two weeks.

The night of the show, while the boys were performing, a message for the fans (in both English and Italian) would flash on the big screens behind them: "Don't tell Blake, Drew, Chase, or Quinn, but they are about to get a huge surprise from their Valentines!" The boys never looked at the screens so they would never notice the message. But the arena would be wild over it. This, at least, they were all sure of. When the time was right, the show's producer would speak to the boys through their ear pieces and tell them that there was a surprise for them, and that they should look back. If all went according to plan, they would see the girls stepping out through the fog.

The two moms worried that Marguerite was doing too much, because by the time they got home each night she was so tired she just went right to bed. Then she started the process all over again the next day. But she kept saying she was fine and assured them she would never do anything to jeopardize her health or that of the baby.

Right before the last practice, they were trying to decide what to wear. All they knew was that they didn't want to all wear the same thing. The boys never did. They decided that, since it was Valentine's Day, they would all just wear something red. Marguerite wanted to wear black leggings with black ankle boots with no heels—so she could move around the stage easily—and some kind of red top. They went shopping together to pick some things out. Marguerite found a red top that had the shoulders cut out and long sleeves trimmed in red lace. That was a load off her mind. She had been worried that she wouldn't find anything. She finally had a baby bump, and the top showed it off, which thrilled her. Cara found a red and black checked top, and was going to wear black tights and boots too. Jeanine decided on red shoes and tights and a black lace top, and Abby went with a striped red and black top, with black tights and red boots. They were all ready.

The time came for them to go to Verona. The mothers went home and the girls headed onto the plane for the trip. They were going to stay with the guys for a few days after the show, so they had some luggage with them. They were arriving in the morning, at which time they would go right to the arena to practice with the live band. The boys would not be there, as they would probably be sleeping at that time. Everyone knew they were coming and were told specifically not to spoil the surprise for the guys.

They got to the arena and started shaking. It was so big. They all started panicking and Jack could see it. "This is why you came here to practice now," he said, "so you can see what to expect." They even taped crowd noise (screams in this case), so they could see how to react.

They said hello to the band, who said they would do their best to follow them and help them out if they forgot anything, and told them not to be nervous. It always turned out all right. The girls felt better after talking to them.

They got on the pop-up ramp and Patrick told them to watch for him this first trial, hoping to make them feel more at ease. Then Jack cued the stage manager and up they went, just as they had practiced. They heard the screams just like in practice. Then they started strutting—they had *really* practiced their strutting—through the fog and to the microphones. As soon as they reached the microphone stands, the music started.

They ran through all of the songs without stopping. It was going so well that Jack just kept them going so they could see how the rhythm of the songs went together. He just had to remind them to wave and acknowledge the crowd. They had spoken about that when they first stepped off the pop up and arrived on stage, deciding if they should wave to everyone before moving forward, reacting to the screams. Jack thought that would be a great idea. Acknowledge the crowd first.

The girls spoke about it and decided they would pop up on stage with their arms around each other. They felt if they did that, it would keep them calmer. Jack and Patrick both agreed with that. Patrick said that he was thrilled with their dedication to the performance. He was amazed by how good they sounded and how good they looked. He was confident that they would be fabulous that night. Then they thought about the boys. They had been so focused on the performance that they'd almost forgotten why they were there.

They ran through it again two more times, and Jack and Patrick decided they were ready because soon the boys would be there to run through some songs.

The girls were whisked off to the hotel and into their rooms. Marguerite needed to rest and the girls lay down with her to make sure she did. Then they ate supper and rested some more. They couldn't go to the arena until the concert was underway, so the boys wouldn't see them.

Finally, it was time and the cars were waiting for them. They had a police escort so they could get through traffic quickly. It worked out perfectly. Vita was waiting for them to do their hair and the stylist, Lisa, was waiting to help them get dressed. She loved everything they had chosen to wear. When they saw the baby bump, they were excited for her. They both bent down and kissed the baby. It was so sweet.

It was just about time for them to go to the stage. Jack said that they had just started flashing the message to the crowd and that was why they were going wild. The boys were used to the noise so they didn't think anything about it.

Peter was waiting for them at the stage. He was thrilled now that they had decided to do this. Now all they had to do was get through it.

At the last minute, Jack asked Marguerite about possibly speaking Italian to the crowd, since they were in Verona. She said that she had taught all the girls some phrases to say to the crowd when the songs were over. He couldn't have asked for more, and was thrilled. "Make sure you do that," he said. "It will be perfect."

Lots of Love

Show time! They stood on the pop-up platform and could hear the crowd screaming. They all grabbed a hand-held mic, and then the platform started to rise. When they popped up on the stage with their arms around each other, they heard the full volume of the screams for the first time. It was deafening. Smiling from ear to ear, they waved to everyone. In their earpieces, they heard the producer tell the boys to turn around, which was their cue to start strutting. The boys looked back, seeing them strutting out of the fog towards them, and their confused looks turned to expressions of wonder. Their mouths hung open, as they watched their women line up behind the mic stands, each in the place normally reserved for their male counterpart. As they placed their mics onto the stands, they smiled at the boys and were rewarded with huge face-splitting grins in return. Then the music started and they started to sing.

The songs were beautiful and their voices were clear and strong. Each had captured the band's moves, and even their individual styles, beautifully. The first song led directly into the second. The boys seemed mesmerized, standing there staring and grinning.

On the last song, they motioned for the boys to join them and they all sang it together, each couple standing together, sharing a mic, and enjoying the moment. The electricity in the building was amazing. Cameramen were taping every move they made. During the final song, they were supposed to leave the mic stands and make their way to the end of the stage to sing to all the fans, switching sides occasionally, so as not to leave anyone out.

The boys just followed their lead. Chase and Marguerite walked from side to side, singing together and waving to everyone. Every time they switched sides, he patted Marguerite's baby bump, as if to show the crowd, and they went wild each time.

During the last chorus, streamers shot up from the sides of the stage out into the seats. Fireworks went off on the back of the stage, and thousands of red and white balloons were dropped from the ceiling. It was a scene no one would forget for the rest of their lives.

Then Marguerite and the girls each said something in Italian to the crowd, and thanked them for letting them sing to the boys, and to them. Then they all kissed their guys for an amazing few seconds, which the fans *really* seemed to appreciate. Marguerite couldn't wait to kiss Chase again, and told him so. "See you later and be ready!"

He laughed, nodding enthusiastically as she followed her sisters back upstage. They went to the halfway mark on the stage, as the boys always did, and waved to all sides; then they continued upstage to the platform and stopped right at the top, lined up, and took a bow with their arms linked around each other's waists. Before the platform started descending, Jeanine lifted her mic and said, for all of them, "We belong to the Band 4 and we are so happy to have joined you tonight. Thank you all for being so kind to us."

As the crowd cheered and the platform started to descend, they waved and threw kisses to everyone. Then they were gone, and all they could hear were screams. People in the audience were crying and carrying on.

They heard Drew say to the crowd, "I don't know how to follow that!" The roar of the crowd got even louder. The band started on the next song immediately, so as not to delay the concert any longer.

When the girls got off the stage, everyone was waiting for them with water and cold towels. They were dripping and they had only done three songs. They went right to the dressing room to change and clean up—they felt yucky and sticky. Peter, Jack, Patrick, and Vita all came in to see them. They were beaming.

"That was the greatest success I think we ever had," Jack said. "What you girls just did will be all over the Internet and the news worldwide."

The girls were still buzzing as they got changed. Now they understood what the guys meant when they said it was a different feeling when you come off stage. The adrenalin was pumping.

Chase used to say, "You can hear the quiet after it being so noisy on stage with the music playing and the fans screaming." Now she knew what he was talking about.

The concert was over. The boys were thanking everyone and the girls waited at the bottom of the pop-up platform for them to come off stage. Marguerite had the cold towel and extra shirt ready for Chase. When he got offstage, he made a b-line to her, picked her up in his arms, and hugged her tight. Mike and Alex tried to get them to move to the car, so he changed his shirt on the run while Marguerite wiped him down with the cold towel. Mike held Marguerite's hand to keep her moving, and Alex had Chase's back.

They made it to the car. Mike and Alex ushered them into the back seat and climbed into the front beside the driver. It was a luxury vehicle, with more than enough room for them in the back or front, but they knew how much the band-mates appreciated quiet alone time after the chaos of being on stage. Once they were on the road, Chase told Mike and Alex to turn around because he didn't want them to see him making love to his wife. They all laughed. He did too, but he wasn't really kidding. "Eyes front! Eyes front!" He kissed her hard and then pulled back to look into her eyes. She swallowed nervously at what she saw in them, and then grinned.

Mike and Alex were still laughing in the front, when Marguerite called up to them, "All right, you heard the man. Eyes up front. Not kidding." The laughter from the front seat kicked into an even higher gear, but before she knew it, a privacy screen was raised between them, cutting off the howls of laughter as if they had never been. "Well," she said, "that's more like it."

It was the last thing she said for a while.

When they finally made it to the hotel, they couldn't get to the room quick enough. As soon as they closed the door, they ripped each other's clothes off and started to make love again. Afterwards they took a shower together to get cleaned up, and just as they finished, they heard Quinn and Jeanine outside their door giggling like two school kids.

They quickly got dressed and then opened the door to let them in. They saw that all the doors on the floor were opened up and everyone was walking in and out of each other's rooms. It was like a big block party. The elevator and stairs had been sealed off by security, so the floor was reserved for their people alone.

"We have been waiting for you two," Jeanine said. "Everyone is in Blake and Abbey's room. We want to talk about the concert."

Marguerite and Chase followed them into Blake's room and everyone started hugging and laughing. All the boys patted the baby bump. Chase was extremely proud.

Then they started talking. The girls told them how Patrick had made them practice all day, every day, for two weeks, and that they'd had to know the songs before they even started going to practice.

"Is that why you were walking around with your iPod on every time I saw you?" Chase asked.

"Yes, I had to get your part down. It was like homework, but more fun."

They told them that they'd had to learn all their moves, and were even prepared for the crowd noise.

"We saw the cameramen filming us," Drew said, "but since no one had told us they'd be doing that, it confused us a little."

Eventually, they got onto the subject of the car rides to the hotel, and the laughter started building as the details were shared.

Cara said, "Drew was all over me in the car."

Abbey nodded. "Blake dragged me down on the floor of the SUV so our bodyguards couldn't see us."

"You're lucky," Jeanine said. "Quinn pulled me on top of him right there in the seat!"

The guys had the decency to look at least moderately ashamed of themselves, but they couldn't stop grinning and laughing.

Then they looked expectantly at Marguerite, who was smiling from ear to ear, and didn't answer for a long moment, drawing out the suspense. Finally, she shrugged. "We just did it in the back seat."

Everyone went wild.

"We couldn't wait for the hotel," she continued laughing saying it. "Chase kept yelling to Mike and Alex, 'Eyes up front! Eyes up front!'"

Picturing the scene, everyone was laughing so hard they practically felt sick. Drew fell off the bed, dragging Blake with him, and they started rolling around the floor like idiots. Eventually, when people settled down, she explained about the privacy screen, wanting to salvage at least a small shred of dignity.

Eventually they settled down into safer topics. "So," Cara asked, "what were you all thinking when you saw us up at the top of the stage?"

Drew spoke first, staring into Cara's eyes. "My first thought was that you were just coming down the ramp to kiss me and say Happy Valentine's Day. Then you started singing and it blew me away."

Blake looked at Abbey. "You looked so hot I didn't know if you would make it down the ramp without me going after you first."

Quinn nodded, looking at Jeanine. "I wanted to rip those red tights off you. You looked so hot, strutting out of the fog like that."

"I just wanted to go kidnap you and bring you back here," Chase said.

They'd all loved strutting through the fog and down to the mics. They'd felt sexy, and seeing their men's reaction only added to it. All of them had needed to hold themselves back so they could get on with their performance.

As for the men, when the girls had started singing they'd been just so amazed and proud of them that they'd wanted to run up to them and kiss them. It was the most romantic moment they could have ever thought of. They couldn't believe they had gone through all that trouble for them. As they were trying to describe how they felt, the feelings all came back in a flood.

Blake suddenly pulled a box out of his suitcase. He knelt down on one knee in front of Abbey. There were gasps of surprise all around, which Blake ignored. He was too focused on what truly mattered to him. "I was going to wait till we got home to do this, but I don't want to wait anymore. Abbey, I promise to love you forever. I can't live without you, so will you marry me?" He opened the box and revealed a beautiful diamond engagement ring. She started crying, and as she said yes (in a small voice that cracked with emotion), everyone started screaming. Then we all ganged up on them, hugging and crying.

As everyone started calming down, complimenting Abbey on the ring and Blake on his choice, Drew slipped off to his room and then hurried back. When he knelt down on one knee in front of Cara, everyone's jaws dropped. Everyone seemed to grab hold of someone else's arm or hand or shoulder, and bit their lips to keep from interrupting, as they stepped back a bit to give them room.

"Cara, you are the love of my life, and I know it might seem like I'm just following along here, but I have been wanting to do this practically from the day we met. I guess I was just waiting for the perfect time. After tonight, after everything you've done for me, I don't see how things could get any more perfect." He looked up at her with his pale blue eyes, which she could never resist, brimming with unshed tears. "I know that we're supposed to be together forever, Cara. So I need to ask, will you marry me?" There was a moment of silence, which was entirely too much for everyone to take, and then she screamed "Yes!" and jumped on top of him.

Then they were rolling around the floor, hugging and kissing and crying. Everyone piled on, slapping him on the back and congratulating them. Only Quinn held back.

"Okay look," he said... and was ignored in the chaos.

"LOOK!"

Everyone paused and looked up at him. He had a small box in his hand, holding it out for them all to see. No one moved for a moment, trying to wrap their heads around what they were seeing, then Jeanine gasped and covered her mouth with her hands.

"It's my turn." Everyone laughed at that, but then quickly quieted down when they saw that he wasn't kidding.

Jeanine was already kneeling next to Drew and Cara, so he approached her and slowly knelt down in front of her. He was shaking noticeably. The rest of them scooted out of the way. He took a deep breath and let it out slowly, trying to calm himself. When he started speaking, his voice was quiet, but strong. "Jeanine, I know that people will say we're too young, and that's part of the reason I've been holding off, but I know for a fact that I want to be with you forever." He looked into her big brown eyes and lost himself there for a moment before continuing. "I love you, and I will love you until the end of time. Will you please say that you'll be my wife?"

Jeanine nodded solemnly and said yes.

By this time, the excitement and hysteria had died down, leaving them all deeply moved and affected by the commitments that had been made. Slowly, they moved into another group hug, and it all just felt right. Perfect.

No one could sleep after that. They settled down comfortably together and kept talking about the evening, from the concert to the engagements. They chuckled when they argued over who was going to tell Peter.

"Just send him a text," Marguerite suggested. "Hit send all at the same time. He'll think it's a joke." They all loved that idea but thought Peter would have a heart attack if they did that.

It was about five in the morning before they started to wind down and get tired. Chase started to worry about Marguerite doing too much that day, and she admitted that she was finally tired. They were the first to say goodnight, hugging and kissing everyone, and telling them how much they loved them. The feeling was mutual.

Chase asked, "Doors opened or closed?"

"Closed!" they all said in unison, and started laughing.

As soon as Marguerite's head hit the pillow, she was ready for sleep.

"I can't believe how much I love you," he said.

She felt the same thing and told him so.

He smiled and then yawned. "I'm going to hold you all night. I don't want to let you go."

Marguerite liked that idea.

30
Back Home in Pennsylvania

It was hard to return to normal after the Valentine's event, but the girls all went home to try to get back to normal. As expected, the Internet exploded with their performance. MVTV (Music Video Television) asked for the rights to the thirty minutes of the concert that had been recorded in Verona. They were the highest bidder so the film was sold to them.

More importantly though, the boys told Peter they'd all gotten engaged over the Valentine's holiday and that he needed to issue a statement to the press about it. He thought for sure that social media would blow up with the three of them getting engaged at the same time. Peter almost blew up all on his own. Chase said he believed Peter's exact words were, "I want to jump off a bridge."

They didn't know whether they should laugh or run. The fans were used to seeing all the couples together and knew it was only a matter of time. The reason everyone had gone so bonkers when Chase got married was because he was never with anyone. He'd been the one all the teenaged girls were hoping to catch for themselves.

Chase was home on a break for March, so they headed to Pennsylvania and an extended stay with Donna. She couldn't wait to see them. Everyone was thrilled Chase would be with them, and were eager to see Marguerite's baby bump.

Chase went with Marguerite to her parents' house. She wouldn't go inside. Gail and Donna had made all the arrangements to knock it down the following day. They met with the builder, also arranged by Gail and Donna, to pick out plans for the construction of a new one. They had to pick out a house with enough bedrooms.

Before they'd left London, they'd had dinner with the others and Marguerite had told them about picking out plans to build a house for them near her family in Pennsylvania for when they were in the US touring or just for vacations.

Blake informed them, "Well you need at least four bedrooms."

And Quinn said, "No, we need more than that. We need five."

And Drew asked, "Why more than four? There are only four of us."

It made Chase laugh. "And where would you like us to put the baby?"

"Oh right. The baby."

"I told you we'll need five," Quinn said.

"*We* will need five bedrooms," Marguerite said. "Would you be wanting en suites with your rooms as well?" That cracked them up. "Please let me know and I will send you the bill for your quarter share of the building costs." They paused and looked at her, unsure of whether or not she was kidding. But then she and Chase burst out laughing, and everyone else followed suit. They were all going to miss being together while they were away.

The builder was great and they picked out a traditional five-bedroom Victorian house. He showed them what he was thinking about for the landscaping and driveway and fence. A fence was very important. They would need it for security.

They had an amazing visit. They got to spend a lot of time with her family and friends, and had found the demolition of her parents' house very cathartic and freeing, but now Chase had to get back on the road. He took his wife back to London first.

It was hard for him to leave her. They used webcam a lot when he was on the road. They would even set their computers up next to their beds so that they could go to bed with it on and fall asleep together. It was pretty cool.

She thought that when the baby came and he was on the road, they would have the camera on all the time so he wouldn't miss anything.

Genius!

31

Unbearable

April and May flew by. Chase was home for some of May and the first few weeks of June. Marguerite was due in July, but they hadn't told many people the actual date because they didn't want anyone camped out at the hospital, or their house, waiting for her to go into labor.

Then the unthinkable happened. Chase was sleeping next to Marguerite in their bed when he woke up because he felt something strange. It was around five in the morning. He looked at his wife and saw that she was so white she almost looked gray. He touched her and she felt like ice. He panicked. Running quickly to the door and calling for the bodyguards at the top of his lungs, he grabbed his phone off the dresser and dialed 999, London's equivalent of 911. He was frantic, trying to explain what was happening to the person who came on the line but hardly able to think. The bodyguards, who had stayed over after a late-night planning session for their next trip, came running.

Marguerite wouldn't wake up. Chase pulled the covers back and saw that there was blood all over the sheets. He doubled over. He thought he was going to die in that moment. He couldn't breathe. He handed the phone to Alex, who took over the communication.

Mike, in the meantime, had started CPR. She did have a pulse but it was weak. He kept up compressions and tried to tune out Chase's desperate cries and the terrifying color of Marguerite's skin. He focused on just keeping her alive for one more heartbeat, and then another...

Agonizing minutes passed before the 999 operator told Alex that the ambulance should be pulling into their driveway as she spoke. He hung up the phone and ran off to let them in.

Chase was bent over his wife, crying and screaming. "Please don't leave me! Please, I'll die if you leave me!"

Alex burst into the room, followed by the paramedics, who quickly went to work to get her stabilized enough for transport to the nearest hospital. Chase wouldn't leave her so they let him ride with her in the back of the ambulance, although they told him he would have to stay out of the way.

As Mike and Alex followed behind the ambulance in Mike's car, Alex quickly called everyone, explaining the situation, and giving the name of the hospital. Gail immediately alerted the hospital about who the incoming patient was, warning them about possible complications due to the press. She also called Marguerite's OBGYN, who was waiting for them at the hospital when they arrived.

Chase and their huge extended family had taken over the hospital's waiting room. A portion of it had been partitioned off to keep them segregated from the other families—Gail had been very busy behind the scenes, although none of them even noticed or gave the matter any thought.

It was a nightmare, as the wait seemed to go on and on, with everyone breaking down and trying to hold each other up at the same time. Chase was sitting very still, off by himself a bit. He felt removed from everyone and everything, as if part of him was fighting for its life right alongside his wife. Finally, Doctor Robbins came in to give them an update. Chase couldn't seem to hear it. Nothing she was saying seemed to pierce the creeping numbness he felt, until something finally did.

"... afraid that the baby did not have a heartbeat. Marguerite's body was trying to abort..."

They all just stood there like zombies as the words sank in. No one spoke. No one moved. The color drained out of their faces, and no one could control their tears. *The baby didn't make it.*

In Marguerite's room, a million thoughts and emotions were going through Chase's head. His wife was finally coming around, but he was a mess. *How can I tell her this?* He couldn't take what had happened, so how would she? When she finally opened her eyes completely and looked into his, she could tell that he'd been crying. "What's wrong?" she said, sounding terrified. "Something with the baby?" As her blood pressure started to rise, the doctor counseled her to slow her breathing and try to remain calm, but she couldn't or wouldn't rest until she'd been told the whole, horrible truth. When she had been brought into the hospital, unconscious, her baby had no heartbeat. It had passed away in the womb, and so her body had apparently been trying to abort it.

In the nearby waiting room, the others heard her scream of agony, and knew that Marguerite had just been told what had happened. They were all completely shaken. Peter had just made it in to the hospital, and when he heard the scream, and looked to the others for understanding, the boys filled him in. They could barely speak they were so upset. The girls were inconsolable.

Because the process had already started, the medical team told Marguerite that it would best for her to finish delivering the baby naturally, allowing it to be born before they would have to say goodbye. She and Chase agreed and they wheeled her into a delivery room. Chase would be there with her every step of the way. The others followed and just stood outside the door, waiting.

The baby came, and Chase stood there holding her hand. "You should see her," Doctor Robbins told them gently, "or you will always regret it." They both nodded. Then they were asked if they had picked out a name.

"Yes," Chase said, but could barely get out the words. "Margaret Abbey Cara Jeanine Martin."

The nurses cleaned up baby Margaret, wrapped her in a beautiful pink blanket, and put a tiny pink cap on her head. Then they somberly walked over to Chase and Marguerite and handed them their daughter. She looked like she was sleeping. Even at seven months, she was beautiful. They kissed her and hugged her and told her how much they loved her and always would.

"Do you want your brothers to come in to say goodbye as well?" Doctor Robbins asked. They looked at each other.

"Only if they want to."

They came in and one couple at a time, holding the baby, kissing her, and telling her that they loved her. They were all crying. The doctor told them the baby's full name and the girls cried even harder.

Then the second nightmare began. Marguerite passed out. Her blood pressure dropped and the alarms on all the instruments she was hooked up to started going off. The doctor started yelling to the nurses, "Get them all out! Now!"

"NO!" Chase yelled. "Mam! NO! I am not leaving." The doctor wouldn't bend though. The brothers had to carry him out of the delivery room.

They waited and waited for news. It seemed like forever. Chase's mom was finally there and saw the condition everyone was in. *I have to be brave for everyone here,* she thought. *They need me!*

The doctor finally came out with news. "Mrs. Martin started bleeding again and I had to pack her uterus to stop it. She's in a coma, but that's actually good. I want her to stay that way while her body starts to heal itself. Once the bleeding has stopped, and we have her stabilized, I will work on bringing her around."

Words cannot describe what was going on in that waiting room. The doctor thought she would have to sedate all of them. She said that she would get her the biggest room in the hospital, because she knew that none of them would be leaving Marguerite's side. Somehow, Chase managed to say a quiet thank you to the doctor.

There was one more thing. As if things weren't bad enough, they knew that funeral arrangements would need to be made for the baby. Peter stepped in and took over. He said that he would handle everything. Quinn had already called Father Cummings, who was on his way over as they spoke. Chase just nodded. He was mostly incoherent.

They wheeled Marguerite to her room, and as promised, it was big enough for all of them. Dr. Robbins had maintenance bring in extra furniture from the waiting room so that everyone would have somewhere to sit. They really didn't care. They were used to the floor. All they knew was that they were not leaving her or Chase.

Peter had to issue a press release. He didn't even tell Chase what he was going to say, since he wouldn't have heard a word of it anyway.

It read:

At 5:30 this morning, the 18th of May, Marguerite Martin, wife of Chase Martin of the Band 4, miscarried their baby girl, whom they named Margaret Abbey Cara Jeanine Martin. They are pleading for privacy during this tragic time. Mrs. Martin is in a coma due to complications during the delivery and Chase has been sedated. The whole group is with them, as well as Chase's mother, Jessica, and will not leave their sides. Mrs. Martin's mother and father are on their way to London from Pennsylvania. Again, we are asking you all to please respect their privacy. Statements will be issued as soon as something changes.

The police were alerted because they knew fans would likely come out by the thousands to camp out at the hospital, waiting for word. They had to issue additional statements telling everyone to please stay away from the hospital. Blake, Quinn, and Drew issued a statement of their own, reiterating this request.

Marguerite's parents arrived with Donna and Sue at around nine that night. When they walked into the room, they saw everyone draped over the furniture, passed out. In the end, the doctor had given them all something to help calm them down. Jessica was up and alert however. In the bed, they saw that Chase was lying next to his wife, cradling her. He would not let her go. Quinn and Jeanine were holding her hand, sleeping in a reclined chair at the side of the bed. Everyone who entered the room started crying and Marguerite's family was no exception. Jessica had been in contact with them during their trip, keeping them informed right from the beginning.

A day and a half later, there was finally some good news. The doctor told Chase that the bleeding had stopped and she was going to try to bring her out of the coma. She asked everyone but Chase to leave the room. She had a hard time getting everyone out, but finally they did as they were asked. Father Cummings was allowed to stay with Chase as long as he stood off to one side, out of the way. They administered the medication that they hoped would wake her up. After a few tense minutes, it seemed to have done its job.

As she started to come around, she looked for Chase and their eyes met. She smiled. Then her hand went to her abdomen and it all started coming back to her. She let out a cry that cut right through everyone in the room and carried out to the others in the hall. It was like it was happening all over again. Chase cradled her and rocked her back and forth. Even the doctor was crying, although as discreetly as she could manage.

She suggested that they have someone come and talk to them for grief counseling, and that they talk to her family. "I've never seen a family like yours, Marguerite. No one would leave your side, and your husband would not let you go. He has been holding you for thirty-six hours now."

She looked at her husband and grabbed his shirt, pulling him down to her. She kept repeating the same four words. "I am so sorry; I am so sorry…"

The doctor shook her head. "This was not your fault. Do not blame yourself. It just happened."

Chase was trying desperately to reassure her, nodding along with what the doctor was saying. "It's not your fault, Mam." He started rocking her again. "It's not your fault." The doctor wanted to give her something to calm her down, but she wouldn't take anything.

The next evening, after a barrage of tests, the doctor decided that she would be well enough to go home the following morning. Earlier that day, with the help of Father Cummings, Chase had told her about the statement Peter had issued and how Peter had taken care of all the funeral arrangements. Together, the two of them would take care of everything else later. He did not want her to think about it now, or worry about anything. They had cried a great deal, and more tears were surely to come, but Father Cummings blessed the both of them, laying his hands on both of their heads and praying for God to give them the strength to get through this difficult time.

The fans had organized a silent march to the hospital to take place as soon as it got dark. It had been decided upon by the organizers and participants that there would be no talking, so that no one could say they were disturbing the people who lived around the hospital or the sick people actually in the hospital. They wanted and needed to show Marguerite and Chase that they were there for them. Thousands of people marched. The streets were full of people, and for the longest time, no one made a sound. Then, almost organically, they all started to sing in whispered voices, a song Chase had written for his wife, entitled, "It's the Little Things."

Up in the hospital room, everyone heard the haunting chorus, and looked out the window. They were amazed at what they saw. They watched and listened until the song finished and faded away, and then (invisible to the fans behind the room's tinted windows) Marguerite and Chase asked for someone's phone. With their arms around each other, they turned on the flash and waved it back and forth so that the group outside could see. Then Blake and Abby, Drew and Cara, and Quinn and Jeanine did the same. They wanted to acknowledge that they had heard their song, appreciated everything they did, and how much they loved them. The thousands of people on the street saw it, and they all turned on their flashes and held their phones in the air, signaling the same message back to them. News stations were there recording it too. Before long, it was all over social media and being talked about on every show on TV.

Marguerite asked her mom if she would do her a favor and go to their house. She wanted her to bring her a certain shirt that she wanted to wear when she left the hospital the next morning. Then she told Peter that she actually wanted the press to see her leaving, because she wanted to pay tribute to all of those people who had sung to her the night before. She was more grateful to them than she knew how to express.

He was confused, until he saw her shirt.

It read: *"It's the Little Things* that get you through."

Healing

Mike, Alex, and Gail escorted them to the car, where Nick was waiting to drive them home. Everyone they came into contact with expressed their condolences. Ed was in the US again touring, and Victoria and David were overseas as well, but they all sent word as soon as they had heard what happened, and said they would visit as soon as they got back to the UK. The couple braced themselves for that. They wanted to see them of course, but didn't know if they could take it.

Marguerite's mom and dad were at the house with Jessica waiting for them. Marguerite just wanted to go right to bed, so they let her. She slept and slept, and did not get up until Chase actually pleaded with her to do so and eat something with them. He rarely came out of their room either while she slept. He wouldn't leave her. She kept grabbing for his hand and he wanted to always be near her if she needed him.

Three weeks went by and Marguerite started forcing herself to get out of bed every day and rejoin the land of the living. She wanted to come back to the life she loved with Chase. She wanted to come back to Chase, but it was hard. She knew he had to get back to work though. It was almost time for him to go back on the road, and she knew that if she wasn't better, he would never leave her and do what he had to do. He had to go.

She called the girls and told them that it was time she went out, so they made arrangements to go to dinner down the street at their usual spot. She made the reservation herself, alerted Gail and Mike, and told them she wanted Chase to drive them this time. They were hardly going to refuse her, so they said okay.

Chase was pleased that she wanted to get out. They both got dressed up and it felt good. They met everyone and managed to have a good time. No one mentioned Baby Margaret.

Before Chase went back on the road, she took his pendant to the jeweler and had him engrave "Baby Margaret" on it so that she would always be with him. The jeweler told her how sorry he was for their loss and prayed for her.

Then she went to see the grocers, Franco and Anna, and they met her with hugs and kisses. She thanked them for all the food they had sent for them. She didn't know how she could ever repay them for their kindness and they responded by saying they were just so happy she was well again.

She didn't bother to correct them, knowing that she would get there someday.

The day before Chase left, Marguerite had a doctor's appointment. She asked him if he would drive and he gladly did. She just wanted to be in the front seat with her husband driving her, like a normal couple.

The doctor came in and saw them holding hands again, so tightly that there was no blood in either of their fingers. She told Marguerite that everything looked good. The problem with Baby Margaret had been something that just happens sometimes, and not something anyone could have predicted. Everything was back in place and she was healthy again. "There is something I have to advise you against, however," she said.

They both looked scared, bracing themselves. The doctor noticed. "No, it's nothing bad."

They both let out a sigh of relief. She just wanted them to wait at least a year before they tried for another baby. She wanted Marguerite's body to heal completely and be as strong and ready as possible for the next time. She felt it was best because of all the bleeding that had happened after delivering Margaret. They both understood and agreed. She made them promise. She told them that when couples miscarry, they often want to get pregnant again immediately, and she did not want them to. They were going to do whatever the doctor recommended.

Marguerite and Chase were lying in bed. "What did you think when the doctor said she had something she wanted to advise us against?" Chase asked.

"I thought it was the worst possible thing. I thought she was going to say I couldn't have any more children."

He nodded. "I thought that too."

Chase felt almost desperate to make love to his wife. He had come so close to losing her that his need to be as close to her as possible almost took his breath away. When he asked her though, she just shook her head and started to cry. He told her that he understood, and promised that it was all right. He just held her all night instead, and that was good enough. He would do anything, or give anything in the world, to make her well and happy again.

A Future Plan

Marguerite was all better except that, for some reason, she didn't want Chase to make love to her. He kept coming home from touring to make sure she was all right, and they spoke like they always did and cuddled and kissed, but when it came to him making love to her, she froze up. He even went to see the doctor about it.

"Just give it time," she said. "One day she will snap out of it. It can't be forced though, or she'll blame you if she melts down."

Chase wanted to make love to his wife, but not if it would hurt her in any way. He loved her and adored her, and wanted to show her that, but she just couldn't. She couldn't even explain why, which upset her to no end.

Then one day Marguerite woke up and he wasn't beside her. She panicked and then heard him moving around in the bathroom, brushing his teeth. She rushed in to join him and brushed her teeth as well. She found herself just standing there gawking at him.

"Why are you looking at me like that?"

"I want to shave your beard off. Will you let me?"

"Yes, I would love that." His hair was quite long too.

"Do you want me to trim you hair as well?"

He nodded, so she got the shears Vita gave her, and with his hair still wet from the shower, she trimmed all around the bottom. Then she asked if he wanted to go shorter.

"I don't know. How do you like it?"

"I love it when you pull it back into a ponytail. Makes you look hot!" Then she started to giggle, hiding her face behind a towel.

"If I had known that, I would have been doing it for months now." They laughed together and it felt wonderful. "Better leave it long then."

She nodded and then got his razor, lathered him up, and started to remove his beard and mustache. *God, he is so gorgeous!* Those blue eyes and his curly blond hair. Slowly and carefully, she shaved him.

He did not know how he was going to control himself much longer with her in front of him, leaning into him like that. *She is so beautiful!*

When she finished, she wet a wash cloth with warm water, sat on his lap facing him, and wiped away all the soap and bristles. He put his hands on her hips to hold her so she wouldn't fall, and then it happened! Their eyes met and something finally snapped within her. He noticed it immediately. She was melting. He felt it. He felt her. And she felt him again. She bent down and kissed him and it was almost more than he could take. He prayed that she was ready for him.

He picked her up and carried her to bed. As they got undressed, he made himself ask her if she was sure, remembering what the doctor had said, but she just pulled him down on top of her. They held each other tight and couldn't get enough of each other. She couldn't get enough of him. Both of them were thinking the same thing: *Finally!* They spent the rest of the day showing each other how much they loved one another.

They lay in bed afterwards, talking for hours, and realized once again how strong they were together. Why hadn't they remembered that before? They were able to discuss Baby Margaret for the first time without falling apart, and even talked about when they could start trying for another baby.

Marguerite told him how sorry she was for what had happened, but he grabbed her face in his hands and stared fiercely into her eyes. "You have nothing to be sorry about." He would have died if anything happened to her. She really was his life and the air he breathed. He wanted to make sure they were going to follow the doctor's orders exactly, as they promised they would, and she agreed.

"When the year is up," she said, "and the doctor gives us the green light, if you're on the road I'm just going to call you and say, 'I am coming to you.' That will mean it's time." He loved that plan. "You are the very air I breathe."

She smiled softly, kissed his cheek, and cuddled down into the circle of his arms.

"And you are mine."

34 Surprising

Time really flew by for Marguerite and Chase. So much had happened in the first year they were married. His band-mates had all finally married their partners, one after the other, in beautiful and romantic ceremonies that made everyone cry. Chase and Marguerite made it back to Pennsylvania quite a few times to see how the new house was coming along.

They realized that they had made a mistake in counting the number of bedrooms they would need. They had forgotten about all their bodyguards. While the brothers and sisters often arrived at their London house without them, or at least with arrangements having been made for their accommodations while their charges were safe and sound, it was different when they were out of the country. They each had an assigned bodyguard of their own, and they would need to stay close at all times.

Chase thought about it for a while before coming up with a solution. "Why don't we build a massive garage and put rooms above it?" They met up with the builder and made additional plans to construct another building beside the first. It would take up more space on the lot than they would have liked, but they would still have a large backyard. They were okay with the compromise. However, it meant that they had to pick out more cabinets, flooring, fixtures, and furniture. They were very busy.

Once back in London in their own bed, Chase was trying to calculate when the year would be up so he and Marguerite could try for a baby again. He realized that it was coming up soon.

She grinned at him. "Remember what I said I'll do when we get the green light?"

Chase nodded. "I'll never forget it. I'll be waiting to hear those words: 'I am coming to you!'"

35

I Can't Breathe

It was May. Chase was on the road and Marguerite was still fixing up the house. Springtime in London was just beautiful. Everything was vibrant green, probably because of all the rain they got. Chase had a big backyard enclosed by bushes about ten-feet high. They had a gardener to take care of it, because neither one of them had the time and Chase barely knew what a lawnmower was. She planted some flowers in pots all around the patio off the dining room, and was pleased with how they all looked. When she looked at the backyard, she pictured all their kids playing and kicking balls around. Thinking about it made her smile and warmed her heart.

She had a doctor visit coming up, but Chase was on the road so he couldn't go with her. Instead, Jessica accompanied her (along with Gail, Mike, and Nick, of course—*the shadows*). Gail knew that if she got a clean bill of health from the doctor, she would want to get to Chase immediately, and she had made preparations to make that happen. Marguerite went in for her appointment while Mike guarded the door. Gail and Jessica stayed in the waiting room.

When Marguerite finally came out, she was six shades of purple. No one knew what had happened, but she flew out the door ahead of everyone, rushing to the car. They all ran after her, extremely concerned about what had happened.

All she kept saying was, "I can't breathe... I can't breathe..." and she looked like it. Before she got to the car, she fainted. Luckily, Mike was there to catch her. He scooped her up and put her in the car, where they tried to revive her. Jessica ran back to get the doctor.

Chase felt her distress and called on her cell phone. She was obviously in no condition to answer, and no one else even noticed it ringing, focused as they were on waking her up and taking care of her. When she finally came to, she kept saying, "Gail, please get me to Chase!" She was crying. They all tried to calm her down, but could hear the urgency in her voice. She was starting to hyperventilate, and they were afraid she would pass out again!

They kept talking to her as they waited for the doctor to arrive. When she finally did, she shook her head and knelt down in front of her patient. "Okay Marguerite, take a deep breath for me. Come on."

After a moment, she started to follow instructions. The others took their cue from the doctor, who didn't seem particularly stressed out or somber. Once everyone was breathing relatively normal again, even Marguerite started to calm down, although she was still crying. It was then that the ringing cell phone finally registered.

Mike helped her dig it out of her purse. She had to swipe the screen several times before it connected, but when it finally did, she didn't wait for a response. It was hard to make out her words through her tears, but Chase understood in an instant. "I'm coming to you!" A smile broke through her tears at his response, whatever it was, and it quickly became apparent that Marguerite's tears and hysteria had been built on something positive.

Doctor Robbins smiled at the group and nodded discretely. "She's fine everyone. Or she will be, once you get her to her husband."

Marguerite wasn't saying anything, so Gail gently took the phone from her hand and told Chase that the plane was waiting and his mom had already packed Marguerite a bag. She and the rest of the girls would be at the hotel around midnight.

Chase had been getting ready to go on stage when her distress had hit him like a brick, and the concert was put on hold. The fans were chanting, calling for them, eager and impatient for the show to start. The brothers knew he had been waiting for a phone call, and knew the couple well enough to realize he had sensed something through that weird bond they shared. Without hesitation, they had delayed going on stage until they found out what was going on.

Chase's hands were shaking too much, so his brothers dialed and redi-aled his phone for him, holding it up to his ear until he signaled that it had disconnected again, and then waiting desperately again for her to pick up. Jack finally yelled to them, "Guys! Up on the platform! Now!"

Drew, Blake, and Quinn whipped their heads around to face him, and yelled, "One more minute!" in perfect unison. That was when Jack knew something was wrong. They all saw the condition Chase was in and knew they couldn't go up yet.

Finally, Chase's call was answered, and almost immediately, he started smiling from ear to ear and relaxed noticeably. They pressed his phone back into his hand and all started breathing again, not realizing how much they had been holding their collective breath. They loved Marguerite almost as much as Chase did, and seeing their brother's distress as well had almost been too much for them. They knew everything was all right now though. Finally, he said goodbye and disconnected the call, telling the brothers that the girls would be there that night. They all grinned at each other.

"Okay!" Jack interrupted, seeing their relieved smiles and clapping his hands loudly. "So what are we waiting for? Get up there! Now!" They practically sprinted to the pop-up platform.

They all had their arms around one another, and on the way up, Blake laughed. "So Chase, we won't be seeing you for about two days then. Right?" They were all grinning.

Chase shook his head. "Better make it three."

By the time they got to the stage, they were all laughing and grinning from ear to ear.

As predicted, at midnight Marguerite and the girls arrived at the hotel. The boys were waiting for them in the lobby and didn't even worry about who might see them. It was late enough and the lobby was fairly deserted. When their eyes met, Marguerite flew into Chase's arms, he just picked her up and carried her to the elevators, not even waiting for the rest to join them. They knew what was going on with them and let them go. They also knew they wouldn't be disturbing them. When they were both ready to see everyone again, they would let them know. After what had happened a year ago, losing Baby Margaret, no one wanted anything but the best for them and would give them all the time they needed.

Marguerite asked Chase if he could just hold her. She was so stressed out from the long day. With all kinds of emotions still running through her, she really wanted to calm down and needed Chase to help her. He knew how she was feeling because he felt it himself, through their bond.

He kissed her. "Anything you need from me, I will do for you." He just held her and stroked her hair, while they talked about the day's events. He told her how he had sensed her distress, flipped when he couldn't reach her, and described how the brothers kept redialing the phone for him because he was shaking too much.

She told him that when Doctor Robbins had told her she was in good health, and thought it would be a good time for them to start trying for a baby, she couldn't wait to leave the appointment. But then she had just kept on talking to her and talking to her, and as she did, Marguerite had gotten more and more aware of how far away he was, and how long it would take her to reach him.

All she had wanted to do was run out of there and call him. She hadn't wanted to be rude, but she started feeling more and more trapped, and by the time she got out of the office, she couldn't breathe. She told Chase about passing out and upsetting everyone. She felt horrible for that. He squeezed her reassuringly.

"Don't worry. They're all just glad that you're okay."

He then went on to tell her what the brothers had said to him on the platform, going up to the stage, about them not seeing them for two days, and that he'd told him three would be better.

She blushed and kissed him, laughing.

He kissed her back and then, finally relaxed and comfortable in each other's arms, they made love.

While it might have had a larger purpose this time, for the most part, it was just for them.

Gifts

Marguerite was pregnant! Everyone was excited and thrilled again for them. They were also nervous and cautious about it though. You could tell that they all wanted to be happier for them but were holding back. The hurt they'd all felt the last time was something they would never forget. It wasn't just about losing Baby Margaret, although that was certainly the worst, it was also watching what it had done to Chase and Marguerite.

Again, they were careful about who was told before she had her first doctor's appointment.

They called Doctor Robbins to make an appointment, but she wanted Marguerite to come in for an ultrasound first.

The brothers and sisters asked if they could go to the appointment as well. Chase knew that even if they told them no, they would show up, and he wouldn't have it any other way. They were family.

They knew the drill, but Chase and Marguerite were still nervous and the doctor noticed. She talked to them both, asking questions about how far along they thought she would be. At the same time, they both said, "About eight weeks."

The doctor continued her examination, studying the screen for a long moment before giving her assessment. She was actually further along in her pregnancy than they had thought. Not only was she about twelve weeks pregnant but the doctor had an additional surprise for them as well.

Chase and Marguerite thought they knew what they were looking at, and what they were looking for, but they were confused by the images they saw on the screen. "Sorry doc, but I guess we'll need you to walk us through it again."

The doctor smiled. "Okay, well here is Baby Martin number one..." Chase and Marguerite glanced at each other and then quickly looked back at the screen. "... and here is Baby Martin number two."

Their eyes went wide. Twins? They didn't know what to say. Chase was all over Marguerite then, smiling and crying, and she was just stunned, and more happy and terrified than she could ever remember being in her life. *Twins!*

She kept asking the doctor if she was sure, and the doctor kept showing them, over and over again on the screen, and laughing. Their joy was infectious, and she was reminded of why she loved her job so much. *Twins!*

"So," Doctor Robbins said, clearing her throat, "Do you want to know the sex of the babies, because they are positioned just right and I could tell you?" They both nodded at the same time.

"Well, you appear to have two healthy baby boys." *Sons!* Chase was beaming with pride and Marguerite didn't think she could be any happier. Not that there was anything wrong with girls, of course, and they would always love Baby Margaret with all their hearts. It just seemed different this time.

This time, the doctor knew the drill. "Did you want the others to see?" She wasn't surprised when both nodded. The nurse went out and got everyone. When they walked into the room, they saw the huge smiles on their faces and were relieved.

Then the doctor moved the wand over Marguerite's abdomen again. "Here is Baby Martin number one..." Everyone looked quickly from Chase to Marguerite to the doctor and then back to the screen. "... and here is Baby Martin number two."

The whole room erupted, with everyone yelling, "Twins! Oh my God, twins!" Then, of course, there was the icing on the cake. "BOYS!" they all screamed. "BOYS! Oh my God!"

They were on Chase and Marguerite like flies. The brothers especially couldn't stop going on about the twin boys.

Men and their sons, Marguerite thought. *Geez!*

They were already talking about soccer games in the backyard, now that there would be six of them. The conversation never stopped. Who was going to teach them how to drive? Who was taking them to soccer practice? Everybody's hands kept going up, as people volunteered, but when Jeanine jumped in, and asked, "Who's going to help them do homework?" all the hands dropped. No way. No homework. They would leave that up to the women. They all started laughing.

As they did the last time, Peter issued a statement that was prepared with the help of the doctor:

Chase Martin of the Band 4 and his wife, Marguerite, are expecting twin sons in March. Mrs. Martin is in good health at this time and will be closely monitored by her doctor, who is being extremely cautious because of the difficult time they experienced during her first pregnancy. The Martins are very happy and excited about the pregnancy, as are the rest of the band members and all of their families.

Peter didn't think they needed to say more, and Chase agreed.

When they got home, Chase said to Marguerite, "Our life is so full of strange things."

She had no idea where he was going with that. "What do you mean?"

"Well, like the way we can feel each other. Does that scare you sometimes?"

"Yes, because I don't understand how it could happen. How can we be so connected?" Tears welled up in her eyes. She turned away from him so he wouldn't see. "But what scares me the most is that, if we lose that connection, you won't want me anymore."

Chase scooped her up in his arms. "I could never not want you, Mam. You're my life. I promised to love you forever when we got married. You're my wife. How could I ever not want my wife?"

The sentiment brought more tears to her eyes, but she could see he was holding something else back, something strange, that he wanted to talk to her about.

"What is it? What else do you want to say?"

He just smiled. "Let's call Quinn. I think we need him now."

That was their connection to Quinn. When Chase had questions about God, he knew Quinn could answer them and help them. Quinn had known all along that they would need him, and the time had come.

Quinn and Jeanine came over as soon as Chase called. The two of them were always smiling. There was a peacefulness that surrounded them.

After they all got comfortable in the living room, Quinn said, "Okay, I know you want to talk about something with me. What is it?"

"Do you think God gave us twins to make up for Baby Margaret?" Chase asked, taking the words right out of Marguerite's mouth.

Quinn and Jeanine were not surprised they had asked that. "We wondered the same thing," he said. "We were with Father Cummings when you called me, and I knew that was what you would be asking."

"Jeanine and I felt that the twins were a gift from God to begin with. So while we don't actually think he was trying to make up, so to speak, for Baby Margaret, he's still giving you a gift. One that's even bigger than the first time."

Chase and Marguerite both smiled through their tears, and so did Quinn and Jeanine.

"Do you think Father Cummings feels the same way?" Marguerite asked. They both nodded. He absolutely did.

Chase and Marguerite asked Quinn and Jeanine if they wanted to stay the night. They hadn't needed to ask. They already had a bag packed and weren't going anywhere.

"I knew you would be needing me. I'm going to stick around in case either of you have more questions."

Los Angeles

When Marguerite was five months along, Chase said the band had to go to LA to record something in a studio there. All the girls decided they wanted to go with them.

Joe and Mary were overwhelmingly worried about her traveling to LA. They didn't want anything to happen to her or the twins. Marguerite assured her that the doctor had sanctioned the trip and that she would be fine. They also had a doctor on alert in LA in case anything happened. She told them that she would stop and see them on her way back to London, because she would not be traveling much more until the end of her term. That seemed to calm them down a little, but they told her that parents always worry and that she and Chase would know soon enough what that felt like once the twins were born.

The trip to LA had taken longer than they thought, and they were both so exhausted they just ate in their room and crawled right into bed.

Chase asked her what her plans were for the next day and she said that she was actually meeting Victoria for lunch. She was in LA as well and had said she wanted to talk to her about something. He was happy for her. He loved her friendship with Victoria. Actually, the girls would all be going their separate ways tomorrow. They all had something to do or somewhere to go.

Chase had to admit that made him a bit nervous. "Mike will be with you, right?"

"Yes, the shadow will be right there with me." They both chuckled at that and settled down to get some sleep.

"You are the very air I breathe," Chase said.

"And you are mine."

Marguerite met Victoria for lunch. It turns out Victoria had a surprise for her. She had designed a maternity dress just for her. It was beautiful! It was black, off-the shoulder (her favorite), and would hug her body down to about her upper midriff before flaring out a bit with a swing skirt covered with a layer of chiffon. It was gorgeous. The material was soft and it shined. She loved it.

Just as she was gawking at it with her mouth hanging open, Chase called to say that there was a wrap-up party that evening that they would be going to—assuming she was interested. He went on to suggest that, if she didn't have anything to wear, maybe she could shop with Victoria for something. When she hung up the phone, she told Victoria and they both laughed. She thought the dress would be perfect for the party. She knew Marguerite hated pumps but told her that she would have to suffer and wear them with that dress. Luckily, she just happened to have packed them for the trip.

Then Victoria hit her with something else that was unexpected. "Would you come to my office in London and design a maternity line for my fashion house?" She didn't know what to say or think. She was always complaining that there was nothing she really liked when she was out buying maternity clothes, and nothing reasonably priced. She thought that, since maternity clothes were only a temporary wardrobe, they should not cost an arm and a leg. She'd said that to Victoria many times. Apparently she had heard her, because she quickly told Marguerite that she wanted to keep the cost of the maternity line down. That made Marguerite smile warmly at her.

"Is that a yes?" Victoria asked.

"Yes."

When she got back to London, she would call and they could set something up. In the meantime, Victoria told her to think of what she would like to wear, being pregnant, so she could explain it to the design team. Victoria also told her to make sure she got a picture of herself tonight, in the new dress, so she could see how it looked. Marguerite promised that she would.

She couldn't wait to tell Chase. When he got back to the hotel, she was so excited that he couldn't follow her and kept saying, "Slow down, slow down. I'm trying to take this all in." She was so happy. She would have a job again! Chase was amazingly proud of her.

While they both got ready for the party, he told her about his day. He hadn't seen the dress. She let him get ready first. *He is so gorgeous.* She thought that every time she looked at him. Especially when he was dressed up. He was clean shaven and had a white shirt on with black pants and a black suit jacket. She had to suppress her raging hormones because there was no time for fooling around. Then she put on the dress. It was amazing. She felt like she could walk down a runway in it. That was how beautiful she felt. It hugged her body, leaving her shoulders bare, and the skirt flowed and swayed with her every movement. It was stunning. Her long brown hair styled perfectly, as she pulled it back off her face and let her curls tumble down her back. Her makeup looked beautiful. The smoky liner and eyeshadow brought out the brightness in her light brown eyes. When she walked out of the bathroom and Chase took one look at her in that dress, and at those legs in those pumps, he stopped dead. He couldn't take his eyes off her. She was beaming. That was the reaction she'd wanted from him. He walked towards her. "You are so beautiful." He just kept shaking his head, as if he couldn't believe what he was seeing. "I don't think I should let you out of my sight tonight."

"Yes," she laughed, "because everyone is just waiting to steal your pregnant wife away from you." He laughed too, but said that if he didn't have to be at that party, they would not be leaving the room. She just grabbed his hand and pulled him out into the hall before she was the one who wouldn't let *him* leave.

Cameras were everywhere. Peter told them to be seen on this trip and let everyone and anyone take their picture. They had all been told to go to the party separately so they could be photographed separate from each other for a change. When Chase and Marguerite walked off the hotel's elevator holding hands, all heads in the lobby turned to look, doing double-takes at how amazing Marguerite looked. She saw everyone smiling at them as they walked by. They looked like they had both just stepped off a magazine cover, and were both smiling from ear to ear.

When their car pulled up to the front entrance of the party, Mike jumped out and got the door for them. The camera flashes were going off like little explosions. Chase got out first, then turned back and held his hand out for Marguerite. She exited the car with amazing grace for a pregnant woman, and stood for a moment, resplendent in her dress and heels. If she had thought the flashes seemed like explosions before, then this was an all-out nuclear war. It was blinding. Chase was holding her hand, and while everyone watched, he brought it up to his lips and kissed it. The press were going crazy, shouting for them to look to the left, look to the right, look to the front! They didn't know where to look first, so Chase just looked down at her and smiled. He leaned in and whispered in her ear, "You are so beautiful." Then he patted the baby bump as the cameras kept flashing away. They were both beaming.

Marguerite didn't know she was going to have to speak to anyone on the red carpet, but they interviewed them both and asked her whom she was wearing. "I'm wearing an original made for me by Victoria Baker," she said proudly.

Then they asked Chase the same question. He shrugged. "Marguerite Martin. She made me put this on tonight. " Everyone laughed.

They started looking for the others along the way. One couple at a time, they found everyone. They all looked amazing! Cameramen wanted pictures of just the women, and then just the men, and then all of them together. The girls loved her dress and she told them that Victoria had just given it to her, and had asked her to come help her design a maternity line! Everyone was thrilled for her.

They all walked into the building together. It was amazing to Marguerite how they all just gravitated towards one another. Always! With even one of them missing, they felt incomplete. She had always loved the bond between the brothers, and between the sisters as well.

When they entered the reception, all heads turned to see them. They rarely got out to formal functions, partly because it seemed like it wasn't their style, and partly because they were always worried trouble was just around the corner.

Little White Pill

The party was in full swing. The banquet room was huge and wildly decorated. The party was being given by the recording studio, and many musicians and celebrities were there.

The sisters were drinking wine and Marguerite was drinking a Shirley Temple. They all understood, but they still laughed. Chase rarely let go of her hand, but when someone called all the boys over for a drink, they agreed reluctantly and said they would be back soon. They came back a short time later, each carrying a beer except for Quinn. They had some appetizers, which were outstanding, and just stood around talking to each other, and to everyone who came over to them. Everyone seemed to be having a great time.

Then, seemingly out of the blue, Blake seemed to get agitated for some reason. He grabbed Abbey's hand roughly. "We are leaving. Now."

Then Drew did the same thing, inexplicably grabbing Cara's hand and dragging her out.

Quinn looked confused. That was when Marguerite noticed that Chase was sweating profusely and seemed really jumpy. She started to feel strange herself, but could tell that it was actually coming from him, through the bond they shared. "Chase? What's wrong?"

"What's wrong is that I never should have let you out of the room with that dress on."

Her eyes grew wide and she took a step back from him. Something had clearly happened to them all when they'd been gone for a few minutes.

Could they just be drunk? Quinn was the only one not drinking, and he was fine. Marguerite just looked back at Chase and he grabbed her arm. She tried to pull away from him but he had a strong grip on her and ushered her firmly out to the car.

"Get in the car now!"

She did as she was told so as not to make a scene.

Quinn and Jeanine were running to their car, because they knew something was wrong and they had a good idea what it was. Chase had dropped his beer when he grabbed Marguerite, and Quinn noticed the remnants of a little white pill. Someone had laced their beers with a drug of some sort.

As they ran after them, Quinn called Peter to tell him everything that had happened, and was still happening, as they watched the cars pulling away from the curb. They looked frantically around for the bodyguards, who were nowhere to be seen. Quinn and Jeanine were panic stricken, terrified of what the drug might do to their brothers, and at what their brothers could do to the girls. They were rushing, preparing to follow them back to the hotel, knowing that someone needed to do something! Peter had told them he would call the police right away, as well as the hotel, and get security and medical personal involved as fast as possible.

Quinn tried to call Mike and the other bodyguards, but couldn't get through. *Where are they?*

Chase and Marguerite got to the hotel and he all but dragged her to the elevator. Chase was still sweating and agitated. Once inside the room, he slammed the door and glared at her. Marguerite was shaking.

"What's wrong? Please, let me help you!" When she tried to touch his face, he slapped her hand away and then grabbed her arm again.

"Get out of that dress now! You made me wait long enough, prancing in front of me all night. Now you have to pay the price!" She backed away from him. He tried to shove her down on the couch but she fell, hitting the arm of the couch with her back and hip, before rolling to the ground. She was so frightened! She crawled backwards towards the corner of the room and brought her knees up to her chest, wrapping her arms around them and holding them tight, trying to protect the twins.

Just as he was going for her, Mike and Nick burst into the room. Nick grabbed Marguerite and carried her out of the room. She couldn't walk. The other bodyguards rescued Cara and Abbey at about the same time, and brought them all into Quinn and Jeanine's room for safety. Marguerite could still hear Chase yelling, "You can't get away from me!" as Nick carried her away.

The doctor came, with the police, and Mike gave them a sample of the laced beer, which he had picked up once he and the other bodyguards had arrived on the scene, too late to have done the girls any good at all. He also had what was left of the pill that was found in Chase's beer.

Mike felt sick that this had happened on his watch and knew that he would always blame himself for everything that had happened. The others would as well. He and the other bodyguards had been tricked by someone posing as a security official from the recording studio, with an elaborate story about procedures and authorization requiring signatures or documentation or... Mike didn't even know anymore. In hindsight, he had to wonder if he hadn't been drugged as well for ever falling for it, and actually considered having himself tested for opiates or narcotics once everything settled down. In any case, he and the others had been kept out of the way just long enough for the damage to have been done.

Back in London, Peter was frantic, and for good reason. First, he was worried that the girls might be physically hurt—he already knew they had been emotionally. Then there were the guys. He had no idea what danger they might be in, or what drug had been slipped into their systems. Could it kill them? Change them permanently somehow? Heaven forbid, what if they were fine but the girls weren't? How would any of them live with it? He did not know how he was going to fix what happened. Once the boys came out of the state they were in, assuming they would, he didn't know how they would ever forgive themselves. Especially Chase. He could have really hurt Marguerite and their unborn sons. He just hoped that the twins would be fine, and if they were, he prayed that Marguerite would have the strength to get over what he had done to her, and the strength to bring him back from this nightmare the way she had brought him back to life when they'd first met.

What about the others? He knew Drew would never be able to forgive himself for hurting Cara—the love of his life. Blake would always blame himself for hurting Abbey, whom he'd just married less than a month before.

Then there were the career issues to contend with. He was worried that news would get out that the boys were on drugs, when they barely even drank! He knew that someone had sabotaged that party. It was too soon to know for sure, but he found it hard to believe that they hadn't been targeted specifically. He had to find out why this happened, and who they were after.

Back in Quinn's room, the women were all but hysterical. Blake had been alone with Abbey the longest. Jeanine kept asking her, "Are you hurt anywhere else?" Abbey kept cradling her hand, which was already turning black and blue, but shook her head. There didn't seem to be any other injuries. "Okay, so do you want to tell us what happened?"

Abbey nodded her head, and the words came pouring out. "I punched Blake in the mouth. Then ran and locked myself in the bathroom."

She had tried to talk to him to see what was wrong, and he wouldn't answer. He just kept coming for her. She kept backing away, and then he grabbed her by the throat and she'd just decked him. It threw him off and that was when she ran into the bathroom. He was banging on the door when their security guards barged in and held him down. They called out to her and told her it was okay to come out now, and when she had opened the door, she saw that they had him down on the carpet and were sitting on him to hold him still. Then they took her to Jeanine's room to wait for a doctor.

Cara's story was just about the same. She said she had kept asking Drew what was wrong.

"'Please tell me,' I said, and he looked at me like he wanted to murder me!" She had actually feared for her life. He had thrown her down on the bed and moved to join her there. That's when she kicked him in the balls. He'd rolled off the bed, yelling and cursing at her. Security came in then, grabbed him, and ushered her to Jeanine's room.

Marguerite's story was also a nightmare. How could the one person who swore to love and protect her treat her like that? She told them about trying to help him and being thrown down, hitting the couch and ending up on the floor, desperately trying to shield her twins from whatever was coming next. "The man who was coming after me was not Chase. It wasn't. Not the person who can't breathe without me."

They were all so worried about each other, and even more so about the twins. The sisters were just holding each other crying. How could this nightmare be happening to them? Those men were not their husbands, their best friends. How were they ever going to get over this? That was their biggest concern of all. They were petrified and just couldn't stop shaking.

The doctor came in and examined each one of them in turn. When he saw that Marguerite was pregnant, he looked worried. He made her lie down so he could check the baby's heartbeat.

"Heartbeats," she told him. "Twins." He looked doubly concerned then, but didn't comment. He pressed the stethoscope to her swollen abdomen, and listened carefully for a long time, adjusting the placement of the scope a few times before nodding and taking a step back. "Two strong heartbeats. No irregularities." He asked her a number of questions and took her vitals, and then assured her that she would be fine. They were all relieved. After that he wrapped Abbey's hand and recommend that she be taken to the hospital for an x-ray at their earliest convenience, as he suspected she might have fractured it. Then he examined Cara and found that she had no physical injuries. Their blood pressures were all pretty high, but with what had happened, he told them that was to be expected.

Mike, the rest of their security team, and another doctor came in then, and Mike said, "All of you are packed. You're going to Marguerite's home in Pennsylvania. This is not negotiable."

The girls were confused. "Going? With who?"

Mike told them that they would be traveling together, and he would be accompanying them, but that the boys would be staying behind. In a way, they were happy, but they were worried that the boys might need them. The other doctor, who had been working on the boys, told them they had actually identified a variety of drugs in the samples taken, which had combined into a very dangerous cocktail when slipped into their drinks. For their own safety, they had been sedated and were being closely monitored. There was no other way to counteract it. Until it was out of their system, it wasn't safe to be around them. They would not want to see the state they would be in once they did come around.

"How long will it take to get out of their system?" Jeanine asked.

"At least forty-eight hours," he said. "But with the boys not doing drugs, or building up any defenses or immunities to their effects? Maybe longer."

They would be taken to a home to recuperate, which Peter had rented for them, staffed with the best caregivers. At present, they were working out a plan to get them out of the hotel without anyone seeing them.

They all agreed that Quinn should stay behind—the brothers would need him—while Jeanine would go to Pennsylvania with the girls and help take care of them.

Peter was in London, but he was doing his job. Making arrangements. He was good at controlling every move everyone made. Controlling and monitoring. He had even called Marguerite's parents to tell them that the girls were on the way for an impromptu vacation. They all changed quickly into comfortable clothes and were ushered out of the hotel, to a waiting car, and then quickly to the airport. They couldn't stop crying.

While on the plane, Marguerite kept talking to Chase in her mind. She kept saying the same three phrases, over and over: "Come back to me. I can't live without you. Your sons need you."

Finally, she fell asleep from sheer exhaustion.

Back at the hotel, Chase was completely out of it, but every time Marguerite spoke to him, he stirred. Security thought it was just the effects of the drugs in his system, but even through the doctor's heavy induced sleep, he heard her.

Escaping

The word was out about the party. It turned out there were a number of people involved in what was actually a very organized and malicious scheme, apparently aimed not only at The Band 4, but the other celebrities as well. The police had found the men who were lacing the drinks and arrested them. They had been quick to turn on their co-conspirators, but they were nowhere to be found. In fact many of the drinks had been tampered with that night, and there had been many calls for ambulances and emergency services. It was chaotic!

It was common knowledge that the boys had been there. Peter did damage control by saying they had already left the party before anything happened, so they didn't know about anything happening until they'd heard it on the news. The girls didn't know if he should have said that, because in the end, everything always comes out and you end up having to tell ten lies to cover up one. They spoke about it on their way to Marguerite's home in Pennsylvania.

Many people knew what happened: the two doctors who attended to them and all the bodyguards and drivers. Yes, they were their people, but there were too many of them already. They feared it would get out somehow, but they would never know when.

Marguerite begged everyone not to tell her parents or any of the family. Her parents would go wild over what happened. They would never sleep if they knew. She didn't want that to happen. They all agreed. No one else could know.

When they got to Marguerite's, it was still dark out and the house was all lit up. Marguerite's mom was waiting for them at the door. They all put on brave faces and hoped they were able to fool her. Jeanine ran to her and threw her arms around her. "Mom, we're home!" It made them all smile.

Mom saw Abbey's hand. "What happened?"

"Blake was being silly, chasing me around, and I slipped on the bathroom floor. He felt so bad about it, but it was just an accident."

Mom had food waiting, and truthfully, they were starved. They sat and ate, and then all made excuses as to why they wanted to go to bed. They were tired and it had been such a long night. Mom left and they all went upstairs. They all got in Marguerite's bed, holding each other close and crying. They couldn't get over what happened.

"Can someone please wake me up?" Abbey said. "This can't be real."

Peter called Mike every hour on the hour to see how everyone was. Mike told him truthfully that the girls were in bad shape. Peter didn't know what to do. The man who could fix everything, all the time, did not know what to do.

"Please just take care of them," he told Mike.

Mike told Peter that he should have just told the media the truth, and that the girls were worried it would eventually get out. But he stuck to his guns. He truly believed this was the right way to go, and in any case, the statement had already been made and he couldn't take it back.

Back in LA, Quinn got a message from Jeanine, who said they were at Marguerite's and going to bed. She didn't know if anyone would be getting any sleep though. "Everyone's in Mam's bed, just crying." Quinn was shaken. *How can this be happening to my family?* He was worried about how it was ever going to be fixed.

He called Father Cummings. He didn't tell him what happened but asked him to pray for the whole family. Something tragic was happening. He clarified that it wasn't with the twins though. They were fine. He asked for a private prayer and Father Cummings said one for him while he was on the phone with him.

"Do you think you could come to LA," Quinn asked. "I will make all of the arrangements for you."

"Is it that bad?"

"Remember how devastated everyone was when Baby Margaret died?"

"Yes, I will never forget that."

"This is worse."

"Make the arrangements," Father Cummings said firmly. "I'll be ready."

They managed to get the boys out of the hotel and to the house Peter had rented for them. They were still out cold, but Quinn couldn't sleep either. He just kept walking back and forth between the various bedrooms where his brothers were sleeping. Back and forth. Back and forth. He was so tired. He just kept saying prayers that this would all be over soon. Everyone would be all right, wounds would begin healing, and the family would be back together again. He couldn't wait for Father Cummings to get there. He leaned against the wall outside Chase's room, slid down it, and finally fell asleep right there on the floor.

Marguerite was lying in bed awake. She couldn't close her eyes. She kept talking to Chase. "Come back to me. Come back to me. I'm dying."

Chase sat straight up in bed, jarred awake. The doctor was with him. With the dose of sedative he had been given, he should never have been awake yet, but he'd heard Marguerite talking to him. She'd said she was dying. He didn't know what was going on. He looked around. He was in a strange place and she wasn't with him.

"Please save me," he said aloud.

The doctor nodded, but Chase was somewhere else.

Chills went down Marguerite's spine because she'd heard what he said. She responded, "I will save you, Chase. Your sons need you. I need you. Come back to me. You are the very air I breathe."

Chase didn't feel the doctor give him another shot, and before he could reply, he was out cold again.

How to Fix This

Donna, Sue, and Mary thought something was up. They thought maybe the couples were fighting, but could they all be fighting at the same time? That couldn't be what was going on.

Donna had a moment alone with Marguerite. "Just tell me what's going on. The four of you are walking around like you're at a wake. Something is clearly up, so you should just say it."

Marguerite thought fast. "The boys are working so hard and we barely get to see them. We're all just feeling lonely. We just can't shake it this time. With the twins coming, my emotions are getting the best of me."

She searched Donna's face to see if she bought it. Apparently she did.

"Well," she said, "they can't work like that forever, so hang in there and wait just a little longer. Maybe you should all go back to LA so you can be closer to them."

"No, I wanted to come see everyone," Marguerite said. "And truthfully, so did the girls."

She bought that too. Ten lies to cover up one. She had just told two in less than a minute. Marguerite told the girls what she'd said to Donna and they approved. They thought it was a good story to stick to.

They went to dinner at Mary and Joe's house that night. They hadn't wanted to. They would have preferred to be home if anything happened, and they couldn't talk at Marguerite's parents' house.

They kept hearing from Quinn that the boys were still out cold, and they wondered how long it would take them to snap out of it. That was their first worry: When were they going to snap out of it? Then they worried about what would happen when they remembered what they had done. Or would they even remember that? How were the boys ever going to get over this?

Could the girls forgive them? No one wanted to even think about it, but they had to decide what they were going to do. They definitely wanted to see them get back to normal, but didn't know if *they* could ever get back to normal. Did they want to lose everything they had with the boys? After all the years together, going through all the trials of life together, could they get over what had happened and accept them back into their arms?

What if the drugs changed them? That was another issue they thought about. What if they came back to them different? Not those same loving men from before those stupid drinks.

Three little pills destroyed four sets of lives. Why was this done? *Peter had better find out,* Marguerite thought.

They would demand he find out. They had a right to know why their lives might have been destroyed. It made them so mad every time they thought about the guys they arrested. They were pointing fingers at everyone else, but not saying anything about why it had been done!

A full day had passed. They were hoping for news from Quinn, but there had been no change. They all crawled into bed together again. Marguerite said that she was thinking about how to get over what Chase had done. It wasn't that she had to forgive him exactly, because it wasn't Chase who had done that to her. All the girls agreed on that. It wasn't Blake or Drew either. But they all had the same issue: "How do we get over it?"

Abbey was afraid that, when Blake tried to touch her, she wouldn't be able to let him. Cara and Marguerite had the same fear. Marguerite wondered if she would flinch when Chase tried to touch her.

She started sobbing, just thinking about it. "I want him to just hold me. I *need* him to. I'm dying."

All the girls agreed. They were slowly dying without them. They would all have a lot of healing to do.

They were struggling to control their tears, and Jeanine couldn't take it anymore, watching them suffering so much.

"You *all* have to heal, but you need to do it together. Being away from the guys will only make it take longer and drag everything out."

She had hit the nail on the head. They wanted to be with their men. They had to do this together. Marguerite told them how Chase was always asking her, "Why do we forget how strong we are together?" That made sense to the girls and they quickly started to feel better.

"What if they come back to us different though?" Abbey asked.

Jeanine shook her head. "Doesn't matter. They'll still need to be around you to show them how it was. Yes, you all were victims, but so were they. Yes, you have physical and mental bruises, but they do too. You need to remember that. I'm going to pray that the boys can forgive themselves first, because until they do, none of you will be able to move forward."

The girls decided that they wanted to help their men, and themselves, recover. The only way they could do that was together. Together they were strong. If they came back to them different, well then they would show them how things used to be and how it could be again.

The love they felt would always be there, until the end of time, and they had to show the boys that.

Marguerite had finally pulled herself together. "Tomorrow we should go back to LA and get our men." They all agreed, and with that decision made, they finally got some sleep.

Forgiveness and Healing

Marguerite said that she wanted to send a note to Chase—not telling him she was coming, but something more like a love letter. She felt that if he knew she didn't hold him responsible, he would heal quicker. The girls all agreed it was a great idea, and would do the same. She suggested that they keep the notes short, just a line or two, and send one every hour until they got back to LA. This was when the girls finally started coming back to life.

They told Mike they were going back to LA to get their men. He thought it was a good idea too. Gail made all the arrangements, and before they knew it, they were riding to the airport.

They alerted Peter and said that they did not want to speak to him again until he could tell them why this had happened. They were bold and adamant about it. Peter knew he was in trouble.

Mike alerted everyone at the house in LA that they were coming, but told them not to tell the boys. The doctor didn't know if their coming was a good idea or not, but couldn't stop them either way.

It would take about six hours to fly to LA, so they needed to come up with six messages each. When they were done, they all read each other's messages and loved them. They thought, and hoped, that they would help bring their men back to life. Jeanine called Quinn, who confirmed that they were finally awake, although not handling things very well, and told him what they were doing. Quinn thought it was brilliant. He would make sure that the brothers saw each message as they came in, although for security reasons, they weren't being allowed to hang onto their phones just yet.

Father Cummings was still there and felt he was making progress with them. He felt the girls were doing the right thing by coming back to get them.

The doctor said that they were slowly getting back to normal, and was hoping that, physically at least, they would be themselves again by the time the girls arrived. Mentally though they would likely still be a mess, because they were all starting to remember what they had done. One by one, it was all coming back to them.

Drew could not believe he had attacked Cara. He remembered distinctly that she had kicked him in the balls to escape from him and keep him from hurting her. He was so grateful she had done that, and incredibly proud of her. *She is so strong!* But how could she ever forgive him? He loved her so much and was quite distraught at the thought of her leaving him, although he knew he would deserve it.

Blake was sick over the fact that Abbey had fractured her hand punching him in the face to protect herself from him. He had the bruise to prove it too. He couldn't believe he had done that. *How scared she must have been!* He could still see the fear in her eyes and it was tearing him up. How could he say he was sorry and beg her not to leave him? What could he possibly say to make her understand that it wasn't him? But if it wasn't him, why did he hate himself so much? He asked Father Cummings to pray for him, to give him the strength to get his life with Abbey back together.

As bad as it was for the others, Chase took it the hardest. He had gone after his pregnant wife. The person who saved him, he had tried to destroy. How could she ever forgive him? He couldn't feel her anymore. He thought he'd heard her when he was drifting in and out of sleep. He could have sworn he heard her say, "Come back to me. I am dying."

He prayed with all his heart that it *was* her speaking to him, and not some drug-induced hallucination. How could he ever make this up to her? Would she ever be able to trust him again? How could he trust himself? He could have harmed his sons! That would have been absolutely unforgivable! Thank God they were safe.

They all had so many questions! None of them knew that, one by one, they would soon be answered.

One by one, Quinn showed them their individual messages from the girls. Every hour, another message arrived. Between the messages, Quinn had been ordered by security to take the phones back. They didn't get to respond, and were more than a little miffed, but Father Cummings counseled them to just go with it and told them that it would be worth it in the end.

Message one from Marguerite:

Being away from you will only delay the healing process.

Chase started perking up at her words. He thought that maybe there was hope for them. Was she willing to come back to him?

Message two from Marguerite:

My arms are open for you. All you have to do is let me wrap them around you.

As he read those words, Chase's heart was breaking. He needed to see her so badly. He wanted her to wrap her arms around him, but didn't think he deserved it.

Message three from Marguerite:

I am dying a slow death without you.

Chase felt the same way. The pain was so deep, he didn't know if he could ever get over it.

Message four from Marguerite:

Why do we keep forgetting we are stronger together?

He was almost pushed over the edge by that one. He started crying and crying. He needed her! He *needed* her!

Message five from Marguerite:

With all my heart, I forgive you. You are the very air I breathe. I am suffocating without you.

She forgave him. How could she? She forgave him! He fell on his knees, thanking God.

Quinn and Father Cummings were smiling from ear to ear. It was working. They were coming back to life. Love had done it. So far at least, love was winning.

Message six from Marguerite:

Your sons miss you! We are coming to get you!

That was it. Chase snapped out of whatever had been holding onto him and ran out into the hall. So did Drew and Blake. They were all upset and shaking. They needed to get out of there. They needed to go find their wives!

Father Cummings said to them. "Go to the garden. Now."

When they did, Marguerite, Cara, and Abbey were all standing there crying. Then all at once, they opened their arms for their men to come to them, and let them be loved again.

As the couples came together, Father Cummings, Quinn, and Jeanine stood there crying.

It had worked!

Chase hugged Marguerite like he wouldn't ever let her go. He felt the twins kicking at him, and dropped down briefly to his knees to kiss them. "It's okay boys, I'm here. I missed you both." He stood back up to kiss Marguerite but hesitated at the last moment, still unsure of his welcome after everything he had done. She was having none of that, and quickly pulled him in. It was the best kiss in the world.

There was a lot of talking to do, but they all decided to go home to London and work it out. They wanted to be home, around familiar things. They thought that would help.

On the plane back to London, Chase said to Marguerite, "I swear I heard you talking to me."

"I was. I was trying to tell you that I was dying without you."

"I heard you, over and over again, saying, 'Come back to me.' I was thinking the same thing, but the doctor knocked me out again before I could say it."

She shook her head, realizing that if they'd only had another minute, she would have gotten his message as well and been comforted by it.

But he had heard her. That was what was important. Even through all the drugs, he had heard her. She was amazed by how strong their connection was. She smiled at him, and just kept him wrapped in her arms, stroking his face and hair like a child, and taking his pain away.

"You are the very air I breathe," she whispered.
"And you are mine."

Family by Mam

Weeks had passed since they had gotten home from LA back in October. Everyone had tried to get back to normal. The boys were still having a hard time dealing with what had happened to them, and the whole situation. The girls could tell something was still off with them; something was not quite right. They were afraid that the drug might have done something to them.

The girls all talked. Then they sat the boys down and told them that, whether they liked it or not, they were going to have to see someone professionally about what had happened in LA—even if it was just Father Cummings. They needed to take whatever was going on inside and say it out loud. Maybe if they could hear themselves speaking about it, they could figure out what thorn had been left in their sides.

Marguerite and the girls still wouldn't speak to Peter. He had come to visit Marguerite multiple times since they'd gotten back, but she would just lock herself in her office at the house or go upstairs until he left. He knew what she wanted. It was the same thing everyone wanted: Answers. Why did those men do that to the boys? Were they the initial targets or just random victims of what they were doing? They had hurt so many people, and their own eight lives had nearly been destroyed. That was the thorn still stuck in *their* sides.

Marguerite threw herself into her work, designing a maternity line for Victoria, and she enlisted the help of all the girls. Victoria told her she was okay with Marguerite hiring them to help. Ultimately, the line would belong to Marguerite, and she could do whatever she wished. They had all needed a distraction, and this came at the right time. They had so much fun working together and would be forever grateful to Victoria for giving them such a once in a lifetime opportunity.

They planned a huge maternity fashion show and wanted Marguerite to model. "Absolutely no way!" That was her answer whenever anyone tried to talk her into it. She would laugh and say, "Victoria would make me wear six-inch heels and I would be falling on people's laps in the audience!" Then everyone else started laughing too.

Victoria came to see Marguerite and the girls at the maternity offices to pick out a name for the line of maternity clothes. Marguerite and the girls were blown away when Victoria said she wanted to name it "Family by MAM". She told them it was an easy choice. Every time she came to the offices, all she would see were sisters working and brainstorming together. She could see the love between them and that they were obviously a family.

A press conference was held about the new line:

Victoria Baker would like to announce a new line for her fashion house, which is being designed solely for pregnant women by Marguerite Angeli-Martin, with the help of Abigale Adams-Thomas, Cara Goodwin-Bishop, and Jeanine Mercer-Howard. The line will be reasonably priced and carried exclusively by Darcy's Department Stores. The name of the new line is "Family by MAM".

The boys were all at the studio listening to the news when the line was announced. They were so proud of the girls, who were right beside Victoria on the podium when the announcement was made. Victoria turned to Marguerite and asked her to say something. She didn't know that she was going to speak, so she had nothing prepared. She took a deep breath and then grabbed the hands of Abbey and Cara, who grabbed Jeanine's hand in turn, and together they walked to the microphone. The camera flashes all seemed to be going off at the same time. She didn't know if she would ever be able to see again.

Blinking and taking a moment to compose herself, she said, "We want to thank Victoria first and foremost for giving us all an opportunity to create something." Then she looked down at her baby bump. Everyone laughed. She cleared her throat. "Of course, I meant professionally!"

The audience laughed again. The girls were beaming, standing next to her. "I always complained to Victoria that women needed a maternity line that would be fashionable and affordable. Maternity clothes are temporary clothes. They should be reasonably priced so that women can afford them with all of the other expenses they have coming up in their lives when their babies are born."

Everyone started clapping and agreeing. Then she said, again to Victoria, "Thank you so much for naming the line after my sisters and me. It means the world to us. We can never repay you for the kindness you have shown us, and the opportunity you have given us. I speak for us all," she said, as she looked at the girls and then back to Victoria, "when I say that we love you with all our hearts."

Victoria was beaming and hurried over to Marguerite and the girls, who grabbed her and pulled her into a big group hug. The cameras kept clicking away.

Back at the studio, the boys and Peter were watching the press conference. "Can you believe they did that?" Blake asked. "Developed a line of clothing for Victoria Baker's fashion house?" They all just shook their heads. They were so proud of them and constantly amazed by things they were doing and thinking about.

"This came at the right time," Chase said. "It gave them all something else to think about and helped them forget about LA." All the brothers agreed. They couldn't wait to get home to see their women.

I have to find out what happened in LA, Peter thought. *I owe it to them all.* He missed talking to the girls. He was so fond of them and his life had felt empty since they stopped speaking to him.

Chase got home before his wife. When she arrived home, he ran to her for once, instead of the other way around. He wrapped her in his arms and buried his head in her hair. "I saw the press conference! You were amazing."

She told him that she hadn't known she would have to speak and had nothing prepared.

Chase chuckled. "You're always prepared. Somehow." He told her how proud of her he was and how much he loved her. They could *feel* each other strongly in that moment, and said so at the same time. "I feel you!"

Then the boys kicked their dad in the stomach while he had their mother in his arms. They just laughed. So he bent down and spoke to them. "Yes I know, you are here too."

43 Reasons

Marguerite wanted to get rid of her hair. It was too long and she wanted to shorten it drastically before the twins were born. She called Vita and asked her if she would do it, and she was thrilled. She felt it was time for Marguerite to change her style as well. When Chase came home from the studio, she told him what she was going to do.

"Your mind is already made up, so just do it."

The way he said it bothered her. They usually talked about everything and she realized she hadn't talked to him about this. She'd just made the decision. She followed him into the office and stood there looking at him. He wouldn't look up at her.

Something was happening. "What's wrong? It's not about me cutting my hair." She felt that something was wrong with him.

"Peter will be here in about five minutes to talk to you. The girls are coming over too, so he can talk to you all at once."

The couples started arriving. The girls were all wondering what Peter wanted, and hoped it wasn't just to ask them to please start talking to him again. They knew it upset him, but he knew how they felt and why.

When Peter arrived, they all sat around the big table in the kitchen. "I want to tell you again how sorry I am about what happened in LA. You said you wouldn't speak to me until I found out what happened. And so I did. I have that information, but you are all going to be very upset."

They braced themselves.

"The boys were not the target." They were all relieved at first, but noticed that the boys had their heads down, as if they couldn't look at any of them. That's when the panic started to set in.

"You girls were the target. The bartender was supposed to lace your drinks. Not the boys'. When you all got your drinks from a different bar, the bartender panicked and went after the boys instead."

The room started to spin. They all turned white. Marguerite got up and ran to the bathroom. Chase followed her and held her hair back from her face as she got physically sick. She started freaking out then, as it all started sinking in. She felt like her skin was crawling and suddenly couldn't bear to be touched. Sobbing desperately, she pulled away from Chase, barely even registering that it was him.

"Don't touch me! Don't touch me!"

There were similar cries of distress coming from the kitchen. They were all upset. Peter had his head in his hands. He didn't know what to do. Eventually Marguerite came back out, wanting to be with the sisters. They ran to each other and just hugged and hugged, crying loudly. No one knew how to help them.

It didn't make sense. Why them? They didn't bother anyone. They rarely even went out. What if something had happened to Marguerite and the twins? *My god, the twins!* That thought really put them all over the edge. If that drug had laced her drink, would it have killed her twins? Would she have done it herself, in some fit of violence? They were all close to collapsing when it hit them: The boys had taken the hit for them, not even knowing that they were doing so.

They asked Peter to explain why they were targeted. "Competition, I suppose. The arrested bartender finally started to tell the story last night. A small group of female fans wanted you all out of the picture, thereby freeing up the boys. Unfortunately, they had the financial means to make it happen. The young women were arrested this morning. The men who posed as security personnel are still unaccounted for. They figure they were just hired hands anyway though, with no real stake in things, and that they likely won't surface any time soon."

Now it would be all over the news that the band and their spouses had been the targets of the incident in LA, which had caused quite a commotion in the news and social media at the time. "I know you won't be happy about this, but I'm reconfirming our original story that you all left the event before anyone could get to you."

The girls were so upset that they couldn't even argue with or reject his plan. They thought he should have told the truth the first time. Regardless, enough other people at the event were harmed and put at risk—some fairly powerful and well-known—that the young women would be going away for a long time.

No one wanted to go home. They wanted to talk it out, but needed to compose themselves first. Marguerite suggested that they all go and lie down for a while. She was wrecked and saw that the others were also. She and the girls staggered to her bedroom and crawled into her large bed together, hugging and just quietly lying there. The boys settled down on the couch beside their bed, not wanting to leave them.

After they had rested a bit and calmed down, Marguerite said, "Why don't you boys go downstairs and whip something up for diner?"

Chase knew they wanted to be alone. He and his brothers climbed to their feet and stood there for a moment, looking down at them. The girls didn't even look up at them, so they turned around and left.

At the last minute, Marguerite thought, *I love you, Chase.* He turned back around and nodded his head. He'd heard her.

Chase closed the door to the bedroom, but they didn't go downstairs. Instead, they sat down on the floor outside the door. They would not leave.

Panic

Lying together on Marguerite's bed, the girls had so many questions going through their minds all at once that they had to force themselves to stop and just address one at a time.

Judging by the way Chase wouldn't look at her, Marguerite thought that maybe the boys were blaming them for what had happened in LA. The girls all suspected the same thing, and it was tearing them apart. They talked about it and decided that they would just have to ask them as soon as they got the chance.

"What made you go to that other bar all the way across the room in the first place," Jeanine asked, because that's what had saved them.

"I just didn't notice the one closer until we already had our wines," Abbey said.

Then they began to cry again, thinking about what would have happened if Marguerite had taken one of those toxic drinks. "I would have killed my sons."

Just like that, they were on the verge of hysteria again.

They couldn't control themselves, and the boys couldn't take it anymore. They ran back into the room and grabbed their wives. All they could do was hold them. This time, the girls clung to their men tightly, as if they were hanging on for dear life. Eight people were draped over the one bed. It was quite a scene.

One at a time, they asked the boys questions, starting with the most important one: "Are you blaming us for what happened in LA?"

They were all stunned that they would even think that. "Absolutely not," they assured them, fiercely. They were just glad it had been them and not the girls.

Then Jeanine told Chase, "Mam feels that, if she had gotten that drink, she might have killed your sons." Chase looked at her. "I'm glad I was the one who got it. She protected them from me instead, just like I would have protected them from her. I would have done anything to protect my sons and my wife. I will do anything I can to protect them."

One at a time, the men started to confess some of the feelings they had been dealing with.

First, Blake said to Abbey, "Every time I looked at your hand bandaged up, because you had to protect yourself from me, it tore me up inside. Now, knowing what I know, I realize that *that* bandage was actually thanking me. Thanking me for taking that drink instead of you. That's the way I will think of it from now on. I know you've all felt we've been a little off, well, that's what was off about me. Seeing what I did to you." He sighed. "I would gladly take that drink for you every day if it would have kept you safe. I love you, Abbey, and I can't live without you." Blake drew her up onto his lap and engulfed her in his arms.

Drew talked to Cara next. "I had no idea what a strong woman you were. I mean, I knew you were strong, but you actually kicked me in the balls to protect yourself from me! Even how much I love you could never account for how proud I am of you" Just like Blake, he assured her that he would take that drink for her every day if it meant keeping her safe. Cara was crying profusely. He brushed away a tear from her cheek. "Please let me take your pain away my love." She rolled closer to him so his arms could wrap completely around her.

Chase looked at his wife. He was slowly shaking his head with tears streaming down his face. "Thank the good God above that you didn't get that drink." He could barely talk, but they all heard exactly what he was saying and thinking. *The twins!* "When we first came home and I saw that you were black and blue, from your back right down to the back of your knees, knowing I had done that to you, that I had pushed you and could have killed you... You! My sweet wife, you did the right thing. You wrapped your arms around your legs to protect our sons... to protect them from me." He squeezed his eyes shut, unable to look at her. "I thought, how could she ever forgive me for that? Then you sent that note saying you forgave me, and I couldn't believe it. How could I be so lucky?" He looked into her eyes. "Sometimes I worry that you'll get tired of saving me."

She leaned in a bit closer. "Don't you know?" She reached out and touched his cheek. "We're supposed to keep saving *each other.* I thought you understood. That's who we are, Chase. Until I take my last breath, I will keep saving you, and I expect the same from you in return."

Quinn and Jeanine were smiling, watching the healing that was taking place, and told each other quietly that they thought they would all be fine now.

They all finally felt that the tragedy was behind them, but they wondered whether the details were going to be released to the media, unable to remember what Peter had told them. He had quietly gotten up and gone home when the girls had headed upstairs to bed. Quinn called him and Peter told him that he'd made sure that no details would be mentioned now. As far as the press (or the world) knew, they had left the party before they could be hurt. It would stay that way. Now that they had finally started to heal the wounds, they thought it was probably just as well. Peter was glad. Keeping those events firmly in the past was the least he could do for them.

They finally got up and decided to order pizza and have it delivered. No one wanted to go out and no one wanted to cook. Instead they ate pizza and drank cola. They actually laughed about it, which made the girls feel better. It would be a long time before anyone felt like drinking alcohol again, but it was okay. They were finally putting it behind them. They had a nice quiet evening, and then they all went up to bed. No one was going home. It had been such an emotional day and they were all drained.

Jeanine and Quinn knocked on Chase's door and walked in. They were just getting into bed. Chase nodded his head toward the empty side of the bed, motioning for them to join them if they wanted, and they did. Marguerite knew they wanted to talk some more.

"You know I have another question for you, don't you?" Chase asked.

"Yes," Quinn said. "That's why we're here."

"Do you think we have guardian angels?"

Both Quinn and Jeanine nodded their heads.

"Do you think it was our guardian angel who saved Mam from that toxic drink?"

They nodded again. "Absolutely," Quinn said, with a smile.

Chase and Marguerite told Quinn and Jeanine that they loved them, and they responded with the same sentiment. As they turned off the bedside lamps, and all settled down for a well-earned sleep, Chase kissed his wife tenderly and whispered in her ear, "You are the very air I breathe."

She smiled softly in the darkness. "And you are mine."

Ed

Chase felt he wanted to tell his best friend Ed what had happened. He talked it over with Marguerite and she felt that, if he wanted to tell Ed, he should. The two men knew everything about each other's lives anyway, and had for years. Chase thought everyone should have one person outside of their family who they could say anything to, if only for an unbiased opinion every now and then. Ed was that person for Chase, and vice versa.

He told Ed the whole story. It took hours, and many breaks were necessary because of how upset it made him to talk about it. Ed was stunned, and when he told him about his drink being meant for Marguerite, pregnant with his sons, it sent them both over the edge. All either of them could think of was that Chase's sons and possibly his wife could all be dead today if they had gotten the drink instead of him. Ed was so shaken. It was so hard for him to take it all in. He got up and kept pacing back and forth, thinking about what he had just found out about Marguerite and the boys. He loved her like a sister, and Chase was his best friend and a brother to him.

Eventually, after talking everything out and spending some time making each other feel better about it, the conversation drifted to less upsetting subjects.

"The band and I have to go to the US for an appearance on Friday Night Live," Chase said. His wife was upset she couldn't go with him, but her traveling days were over for now. She still felt great, with no complications or problems with the pregnancy, which they were thankful for.

When Ed heard the dates in question, he realized that he could help take her mind off Chase's absence. "I'm doing a concert at Wembley Stadium while you're away in the US. How about I pick up Mam and take her with me. I want to spend some time with her anyway, after everything you just told me. I'll make sure she's safe and then I'll personally take her home afterwards. It will get her out of the house a bit while you're gone."

Chase thought that was an excellent idea. He would only be gone two nights, but it still bugged him not to be there with her. He knew she felt the same. The girls had chosen to stay behind with her and would spend the first night at the house to keep her company. They were busy the second night though, so she would be on her own. Chase felt much better that Ed could be with her that night.

Chase went to the US, flying into the Scranton/Wilkes Barre Airport in Pennsylvania, because there were fewer crowds than at JFK and they found it easier to arrive unnoticed. More importantly, it allowed Chase, his brothers, and their people to stay in the Pennsylvania house. They would rent a bus from there and commute to New York in relative comfort and anonymity.

Donna and Sue were thrilled they were coming and planned to cook for them. Mary and Joe would also be around. The happy parents would air the house out for them and would be there waiting for them when they got in. Marguerite was happy that they would be with family.

Chase webcammed home the first night and Marguerite was wild with frustration at her pregnancy. "I feel like a moose! And these boobs are so big, I can't take them! They hurt!"

"Wait!" he said. "How big did they get since I left this morning?" That made her laugh, and he joined in.

Chase could hear Drew behind him, yelling, "Let me see! I'll tell you if they got bigger!" Everyone got a good laugh out of that.

Chase knew she was starting to feel uncomfortable. She was eight months pregnant and completely over it. She had two sets of arms and legs punching and kicking her insides around. When he held her, the boys never stopped moving. He'd asked her one day, "How do you sleep with all of that going on in your body?"

She would just laugh "Exhaustion just takes over and you pass out." Once again, he was amazed at how strong she was.

The second night Chase was gone, Ed picked up Marguerite and Mike at the house. She had told Ed that she felt like a moose too, and that he should not be surprised when he saw her. But when he looked at her, all he could see was joy. Her happiness made her glow. As he touched her baby bump, she looked down and said, "Uncle Ed is here boys, and we're going to his concert. He's going to sing to you."

All of a sudden, they started kicking up a storm. Ed's face turned red when he felt the movement. *Even though she's big,* Ed thought, *she still looks beautiful.* He couldn't get over how lucky his best friend was to have her as his wife. Ed took her by the hand and led her to the car. He opened the door for her, helped her climb into the back seat, and then moved around to the other side, climbing in beside her. Mike, who had followed discreetly behind, climbed into the front seat next to Ed's driver, who acknowledged him with a nod. Mike would be there with Marguerite at the concert, keeping out of the way in the shadows. He wasn't letting her out of his sight again.

All of Ed's people knew she was coming to the concert. He'd told them so they'd be expecting her.

They got to Wembley and were met by his manager. He and Marguerite had met on a number of occasions and he was quite fond of her. He kissed her and touched the baby bump.

"Twins," he said, shaking his head. Marguerite just laughed. They still had a long walk ahead of them, so Ed took her by the hand again. They had wanted to get a cart for her but she refused. They had to stop once or twice but made it to the lounge okay. There she got to sit down and rest while Ed went to get ready.

A few famous recording artists who were at Ed's concert came in to see him. Ed introduced them to her. She told everyone that she loved their music and it was a pleasure to meet them.

It was time to walk to the stage. Ed was so protective of her that he helped her out of the chair and took her by the hand to walk with him. He told her that he thought she looked beautiful, and how happy he was that she was making him an uncle. He couldn't wait for the boys to be born.

"I love you as much as I love Chase, you know," he said.

She stopped walking, as her eyes welled up with tears. "You cannot do that to a pregnant lady," she said, and kissed him on the cheek. "I'm very emotional right now." They both smiled and resumed the trek to the stage.

Ed's cousin was going to be in charge of her when Ed was on stage. He was going to sit with her every moment. Marguerite was happy that she wouldn't be alone. Then the stage manager said, "It's time." Ed went over to her and kissed her again.

"Have a good show," she said.

"I am so proud of you, Ed. And I love you too." He smiled wide as he walked out to the stage and waved to the audience.

The show was amazing. In the middle of it, he asked the crowd, "Do any of you know who my best friend Chase Martin is?" They cheered and applauded.

"Okay now, do any of you know his wife Marguerite?" Now they really went wild. She was touched, as always, by people's apparent affection for her.

"You all know they are going to have twins right? Well, unfortunately for Chase, he's in New York tonight, and so Marguerite is here with me." The volume went up a notch or two.

"I'm kind of wife-sitting for him. Do you want to meet her?"

Marguerite was shaking her head wildly. *No, no, no!* She was huge. She was *not* going out there!

But Ed wasn't done. "We'll have to ask her nicely though..." He was having trouble being heard over the crowd, and had to keep pausing to catch his breath. "... And make her feel better... because she says she feels like a moose right now. In all honesty though... when I look at her carrying my nephews... I only see a very beautiful woman. Mam, I am coming down to get you!" Everyone was screaming for her.

He had to drag her up the ramp to the stage, leading her by the hand. When she appeared, everyone started screaming even louder. She was shaking her head and had her hands over her face. She couldn't believe he had done this.

Resigned now, she took the mic from him and started talking to the crowd. "I cannot believe he just did this. I was trying to stay hidden! I'm a cow!" At first she thought they started booing, but then she realized that everyone was screaming "Nooooo!"

Ed stepped up beside her, talking into her mic. "When Marguerite and Chase got married two years ago, I sang "Thinking of You" to them for their first dance. Now I'm going to sing it just for you, Mam, and we can dance to it. Okay?"

She was in no condition to run. She could barely walk. So what could she say? "Okay."

Of course, when he started singing, and then dancing with her, her water works started and the crowd melted and let out a collective "Aaawww!"

She cried throughout the whole song, and when it was over, he just hugged her until he felt she was okay. He whispered, "I love you, Mam," while her face was buried in his shirt. The crowd was pleased. Everyone had been recording the song, and the whole exchange, on their phones.

"You know," she said, sniffing and wiping her face as she smiled up at him. "I have to tell Chase that you love me now and I love you. I don't know how he is going to take it."

They both laughed, getting a kick out of that. With a final wave to the crowd, he walked her back to his cousin and then went out to finish his concert.

When the concert was over, she had a change of shirt for him and a cold towel. His cousin thought she was crazy for asking that the towel be put in the fridge. When Ed came off the stage, she asked him if he wanted to change his shirt and he nodded. So she helped him out of the one he'd had on, which was drenched.

Then she said, "Okay this is going to be cold." She wiped his face with the towel. After a moment, she paused, frowning. "You're staring at me. Is it too cold? Do you want me to stop?"

"No, don't stop! No one ever did that for me before." She smiled and put the cold towel on the back of his neck to cool him down. It was a nice moment between them.

"Okay," he said and took her hand, "we have to go now or we won't get out."

Bonding

As Ed took Marguerite's hand to lead her back towards the car, she doubled over in pain and let out a scream. Mike rushed over to her and both he and Ed asked what was wrong. The pain stopped as quickly as it had begun, and she stood up straight. She was shaken though, pale and trying to catch her breath.

"Um... okay," She shook her head and shrugged uncertainly. "Let's walk now; I'm fine." They started moving again, with Mike and Ed at her sides and watching her like hawks. Right before she got to the car, she doubled over again. The pain was excruciating. "Okay, get me to the hospital. Now."

Ed picked her up in his arms and put her into the waiting car, telling his driver, "Get us to the hospital and quickly."

The police were already at the stadium, prepared for crowd control issues, and so the driver pulled up alongside a patrol car that was idling near the closest exit. He rolled down his window and quickly told the officer the situation. He turned on his siren and flashers and gave them an official escort.

Mike called Gail and told her to call the doctor and everyone else. They were headed to the hospital.

Chase felt her. He knew something was wrong. He turned white. "It's Mam," he said. The boys all looked at him. "Something is going on."

They were always amazed at the connection those two had. "Well," Quinn said, as they looked around the airport. "It's a good thing we're already getting on the plane home then."

Chase nodded.

All their phones went off at the same time. It was a message from Gail:

Mam is going to the hospital. We think she is having contractions. The doctor is waiting. Ed is with her and will not leave her alone.

Oh thank goodness, Chase thought. *Ed is with her.* That made him feel better.

They got on the plane and knew it would be the longest seven hours to London in history, so he closed his eyes and tried to feel his wife. "I am coming, Mam. I am coming."

At that moment, Marguerite turned to Ed. "Chase is on the way."

"How do you know?"

"I feel him and he just told me. He said, 'I am coming.'" Chase had always told Ed about their connection, but this was the first time he got to experience it first-hand. It was kind of spooky.

Mike nodded. "It is weird, but it's somehow true. I see it all the time with them. It makes me realize how lucky they are to have found each other."

Chase's mom was already there when they arrived at the hospital. The girls were on the way and one by one they started to show up. Doctor Robbins was there too, and quickly ushered Marguerite into an exam room to take a preliminary look.

"The twins are fine!" That was the first thing she confirmed. It put everyone at ease. Peter ran in next and they filled him in too.

"Where is Chase?" Dr. Robbins asked him.

"In the air coming from the States," he said.

She nodded and talked to Chase's mom about Marguerite's condition.

"Marguerite was going into labor, but I really didn't want her to deliver yet. With twins we always like to let them go as long as possible. I gave her medication to try to stop the contractions, and they're taking her to a room now. If we can get the contractions to stop, which is what I am hoping for, she can go home tomorrow."

Everyone was relieved. Jess called Marguerite's mom and dad back in Pennsylvania, along with her cousins, Donna and Sue.

They were able to contact Chase on the plane. They told him what was going on and he was relieved too. He was doing his best to stay calm, and all the brothers were doing everything they could to support him.

Back in the hospital, Marguerite was in her room and had been sleeping for a while. Ed was sitting at the side of her bed, holding her hand, while the girls were spread out around the room, sleeping wherever they could find a place to sit or lie down.

When Marguerite woke up and saw Ed sitting there, she felt her eyes welling up with tears. "I am so sorry."

"For what?"

"For all the trouble I caused you."

"You are no trouble at all. I learned a lot today about loving someone and being there for them when they need me."

Marguerite just laughed. "Isn't that in one of your songs?"

"Not yet but I'm thinking of putting it in one soon." Chuckling, he leaned forward in his chair.

"Thank you for everything, Ed." She squeezed his hand. "Oh, and we have a surprise for you by the way."

"Oh yeah? And what would that be?"

She gave him a big smile. "You'll see." Then she closed her eyes and fell quickly back to sleep.

The doctor came in to check on the twins and Marguerite. She saw Ed sitting there holding her hand. The friendships Chase and Marguerite had always amazed her. These were not just friends, they were a family.

Ed looked up at the doctor. "How is she doing?"

"Really well. Every time we check, her vital signs are good, and the twins' heartbeats are strong. Everything looks really good so far. But of course, with twins anything can happen at any given moment. That's why I want her to stay overnight."

Ed sensed that she wanted to say something more. "What's on your mind?"

She seemed reluctant to share it, but eventually nodded, stepping closer and speaking quietly. "I was remembering coming into a room similar to this over a year ago, and the terrible outcome. I remember giving everyone in the room something to calm them down because of the distress they were all in. Later, I remember coming into the room and finding everyone passed out wherever they landed—on the floor, on chairs, couches..." She shook her head. "Chase cradled his wife for hours and hours. I had never seen anything like that before, and believed I never would again."

The doctor looked over and saw all the girls there, sleeping and holding each other. "Yet here we are. I will do everything in my power to ensure that this time they all go home smiling. They deserve it."

"I know," he said. "What a group of amazing people they are. I've never met a family like this one either, and I feel privileged to be part of it. I was actually babysitting Mam for Chase when the pain started. I brought her to the hospital."

Doctor Robbins smiled, raising an eyebrow at him. "Babysitting?"

"Well, sort of. I had a concert at Wembley tonight, and I took Marguerite to help get her mind off of everything until Chase got home. I was just thrilled I could help my best friend out. And you know what?" He looked at her with a disbelieving smile on his face. "I'm happy to get to sit here for hours until he gets here. It's these people, or maybe it's just her and Chase. I don't know." He grinned at her. "But I do know that either one of them would do the same for me in a heartbeat." He looked at Marguerite and kissed her hand.

"It's a good thing you weren't here the last time," the doctor said. "It was devastating. Even I cried, and doctors are supposed to distance ourselves from our patients. I've been managing it perfectly well for years but, when I saw all of them, so distraught and heartbroken, I couldn't help it."

"I was in the US when it happened," Ed said. "I flew back as soon as I could. I remembered thinking, 'I hope they can recover from this', because when I saw the condition they were in, I didn't know if it would be possible. They bounced back though. Stronger than ever."

The Delivery

Chase's plane finally arrived. The car was waiting for them, and as soon as the plane's door opened, the boys flew out of it and climbed into the car. It took twenty minutes to get to the hospital. Everyone kept looking at Chase, but could see he was calmer this time.

They got to the hospital in record time, and when they got to the floor Marguerite was on, Blake told the others to go find the room while he got the update from the nurse. They already knew the room number, as Peter had texted it to them as soon as they had Marguerite settled in.

Chase walked into the room and didn't see anyone but Marguerite sleeping in the bed and Ed holding her hand. Ed looked up at him and Chase felt his eyes well up. He reached across the bed to squeeze Ed's shoulder. "Thank you," he whispered. "Thank you for taking care of my wife."

Chase took off his shoes and jacket and lay down next to Marguerite. He put his arm underneath her and slid her over to him. She turned a bit in her sleep and settled down into his arms. Quinn and Drew watched this all from the doorway, incredibly happy that everything looked under control. Then they both moved forward and hugged Ed, thanking him. At that moment, Ed thought, *I really am privileged to be in this family.*

Quinn pulled up the rail so that Chase would not fall out of the bed. Then Blake came in and gave him the update on her condition. "Okay, so she started going into labor. The doctor stopped it because she wants her to last about two more weeks if she can. The twins' heartbeats are strong and she is not in any distress at the moment. All is quiet."

They all let out a big sigh of relief, and when they saw the girls all sleeping on the couch, they went over to join them, but not before leaning carefully over the bed to kiss Marguerite.

She started to stir, and when she opened her eyes, she found Chase looking at her. She started to cry and he just stroked her face. "No tears now. I'm here. No tears."

And then she fell back to sleep.

Early the next morning, the doctor came in to see them. Once again, people were passed out everywhere. Chase was back in bed holding his wife, and Ed was still holding her hand and sleeping at the foot of the bed. That really made her laugh. Marguerite started waking up. She had to use the bathroom. She woke Chase up and let go of Ed's hand. Chase jumped up, thinking something was wrong, but Marguerite shook her head.

"I only have to wee."

He smiled and kissed her, then helped her up. She was able to stand on her own and walk to the bathroom, but she didn't get far. Her water broke. She was glad the doctor was there when it happened.

But I still have to wee, she thought. Her expression made that clear, so they let her go. Chase took her, and by the time she got out of the bathroom, everyone was up. She was walking back to the bed when a contraction hit. She doubled over in pain. Her face turned almost purple as she fought against it. The doctor got her back in bed and checked the twins' heartbeats. They were strong, but their rates were quite elevated. Then she ran some quick tests on Marguerite, muttering under her breath the whole time. Finally she stepped back, nodding firmly and putting her hands on her hips. "Okay, new plan. You're having your babies today."

"Today?"

"Yes. Excuse me for one moment please." As she stepped out into the hallway and spoke briefly to someone outside, Chase and Marguerite stared at each other with wide eyes, excited but terrified at the same time. Doctor Robbins stepped back into the room and moved to the foot of the bed.

"Okay, they are prepping the O.R. as we speak. I know we talked about the possibility of delivering the twins by Cesarean section, and that you were hoping to avoid it, but I'm afraid that is the route we will be taking." The doctor could see the fear and tension in their expressions and took a deep breath. "You're in full labor now. The babies' heart rates are elevated, and your blood pressure is rising more rapidly than I'm comfortable with.

I know it's not ideal for you, and scary to think about, but C-sections are a common practice now, and in many ways, are much easier on you and your babies. Now, I need you to take some deep breaths and get yourself as calm as possible. Okay?"

Marguerite nodded and tried to do as she was instructed. Chase stayed as close as he could, offering as much comfort as he could manage.

"Chase," the doctor said, "you were at the appointments and know the potential risks. Do we have your consent to proceed?"

"Yes, of course. Do whatever you have to do to keep them all safe."

"Marguerite?"

She nodded as well, and took yet another deep breath, letting it out as slowly as she could. It was shaking.

Porters and nurses came in, transferring her to a new bed, and wheeling her to the operating room. A different doctor came in and gave her a spinal block. He explained to Marguerite and Chase that it would numb her from her chest to her toes. That way she could be awake for the deliveries.

The rest of the family were waiting outside. They just sat on the floor outside the operating room, leaning against the walls in between the various pieces of equipment stored there. Nurses tried to get them to move but Dr. Robbins, looking back at them all, said, "Let them be. Trust me. They are not moving."

Then she went into the operating room. They put Chase in scrubs and made him cover his hair. *He looks like a doctor,* Marguerite thought.

She was having one contraction after another and wasn't feeling them at all, which is what the doctors had explained and expected. They were ready to start. "Okay," Doctor Robbins said to Chase and Marguerite. "Are you ready to meet your sons?" They both were excited and had tears in their eyes. Chase stood beside his wife's head and held her hand.

They tried to ignore what they were hearing, and not think too much about what was taking place on the other side of the screen that separated them from the surgical procedure. They focused instead on the love in each other's eyes, and the impending arrival of their children. Suddenly, they heard a baby start to cry.

Marguerite was squeezing his hand almost as hard as he was squeezing hers.

"Chase?" Dr. Robbins held up a pair of surgical scissors and asked him to come cut the umbilical cord. Chase froze. He hadn't known he was going to be doing that. But he took a deep breath, steeled his shoulders, and then moved forward and cut the cord. The doctor showed Chase the baby, and his face lit up. He was smiling from ear to ear. Incredibly proud. Then she handed the baby to a nurse, who wrapped him up quickly and brought him to Marguerite to see. Both parents were crying.

"What's his name?" the nurse asked.

"Zachary Quinn Edward Martin."

The nurse repeated it, and Baby Martin number one officially had a name.

Then the doctor pulled out the second baby. Again they heard a cry. Chase went over and cut the umbilical cord again, still beaming from the first. She showed him his second son, and then the nurse showed him to Marguerite. She took him to clean him up also. "And what is this little one's name?"

Chase answered again. "Zeke Blake Drew Martin." And so Baby Martin number two had a name as well.

Outside the O.R., where the family was sitting, the nurses came out with scrubs for everyone. She told them to get dressed fast if they wanted to go in and see the babies. They did so in a flash and were just waiting for someone to come and get them.

The nurse in the O.R. handed one son to Chase and one son to Marguerite—once they made sure she was strong enough to hold him securely. They stayed close just in case. They were both so happy they were crying. "Look what we did!" Chase said, smiling at his wife through his tears.

The babies were beautiful and looked just like Chase. They had a thick head of hair already. The doctor said that Zac was 7lbs 2oz and Zeke was 7lbs, which was large for twins.

"No wonder you felt like a moose," Chase said. The operating room was suddenly filled with laughter. They looked at their sons. Their lungs were clear and their heartbeats were strong and steady. Once the family came in to see them, they would be taken for a more thorough exam, but so far everything looked perfect.

The nurse finally went out and got everyone. They were all shaking. When they walked in they saw Chase holding one son and Marguerite holding the other.

"Boys," Chase said to his sons, "your Godfathers and Godmothers are here." He gave his first son to Quinn and Ed. "This is my son Zac Quinn Edward Martin." Quinn and Ed started crying like babies.

Then he took his second son from his mother and handed him to Blake and Drew. "Meet your new nephew, Zeke Blake Drew Martin." They were all crying now. The girls were over the moon because they would be Godmothers to the two boys. They passed the babies around carefully, kissing them gently.

Then the nurses came and took them. The doctor said that they had to leave now so they could finish their work. They all did except for Chase. He kept just crying and kissing Marguerite. He kept saying, "I love you; you are so brave and strong. I love you..."

And she kept saying "I love you!" back.

Marguerite was back in her room, but in her bed alone this time. The doctor had told Chase, "Absolutely not! You cannot get in bed with her. She just had an operation!"

So he had pulled a chair up next to her, kissed her hand, and then rested his head beside it on the mattress. She kept stroking his face and hair to get him to relax, and that did it. After a few minutes though, he grabbed her hand and held it next to his heart. "My heart is only beating because of you, and only beating for you and now for our sons."

She smiled from ear to ear, as did everyone else who had heard him. *What a day!*

Quinn said to Chase, "You were so calm this time. We all noticed it."

"I knew everything would be fine this time," he said. "I just felt that God wouldn't let anything happen to my family again."

It made Quinn happy to hear him say that.

The Z's

Peter needed to release a statement. He ran it by Chase first:

> *Chase Martin of the Band 4 and his wife, Marguerite, are proud and excited to announce the birth of their twin sons, Zac Quinn Edward (7lbs 2oz) and Zeke Blake Drew (7lbs) today at 6:05 a.m. and 6:12 a.m. The babies were delivered by Cesarean section and mother and both babies are doing well. Chase and his brothers were on the way back to London from the US when he got news that Mrs. Martin had gone into labor. She was taken to the hospital by their best friend, Ed Mehan, whose concert she had been attending. The rest of the group's members, whom as you all know are family to the new parents, were at the hospital with them, as was Chase's mother. Mrs. Martin's mother and father are on the way to London this morning.*

Everyone thought he had given out more information than usual, but they liked what he said.

When it came time to leave the hospital with the twins, Peter asked if they would allow the press to be present. They had to be coaxed but agreed in the end. It was quite a sight, as Marguerite and Chase—surrounded by brothers, sisters, Ed Mehan and numerous bodyguards—exited the front entrance of the hospital with their twin boys and found themselves faced with more cameras, microphones, and reporters than they had ever seen. Their joy was obvious to everyone present. They were each holding one of the twins until Jeanine and Quinn came with a baby carrier and took Zac from Chase, while Blake and Abbey took Zeke from Marguerite. They each placed their nephews in the carriers and walked to the waiting SUV as flashes went off around them left and right. They had all practiced how to safely secure the babies into the carriers and the carriers into the car. Drew, Cara, and Ed stood and watched with Marguerite and Chase.

Chase held Marguerite's hand while everyone was fussing over the twins in the car.

"Marguerite," a reporter called, "how are you feeling?"

"Great, and happy to be going home with my husband and sons."

"Why did you choose those names?"

Chase answered that one. "Mam and I felt the boys were gifts from God, so we chose biblical names. It was that simple."

Before any more questions were thrown out there, they were in the car and taking their sons home. Their friends and family climbed into their waiting cars and followed close behind. Marguerite and Chase couldn't wait to get home with their sons.

Jess, Mary, and Joe were all there waiting for them. Franco and Anna had sent tons of food for them all, because they knew everyone would be at their house.

Life seemed to fly by for the Martins. Chase spent the next six months at home with Marguerite and the boys. He was so happy to be with her and his sons. He watched every day as his boys grew and changed, and couldn't believe how much he loved his children and his wife.

Before he knew it though, he would have to get back out on the road again. It pained him to even think about leaving them. Marguerite could feel him and his distress whenever he thought about going back to work. She tried to ease his mind, reminding him that the sisters would be there with her, along with his mom.

On nice days, the guys would pack the twins up and take them to the studio with them, where they were cooed and gooed on by everyone. They sang to them, about them, and for them. The twins were like community property. Sometimes Marguerite had to stop and think about where they were and who had them. It was great to have so much support, and the twins loved all of their uncles and aunts, as well as their Grandma Jess.

Marguerite wanted to plan a trip to Pennsylvania so she could see her family and all of their friends (who were dying to meet Zac and Zeke).

Chase was hesitant but finally agreed. They would start with a week in the States and take it from there. It was summer, so they thought it was a great time to go.

Everyone else just about had coronaries when they heard they were going to go to Pennsylvania. They would miss them too much, and what if something happened? Finally, Chase and Marguerite let them off the hook.

"You know you can come with us if you want, right?"

They all breathed a sigh of relief at that and went home to pack. Marguerite and Chase looked at each other and shook their heads, laughing. In all honesty, having the others around made it easier on them. Someone was always there to help. It felt good, and they always felt the love everyone gave to their sons.

On the plane, Quinn and Jeanine had Zac and Drew and Cara had Zeke. Marguerite kept watching to make sure they didn't need her.

"It looks like they got the Z's to sleep," she said to Chase.

"Hey!" he said, smiling at her nickname for them. He hadn't heard her use it before. "That's what *I* call them."

They just looked at each other and laughed. They were always on the same page. They kissed and kissed until they heard one of the Z's crying, and of course, then the other one started.

"They're trying to keep us apart," Chase said.

Marguerite nodded. "They don't want any siblings yet. They're not ready."

Smiling, they touched foreheads and went and got their sons.

Family

Back in Pennsylvania, everyone knew they were coming. Chase looked out the windows and saw that reporters and fans were already at the hanger when the plane touched down. They agreed that Marguerite and Chase would exit the plane last, carrying the Z's.

Everyone stopped talking and looked at them. "What did you just say?"

Chase frowned, looking confused. "Mam and I will go last?"

"No, you called them the Z's," Drew said. "That's what *we* call them. We didn't want you to be mad."

They just laughed. "Don't be ridiculous. We're not mad. It worked so we use it. The Z's."

The local stations were filming before the doors even opened and captured a lovely moment between the band and the pilot. Chase had shaken his hand first and said, "Thank you for getting my family here safely." The pilot had nodded politely. "It has always been a privilege." He looked down at the baby in Chase's arms. "Now even more so." One after the other, they had shaken his hand and expressed their appreciation.

Marguerite was always amazed at the boys' manners. Especially considering they had been away from their families from the time they were 16, 18, and 19 years of age. As famous and successful as they were, they weren't spoiled at all. They were always so grateful for every kind gesture shown to them, and she loved them for it.

As they all headed down the ramp towards the waiting cars, the reporters started yelling questions to them all at once. They asked Marguerite,

"How are you feeling?" and she said, "Great. No problems at all. I feel back to normal after the delivery."

Chase said, "Yes, and I am feeling great as well." Everyone laughed. "Well," he chuckled, "everyone asks how my wife is feeling but nobody asks me. I went through it too!"

Marguerite patted his cheek. "Glad you feel that way, because next time you are going to carry the babies."

Everyone got a big kick out of that. Then they asked all the usual questions: How long would they be in town? Were they excited to see their family and friends? Any big plans?

They answered them all politely, but kept moving towards the cars. As they always did, Quinn took Zac and put him in his car seat and Blake took Zeke and put him in his car seat. All the cameras were rolling, as they loaded up in the cars, climbed inside, and took off.

Everyone was waiting for them at their house. Donna, Sue, and the little cousins Ashley, Marie, and Kristen were all waiting to meet the babies. Marguerite's parents, Joe and Mary, were there also and were cooking up a storm.

It was six o'clock by the time they got there, and they were tired and hungry. The Z's had made the trip with no problems. Donna had the nursery set up and ready for them. She had the baby monitors up and running, and all they had to do was put them down to sleep. Mike, Gail, and the rest of the security team headed to their new digs too. They had already discussed who was going to be on duty and when so they were all set. Donna had their refrigerator stocked and ready to go too. It was a massive production coordinating everything and everyone.

Every day they had company over to see the Z's. Marguerite's friends all came over, a few at a time. One day Donna invited her, the babies, and the sisters over for lunch. Marguerite thought it was going to be some nice girl time, but her cousins had planned a big baby shower for her. It was great! Marguerite was incredibly happy, and the Z's got so many presents, she didn't know what she was going to do with them all.

The Z's slept through the whole party. "They are just like their father," Marguerite said. "He could sleep through an apocalypse." Everyone laughed.

When it was over, all the guys came by to eat the leftovers. They went straight to the Z's though, who were just starting to wake up.

"Just in time to feed them," Marguerite said. Everyone laughed but the guys did it without any hesitation. They knew exactly what to do. They heated up the baby food, got the juice ready, and fed them while keeping them entertained. The Z's loved them. The guys made them laugh and laugh. Donna and Sue just looked at Marguerite.

"This goes on all the time," she said. "I don't know whose kids they are anymore."

She smiled when she said it, but Chase felt something was on her mind.

Later that night, Drew and Cara had Zac and Blake and Abbey had Zeke, so everything was quiet. When they were alone, Marguerite told Chase, "We have to make more alone time for each other. I'm just realizing how much I miss you. I want to feel your body next to mine. I actually crave it." Tears started to well up in her eyes.

Once again they were on the same page. Chase admitted feeling the same. "I miss the intimacy we always shared." He kissed her softly. With that, they went to their bed and just lay in each other's arms with the door open so they could get their sons when it was time for them to go to sleep.

Tired

Once back in London, the guys all asked to meet with Peter and Jack. They wanted to discuss slowing down a little. They were tired and being off for six months had made them realize that their lives were passing them by, especially when they saw Chase with his sons and knew he couldn't be home every day with them. They didn't want to leave the twins either. They were constantly at the house, and babysat while the girls took Marguerite out to get a break. They were expert diaper changers and they knew that when the twins cried, they always just wanted to eat. They felt pretty good about themselves.

Peter was concerned about them slowing down. He felt they had to keep going out there or the fans would lose interest and find a different group to follow.

Quinn asked Peter, "How much is enough for you? We have been at this for seven years. You haven't been on the road all of those years. You sit at your desk and go home to your wife while we webcam our wives, and now our children!"

Peter saw that they were all agitated. They were tired, and were getting older, and wanted to settle down to some kind of normality.

"I hear what you're saying, but you have to strike while the iron is hot and right now you are still a hot commodity."

Blake shook his head and turned away from Peter. Actually angry now, he looked at Jack instead. "Trim down the schedule! Leave time between all the shows so that we can come home for a few days."

With that, they all got up and left.

Peter and Jack looked at each other.

"What just happened?" Peter asked. They shook their heads and sat in silence for a few minutes, processing.

"Okay." he sighed. "Maybe it's time to let them go and do things on their own. If we force them on the road, the shows would be horrible anyway, and people would start talking, saying they're not interested anymore, and don't want to be together, and are fighting, and blah blah blah." They both knew that nothing could be further from the truth. They still wanted to tour; they just wanted to tour less.

Jack nodded. "I'll look and see what I can come up with, schedule wise, to keep the guys happy."

The guys went home and told the girls what they had done. The girls were amazed that they had stood up to the managers like that, and thrilled that they felt so strongly about not being on the road so much and being home with them more. They had assumed that this was how their lives would always be and had accepted it, but underneath those brave faces, they had always wanted more. More of their husbands and more normal.

They were so happy, but Blake was afraid they would be disappointed. "Don't get your hopes up too soon okay? Jack still has to look and see what can be done." The tour dates had already been announced, and depending on contracts and whatnot, it might not be as easy to get things changed as they would like. But they were all still hopeful and would continue to be.

A few days after their initial meeting, Jack called them and asked to see them all—the guys and the girls both. Their first instinct was to think they were going to be scolded like children. The girls wondered if he was going to blame them for the shortened schedule the guys had requested. Knowing how the guys would react to such a response, they hoped that wasn't the case. No one wanted things to get ugly.

With a fair amount of trepidation, they agreed to meet at the studio. Vita and Gail were thrilled the eight of them were all going to be a part of the meeting, eager for the opportunity to watch the Z's for them!

They went in and closed the office door. Jack and Peter were waiting for them. Jack had a copy of the schedule for each one of them, and handed them out without saying a word. The eight of them huddled together, examining it closely. They were amazed.

It was better than they could have hoped for. Jack had them home for every one of their birthdays and anniversaries, for holidays—even the American ones for Marguerite—and every function that the Z's would be involved in. Each time they were home, they were home for at least four days. The girls started crying, and jumped up and hugged Jack. The schedule was fantastic. Then they looked at the boys, who had huge grins on their faces. They got up and shook Jack's hand, and then Peter's, and apologized about the last meeting they'd had.

"It needed to be done," Jack said. "The concerts wouldn't be worth going to if you were unhappy doing them. In the end that's what would have happened."

"For the record," Blake said, "our wives had nothing to do with this. It was just us. So I don't want either of you blaming them. They had no idea we were going to ask to shorten the schedule."

Now Peter spoke up. "We knew it wasn't them. Your relationships have always surprised us. The girls never gave any of you a hard time about being on the road, and we know we were really pushing you hard. We can't tell you how much we admire them for that."

To celebrate their newfound freedom, they went to dinner with the Z's through the kitchen of their favorite restaurant. Rocco was happy to see them as always. The Z's slept right through dinner, even with all the talking that went on, proving once again how much like their father they were.

Zac and Zeke were ten months old already, and one Sunday in December, everyone was at the house watching a football game. Ed called to say he was on his way too so they left the door unlocked for him so he could come in. Mike and a number of other security personnel were nearby of course, keeping a discreet eye out. The men were on the floor and the Z's were sitting in between Chase and Blake's legs. When they heard the door open, Marguerite said, "Uncle Ed is here to see you!"

Zac and Zeke both climbed clumsily to their feet and wobbled over toward the kitchen as if it were the most normal thing in the world.

Quinn was quick enough to catch it all on his phone.

Everyone went wild. The twins were walking!

When Ed heard the commotion, and then saw the boys heading his way, his face turned bright red, as it always did when he was at his happiest. When his two nephews got to him, giggling excitedly, he scooped them up in his arms and hugged them.

"Those are my boys!" Chase said proudly.
Everyone just smiled at him.

51

Another Surprise

When the twins turned 1, their uncles bought them both battery-operated cars that they could actually sit in and drive. *They were 1!*

Drew, Blake, and Quinn had gone to the store together to pick them out. It had taken hours, because they couldn't choose between army trucks or sports cars. They didn't want to get one of each, because they were afraid the twins might fight over who got which. They had to check with Ed to see what he wanted (since the cars would be from all of them); unfortunately, all his opinion did was make it a solid tie. The girls finally said, "That's it. Make up your minds and like what you choose."

They picked the army trucks. It would be a while before the twins were old enough to do more than putter around in them with an adult hanging frantically onto them, ready to pull them out of any looming disaster.

When the twins were eighteen months old, all the men started taking them into the bathroom with them because they were getting tired of changing diapers and hoped they would want to mimic the grownups. Believe it or not, it worked. The Z's wanted to use the toilet just like Dad and their uncles. It was cute.

When they were four years old, no one could fathom where the time had gone. They were still driving the army trucks and had to park them in the garage just like their father did with his car.

They loved going to the studio with him because they felt like they were going to work too. They were always a big hit. Chase would say to them in the morning, "We are working today boys; are you coming?" They would both be up and dressed for breakfast before anyone knew it, and then heading to the car with their dad to go to work.

When Chase left to go on the road, he would give them a big speech and tell them that they had to take care of their mother while he was gone. When they webcammed, he would ask them how that was going and they would tell him that they had helped fold the clothes or take out the garbage. They weren't just little men; they were miniature Chases. They looked just like him. The resemblance was uncanny. He occasionally even called them "the mini me's".

Marguerite and the girls still worked at Victoria's fashion house a few days a week. They really weren't needed there that much but enjoyed getting out. It made them feel like they were accomplishing something.

Jack had made good on his promise to trim down the touring schedule four years ago, and every January, they all got together and planned it out for the following year so they wouldn't miss any days they wanted (or needed) to be home. Everything was going along well.

Then one morning Marguerite woke up because her stomach turned. Chase wasn't home. He was on the road in Mexico. He felt her though and woke up right away. He remembered that feeling from before but didn't say anything. He just waited. On this trip, they had agreed to be gone for two straight weeks because after Mexico they were touring South America, and didn't want to be going back and forth. The ladies had agreed and didn't have an issue with it.

Chase patiently waited for the next day, to see if he could feel Marguerite's discomfort again. Sure enough, the next morning as soon as she woke up her stomach turned. She knew that feeling too and what it was about. *Four years.* The kids would be four years apart. *No,* her eyes widened at a sudden realization. *It'll be almost five years, once the new one arrives!* She and Chase had always wondered when or if they would be blessed with more children. After so many years, they had started to assume that two would be it.

She webcammed Chase right away because she knew he would have felt her. He was waiting with the biggest grin on his face. She shook her head. "You felt it, didn't you?"

"Yep."

"I'm not taking the test until you get home."

He was glad. He wanted her to wait for him. Now there was a sense of urgency for him to get home. He went to breakfast with all the brothers that morning with the stupidest grin on his face, and they all questioned him about it.

"It's nothing, just happy I guess, and glad the tour's a short one. I'm looking forward to getting back home soon."

Chase flew in the house to see Marguerite. He couldn't wait to just grab her and hold onto her. The boys saw him coming and ran out to the driveway to meet him. He swooped them both up in his arms and they hugged and kissed him as he continued walking to the house. Marguerite was standing waiting for him, amazed as always at how much love she felt for him. He was so good with the Z's and enjoyed being a father. Not to mention being a great husband. *How lucky am I?*

Once the Z's were sleeping, they couldn't wait to get to bed so that they could hold each other and make love. Chase felt as if he could go all night, fueled only by his love for her. She smiled knowing he was in that kind of mood. She knew Chase loved her more than his heart could hold, and it warmed her heart.

Again

Marguerite had the pregnancy tests waiting the next morning. They got up and smiled when her stomach flipped. They read the test results together, one at a time. Test number one—positive. Test number two—positive. Test number three—positive. They embraced and cried. Chase picked her up, carried her back to bed, and held her tightly. Before he could think of making love to her again, the boys were up and jumping into bed with them. They put the two of them between them and coaxed them into lying down with them for a little while. Marguerite and Chase kept staring back and forth between the twins and each other. They joined hands across the Z's and enjoyed the moment with them.

They didn't tell anyone yet. She thought she was only maybe six weeks along but she seemed to have the beginnings of a baby bump. They didn't think it could be twins again and assumed that maybe, because her abdomen had been stretched out so much with her last pregnancy, it just had more give to it now. In any case, they waited for six more weeks, and once she started really showing, they felt they had to tell everyone. Everyone was thrilled, of course. They all knew Chase and Marguerite wanted a big family, and as far as they knew, they were trying. It just hadn't happened. They had decided to just let it happen or not happen, as it was supposed to.

Marguerite called Dr. Robbins' office and made an appointment to see her. She asked Chase if he could drive them, instead of Nick. She loved it when he drove them places. Sometimes they would just pack up the twins and take them to visit his mom or Ed. It made her feel normal.

The doctor examined her and said that she was about twelve weeks along, and scheduled an ultrasound for the next day. Chase told everyone, and just like before, they were there in the waiting room before Chase and Marguerite arrived. Grandma Jess was watching the Z's for them.

In the dimly lit room, the doctor did her thing while they all studied the screen. They saw nothing at first, but then the doctor did something that brought everything into sharper focus. This time they knew what they were looking at. *No way!* Their jaws just dropped as they looked at each other in disbelief. *Twins again!*

Then Chase's face lit up and he kissed Marguerite, thanking her over and over. She was crying. The doctor was pleased for them. She didn't ask this time; she sent the nurse out to get the others. In the waiting room, the nurse's smile told them that everything was all right. They all piled into the room and the doctor proceeded to show them. When they saw two babies again, they all went wild, hugging and kissing Marguerite and Chase and each other and even the doctor, as if she had given them the miracle.

As if sensing that they were the center of attention, the twins moved, turning *in utero* even as they watched. The doctor smiled. "Do you want to know what sex they are? They're in full sight now." Marguerite nodded eagerly.

Doctor Robbins looked at everyone in the room, and after a dramatic pause for effect, said, "Boys! Both boys!"

Oh my God, boys again!

It was pandemonium in the small office, with hugs and kisses and excited screaming and chatter. "Now we have four on a team for soccer!" Drew yelled. Everyone laughed and high-fived each other.

They called home and told Grandma Jess, who was ecstatic. She said that the Z's were napping, so they could stay out and have fun to celebrate. They all went for an early dinner at their favorite restaurant, entering through the kitchen, saying hi to Rocco, and heading right to the private dining room where they sat in amazement at what had just happened.

Chase and Marguerite were standing in the Z's room looking at their sons. They were in their sports car beds, which had been the compromise the brothers had come to when they'd decided on the army trucks three years earlier. They would give them army trucks for their first birthdays, and sports cars for their beds when they could no longer fit in their cribs. They were so good to them—giving them all the love and time they had to give. They could have never imagined how much love would be shared between them all.

Chase and Marguerite went to bed. "I am so proud of you," he said. "Thank you for loving me the way you do."

She kissed him softly on the lips. "You are the very air I breathe."

"And you are mine."

Worry

"Chaaase! Noooooo!!" Marguerite was screaming, as a contraction hit. Finally, after a few more long, horrible moments, she let her head fall back on the pillow, gasping and trying to catch her breath. "If I ever make it out of this bed, I'm going to kick you!"

He leaned in and kissed her hair, wishing he knew what to say or do to help and enjoying the temporary lull.

"Ohhhhhhhhhhhhhhhhhhhh!!" Another contraction had arrived. "I do *not* want to do this anymooooore!"

She fell back gasping. Three deep breaths were followed by yet another contraction. "GIVE ME DRUGGGGGSSSSSS!!" Crying she clung to him. "Chase, I want drugs."

Chase was beside himself. He didn't know what to do to help his wife. She was in so much pain now, but it was too late to give her the epidural so she had to endure it. She had been in labor for twelve hours.

There were surrounded by medical personnel. The doctor finally said that the babies were coming and to get ready. "Okay, Marguerite," she said, "push hard."

Chase was holding her up a bit, supporting her back as she gave a big push and Baby Martin number one arrived. Marguerite heard her son crying and said to him, "Oh, I'm sorry, I don't know what you mean!" Everyone in the delivery room started laughing.

The nurse showed Chase and Marguerite their son. Proud as a peacock, Chase cut the umbilical cord again. Doctor Robbins asked what his name was. "Matthew Joseph Martin. Matthew's from the bible, and Joseph is for Mam's adoptive father—"

"CHAAASSSSSSE!!" Another contraction interrupted the discussion. Baby Martin number two wanted to join the party and didn't want to wait.

"Uh oh," the doctor said quietly.

Both Marguerite and Chase's ears perked up at that. "What?

"What do you mean 'uh oh'. Uh oh, what?"

"The baby's breech. Must have slipped into it as his brother slipped out. Don't push for a moment." Marguerite swallowed hard and focused all her energy on resisting the urge to push. Another contraction hit. Chase could see the muscles ripple all through her body.

"Don't push, Mam," he said, but her body seemed to have other ideas. She started taking shallow breaths. After a few long shaking moments, her muscles relaxed again, but she was starting to panic.

"Okay," the doctor said with a resigned sigh, "he's not taking no for an answer."

"But—"

"The only butt I'm thinking about is this one. Your baby's coming butt first into the world, and there's no time to talk him out of it." There was a flurry of activity going on down there, but Chase didn't let himself panic. He couldn't. He focused instead on finding some sort of calm for his wife's sake, taking deep breaths and letting them out slow.

"Okay Mam, with the next contradiction your gonna push like there's no tomorrow. It's gonna hurt like hell but you'll get through it fine and have an amazing story to tell all your friends. Deep breaths now, get yourself as ready as you can."

Chase moved closer to her side and looked her in the eye as she squeezed his hand till it creaked. Then she reached out with her other hand, grabbed him by his shirt, and pulled him towards her. "When we're done here, you're going to owe me the biggest Spa Vacation Package out there."

"I will gladly *buy* you a Spa if it will make this any easier."

"Oh God! Here it comes!"

"Okay, Mam," Doctor Robbins said firmly, "Now push!"

Marguerite gritted her teeth against the scream that tried to escape and pushed for all she was worth. "That's right," the doctor said approvingly, "just a little bit more. Let's get this little guy out so he can say hello."

Marguerite couldn't hold it back anymore and an agonizing scream escaped her, echoing around the room like a stray bullet.

"You're doing amazing, Mam!" Chase said, looking at her through his tears. "You're amazing!" He had never been so proud of her or loved her more. He was dying inside, feeling her fear and distress through their bond, as well as just the faintest hint of the pain that was ripping through her—but still enough to almost drop him to his knees.

Suddenly the baby was out. "That's it!" Dr. Robbins said. "I've got him."

Sobbing with exhaustion, pain, and astonishment, Marguerite collapsed back onto the pillow. Chase held her face to his chest, kissing her hair, her forehead, holding her as if he were afraid to let her go.

Out of the corner of his eye, he saw the medical personnel taking care of the baby, cleaning him, checking him out. His heart nearly jumped out of his chest when he realized his son had yet to make a sound, but before panic could get a grip on him, a high-pitched wail sounded loud and strong, bringing smiles to the faces of the nurses gathered round.

Doctor Robbins gestured him toward the umbilical cord, but Chase just shook his head, hoping his wife wouldn't notice. He was shaking so badly that he knew it wouldn't be safe, and he didn't want to leave his wife's side in any case. The doctor took care of it, and once the baby was carefully swaddled, she held him up to show Chase and Marguerite, asking what his name was.

"Mark David Martin." Mark from the Bible, and David after Chase's father, who had died when Chase was four years old.

Marguerite was watching everything with tired, tear-filled eyes that conveyed every ounce of the joy and contentment she was feeling. She looked at Chase and smiled. "Okay, I'm done now."

Then she passed out.

Her blood pressure had dropped abruptly, but this time they were ready. The doctor had told them that she was almost certain this would happen. She'd also started bleeding again, and as they feared, the steps they had to take to save her life meant that she would no longer be able to have children. The strain and stress of carrying and delivering twins twice was just too much on her system.

Even though Dr. Robbins had prepared them for the eventuality—and even though they knew what a blessing it would be to have four healthy sons—coming up to her due date, Marguerite had felt as though the surgery would take away what made her a woman. She was afraid that she would lose her attraction to Chase or that Chase would lose his attraction to her, which was ridiculous. The doctor told her as much.

Chase tried to tell her that he didn't (and wouldn't) care, and the doctor reassured them that nothing would be different about her. She told her that a hysterectomy would in no way impact her sexual attractions, and that men don't lose interest in their wives just because they can no longer bear children. Chase agreed, and once they were alone, told her over and over that she was the very air he breathed and that nothing on this earth would ever stop him from breathing her in. She was relieved, and had started to feel better about it, but now that it had actually happened, he knew that she would still probably be upset.

Everyone was waiting in Marguerite's room, including Joe, Mary, and Jess. No word was coming and she had been gone so long. Finally, the head nurse came out and filled them in on everything that had happened. They had been prepared for it because Chase and Marguerite had warned them what might happen after the delivery this time.

She also told them that Chase was not coming out until Marguerite could come back to her room, and that he didn't want to bring the babies until she was present as well. He didn't want to take that moment away from her. They all understood completely. They just had to wait.

The nurse said that both babies were fine, and that Chase and Marguerite wanted to tell them the names they had chosen themselves, but that did not stop them from pacing and worrying.

Four hours after that update, they wheeled Marguerite to her room. Everyone crowded around her, so happy to see her that they had tears in their eyes.

Marguerite was awake and sitting up in the bed when they wheeled her sons in.

Everyone was so happy to finally see them. They remembered when the Z's had been born, and how thrilled they were to be aunts, uncles, and grandparents. Now they were again!

Chase handed Joe and Mary his older son, Matthew Joseph. Marguerite watched her father's face as they introduced him. Then Chase handed Mark David to his mom, and introduced him. Jess and Joe were both very proud and moved by their choice of names. Mary, Joe, and Jess were all beside themselves, and the tears started to fall once again. Then everyone joined in.

Chase looked around at everyone and said, "I'd like to introduce you to the M&M's." Everyone laughed. Now they had the Z's and the M&M's.

Cara had Matthew and Jeanine was holding Mark. Marguerite told the men to go get something to eat, and they knew immediately that she wanted to talk to the girls and that the girls wanted to talk to her as well, so they left without asking questions.

As soon as they left, Marguerite broke down in tears. The girls all flocked to her to calm her down. They knew she would be upset over what had happened in the delivery room.

"We talked this all out," they said. "Nothing is going to change with you and Chase. You'll still have the drive you always had, and Lord knows Chase certainly will." They all started laughing, even Marguerite. Especially after they reminded her about what she and Chase had done in the car after the Valentine's Day concert.

Her mother and Jess looked at each other. "What happened in the car?" That broke the ice and she started feeling better.

Chase was with his brothers but could still feel his wife's distress. He had told her that he'd make sure she never lost her desire for him. Even if he had to dance naked on the table to get her going. Thinking about that conversation made him smile.

"Is she still upset about not being able to have more kids?" the brothers asked. They had seen Chase's expression turn serious for a moment. After all this time, they could always tell when something was wrong with their brother.

"Yes, I have to keep reassuring her that she's still the person I married." And the guys said they could understand how she felt, but that if it were their wives, it wouldn't make a difference to them either. They guessed it was a women thing. And they were right. It was a women thing.

Chase, Marguerite, and the twins were finally alone late that night after everyone left. The boys were sleeping soundly and Marguerite and Chase kept staring at them. As he had done the last time, Chase turned to Marguerite and said, "Look what we did." She smiled, but he still felt her despair.

Finally, he took her head in his hands and forced her to look at him. She melted. She could never resist looking into those beautiful blue eyes of his.

Tears started rolling down his cheeks. "Why can't you believe that I would die without you?" he asked. "This body would be a hollow shell without your love. Even having four sons to keep me going wouldn't be enough."

With that, it finally hit her: She would die without him too. Crying as well now, she kissed him, and then pulled him in for a huge hug.

He kissed her hand, her abdomen, and then the babies. The doctor said that he couldn't get in bed with her, so he just bent his body down over her chest as she held him, stroking his face and hair like a child until she felt him relax.

Full House
54

Peter needed to release a statement and Chase asked to approve it, because they wanted to keep it short:

> Chase Martin of the Band 4 and his wife, Marguerite Angeli-Martin, welcomed their second set of twin sons, Matthew Joseph Martin (6lbs 4oz) and Mark David Martin (6lbs 2oz), at eleven o'clock this morning. Mother and both babies are doing fine.

Chase would not let him get into the complications that occurred after the delivery. He asked Peter to just leave it at that. Peter pointed out that everyone would know something was wrong, because she wouldn't be going right home like she had the last time, but Chase was adamant about it, so he just left it at that.

And everyone did notice. The media was pressuring the staff at the hospital, Peter, and anyone else they could find for information. Speculation about what was going on was all over the Internet. So many people cared about them and were anxious to hear if everything was all right that the doctor finally stepped in and released a statement:

> Marguerite Angeli-Martin and her sons are all doing well. She just had her second set of twins, was in labor for twelve hours, and delivered them naturally, so please just let her rest.

Everyone seemed content with the statement. Chase and Peter thanked the doctor for her help.

Chase spoke directly to Ed, and to Victoria, so that they knew what was going on. He didn't want them to worry. Both were in the States at the time.

The next morning, the three grandparents took Zac and Zeke to meet their new brothers. They were incredibly excited to see them and couldn't wait. They ran into their mother's room and were shocked when they found her in bed, which Marguerite and Chase did not expect.

At four years old, they didn't understand. They started to cry. "Mom, are you sick?"

She had to keep from crying herself. So did Chase, who was so moved to see how worried his sons were about their mother.

"No," she assured them. "I'm just resting." They both ran to her. They tried to crawl up into bed with her but Chase had to stop them, explaining that her tummy was very sore right now and they needed to be careful. Marguerite couldn't resist holding her first two sons though. "Wait a minute. Chase, put them up here with me." She bent her legs and brought them up to protect her abdomen. "Just put one on either side of me so I can hug them."

Chase did as he was told, warning them to be very gentle with their mother and "no bouncing around." Marguerite wrapped one arm around each of her sons and hugged them, starting to cry as she told them how much she loved them. She thanked them for being so worried about her, and when she saw that they were calm and content, asked them if they would like to meet their brothers. They both just smiled and said that yes they were ready. The nurse brought in Matthew and Mark, and the look of wonder in the young boys' eyes when they looked at the babies brought smiles to their parents' faces.

When they left the hospital the second night after her surgery, Peter asked if she would be able to walk and she said she could. She knew that he wanted to have the press there, but regardless of her wishes either way, there would have been no stopping the press. They were already there and waiting. She and Chase were prepared for it.

The same ensemble left the hospital with Marguerite and Chase as the last time. The happy parents were each carrying one of the twins. Cameras were flashing everywhere, video cameras were rolling, and reporters were calling questions out to them all at once. As they stepped towards the car, Quinn took Matthew and Blake took Mark, and they placed them in their car seats. They'd had a lot of experience strapping babies into car seats now. Their wives were grinning from ear to ear at how good they were at it.

Reporters asked Marguerite how she was doing and she smiled. "Well. Just very tired."

They asked about her labor and she said, "It was twelve hours long, and I definitely feel bad for all women who are in labor longer than normal."

Someone asked if there had been any complications and she just shook her head and said that "the only complication was wanting to get home so badly to be with her husband and four sons and the doctor not releasing her fast enough."

Then they all loaded into their cars and took off for home. Marguerite couldn't wait.

Gathered around the table for a late dinner, Marguerite told everyone how Zac and Zeke had reacted to seeing her in bed in the hospital. No one seemed surprised. They all thought that the twins not only looked just like Chase but were as sensitive as him too. Marguerite and Chase realized this of course, but had just never thought about it like that. They knew they were sweet boys, but didn't take it as meaning they were sensitive really, until just then, when the others had mentioned it. All three of them wore their hearts on their sleeves. It made them both smile. Marguerite leaned towards Chase, who put his arm around her and kissed her head.

Then they spoke about the M&M's. While the Z's were Chase to a T, the M&M's were Marguerite to the T. The Z's looked so much like Chase, the joke had always been that she'd had nothing to do with giving birth to them at all. Not one of her features were on the boys.

When the M&M's were born, they all thought she'd finally gotten back at him. These twins looked just like their mother. There was not one of his features on them, at least not that could be seen yet.

Marguerite got everyone to sleep with the help of her parents and Jess. They were all staying with her, and so were the fantastic six, as she had begun to refer to the brothers and sisters. They were draped over couches; on the floor—anywhere they felt comfortable. Because so many people always stayed with them, Marguerite and Chase had purchased couches that pulled out into beds. They'd felt bad when they saw them sleeping on the floor, but no one else minded. Even with all the couches pulled out into beds, some still hit the floor to sleep.

Chase finally got to get in bed with his wife. It felt like forever, although it had only been two nights. He gently pulled her over to him and wrapped her in his arms. He immediately felt her relax as her body melted into his.

"Even like this," he said, "when I can only hold you, I can feel your love for me. Please tell me that you feel my love for you, Mam."

"I always feel your love for me." It was so strong and she knew it. "I love you so much, Chase. You are the very air I breathe."

"You are the very air I breathe. Please don't ever take that away from me," he said, then finally fell asleep, which he hadn't done during the two days Marguerite was in the hospital.

Scholastico

Marguerite was puttering around the house and decided to go up to the attic to see what was there, thinking that maybe they could convert it into bedrooms or a big playroom for the Z's and M&M's. When she got up there, she thought, *This is wasted space.* There was definitely space for a big playroom. They could put a huge TV up there with some couches for the kids and maybe some large, built-in toy boxes. *Maybe we could even have a bathroom put in.* She pitched the idea to Chase.

"I have an attic?" he asked first, just to make her laugh. Then he went up to see it and loved the idea. He felt that the kids would need their own space soon so that there wouldn't be toys lying all over. After all there were four of them now, and he knew that Marguerite liked things in their place. She didn't like clutter. Maybe the kids' couches could pull out into beds as well, since they never seemed to have enough. Their house was like a bed and breakfast sometimes, especially around the holidays.

Just like with the Z's, it seemed like time flew by. When Chase was on the road, they webcammed a lot. When it was time for the M&M's to take a nap, Marguerite would call Chase and webcam him on a small TV with Wifi in the boys' room so they could see him. He would say, "Let's take a nap now!" And they would all go to sleep together. Even if Chase only had a few minutes, he would wait for them to fall asleep before signing off. It was the same with meals. They tried to have at least one meal together every day, so Marguerite would webcam him on another TV (this one a big screen) in front of the table and they would all sit down and eat together.

One day when the M&M's were about six months old, Marguerite was feeding them puréed chicken and peas and Chase was calling on the webcam. With a straight face, he said, "I wish I was there, because that is my favorite dish." This was just seconds after texting her: "That is so wrong, feeding them that!" Marguerite had to turn her face away to hide her laughter. The boys looked at her, not getting what was so funny.

The Z's helped feed the boys too. They loved doing it. Especially since it was their job to take care of their mother, and now their brothers, when their dad was not at home. They took that responsibility very seriously.

When it was time for Zac and Zeke to start school, Marguerite was in a panic about letting them go. She knew they had to go to school though. She and Chase visited the local schools to see which ones they liked and which ones would be safe. The aunts and uncles insisted on joining them so they could see for themselves. They all had to agree, just like with everything else they did. It was like a democracy.

Of course, this only really worked because they tended to be in agreement about pretty much everything to do with the kids anyway. Intellectually at least, they all knew the kids were really Marguerite and Chase's, but it didn't feel that way, and they didn't like to think about it. They finally found a school they were happy with, and then spoke to their security team, who got together with the school's security staff to ensure the boys would be safe there. When the boys had recess, Mike would always be present if they were outside playing. He'd be somewhere hidden, but he would always be present until they went back into class.

Chase was on the road for the first day of school, but he and the brothers all webcammed them that morning and told them to have a good time but to behave, because the teacher would let them all know if they didn't. Chase followed up with one last piece of advice: "Be respectful to the teachers. They are very smart and want to teach you all they know." The Z's understood.

Mike and Nick would be taking them to school and would pick them up when it was done. They had already told the school that under no circumstances were they to go home or leave the school grounds with anyone but them. If they saw anyone different, they were to keep the boys in school and call immediately. Marguerite wondered if the school they chose had known what they were getting into.

All the aunts were also at the house that morning for the Z's first day of school, taking pictures. When it was time for the boys to go, they all hugged them and tried not to cry when they were leaving. Marguerite got the last hugs and the twins could tell that she was feeling worried. They squeezed her extra hard to make her feel better.

They got in the car with Mike and were off. Mike came back ten minutes later after dropping them off, and reported to Marguerite that he walked them right to the door of their classroom. He told her that they were excited to be going to school with other kids and looked happy. Marguerite looked at Mike seriously for a moment and then smiled. "Nice job trying to make me feel better." They both just laughed.

Then there was a knock on the door. It was a local florist—who had been given clearance to pass the perimeter security by Mike—carrying a massive bouquet of flowers. Marguerite assumed that Chase was sending them because he couldn't be there for the boys' first day of school. She opened the card attached and gasped when she saw that it was from Zac and Zeke.

It said, "Don't worry, Mom, we will be fine. We love you!"

She sank to the floor, crying like a baby. She handed the card to her sisters and they did the same thing. They all met on the floor, sobbing. Their babies had gone to school.

Chase and the brothers were trying to webcam her but couldn't see her. He called her name, and was startled when she pulled the camera to the floor and all the brothers saw them there crying.

Marguerite explained why they were crying.

Chase told her they had called him and said, "Dad, we know Mom is going to be upset when we leave tomorrow. We're worried about her. Can we get her some flowers or something to make her feel better?"

He had said, "Yes absolutely! What do you want the card to say?"

They'd told him and Chase said they had blown him away. He'd almost cried in front of them. When he'd told the brothers, they'd just stood there with their mouths open, shaking their heads. The boys always amazed them. Chase told them that they always amazed him too.

Now, looking at her on his computer screen, so far away, he said, "I wish I could be there with you, Mam," Chase said. "I am so homesick."

"I wish you could be here too." That was all Marguerite could get out through her tears.

Marguerite had as much help with Mark and Matthew as she did with her first twins. The sisters all helped out, and for the most part, everything was stress free, even when Chase was on the road. Knowing that his wife was in good hands, with the girls and his mom, helped Chase to relax when he couldn't be there.

Before they knew it, the Z's were 8 and the M&M's were 4. It had happened in the blink of an eye. Now Chase and Marguerite would look at them playing in the yard and wonder where the years had gone. The uncles were always over at the house, teaching them how to play soccer and practicing, and the boys loved being with them.

If the streets looked quiet enough, they would take the four of them for a walk to the grocers to see Franco and Anna. The kids would always run to them when they got in the store and say something to them in Italian, like '*Buon Giorno,* Franco and Anna.' Marguerite and Chase would be so proud they would glow.

How did we get so lucky? They had the sweetest kids, and Franco and Anna spoiled them. In the summer, they would leave their store with ice-cream and in the winter, they left with candy.

Marguerite wanted them to know how to speak Italian, which was her heritage. She taught them words like *Salve* (hello), *arrivederci* (goodbye), *buona sera* (good evening), *ciao* (hi or bye). When they were a little naughty, they heard and understood commands like *stare fermo* (sit still), *impuntarsi* (stop dead), and *silensio* (be quiet).

The first time everyone heard her say something to them in Italian, they did a double take, because the four of them understood! They were getting a little rowdy and kept interrupting someone who was speaking at the table during dinner one night.

Very calmly, Marguerite said, "Un momento per favore. Aspetta il tuo turno." They stopped and sat quietly. Everyone looked at Marguerite, then at Chase, and then at the boys who had settled right down. They didn't ask what she said until later, because they didn't want to embarrass the boys.

After Chase put them to bed, they were all sitting in the family room and asked him what she had said to the boys at dinner, to calm them down like that. "I have no idea," Chase said, "but it worked." They all laughed.

Marguerite shook her head at them, smiling. "I told them to wait a minute and to wait their turn to speak."

"And they understood that?" Blake asked.

She smiled. "Yes, we practice the behave commands a lot. I have four boys, not four saints."

Chase planted a big kiss on Marguerite, and she said to him, "Your training starts tonight."

Laughing, Blake said, "Well, we better be going. We don't want to be around for that."

They all started climbing to their feet, and still smiling, they gathered their things and headed home.

Marguerite and Chase were finally alone. The boys were sound asleep and the house was quiet. They had learned to lock the door to their bedroom when they were having sex because they had almost been caught by one or both of them on more occasions than they wanted to remember. They opened the door when they were done.

"Ti amo con tutto il cuore," Marguerite said to him.

"Tu sei l'aria che respiro molto," he replied.

She just looked at him and decided he didn't need any more lessons. He had just passed the test, even outdoing her. She had said, simply, "I love you with all my heart."

He'd told her that she was the very air he breathed! In Italian!

With that, well, there's no other way to say it, she jumped him. She had been waiting all night to get him alone and just wanted to feel him next to her. He was right on the same page, and was ready for her.

Afterwards, they opened the door again, climbed back into bed, and fell asleep with their arms and legs wrapped around each other.

Bad Dreams

Marguerite had just gotten home from work from her job in Pennsylvania. Her mother and father were impatiently waiting for her so they could start dinner. When she walked through the door five minutes late, they both yelled at her.

"You are lucky we waited for you! We told you we were not waiting if you couldn't make it home on time! You know we eat at five every day! It shouldn't be a surprise!"

Meekly, Marguerite said, "The traffic was horrific and I'm lucky I was only five minutes late."

Her father started screaming, "I don't know why you are even working!"

"If I didn't have work, I would have nothing."

"What do you mean nothing? I worked my ass off providing a house for you to live in!" He was going to say more, but her mother stopped him with a pleading gesture.

"What am I going to do all day if I don't go to work?" Marguerite asked. "Cook and clean all day? I already clean. I clean, I cut the grass, I plant the flowers, and I plant the vegetables! I don't know what else I could possibly do to please you!"

That day, Marguerite had been stressed out because her boss, Joe, who always looked after her at work, had asked her to take some courses that were offered by Penn State University right in her office building. The classes would be two nights a week, starting right after work and lasting until around eight o'clock. She didn't know how she was going to approach her parents about it. She knew they would forbid it, but she was deter-mined to take the classes.

During dinner, she told them she was going to take the classes, and that's when her father threw his dish of spaghetti against the wall, breaking it and making the biggest mess she had ever seen. Her mother just got up and walked away.

Marguerite was shaking and thought she would pass out. She knew she was the one who had to clean it up. She couldn't breathe.

∞

In London, Chase was with his brothers at the studio, just looking out the window. It was gray and cold and had been raining all day. *This is about the tenth day in a row it's looked like this outside.* It was depressing. Drew was saying something to him, but he didn't hear him. He was in another world. Drew called his name. "Chase!"

He came out of his trance and turned around, not looking any of his band-mates in the eye. He moved away from the window, sat down with them, and just looked at the floor. His heart was so heavy at that moment he wished it would just stop beating.

They were going over some lyrics. "Chase, we're stuck with this line. Can you think of anything?" They told him what they had up to that point, and then repeated it, hoping to get him involved in writing the song with them.

"No," he said, almost in a whisper. "I'm sorry. I just can't think of how to finish it."

With that, he got up again and went back to the window. His band-mates were dying inside. They saw his pain and knew what was going through his mind, but they didn't know how to help him. Their hearts were breaking, knowing that he couldn't do this anymore. The band was over for him. They knew he wanted to say it out loud but couldn't. They couldn't bring them-selves to do it for him. They didn't want to lose him. They couldn't.

They were hoping for a miracle, something to turn him around. They had thought of everything they could to help him, but he was already too far gone, and it was killing them. He wasn't just a quarter of the band. He was a quarter of each one of them. No one knew if they could take the heartbreak when he left them. They couldn't breathe.

∞

The sun was just starting to come up when both Chase and Marguerite woke up in a cold sweat, gasping for air. They both sat up and just looked at each other. Marguerite was nearly in tears and the look on Chase's face made it clear he was in some kind of turmoil. All at once, they got the strangest feeling and both flew out of their bedroom. Marguerite went in to check on Zac and Zeke and told Chase to go see Mark and Matthew.

Zac and Zeke were sitting up and gasping for air, when Marguerite burst into their room. They looked at their mother, got out of bed, and ran into her open arms. She just held them for a long moment, and then said, "Okay, let's sit down and see what happened."

Just then, Chase came in with Matt and Mark. One was on his back and the other was in his arms. Marguerite told them the plan. "We are going to sit down and talk about this."

The M&M's looked just as upset as the Z's did.

They settled down on the beds, Marguerite with the Z's and Chase with the M&M's. "Okay, Zac and Zeke first. Do you want to talk about it? Let's see what happened okay?"

They both said they had been dreaming.

"What about?" Chase asked.

"About Mom," Zac answered.

Marguerite tried not to get emotional and took a deep breath. "Tell us what happened in your dream."

"You were somewhere in a room talking to two older people at dinner," Zeke said. "They were yelling at you, Mom."

Zac nodded. "I saw you cleaning spaghetti off the floor."

Chase turned white, but didn't say a word. He looked like he was going to pass out. Marguerite felt his distress, but stayed focused on her sons.

She calmly held the two boys, rocking them back and forth. "It was a dream. Just a dream. We had spaghetti last night and it probably just prompted you to dream about it. That's all. Please don't be upset. It was just a dream." They were holding onto her like she was going to disappear.

When the older boys had calmed down somewhat, they turned to look at Matt and Mark. "Do you want to talk about it too?" Chase asked. They nodded.

"Okay," he prompted, when they didn't continue. "So, can you tell us what happened?"

They could barely get the words out, still shaking quite badly and clearly upset. Chase just held them and rocked them back and forth until they composed themselves.

"I saw you with Uncle Blake, Uncle Drew, and Uncle Quinn," Matt said.

"Really, what were we doing?"

"You were looking out a window at the rain. I think it was at the studio."

Mark chimed in and continued the story. "Uncle Drew called you and you didn't hear him, so he called you again and you went over to sit with them. They asked you to help them and you said you couldn't and got back up and went back over to the window."

Matt said, "I saw the look on their faces when they looked at you. They looked really upset. And you looked upset too and that is what woke me up."

"Me too, Dad," Mark said. "I needed air."

Matt nodded again. "Like I couldn't breathe."

Marguerite turned white and Chase felt her. Chase scooped up the M&M's and started hugging them. Not knowing what to say, but needing to make light of the situation, they all started wrestling and throwing pillows at each other. Finally, they started laughing and feeling better.

After a little while, Chase said, "Okay, you know what? No school today. We need a family day out."

The four boys started yelling and jumped on Chase, pulling him to the floor and rolling all over him. He loved it. His little men. And Marguerite loved watching it.

After breakfast, they told the boys to go and get dressed and then wait for them in their playroom. When they were ready, they would come get them and they would go somewhere for the day. Chase and Marguerite were shaken. It was time now for them to be upset, but they still didn't know the half of it. They hadn't had a chance to tell each other about their own dreams and what had woken them up, not able to breathe.

Chase said to Marguerite, "Okay, you first."

"I dreamed you were in the studio with your brothers, possibly the same night I met you. You were so distressed about being there and not wanting to be in the band anymore. You were looking out the window and it was raining and Drew asked you to come help them. They were stuck with a lyric and you went over to them but couldn't look any of them in the eyes.

You apologized and told them you couldn't think of how to finish it. Then you got up and walked back over to the window. Your brothers looked devastated. Heartbroken. You could see it on their faces and you could feel it from how they looked." She started crying. "That's the same dream the M&M's had." She was shaken badly. "Oh my God, Chase, what if they are channeling me somehow? Did I do this to them? What about the boys? They both had the same dream!!"

Chase wrapped his arms around her. "Just wait. Let me tell you now." His voice was shaking.

"I dreamed you were back in Pennsylvania and you just came home from work and your parents were waiting for you and yelling because you were five minutes late for supper. You said you were stuck in traffic and they didn't care. They kept on you, and your father told you to quit your job and you asked what you'd do then, since you already took care of everything at home. Then you told them Joe wanted you to take some classes from Penn State and they went wild. Your father threw his dish of spaghetti against the wall. That's when I woke up not being able to breathe. That's the dream the Z's had. Oh my God!" He put his head in his hands, just trying to wrap his head around everything. "What is happening? Did we do that to them? Both boys had the same dream!"

They were both crying and upset. Had they caused that pain to their sons? Would they be feeling them next, the way they felt each other? They didn't know what to do. They'd each had a dream about the other, but from the past! At least eleven or twelve years before. Why would they dream about something so long ago, and about things already resolved and out of their thoughts?

What about the children? Why did they have the same dream? Even though the Z's looked just like Chase, they stuck to their mother like glue. Chase just thought it was because he had been telling them since they were born that they always had to take care of their mother when he was gone to work. The M&M's stuck to *him* like glue. Marguerite always thought it was because they were so young and just wanted their father. It wasn't like they played favorites with the boys. They always made sure that they treated them all equally and loved them all equally. They never wanted to make any of them feel like they loved one more than the other, because they didn't. They truly loved them all the same. With so much love for them, their hearts were always on the verge of exploding.

Distressed, distraught, worried, confused—they couldn't describe what they were feeling in any single word, but to say they were upset was putting it lightly.

Knowing that the kids were counting on them for a fun day, Chase suggested that they leave it for now and talk it out later. She knew they would be talking it all out with the brothers and sisters eventually. She felt maybe that they should talk to Father Cummings too this time. He had always been there for them. For all of them. He was like their unofficial spiritual adviser and psychologist.

Marguerite and Chase were watching the kids play in the family room that evening, and they could tell they were getting tired. After a long day at the park and sightseeing, they had gone to see a movie, and then out to dinner. They'd stopped to see Uncle Ed too, and had loved the visit. It was getting late.

"Okay," Chase said, "everyone ready for bed." They all agreed and headed upstairs and put on their PJs before being tucked in by their parents. The hugs and kisses were extra special that night.

"Let's go watch TV in bed tonight," Marguerite said to Chase. "I need to feel you holding me." She didn't have to say it twice. They were both in bed in a flash, holding each other and falling asleep.

57

Reconfirming

Chase had been away for a while on the road and was glad to be home, even though they all webcammed every day. It just wasn't the same as being there. Even after several weeks, he and Marguerite were still thinking about the dreams they had all shared. They couldn't believe it. They weren't ready to bring it up again, but it was always on their minds. They figured they would just wait to see if anything more happened.

They were watching to see if the boys were "feeling" Marguerite and Chase the way Marguerite and Chase could feel each other. If so, how was that possible, since Marguerite and Chase couldn't feel the boys?

They wanted to talk to Father Cummings about it, but couldn't bring themselves to dig that up again. They just decided to see if anything else happened. Maybe it was just a freaky one-time thing.

Again, time had flown by and Mark and Matthew were ready to start going to school. Luckily, all the legwork was already done and they would be attending the same school as their brothers. So now, Mike would be accompanying the four of them to school and would be watching them on the playground at lunch. Marguerite and Chase wondered if they should hire another security guard, but Mike assured them he would be able to do it so they went with it.

The first day of school for Mark and Matthew was as memorable as when Zac and Zeke went. This time Chase made sure he was home, and all the aunts and uncles were there to see them off also. Seeing them get in the car together to head off for school made them all want to cry.

"So," Drew said, "this is the first time in nine years that you're alone during the day, right?"

Marguerite and Chase looked at each other and nodded. "Okay, everyone out." Then they started laughing and so did all the brothers and sisters.

They left and in a hurry, because Chase said, "We only have seven hours, so out!" Laughing, they all ran to their cars.

Marguerite was running up the steps and Chase was fast behind her. All the time she'd spent worrying about not having desire for Chase after her operation was a complete waste. None of that had happened. They both jumped back in bed and kissed and kissed. They loved kissing, but most of all they loved lying with each other. Marguerite loved feeling Chase next to her and he loved when she melted into him.

"Remember," Marguerite said, between kisses, "we only have seven hours." They both started laughing, and then made love.

Marguerite lay next to Chase and kept looking at him.

"What are you looking at?"

"I am looking and thinking."

Chase asked, "Thinking about what?"

"Thinking about why I can't stop looking at you." They both smiled wide. "Why is it I always feel like I can't get enough of you?"

"I feel the same way about you."

Then the conversation got serious.

"When I say I can't breathe without you," Chase said, "I mean it. I truly cannot breathe without you. I can't tell you what you mean to me, because there are no words to describe it. Look what you did for me. You saved me. I was at my lowest and you saved me. You brought me back to life. You gave me my life. And our four beautiful sons. Four! How could I not be the luckiest man in the world? When I look at you, I see how beautiful you are and thank God for you. You're my angel. I know you are. I cannot tell you how much I love you. There aren't enough words."

Marguerite started to cry. Chase kissed her softly on her lips and then on her forehead.

"Chase, I always said we were meant to save each other. I know you saved me, although it's harder to explain. I was over the turmoil in my life. You found me when I was just awakening. But then, when I think about that time in my life, when I was trying to find out who I was and what I should be doing, you gave me that purpose. You showed me who I was. You put love into my life, when I had no idea what it was because I'd never felt it before. You did that. You saved me. You are my angel and I will be forever grateful. I can't find enough words to describe the way I feel about you either. It scares me to think about it. If something ever happened—"

Chase stopped her there. "Nothing is ever going to happen. We've gone through a lot already. It wasn't all fun and games, and I know I ask you to put up with a lot. I'm not home every night for dinner. I can't take you out whenever I want to. We have to arrange everything in advance. You have a shadow and you can't even drive your own car. I'm gone, sometimes for weeks at a time, and yet you found a way for us all to be together even when I'm away. If we didn't have the webcam, I would have missed out on so many important things. You insisted on it. It saved me from going crazy from not being with you and my sons. All four of them!"

Marguerite just nodded and looked in those beautiful blue eyes of his. She couldn't look away, and neither could he. He gave her the softest kiss and asked her how much longer they had.

"Still a few more hours." They both just smiled and held each other tight.

They decided a nap would be better than anything else. After all, they were going to be alone a lot during the day now, and didn't have to rush anymore.

Headaches

Chase had a tour coming up in Italy. It was summer already. They would be in Milan, Verona, and Rome, among many other cities. Marguerite was excited. She loved Italy and she and the sisters planned to accompany them to some of the concerts. Gail made all of the arrangements and they seemed to be all set.

Other than Marguerite, they had all headed to Italy a couple of days before. Marguerite had some things she needed to take care of at home and planned to follow them there on the weekend with the boys.

One night Marguerite had a headache that just wouldn't go away, and Chase felt it. He was in Germany, preparing to head to Italy to meet her and the boys a few days later, but he felt her. He called her right away, and she admitted that she wasn't feeling well, but that it was only a headache.

The next night, she still had the headache. She called the doctor and he prescribed something for her that was stronger than an over-the-counter tablet.

Marguerite was lying down resting, and the boys were worried about her. They went to the family room and talked it out with each other. Eventually they came to an obvious conclusion. "We need to call Dad," Zac said. "He needs to know." They all agreed, so they called him.

"Dad, Mom isn't feeling well. She'll tell you she is, but she doesn't look good."

Chase immediately thanked them for taking care of their mother for him. "I'll come right home. Don't tell your mother though, because she'll be upset."

They kept the secret between them and their father. He told them to call him back in an hour, if they could, and he would tell them what time he would be in.

In the meantime, Chase called his own mother and filled her in.

"Can you take care of the Z's and M&M's for about a week? I'm coming home to get Mam. She's not feeling well. She's been having terrible headaches and I thought that, if she were with me, it would help and I could take care of her."

"Yes, absolutely." Jess was very concerned and happy to help. She could hear Chase's voice shaking when he spoke.

"Please call Mam's parents and ask them if they can come help you also. Then call Gail and ask her to make all the arrangements for them as soon as possible."

Jess did everything Chase asked. She heard the urgency in his voice and was worried.

When he walked in the door, the boys flew to him. They all but dragged him to the bedroom where Marguerite was resting. She had deep circles under her eyes and was sleeping. He touched her face and kissed her. She opened her eyes, saw him sitting there, and for a moment thought she must be dreaming.

"What are you doing here?"

"I feel you. Remember?"

She just smiled and got up. Barely. He was scared by the way she looked.

"Your parents are coming to watch the boys, along with my mom. I'm taking you to Italy with me. Okay?"

She nodded.

The next day, she found that she was already packed. Jess and Mary, who had arrived late the night before, had packed her up and gotten her ready to go. Jess and Mary looked worried. Marguerite looked terrible!

The boys were so happy their mom would be with their dad because they knew he always made her feel better. They saw it and they felt it. They always felt it. The four little men had talked about it amongst themselves, but didn't tell their parents that they could feel them, even when they weren't around.

The flight to their destination near Lake Como in Italy, which was the first stop on their concert tour, took about three hours. Marguerite slept the whole way there. When they got off the plane, Marguerite looked even worse to Chase. She got in the car and her hands went to her head. Tears were streaming down her face. Her head was killing her. Chase didn't know what he could do for her so he just held her in his arms.

Before he knew it, he saw her eyes roll back in her head and she was out cold. "Get us to a hospital now!" he said. He was panicked. Nick didn't know where he was going, but they saw some police shortly after exiting the airport and waved them down. They got them to the hospital in a hurry.

Mike alerted everyone in town about what had happened and where they were going, and then called Gail, who alerted everyone back home to what was happening.

In the emergency room, everyone was barking out instructions in Italian. If Marguerite were awake, she would have known what they were saying, but Chase did not. He called Gail to see if they could get a translator there so he would know what was going on.

Then all the brothers and sisters arrived, as well as Peter. They saw the look on Chase's face as he filled them in on what happened. He was shaking all over. They had known Chase was going to pick her up but not that she was ill.

A hospital translator arrived and introduced herself to Chase and the family. The doctor came out and told them that they were going to take Marguerite for an MRI to see what the issue was. With the help of the translator, Chase was finally able to tell the doctor that Marguerite had been suffering with a terrible headache for four days. Then the doctor fine-tuned the order on the tests to reflect and react to this information.

It seemed like a long wait for the results, but when they came in, the doctor asked them to come over to a private conference room to talk to him. Chase wanted to die. He knew it was going to be bad. His legs did not want to move when he tried to walk. The brothers guided him and the girls took his hands to pull him into the room.

The doctor lit the screens in the room and held up the scans of Marguerite's brain. A blood vessel had burst in her brain and that's what was causing all the trouble. She needed surgery right away if she was going to live. She was being prepped for the O.R, and they had contacted the best neurosurgeon in the country, who was on his way in as they spoke.

Chase was shaking terribly. The doctor asked if he could prescribe something for them all to help calm them down.

"Yes," Peter said.

Chase looked at him, but he was already so out of it that he barely heard the doctor or Peter. All the girls were crying, and the brothers sat with their heads in their hands waiting for the surgeon.

59

Life and Death

Chase asked the translator to ask the doctor if he could go sit with Marguerite. He didn't want to be without her and he looked so desperate that they allowed it. She had already been made ready for surgery, and Chase tried not to look at the various tubes and wires attached to her, some coming from beneath coverings on her head, which appeared to have been shaved. He felt like maybe someone had explained all that to him, but nothing was reaching him. He didn't know what the tubes and things were for and he didn't want to know. He just sat at the side of the bed and held her hand, kissing it and telling her how much he loved her. He said it in Italian also. Everyone around her could hear him and were distraught, deeply impacted by his obvious fear and pain. Everyone knew exactly who they were, and could see that he was dying right along with her.

Back home, the boys knew their mother was in trouble. They felt their father's distress and just knew. They all went upstairs and packed their suitcases. They knew they would be going to Italy as soon as a plane could be made ready to take them. They knew before their grandparents even got the call. They were sitting in the Z's bedroom with their suitcases and just waiting for them. When that call came, Grandma Jess and Nana Mary came in to tell them they were going to Italy and froze when they saw that they were already ready.

"We know," Zac said. "We felt that our dad was upset and knew mom was in trouble. We can't explain to you how we know, but we do."

They all knew Chase and Marguerite had a strange connection like that, but hadn't known the boys had that same connection with them.

"We need to go now. We can't wait. Our mom and dad need us."

Mary and Jess were stunned. Off they all rushed to the airport.

The surgeon came in, saw the scans, and went to talk to Chase. Everyone had followed him to the room when they saw him come in. Chase told the translator to tell the surgeon that they were all his family. The doctor allowed them to be at Marguerite's bedside.

"The bleeding in her brain has to be stopped immediately," he said, "or she might not make it." He told them that he needed to get in and see what damage had already been done. He made it clear that the situation was dire, and that even assuming she survived the surgery, there was no way to predict the type or severity of potential cognitive or physical impairment. Regardless, surgery was her only option.

The family's sobbing was uncontrollable.

"I do not want to paint a pretty picture, because I need you to be prepared. However, I ask you to hope for the best. I will do everything in my power to get her through this and keep her intact. You have my word."

Back at the hospital, everyone was asked to say goodbye to Marguerite before she went into surgery. She looked very pale, but basically like she was sleeping. Everyone tried to put on brave faces, but none of them could. One by one, they kissed her and told her they loved her, hoping that she could hear them. Then it came time for Chase to say goodbye. He was like a zombie. His eyes looked like they were glazed over. He leaned over Marguerite, looked at her for a long moment, and then said, "Please fight for your life. Please don't leave me. Please don't leave our sons. They need their mother and I need my wife. I will love you forever. You are the very air I breathe."

Somehow, that reached her, if only for a moment. She opened her eyes slightly, and whispered, "And you are mine." He felt a glimmer of hope as she took a deep breath, letting it out slowly as she continued, "Tell my sons I love them." With that, she lost consciousness and her eyes closed again.

Chase saw her continued breathing and focused on that, breathing with her. He believed now that she would be fighting for her life, because she had so much to lose. He knew how much she loved him and the boys. All four of them. He knew she would fight to get back to them, and he had to believe it was a fight she would win!

After she had been taken off to surgery, Quinn told Chase that he'd called Ed and Victoria to let them know what had happened. Chase gave one nod to acknowledge that he heard him. Peter had gotten the doctor's prescription filled and forced everyone to take a mild sedative to calm down. Everyone but Chase. He wouldn't take it, so Peter let him go.

The Boys

They had a room booked for Marguerite for after the surgery, so they all went there to wait. The press got wind of what was going on and within the hour it was breaking news everywhere—in every city, in every country. Peter had to issue a statement to the press but was holding off until the twins and parents got to the hospital. It would be the most difficult statement he ever had to come up with. Worse than when Baby Margaret died. He also had to cancel all of the concerts scheduled in Italy. "Until further notice" the statement read.

Ed was on his way. He called Quinn and told him, because Chase couldn't or wouldn't answer his phone. Everyone was sending messages to wish Marguerite well and say they were praying for her.

Quinn and Jeanine told Chase that they were going to the chapel. He hugged Quinn then and nearly collapsed in his arms. Quinn and Jeanine just held him until he had somewhat composed himself. "I know it's hard, Chase," Quinn said, "but you have to pull yourself together. The boys will be here soon." Chase acknowledged that and straightened his shoulders, taking a few deep breaths.

Reassured somewhat, Quinn and Jeanine headed off to the chapel. They felt they needed to talk to God and now! They knelt at the altar in front of the cross and just wept uncontrollably. They prayed for strength for Blake and Abbey, Drew and Cara, and for themselves so that they could support Chase and the boys. They prayed for Marguerite, and asked God to show her what she was fighting for: Chase, her loving husband, and her four sons who all needed her. They prayed and prayed and prayed!

In the operating room, the nurses finished prepping her while the surgeon was studying all the scans and making marks on Marguerite's head outlining his plans. When the procedure started, the nurse went out to tell them and handed Chase Marguerite's wedding ring. He nearly lost it. The nurse explained, "She can't have any jewelry on in the operating room."

Chase held the wedding ring for a moment and then put it on his little finger, where it barely fit. He kept looking at it. He was so distraught, feeling like he'd lost her already. She didn't have her ring on. The ring she never took off. The ring he gave her to show that she was his and was never going to let her go and would love her forever.

Every hour on the hour, they got an update about what was going on in the operating room, but all the nurse was allowed to say was that her vital signs were stable.

Blake looked up at the clock. Quinn and Jeanine were still in the chapel. They had been there for three hours already. "I hope they're making those prayers good ones." Abbey was holding onto him and shaking. She couldn't stop.

Cara was clinging to Drew like she would never see him again. He kept rubbing her back and arms, trying to keep her calm. Unfortunately, someone needed to keep him calm at the same time.

They didn't know how they were going to react when the boys came. They were afraid they'd lose it. They all said they'd try to keep calm, but couldn't promise they'd manage.

Chase didn't hear anything being talked about in the room. He didn't see anything either. He was just staring blankly in front of him. Waiting.

Marguerite was still in surgery eight hours later. Peter kept updating the press, basically saying the same thing over and over:

Mrs. Martin is still in surgery. The only report they've had from the doctor is that her vital signs are stable. Any news like that is good news.

The boys arrived. Chase felt them first. He picked up his head suddenly. Drew noticed. "What is it?"

"I think the boys are here," he frowned, confused. "I felt them."

This is the first time he'd ever felt the boys. They all braced themselves. Sure enough, it was them.

All four of them ran to Chase and hugged him. "Dad, we're here to take care of you," Zac said. "We know you need us, we felt you. And we felt Mom."

Zeke nodded. "We knew she was in trouble. But we're here now and we're going to take care of you and her so she can get better."

With that, the whole room lost it. Quinn and Jeanine had gotten back just in time to hear this announcement, and be amazed.

Chase started crying hard, hugging his sons. They clung to him. The M&M's crawled up onto the chair and hugged Chase from behind as the Z's hugged him from the front, and around the sides they joined hands, front to back, engulfing their father in their arms.

"You and mom do this for us," Matthew said, "and now we're going to do it to you. We want to hold *you,* Dad." Chase buried his head in between the Z's. He couldn't believe what his boys were doing for him.

Joe and Mary and Jess were all crying too. They were still amazed at what the boys had said, about feeling Chase and Marguerite, but also at how determined they were to help their parents. They were the light everyone needed to see in the dark place everyone was in.

The twins all turned to the aunts and uncles and said, "We'll come and see you all too, after we take care of our dad first. We can't leave him right now." One by one, the aunts and uncles went to them and kissed them, telling them they loved them and thanking them for wanting to take care of their parents.

Ed arrived and Quinn filled him in, because Chase couldn't speak. He was sitting with his four sons on a big chair. He saw the boys stroking Chase's face and rubbing his hands and arms. Chase was holding onto them for dear life. He stared ahead and didn't see anyone.

Ed knew it was bad. He looked at everyone else and could see it was bad. He was shaking and wondering what he could do to help. In the end, he figured he would just be there in case anyone needed him.

The boys got up and started talking to each other in front of Chase. Then they were talking to him and he finally answered them. "Yes, I'm so sorry." Once they had reached their father, they went over to everyone else and hugged them all one by one. When they reached Ed, they grabbed him and held on. He was incredibly moved.

Zac seemed to be the spokesperson for the little band of brothers. He said to Ed, "We wanted to thank you for coming to be with us all." Ed was taken back by their manners. *They're 9 going on 90.*

"We need to get something to eat," Zac said. "Would anyone like any-thing?" Quinn and Jeanine said they would take them to the café to get them something. "No," Zac said, "we wanted to order something and have them bring it here. We can't leave our father."

They looked at Chase. He was looking at his sons, shaking his head with tears rolling down his cheeks. The boys always amazed him, and at that moment, he thought of how proud their mother would be if she could just see what little men they'd turned into. They continued. "We need to feed our dad. He has to be well so he can help us take care of our mother." It blew everyone away. They all just looked back and forth between Chase and the boys. Chase couldn't believe it.

Finally, he got up and took the boys by the hand. "We'll all go get some-thing and bring it back here. We can get something for everyone."

At least the boys had gotten a reaction out of him. Everyone was relieved for the moment. Quinn said the nurse had just been there, so they probably had about an hour before the next update.

Chase nodded to Quinn and off they went—five of them all holding hands like a chain.

Unfortunately, a nurse took a picture of them walking down the hall like that and had it posted. Everyone in the world saw it. All the stations picked it up and it was everywhere. Chase looked like a zombie in it and the boys with him. It broke hearts all around the world. Peter was livid, as well as everyone else. They got the nurse who had done that and she was repri-manded. Then they had to tell all the staff that they couldn't do things like that. They made everyone sign confidentiality waivers. But the press ate up that picture anyway, because it was the only thing they had so far from the hospital, other than for Peter reporting every hour that nothing had changed. The whole world knew that it did not look good for Marguerite.

Chase and the boys weren't gone long. They brought something for everyone, and knew exactly what to get. When they asked them how they knew what to get them, Zeke said, "We always watch what you order back home, whenever we go out."

They brought hamburgers for Drew and Quinn, cheeseburgers for Blake and Abbey, salads for Jeanine and Cara, and a turkey sandwich for Ed. The boys all got turkey sandwiches, and got their dad a cheeseburger, just like Blake and Abbey. Settling down in the room, they all started eating, even though they weren't particularly hungry, so as not to offend the boys. Chase stared off into the distance again, so the boys opened up the wrapper on his cheeseburger and said, "If you don't take a bite, we won't either."

Chase didn't know if he could hold anything down, but with those four faces looking back at him, he felt he had to try, so he just took little bites. Everyone breathed a sigh of relief. The boys were hungry and devoured their sandwiches. Chase noticed. "Would you like to get something else to eat?"

"No, we're fine," Zac said. "The nurse should be back soon and we don't want to leave the room."

"Well," Chase said, "I can't finish my cheeseburger; would you help me finish it?" They all took a bite, just to help out, and before you knew it, Chase had finished the burger.

Everyone looked at the boys. Blake leaned in towards Abbey, "If they planned that to get Chase to eat, they are really good." For the first time in almost twenty-four hours, someone smiled.

Chase looked at his sons in complete awe. They were taking care of him. They had told him they wanted to and they did. They had taken charge of the whole situation from the minute they walked in the room. He was incredibly proud of them, and knew how proud Marguerite would be too when she found out. They had come to take care of their dad until it was time to take care of their mother too. Little men at 5 and 9 years old.

Hope

Jess, Mary and Joe had gone to the hotel to get them all settled in. They came back just in time because finally the surgeon himself came in with the update. They were all bracing themselves.

Jess asked if someone should take the boys before the surgeon started to talk, but the four just said, "No. We're staying."

With that, Chase stood up to listen to the surgeon, with his older sons holding his hands, and his younger sons clinging to his legs.

"So," the surgeon said, "she's alive, and as far as we can tell, the surgery was successful. I was able to stop the bleeding, but it took us a while. There was a lot of swelling in the brain because of the blood, which slowed down the procedure."

As the surgeon looked around at everyone, he saw how tightly they were holding onto each other, and knew that they probably didn't even realize it.

"It was hard to find where the bleeding was coming from," he continued. "That's what took the longest. We had to locate the bleed without disturbing the rest of the brain any more than absolutely necessary or else it could have affected Mrs. Martin's cognition or her physical coordination and mobility."

He rubbed his neck, seeming tired, and they all realized that he had been working very hard all this time trying to save her life. "She is in recovery," he said, "and is still under anesthesia because I don't want her to wake up quite yet. Awareness, emotion, pain—these things can all cause blood to rush to the area and create additional swelling. She is being closely monitored, and we are ready to take immediate action should her condition change for the worse. I am cautiously optimistic that she will recover fully, but it is too soon to tell, and there are many variables. But I assure you all that we are being very cautious. The next twenty-four hours will tell us a lot."

Chase tried to wrap his head around what the surgeon was telling him, that basically it had gone slowly but well, and now they just had to wait to see if his wife would have any lasting effects from the bleeding or the surgery. They could only learn that when she was allowed to wake up, which wasn't happening just yet. The surgeon told them they would all have to wait at least until the next day.

Everyone was breathing a little easier, although Chase and the girls were crying. The boys brought him over to the chair he had been sitting in and made him sit back down. They all settled down into the room, with some people dozing off, while others stared out the window or counted tiles in the ceiling.

Hours passed before the surgeon came back in and asked to speak to Chase. He got right up with the boys following behind. The girls all ran after them and stopped them. The twins were fussing and hard to stop. They yelled, "Dad!" while struggling against the hands that were holding them back. Chase came back to them. "I will be right back, I promise." He knelt down before them like they were in a huddle and whispered, "Take care of your aunts until I get back. I think they need you." He hugged them all and kissed them. With that, they let him go and went back to Cara, Jeanine, and Abbey. The surgeon just watched in amazement.

Chase followed the surgeon, who told Chase he wanted to bring Marguerite out of the sleep he'd put her in, just for a few minutes, to see if there were any obvious problems. He felt Chase would need to be there when he woke her up. Chase started coming back to life at that point.

"Thank you," Chase said as they headed into the recovery room. He saw Marguerite lying there. Her head was all white bandages; she looked like she was wearing a turban. He moved right to her side.

"Do not move her head."

Chase nodded and then picked up her hand, kissed it, and placed it next to his face, which was wet from all the tears falling. Then the surgeon injected something into her IV. Less than a minute later, they heard her moan quietly. Chase was amazed.

He was leaning over her, looking at her face, and the surgeon said, "Ask her simple questions like her name and who you are."

Her eyes slowly blinked open, but she didn't seem to see anything. She felt Chase holding her hand, but her eyes stayed fixed in front. She kept blinking them. Chase started to panic, until she finally moved them towards him.

She smiled as widely as she could. "I feel foggy. Am I dreaming?"

"No. I'll tell you all about it, but for now can you answer some questions for me?"

"Yes."

"Do you know who I am?" he asked through his tears.

She paused for a moment and then said, "Yes, the very air I breathe."

The surgeon frowned and looked at Chase, who couldn't control the tears streaming down his face.

"She knows me." He kissed her hand again.

Chase took a deep breath. "And you know who you are?"

"Marguerite Angeli-Martin. Wife of Chase Martin of the Band 4. Together we have four beautiful sons."

The surgeon nodded. "Okay, that's enough for now."

But Marguerite was not ready to stop talking.

"Tell Quinn and Jeanine that I saw them in the chapel and thank them for me." She was falling back to sleep but managed to say one more thing before she did, in a quiet sleepy voice: "I saw Baby Margaret. She is still so beautiful."

That put Chase over the edge. The surgeon waited, letting him compose himself, and asked who Baby Margaret was. "Our first born. She didn't make it." There was nothing either of them could say about that, so the surgeon focused on the patient. "Well, it looks really good right now, but as I said, anything can happen. Only time will tell."

Back at the room, the boys all felt their mom. They jumped up suddenly and gathered together talking, looking at each other but not seeing each other. The others looked on, confused. Zeke noticed and explained. "Mom is awake and speaking to Dad. He feels better now and is on his way back here."

Everyone looked at them and realized that they had the same connection to Chase and Marguerite as Chase and Marguerite had with each other. Everyone looked dumbfounded. Everyone wondered how Chase and

Marguerite's bond could happen, but they never questioned it because they didn't know who they could ask. No one had ever heard of that before, not even Chase or Marguerite.

Now they all just looked at each other and couldn't believe it.

Ed said, "Okay, that's spooky." That was the only word he could think of for it.

They all nodded. "Good word." They couldn't think of a better one.

The surgeon walked Chase back to the room and saw everyone standing there. Chase looked better, but was still crying.

"The surgeon woke Mam up for a few minutes," Chase said, "to see if there were any initial issues with the surgery. There were none so far. She knew who I was and who she was. That's what the surgeon was looking for. So far it's looking good." They saw plain as day that Chase was coming back to life. It gave everyone hope.

Peter and the surgeon held a press conference to let everyone know what was going on and how Marguerite was doing. The world was waiting and now they had some hope to tell them about.

The surgeon told them that the operation had taken approximately sixteen hours and explained why and what had been done. Mrs. Martin was in recovery now and they had woken her up for about five minutes to see if there were any immediate cognitive issues relating to the bleed or the surgery. Chase had been present when she woke up, and she knew him and was speaking to him.

Then they had put her back to sleep.

The press was all over that. "Do you know what was said between them?"

"Yes. I told him what to ask her. Basic questions like who he was and how did she feel. She knew him immediately, and both started crying."

Then Peter said that was enough and both left the room.

The Reveal

Drew said to the boys, "Tell your father what you told us."

Chase was holding them. "What is it?"

"We felt Mom wake up," Zac said. "We felt you feeling better when you talked to her."

Chase was startled. "You did?"

"Yes, we've always felt you and Mom. We never knew what the feelings were though, so we never said anything before. But now we can figure them out and understand."

Mary and Jess chimed in. "Back at the house, when we were waiting for the call about what time to go to the airport, the boys already knew. Without us even telling them anything. They knew their mother was in trouble. When we went to tell them to pack, they were already done, sitting in the Z's room and just waiting to go."

Everyone was shocked.

Chase said to his sons, "Does it scare you?"

"No. It never did."

"Can you feel each other?" he asked, pointing to each of the brothers.

They all nodded. "Yes."

"And you are not afraid?"

"No," they all said at the same time.

Chase was shaking his head. "Is there anything you want to talk about?"

"Yes."

"Now?"

They all nodded. "Yes, because almost everyone is here."

"Here for what you want to say?"

All together again, they said, "Yes."

"Okay, well," Chase shrugged, "you can start when you're ready."

They turned to face everyone, with Chase's arms still around them.

Mark and Matt started. "We had a dream a while ago, in it we saw Dad at the studio with Uncle Blake, Uncle Drew, and Uncle Quinn. He was looking out a window in the studio. It was raining. Uncle Drew, you called him, but Dad didn't hear you, so you called him again and he turned and looked your way. You asked him to come and help you all with something and he walked over to you and sat down. But then he got up and said he can't help you and went back to the window to stare out at the rain. But the look on all of your faces when he said he couldn't help is what woke us up."

"Us?" Drew asked.

Matt nodded. "Yes, we were both having the same dream."

Chase decided it was time they all knew everything. "Mam actually had the same dream at the same time." Everyone started speaking at once, wanting to ask questions, but Chase said to everyone, "Please wait every-one, and let them finish."

Zac spoke up next. "Zeke and I were dreaming that same night as well. We dreamed we saw Mom sitting having dinner with two older people. We didn't know where they were. Then the older man got so angry at Mom that he threw his dish of pasta at the wall. All we could see was how upset Mom was, and then her cleaning up pasta that was all over the floor."

"And I had that same dream the same night," Chase said. "We all had those dreams on the same night at the same time. Mam and I both woke up in a cold sweat. Then we felt funny and flew out of the room and Mam told me to go see Mark and Matt and she would get Zac and Zeke. When we got to their rooms, Zac and Zeke were sitting up in bed gasping for air, and so were Mark and Matt when I got to them. So we all got together to see what they were so upset about, and they told us about the dreams. We tried to make light of it because we didn't want to scare them, so we played hooky from school and went to the movies and stopped by to see Ed." Ed nodded, remembering.

"But what was worse came afterwards, because at the time, I knew I'd had the dream about Mam but didn't know she'd also had the dream about me. To say we were shocked and stunned when they told us would be an understatement. Then we were so worried that we might have done this to them, channeling them somehow, and it upset us. Obviously. We said we would talk about it at a later date, but really we just wanted to forget it because until today we never mentioned it again."

The boys looked at Chase and said, "We can forget it Dad, if you want us to."

Chase shook his head. "It was confusing even to your mother and me. We don't know how to handle what we feel sometimes."

"If we feel like we can't understand something we're feeling, we just talk it out and try to forget it too."

Everyone in that room looked at those four sweet, good boys and thought, *What is going on?*

Chase said to the boys, "How about a nap now?" He knew they were all spent and needed them to rest. He picked them up one at a time, hugged them, and put them in Marguerite's empty bed. He covered them and kissed them. "Thank you for coming to take care of me and your mother."

They fell right to sleep.

He looked at the others and whispered, "What do I do with that?"

They knew what he was talking about, but had no answers for him.

"Who do I call? They'd think we were all crazy, wouldn't they? Would they take the boys away from us, thinking we're nuts? Not to mention what would happen if any of that got out to the media! It's one thing for Marguerite and I to mention that we felt each other when we met, but this?"

Chase was upset and pacing back and forth in front of the bed.

"I don't think you're crazy," Quinn said. "I just think you are so blessed."

They all looked at him.

"The connection you have with Mam is amazing and real and true. Do you think it's not real?"

"Of course not. I know it's real because I feel it and so does Mam."

"Do you think what the boys feel is real?"

"It certainly seems to be and they seem to know it's real."

"Speaking for all of us," Quinn said, glancing around at the others for confirmation, "I don't think you or Mam are nuts. Or the boys. We think it's a gift you have." The others were nodding in agreement. "Everyone has a gift from God. Mine is playing guitar. I'm good at it and it comes naturally. Blake is good at lyrics. He can recite new songs in his sleep. Drew, well, we are still wondering what his gift is." They all laughed for the first time in hours. "Ed's gift is his music, beautiful and simple. He is a one-man band and one-man show. Your gift, Chase, is your natural connection to the woman, and now the little people, that you love."

Everyone was still nodding in agreement.

"As far as the boys, maybe you passed that gift on to them and maybe you didn't, but it's something they should not forget about. Think how lucky you all are! How incredibly lucky!" Everyone started crying.

"I *am* lucky," Chase said, "and I thank God on a daily basis. After the first exam, when the doctor said, 'if she's going to live', I realized I have been in heaven for eleven years now. We've had setbacks, but we always came out of it stronger. I have to believe that we will come out of this stronger too. I can't breathe if I don't think that." He shook his head.

"But when Mam gets better, we will have to talk to the boys. They can't tell people about that connection to their brothers or to us." They all agreed about that too.

There was a ray of light in his voice though. He had said "*When* Mam gets better!" Not if. It made them all feel better.

Drew was still thinking about the dreams. "That dream about you, Chase. That's the night we thought we lost you. We were distraught. We thought you were going to come in the next day and tell us that you quit the band. That you quit us. We were all hoping for a miracle! Then you came in like a different person with coffee for all of us. We just looked at each other and thought, *What happened?* We were so happy and so hopeful. That's why we followed you home that night. We had to see who had done that to you—who had given you life again. That's why we love her so much. She saved our brother. We didn't care about the band. She saved our brother!" With that, they all got up and hugged each other and wouldn't let each other go. Brothers!

"That dream about Mam's parents?" Joe said. "That actually happened too. They treated her terribly and I saw it all the time. She confided in me. It took her hours to clean up all that pasta off the floor and wall."

They didn't know what had triggered the dreams about things that had happened more than eleven years before. In the end, they supposed that it didn't really matter.

Chase was watching the boys sleeping when he remembered something else.

"Oh! Quinn, I have to tell you something. I forgot all about it."

"What is it?" Everyone was listening.

"It's a message to you and Jeanine. When the surgeon woke her up for those few minutes, Mam asked me to thank you."

"For what?" Quinn asked. Everyone was watching the exchange, curious.

"She saw you two in the chapel and said to say 'thank you' to the both of you." Quinn and Jeanine hugged each other and cried. They said they had asked God to show Marguerite what she was fighting to stay alive for.

If that wasn't enough to get everyone going again, Chase told them the rest. "Mam said she saw Baby Margaret, and that she still looked beautiful."

There wasn't a dry eye in the room.

Waking Up

They brought Marguerite to her room and were going to wake her up there. It had been twenty-four hours. The surgeon felt it was time. It came just in time, because Chase was a wreck waiting for word. He paced back and forth. They all wanted to tie him down.

He had somehow talked his sons into going back to the hotel with their grandparents. He said to them, "You will know when it's time for you to come back." They had nodded. He hugged and kissed each one of his sons, told them he loved them, and then they were gone.

Marguerite had color in her cheeks again when they saw her. When Chase had brought her to the hospital, she was a pale white. She looked better now. They administered the drug to wake her up and she started to move. They elevated the bed so that she was sitting up a bit. Chase was at her side holding her hand. Quinn was on the other side, holding the other one at Chase's request. The surgeon suggested that the rest stand back so as not to confuse her, because she would be groggy.

Chase was shaking like a leaf, as were Quinn and everyone else in the room. Then she opened her eyes. As she had done the last time, she stared straight ahead. It was like she was trying to focus. Then her eyes searched for Chase and found him. She started crying and so did he.

The surgeon said, "I don't want you to get upset so try to stay calm." She tried.

Chase said, "Do you remember what happened?"

"I had a headache and you came for me. I wasn't feeling well on the plane ride... and then we got off the plane... and... there's nothing after that."

"Can you tell me where you live?"

"In Pennsylvania."

Everyone nearly stopped breathing. Chase thought for a split second that he was going to pass out.

"And London."

They all let out a sigh of relief.

"Can you tell me about our sons?"

"They are beautiful." She smiled with tears streaming down her face. "Zac and Zeke look like you and Mark and Matt look like me."

Everyone was smiling.

"How about my brothers? Can you tell me about them?"

"Yes, they're my brothers too, and we have sisters."

Smiles were getting wider.

Chase nodded. "Okay, tell me then." He squeezed her hand.

"Blake and Abbey," *Yes,* "Drew and Cara," *yes,* "and Quinn and Jeanine."

"Perfect!" Chase grinned.

"Wait! One more. Ed. You forgot Ed!"

Chase looked at Ed and said, "Yes, I did. Thank you, my love, for reminding me."

Chase took her wedding ring off his little finger and put it back on her ring finger. "In sickness and in health. I will love you forever." He kissed the ring now that it was back on her hand where it belonged.

Marguerite smiled softly at him. "I will love you forever."

"Would you like to see everyone? They are all here."

They were all dying to see her and tell her that they loved her too.

"Please yes."

One by one, they came over, kissed her hand, and said they were so happy to see her and that they loved her. She said she loved them too and thanked them for being there with Chase.

The surgeon said he thought that Marguerite was going to be fine. It might be a long road, but if she was as strong as she appeared, he didn't think it would be too long. Regardless, she would not be allowed to fly anywhere yet. She might not be able to for a few months. She had to heal and the pressure of being in a plane with the altitude might cause her trouble. She should start doing small things daily to acclimate herself to getting back to normal. She would have to take it slowly and come back for weekly appointments until the surgeon was ready to release her from his care.

Everyone was so happy. They knew she would be fine. Chase came back to life and the boys were going to make good on their statements about taking care of their mother and father.

The next thing they had to do was find a home to rent near Lake Como, one that fit the twelve of them—eight adults and four children—and their bodyguards. The brothers and sisters had already said they weren't leaving. They had to be with Chase and Marguerite. They would help with the boys, even though the boys said they were ready to take care of themselves *and* their mom and dad.

Peter stepped up to find them a place to rent for about two or three months. George Dooley, the Oscar winning actor, heard through his people about the Martins looking for somewhere to stay until Mrs. Martin was able to travel again back to London. He and his wife, Amelia, had a house on Lake Como and immediately got in touch with Peter to tell them they could use it. Peter told him they would rent it from him and pay whatever he wanted, but George insisted that he didn't want any rent. He was happy to help. He knew what was happening with the Martins.

Then Peter said, "Before we shake on this, over the phone, you do know that there are at least twelve of them right? Four couples, four children, and assorted help?" George never hesitated. Peter was touched and swore that they would absolutely not trash his house. He gave his word on it. George said he had nine bedrooms in the house and they could use whatever was there. Linens, dishes, pots, utensils; whatever they needed. They accepted. George's security guard at the property would meet Chase's security guard with the keys and take him around the property. It all turned out to be easier than Peter thought it would be. When he told everyone, they were a little nervous about using Mr. Dooley's house, but Peter said that it would be perfect for them.

Marguerite was released and off they went to George's house. The grandparents handed the boys over to the aunts and uncles, because they were all going back home. Ed had to get back to the UK, but said that he would be back as soon as possible. When they left, it was very emotional. Ed did not want to leave Chase and Marguerite but he had to. They hugged and kissed and hugged and kissed and said thank you a million times. The little men did the same thing. Before he actually turned to leave, they walked over and put their hands out to shake his. One at a time. Like men.

The family reached George's house and just stood there and gawked at it. It was massive and beautiful.

The first thing they said to the boys was, "Mr. Dooley is letting us use his house to help out your mom because she cannot travel back home yet. We can't do any damage here. Do you understand that we all have to be careful?"

They said yes and that they would be.

Security was all around and they met everyone, and they showed them where everything was. Then they tried to make themselves at home.

They went out to the back porch, and the sight was a picture right out of a book. The outdoor furniture on the massive porch looked out onto the water, with boats floating calmly in place and others going by. Marguerite loved the ocean and lakes. They had always calmed her but rarely in her life had she gotten to see either in person.

Recovering

Everything was going fine at Mr. Dooley's. Every night they checked to see when it would be sunrise and every morning everyone met on the porch to watch it come up. It was beautiful. The coffee would already be made in a massive coffee pot they found to use and everyone would come out and sit on the porch and watch the sun come up. They loved that time together.

They came out however they got up. Blake and Drew came out in their underwear, which were like shorts, thank God, and the girls came down in long t-shirts or nightgowns. Marguerite loved beautiful nightgowns. She had four boys so she was used to covering up.

The one thing she never forgot to wear was a cap to cover her head and stitches. She had them in all colors and always had one on. Her head was shaved and her hair was just starting to grow back. It still looked like five o'clock shadow. It upset her when she saw herself, especially the deep circles under her eyes, which were finally fading away, and her lack of hair. She did not feel good about herself, but Chase just kept saying she was so beautiful and so did the boys. When she had a new cap on, the first thing they would say was how much they liked it.

The Dooley's had beautiful dishes and so they set a formal table every day for breakfast and dinner. Before they went to bed, they always set the table for breakfast. Lunch was always on the fly, either outside to enjoy the weather and view or just at the snack bar. Dinner was a big deal. It was usually at six every night. If the girls didn't cook, they ordered in, always being careful not to be recognized. There was a massive table outside on the veranda, so if the weather was good they loved eating out there. Marguerite and the girls would light candles everywhere and everyone loved it.

No one knew where they were either. If it ever got out, the place would be mobbed with fans and reporters everywhere, so they kept a low profile.

Mr. Dooley had a boat the guys took out on the water—with his permission of course—and sometimes they took the twins. Marguerite had a hard time with it, and Chase had an even harder time. He hated being in a boat and rarely went with them. In the end, they got used to it though. They knew the uncles would watch over them and they always had their life-jackets on.

Chase took Marguerite weekly to see the surgeon. They went through a battery of tests each time and each time she got a good report. The surgeon asked, "Are you feeling any different with anything? Speech, mobility, memories?"

She said she did. "My left arm and hand trembles a little. Not all the time but it's noticeable when it does."

The surgeon said, "It will likely not get worse or better. It's a side effect of the surgery."

She nodded. "That's a small price to pay to be alive and still here today."

Chase kissed her head and just smiled. *Is it ever!*

Sometimes the Z's and M&M's joined the family in the morning to see the sunrise and sometimes they slept in. They never woke them until it was time for breakfast, which was always at nine. On the big coffee table on the porch where they sat, the coffee would be in a carafe and the orange juice would be out for the boys, so everyone had something to drink. The adults all loved coffee in this family. It was amazing. They blew through at least forty cups every morning. And those mugs were pretty big so one cup was probably the equivalent of three. At least it was decaf. That was its only saving grace.

One day Marguerite and Chase were on the porch waiting for the sunrise. She was sitting sideways between his legs with both her legs draped over one of his. He held her in his arms, exactly where he always wanted her. He treated her like a porcelain doll—like she was breakable. She told him to stop but he felt he couldn't risk her getting hurt until she was all better.

"Let's take your cap off and give your incision some air." She always had a cap on and the doctor and Chase both felt she needed to start taking it off once in a while.

Reluctantly, she took it off and Chase sang "It's the Little Things" to distract her. It was the song he had written for her. Little did they know they were being watched. Mr. and Mrs. Dooley had come home because he needed something from the den, which overlooked the porch. It was early enough that they hadn't wanted to bother them, and had planned to just sneak in and out before they were noticed. Mike was on duty and had let them into the house with no bother. It was theirs after all, and he felt comfortable that they were no threat to anyone (Chase and his family were not the only ones impressed with their generosity). They hadn't meant to spy on them. They were just mesmerized by them. With her cap off, they were able to tell just how serious her operation was. They felt so bad for her and for her family, wondering how they had gotten through it.

When they had walked into the house, they saw that the table had been set beautifully for breakfast. They smelled that the coffee was brewing and a ham was in the oven. Pancake batter was ready to go in the kitchen and the house was spotless. When they walked upstairs towards the bedrooms, they saw that the beds were all made. The twins were sleeping away on blow-up mattresses in someone's bedroom. They looked in their own bedroom and saw that no one was using it. They were amazed.

Drew came downstairs and saw Marguerite's bare head. He almost stopped dead in his tracks, but didn't want to upset her so he just said, "Good morning, brother... sister!" and kissed the top of each of their heads. He was dressed as he usually was: in his underwear with no shirt. He got his coffee and sat down.

As the rest came down, they all handled the surprise in much the same way, kissing their heads and complimenting Marguerite on how good she looked. They were upset by the sight of her scar, being reminded of how close they came to losing her, but were careful not to let on.

Chase mouthed thank you to all of them when she wasn't looking.

None of them knew they were being watched. The Dooleys were amazed at the love and thoughtfulness they were witnessing.

The brothers and sisters were sitting and looking out at the water, when Blake said, "Uh oh."

Chase turned his head and saw Mr. and Mrs. Dooley standing there. He quickly held up his hand and gave them a gesture, asking them for a minute.

Marguerite immediately started to panic. "Uh oh, what?" She was turned facing the opposite way and wasn't supposed to turn her head quickly.

Chase grabbed her cap and put it on her. Jeanine grabbed a shawl that was there and put it around her, whispering in her ear, "Mr. and Mrs. Dooley are here."

Her hand went right for her cap and she started to cry. Chase grabbed both her hands. "It's all right. You look beautiful. Don't cry." Everyone said the same thing.

Quinn grabbed her legs and swung them around, with Chase guiding her back so she could sit up straight. He stood up in front of her and saw that her tears were still falling. He kissed her. "Look at me. It's fine. It's fine. Really! You're beautiful!"

She took a deep breath as Chase motioned them over. He helped her up and she turned to see them. She thought they were the most beautiful couple she had ever seen, and there they were in nightgowns, night shirts, and underwear with no shirts. Marguerite and Chase were the first to go over to them. Chase shook Mr. Dooley's hand. "How can we ever repay you for your kindness to us? To my whole family." He looked back at everyone. "Thank you from the bottom of our hearts."

Marguerite was shaking. Chase felt her. She was hiding behind him. He turned and kissed her. "It's all right." They could see she was shaken, but she stepped up and extended her hand.

Mr. Dooley took it. "You look wonderful. You have nothing to worry about. You are beautiful."

"Thank you so much." Then she looked at his wife. "Thank you both for letting us use your things, Mr. and Mrs. Dooley. We so enjoy it here. We love it." Mrs. Dooley embraced her, and told her to call them George and Amelia. It was the warmest hug ever and she immediately started to calm down.

One by one, everyone came over and introduced themselves and thanked them for everything they had done for them. The Dooley's were impressed by how grateful they all were, and took to them all immediately. Chase offered them some coffee and they all sat down.

"We forgot to apologize for our appearance," Blake said, looking down at himself and Drew in their underwear. Mr. Dooley chuckled. "Not a problem on my end." Everyone got a good laugh out of it.

Then they heard Zac talking to them through a monitor they had set up. He said that they would get the M&M's ready for breakfast. No need for anyone to come up. They were handling it. Marguerite explained that their sons were getting up and thought they were little men now. "They want to help do everything," she continued. "So we let them. It's good to learn responsibility."

After a little while, the four of them came out onto the porch and immediately went to their mom and dad, hugging and kissing them. They said good morning, and then went to the uncles and aunts and did the same. Then they noticed the two new people there.

Chase said to the boys, "This is Mr. and Mrs. Dooley. This is their house. They are the ones letting us use it until Mom is better."

Zac went to Mr. Dooley and introduced himself first, holding his hand out to shake it. "It's a pleasure to finally meet you. My name is Zac Martin. I would like to formally introduce you to my brother Zeke."

Zeke held out his hand to shake. "I am Zeke Martin. Thank you for letting us use your house." Then he turned to Mark. "I would like to formally introduce you to my brother Mark."

Mark stepped forward and held out his hand to shake. "Hello, I am Mark Martin. How can we ever thank you for what you've done for us? I would like to introduce you to my brother Matt."

Matt stuck out his hand and introduced himself. "Hello. I am Matt Martin. Thank you for everything. We didn't break a thing." Everyone burst out laughing.

Their family all had the biggest smiles on their faces at the way they had handled themselves. They could tell the Dooleys were impressed. A short time later, they all went in to make breakfast. Chase was helping Marguerite with the pancakes when he kissed her and said, "I am so proud of you and what you've taught our sons. I am so proud of the four of them. Sometimes I have to wonder if I'm dreaming. You're the very air I breathe."

"And you are mine." They touched foreheads. "Now get back to the pancakes."

He just laughed.

All the while, the Dooley's were watching, mesmerized by how close everyone was and how much love they all shared.

Reconnecting

It was almost time for them all to get back to work. Marguerite was feeling better. Peter saw that too, so he got together with the guys and they set a date for resuming the Italian tour.

Chase knew Marguerite loved being on the water—on a lake or the ocean. It calmed her somehow. "Do you want to look for a cottage we could buy on Lake Como while I'm back at work? We could use it in the summer or whenever we wanted to come back to Italy." They both loved it in Italy.

"I love it here," she said, "but we still have our house in Pennsylvania."

"Yes, and that's our residence when we're in the States. Would you like to see if we could find something here in Italy for when we're here?"

"Yes. Of course! I would love to have a house on a lake in Italy!"

The Dooleys were still there. They were so taken with them all that they didn't want to leave yet. At dinner that night, they set the table outside and lit the candles. It was a beautiful night. The guys cooked on the grill and they had a great time. They sat around the table for hours talking.

Chase told everyone that he and Marguerite were going to look for a cottage on Lake Como because they loved it there so much. The guys all perked up and gave them the same speech as when they were building the house in Pennsylvania. Without missing a beat, Blake said, "You know you need six bedrooms. I don't know where you are going to find a house that big."

"You heard Chase say 'cottage' right?" Marguerite asked. They all laughed.

Chase was getting ready to leave the next day to start the tour in Italy. Marguerite could feel his anxiety kicking in. "Chase, I'm fine. I have four sons taking care of me. They won't let me out of their sight. And my sisters are all here. Please don't make me worry about you? You've done enough worrying lately and I want you to just go and do what you do best. You certainly deserve it."

"What I do best is loving you and my sons." She nodded in agreement, and then she smiled in a devilish way.

"What? Why are you looking at me like that?"

Marguerite closed the door to the bedroom and locked it.

"No, no, no! You are not well enough!"

She took his hand and put it on her heart. "Just follow me. I will tell you if I can't."

Chase couldn't wait to make love to his wife, to enjoy that connection they shared.

She started slipping out of her clothes. "I asked the surgeon and he said that, if I was feeling fine, it shouldn't stop us. So I am telling you, I feel fine. I FEEL FINE!"

She pulled Chase over to the bed and kissed him. "I am going to lie down first and then you can join me."

He took off his clothes and dropped them right there. She positioned herself so that she felt good and he lay down next to her. "I missed you so much," he said, and buried his head in her shoulder and sighed.

She picked up his chin so his face was next to hers. "If you don't kiss me, I will die."

He kissed her softly, and when he saw that she could follow him, the kiss deepened. She began to cry. "Are you all right?" he asked.

"I am now. I needed that kiss. Now please, make love to me."

They took it slow, wanting to really feel each other, both physically and through their bond.

Chase lay with Marguerite in his arms. He'd waited months for that moment and it had finally arrived. Marguerite was in heaven with Chase's arms wrapped around her. It was the best feeling in the world to her, having someone hold her. Someone who loved her. Someone she loved.

She knew that tomorrow would be hard, especially if he got emotional on her. "Please don't make it hard on me or the boys tomorrow by getting upset. You have to go."

He said he would try but couldn't promise. She turned and kissed him again, deeply and passionately. They could have easily gotten caught back up in the moment, but decided it was better not to push their luck.

They got dressed, unlocked the door, and found four little men sitting outside it, waiting to come in. It made them blush, and then smile. "Why didn't you knock?"

"We wanted you to be alone first. You never get to be alone. But if you didn't unlock that door in ten minutes we were going to pound on it."

With that, they all jumped in bed together, with the boys in between their parents, who engulfed them in the biggest hug they could give.

The brothers and sisters looked in as they passed by and saw them. So did the Dooleys. Everyone went to bed smiling.

House Hunting

Chase and the guys left for the tour, and as expected, he was filled with anxiety at leaving. His boys felt it and took him aside. "Dad, we are going to take care of Mom. She'll be fine and we think you know that we'll be fine too. We'll call you immediately if anything's wrong. Call us and let us know how you're doing as well." Chase just looked at them and thought, *how old are these kids?* Then he thought, *They are mine. My boys.* The love he felt for them was immeasurable.

He went and hugged Marguerite, kissed her head, and then kissed her on the lips—the deepest kiss he could give her in front of the boys. He could see that she was happy, so when all was said and done, he was able to stay relatively calm.

Mrs. Dooley called a real estate agent in the area and arranged to show some houses to Marguerite and the girls. Mr. Dooley told the women to go ahead and he would stay home with the boys. He loved being with them. So the day the guys left to resume the tour, she had a number of appointments to keep her mind off of it. Between all their bodyguards and themselves, they would have needed a caravan to get to all the houses they were going to be viewing. They decided instead to take one driver and just two body-guards, so they could all go in one SUV. The real estate agent understood that no one could know they were coming or it would be a zoo, with people everywhere trying to snap pictures.

They looked at three houses that day and that was enough for Marguerite. They could see her wearing down. She got tired and said she needed to get back to the house. They agreed to resume the viewings the next afternoon. They kept viewing houses for a number of weeks to come.

Chase called during every leg of the trip to see how Marguerite and the boys were. They were all doing fine, of course, and Marguerite told him about the house hunting. Then the boys talked and gave him an update on their mother. They ratted her out again. "We think she's doing too much."

Chase told her to slow down and not to do so much. She said that she would try, and that she was just trying to get back to normal.

"You have the rest of your life with me and your sons to get back to normal," Chase said.

She promised she would slow down. She could see the worry on all their faces and realized she had put it there. She would definitely do better.

The next afternoon, the real estate agent took her to yet another beautiful cottage on the lake. This one was yellow with navy blue shutters. There were flower pots on the windowsills filled with colorful petunias. It looked like a picture. Marguerite started to come to life when she saw it. It had a dock out back, and about 150 feet of lake-front property. The backyard was big enough for the boys to kick a ball around and the veranda had a slate floor that almost looked like Pennsylvania slate. It reminded her of home, so they went inside. The kitchen was all white with a huge island, and was positioned so that it looked out at the lake. The family room was huge and overlooked the lake as well, as did the dining area right off the kitchen, which Marguerite loved. There was a powder room on the first floor, and a pantry with an entrance to the outside. Upstairs were three bedrooms. The master had its own bathroom, and the other two bedrooms were connected to a single bathroom, which you could get into from either room. There were bunk beds in one bedroom, which the four boys would love. Marguerite asked if they would be able to add onto the house. The real estate agent said that she would have to find out. Marguerite's wheels were turning. She thought they could probably put wings on either side of the house, but they would have to be angled at ninety degrees. They could have extra bedrooms and a big garage built, like they had done in Pennsylvania. But here they would have a huge veranda to look out over a lake! She didn't need to see more. She had found what she was looking for. She told the agent to find out if they could add onto the house and let her know. That would be the deciding factor. She walked around the house and filmed the rooms, providing a running commentary for Chase, telling him what she was thinking and how she wanted to add onto the house. She walked out back and showed him the slate veranda and told him how it reminded her of Pennsylvania. Then she filmed the dock and lake front. She was excited, and he would hear the excitement in her voice when he saw the film.

Chase looked at the film with the brothers and loved the house. When he saw the first picture of it, with the flowers, he knew she would love it. She had been looking for a cottage, and even though they were going to add onto it, it really did look like one. The agent came back and said that they could absolutely add onto it. The lot was big enough. Chase told her to just buy it. He didn't have to tell her twice.

Within two weeks, the house was theirs, and the girls and the boys all moved over to it. Some of them ended up sleeping on couches and floors again, but they were okay with that. They felt that they had imposed on the Dooleys enough. Marguerite and everyone had one last dinner with them out on the veranda, and could not thank them enough for everything they had done for them. It was a teary goodbye, but they all felt that they would remain friends. Marguerite told Mrs. Dooley she would always stay in touch with her.

They hired a contractor and started work immediately on the new wings. The contractors understood exactly what she wanted and got right to work.

67

Missing You

Marguerite had not seen Chase in three weeks and she felt him getting upset about it. She wasn't able to travel by air, but she could travel by car. The closest the guys would be to Lake Como was three hours away. She talked to her doctor, who approved the trip, and then called Gail to make arrangements. They would meet up at the hotel the boys were staying in, and head back to the cottage the next day.

It would be a surprise though, so they told Peter and Jack to make sure there was no last minute changing of plans on their end, and told them not to tell the guys. Jack's wheels were instantly turning and so were Peter's. They knew everyone wanted to see Marguerite, especially considering she had been missing in action for the past three months since her stay in the hospital. They asked her if she would like to surprise Chase on stage. She spoke to the other girls about it. They thought she should do it, since Peter wanted her to. It would show everyone that she was fine now. So she agreed. Peter and Jack were thrilled.

The boys were excited about going to see their dad. Marguerite said they were surprising him and warned them not to be too excited or he would feel them coming. They had never thought of that so they calmed down. She could hardly breathe but tried to keep calm too. It was hard when just thinking about seeing him made her want to jump out of her skin.

They finally got to the arena and were met by Vita, Peter, and Jack. They were so happy to see her that they hugged and kissed her and all cried together. Except for Peter; he never cried. Then they ushered them all to the waiting room and took Marguerite to get dressed. Vita saw her hair, which had grown in quite a lot, and said, "Don't wear the cap." She said that she would do something with her hair, and if she didn't like it, then they could put the cap back on. The girls agreed that she should see what Vita could do, so she dressed and Vita did her hair and everyone loved it. It was short but so beautiful. It looked like she'd just had it cut like that, not like it was just growing back in after being shaved off.

Right before Chase introduced "It's the Little Things" a message started flashing on the big screens at the back of the stage. "Marguerite is coming, but DO NOT TELL CHASE! Marguerite is surprising him." The message played over and over again in a loop. The other guys all knew. Jack had told them, swearing them to secrecy so as not to ruin Chase's surprise. They knew the girls were there too, and they couldn't wait to see them when the concert was over. They hadn't seen them in three weeks either, so everyone was excited.

Chase started talking to the crowd, but the guys interrupted, calling his name. When he looked at them, Quinn said, "Turn around."

Standing at the back of the stage was his wife without her cap, and wearing the most beautiful summer dress he'd ever seen. She was breathtaking. She started smiling and waving to everyone as she moved towards her husband. It seemed like it took her forever to get to him.

When she did, he dropped to his knees in front of her and wrapped his arms around her waist, resting his head on her heart, and weeping. She wrapped her arms around him and stood there, hugging him. After a long moment, Chase got up, picking her up in his arms so that their faces were level and kissed her. In the meantime, the crowd was going wild. They were all crying and recording the special moment between them.

The guys all came over and kissed both of them. Then they gathered around them in a huddle and hugged them. Peter and Jack were beaming. They knew footage of this would be everywhere by midnight—in every paper and on every TV station. Social media would explode. Everyone had been waiting to see Marguerite and find out how she was doing. Now they knew she was fine.

Chase and the guys asked her, "Where are the boys?"

"They're in the back watching."

"Let's bring them out," Chase said. "I need to see them." The guys agreed. They wanted to see them too.

Chase spoke to the sound engineer through his headset. "Tell Jack to send out the boys."

"Do you want to go see your father?" Jack asked them.

They all said, "Yes!"

He put them on the pop-up platform and they said they knew what to do: Wait for it to stop before they jumped off. Up they went.

Well if everyone was screaming before, they thought the crowd would pass out now. The boys saw their father at the end of the stage with their mother and uncles. They ran to them and plowed Chase down. He was suddenly on the floor and they were all over him. Everyone was laughing and screaming. He had his arms wrapped around the four of them and they were hugging him. Finally, they got off him, and seeing the uncles, they ran to them and hugged them too.

"Why don't we bring the girls out and we can sing "It's the Little Things" to them?" Chase asked. The guys thought it was an excellent idea, so another message went through the headset, and out the girls came, running to meet their husbands. Everyone was beaming.

The crowd was screaming and crying. Holding Marguerite's hand, Chase spoke to them.

"You know what comes next, so everyone take out your phones and put your flashes on. We're going to sing, 'It's the Little Things' to our wives." The lights dimmed and there were thousands of flashes on in the crowd. They look like stars. Blake, Drew, and Quinn sat on the stage and sang to their wives. Chase sang to his wife and sons.

Every time one of the uncles would sing their part of the song, one of the boys would get up and go to sit with them. By the end of the song, there was one of the boys with every couple. It was picture perfect. They didn't know how or why they did that, but it was truly amazing. The cameras were still rolling and flashes were going off.

When the song was over, they all got up to go. The girls all kissed their husbands and the boys hugged everyone. They met in the middle of the stage, the girls each took the hand of one of the boys, and they headed back towards the pop-up platform. It looked like the little boys had the girls' hands and were leading Marguerite and the aunts from the stage. Right before they reached the platform, they stopped, turning around, and lining up to take a bow and wave to the crowd. Then they turned back around and stepped onto the platform to be dropped down off the stage.

The crowd was still screaming for Marguerite though, chanting her name. They had all been so worried about her for three months. So the girls said, "Go take a bow again."

She went back out to the front of the stage and curtseyed deeply, placing her hands over her heart and bowing her head to them. Then she went to the left of the stage and did the same, and then to the right. Then she headed back to the platform, joining the others, and Jack slowly lowered them off the stage.

When the concert was over, Marguerite was waiting for Chase with his clean t-shirt and a cold towel for his face. He was so happy. "Where are the boys?"

Marguerite told him their bodyguards had taken them back to the hotel because they were spent, and it was too loud for them to be there for the whole concert. They had wanted to go. "I think they wanted us to be alone."

Mike and Alex came to get them to the cars so they wouldn't get stuck in traffic. Chase sat in the car just looking at Marguerite and touching her hair. Finally, he glanced at Mike and Alex. "Okay, eyes up front. I want to kiss my wife!" Everyone started to laugh.

Unthinkable

They had to get back to London by the first week of September so the boys could start school on time. The surgeon finally cleared Marguerite for flying again and both she and Chase thanked him to the high heavens for saving Marguerite's life. He would send her records to her family doctors in Pennsylvania and London.

Before they left, the surgeon said, "I have never seen a family like yours. Your sons, your parents, and the friends you consider brothers and sisters. Just being around you all made me want to be with my family more."

They smiled and said they were truly blessed with the people around them. They shook the surgeon's hand and thanked him one more time before leaving.

They had loved their time in Italy, and adored their new home on the lake, so it was with sadness that they packed up and headed back to London. Life went back to normal for Chase and Marguerite. The boys went back to school. There were endless soccer practices and games they all went to watch. They attended school concerts and meet-the-teacher nights. The boys all got good grades (except in math) and were loved by all the teachers. Chase and Marguerite were told that they had impeccable manners, which they rarely saw in the children they taught, and felt that the other children in their classes were learning from them. It made Chase and Marguerite proud.

Chase went back to the studio, but this time to produce songs for new up-and-coming artists. The guys all seemed to want to do their own projects and discussed it together, and they were all okay with it. They weren't splitting up. They were still going to record, but just not as much. They could slow down and take it easy for a change. Peter even agreed. He didn't think they were over yet, but felt they should move on a bit. It was time. They all seemed happy about it. They were still at the same studio and all together, but just doing different projects. They consulted each other on everything and always remembered that they were one quarter of each other, not one quarter of the band.

Again, time flew by. The Z's were 12 and the M&M's were 8. They all wondered how that had happened. The twins were all so in tune with each other. Chase and Marguerite talked to them about not telling people about their connection to each other. People might not understand and take it the wrong way. They understood completely what they were saying. Again, their parents had forgotten how smart the boys were.

Marguerite and Chase had more alone time than they usually did together. With the boys going to school all day, they got out more. They had romantic lunches—sneaking through the kitchens of various restaurants—and Chase would go with her to the grocers to see Franco and Anna as well. Life was good and everyone was happy.

Chase and the guys had to go to LA for a week to record something. The girls told them to leave them all at home, as they didn't feel like going along. LA had left a bad taste in their mouths after what happened the last time they were there. It was only going to be for a week anyway.

Of course, something happened at home in the middle of their trip. Mike came running into the house one day with a basket in his hand. He had been making his rounds, and when he arrived at the gate to the property, he saw that someone had left a baby in a basket in front of their house. The baby was crying and as white as a sheet. Marguerite picked up the baby. "Call the police."

She realized that the baby was dripping wet. She removed the wet diaper, saw that the baby was a little girl, and almost fainted when she saw the severity of her diaper rash. No wonder the poor baby was crying. She was cold on top of it. Marguerite grabbed a towel, wrapped her in it, and cuddled her in her arms. The baby was so distraught. She wouldn't stop crying. She was cold and hungry and her bottom hurt so badly.

Marguerite called Jeanine and told her to get there yesterday with cream for diaper rash and diapers, baby powder, baby formula, and lotion. She told her what had happened. "Oh, and on your way, please call Cara and Abbey and ask them to go get some baby clothes." At first glance, the baby seemed to be around five or six months old. She was tiny and frail, but her arms and legs seemed quite long. Marguerite suspected she was probably older than she looked. "Seven or eight months. Also sleepers, blankets... anything."

Chase felt that something was wrong. It had woken him up. It was only three in the morning in LA. Drew was rooming with him, and hearing Chase wake up gasping - had woken him. He called home immediately. Marguerite's voice was shaking. She told him that someone had left a baby girl in front of their house. He heard the baby crying in the background. "She was in a basket. Mike called the police and they're on the way. She has horrible diaper rash. She was dripping when I picked her up."

Chase was distressed over this. He loved kids and could not believe this had happened.

Marguerite said, "I'll call you when we see what the police suggest. Jeanine's going to the drug store for diaper rash cream and diapers, and Cara and Abbey are going to get the baby some clothes."

"Were there no clothes in the basket?"

"None. Oh, wait a second," she said. Mike handed her something. "Mike found a note. It says, 'Please take care of my baby. I only have a few days left to live. I have no family but know who you are. Please love her for me! I had nothing to give her. I could not even feed her. Please, please love her for me and take care of her!" Marguerite's voice got weaker and weaker as she read the note. Marguerite and Chase's hearts were breaking. At that moment, they both fell in love with the baby.

There was dead silence on the phone. "Try to help the baby as much as you can," Chase said. "What if they want to take her away? Do you want to give her up?"

Marguerite started crying. "No." She definitely did not want to give her up.

"I'll make arrangements to get home now," Chase said. His voice was shaking. "Don't let them take the baby."

"I won't," she said through her tears.

Jeanine showed up twenty minutes later with what was needed. Thank God, she'd remembered baby bottles. Marguerite was so shaken, she hadn't thought of it. She filled the sink with warm water and asked Jeanine to heat up some milk. She put milk in one bottle and the formula in another one.

The baby was still crying. When she put her in the sink, her diaper rash burned and she became hysterical. Marguerite washed her up as fast as she could. Her hands were shaking.

Then Cara and Abbey arrived, running into the house with the clothes. They all just looked at the poor baby and her diaper rash, and at Marguerite crying at the baby's obvious suffering. Their hearts were breaking. Tears were rolling down their cheeks. Marguerite took the baby out of the sink and dried her off. She rubbed the diaper rash cream all over her bottom and the baby immediately felt better. She calmed down a lot. Next Marguerite applied baby lotion and baby powder and talked soothingly to her, oohing and cooing at her. She combed her fine, light brown hair, and then dressed her in pajamas. Then she wrapped her in a blanket the girls had bought, sat in a chair with her and fed her some milk, and then some formula, while rocking her back and forth. She didn't want to feed her too much. If her stomach was as empty as she thought it was, she would just throw it up. The baby seemed to settle down. Marguerite kept looking at her and smiling and talking to her. The sisters did the same. She rocked the baby in her arms to help her to fall asleep, and the baby went out like a light.

The police had come in briefly while they were bathing her, but quickly followed Mike back out of the room. Mike had been talking to them ever since. They looked at the security camera footage but could not make out anything from any angle.

They finally came back in to the room. "Child services are on the way to take custody of the baby."

"Chase and I want to keep the baby ourselves," Marguerite said, "until the mother can be found."

The police officer opened his mouth to argue with her, but Marguerite was having none of it. "I am not handing her over. The child has been through so much already. She is already stressed, and has finally calmed down and is feeling safe and comfortable. I will not hand her over and have her be traumatized again."

The girls all agreed, standing beside her with their arms crossed, almost daring them to argue.

The officer seemed to be at a bit of a loss. Jeanine called Gail to get someone to come to the house to help them. Gail came right over herself, making the calls en route.

Child services arrived but Marguerite told them she would not let them take the baby. The woman argued, "Legally, we can take it, because it was abandoned and is now a ward of the state."

Marguerite and the girls were so upset, desperate to find a solution. One of the child services women pointed out that her husband wasn't even home to support the decision. "What if he comes home and tells you to give her up?"

Marguerite dialed Chase immediately and put him on speaker. "Chase, child services are here and they want to take the baby."

"Do not let them take the baby from you, Marguerite. I am on my way home. I will be there around six."

Child services said, "Look, this is simply not an option. We cannot leave this baby in your care. You have to surrender it or the police will come and take it away from you. It is not personal. It is the law."

Just then, Gail came running in with Judge Powell on the phone. He asked to speak to child services. Gail handed the phone to the woman and the judge told her that he was granting temporary custody of the child to Marguerite and Chase Martin. He was sending a courier for them to sign the paperwork that would make it legal. "Yes, I understand," the woman said and handed the phone back to Gail, who got back on the phone and thanked the judge profusely.

The woman turned to Marguerite. "It must be nice to have friends in high places."

Marguerite turned white. She was devastated by the disgust and condemnation in the woman's voice and expression. She had to sit down. Cara took the baby from her arms.

Gail stepped closer to the woman. "Judge Powell has no connection to the Martins. I pleaded with him to grant this temporary custody."

"I will be watching you to make sure that you are not abusing that baby." Everyone gasped. It was common knowledge what good parents Chase and Marguerite were.

Chase was still on speaker, and the guys were all listening too.

With a voice that was colder than any of them had ever heard, Chase said, "Thank you for your help. Please get out of my house now." There was a pause, and then he yelled, "Mike! Please escort that woman out of my house!" Marguerite had never heard him raise his voice like that. Never in fourteen years.

Marguerite was relieved when she was gone. The woman had been nasty. It was one thing to do your job, but in a case like that, the woman had no compassion at all and acted like they were inconveniencing her.

She took the phone off speaker and told Chase the woman was gone. She thanked him for stepping in. He told her how angry he was and thanked her for being there and standing her ground. Then he told her they would talk when he got home and that he was four hours away.

Marguerite called the boys' pediatrician to see if he could make a house call. She didn't want to stress the baby out by taking her to the hospital to be checked out. He said he could come over, but that it would have to be after visiting hours because he currently had a waiting room full of little patients. That was fine with her as long as he could make it, and Chase would be home by then.

"How do you think the boys are going to take it?" Abbey asked.

"They probably already know." She didn't think her sons would be surprised, and was silently hoping they would understand that they couldn't let the baby go.

Baby Girl Martin

Gail called Peter. He came right over. He was afraid that if word got out that someone had left a baby on the Martin's doorstep, and they were going to try to keep it, everyone who couldn't take care of their child would do the same thing to all of them. When Peter mentioned that possibility, reality set in. He had to get in touch with child services and make sure that horrible woman did not discuss it with anyone. If she did, it would be a zoo out there. They got in touch with the judge who had granted temporary custody and got him to issue a gag order. After that, no one could discuss it publicly, which made them all feel a little better. Marguerite was afraid the child services woman would do something to jeopardize their chances of keeping the baby. She didn't know why. She didn't even know them.

The boys had soccer practice, so they wouldn't be home until around six thirty. She was hoping Chase would get home first, and he did. Thank God! She was waiting for him. The baby was calm and happy by the time Chase got home. He went to Marguerite immediately and embraced her, holding onto her tightly. She apologized for making him cut his trip short and he said that no apologies were needed. All the guys were with him. The girls were making supper.

Marguerite took Chase right to the sleeping baby.

He looked down at her and nodded. "Here is my daughter." He picked her up and everyone started crying. Marguerite loved the baby already and now so did Chase. She saw it on his face and could hear it in his voice when he talked to the baby. So did everyone else. Everyone was hooked.

Then the guys asked if they could hold her and they did, one at a time. They were smiling from ear to ear. After all, they hadn't held a baby for eight years. Suddenly something occurred to them, and they looked up. "Wait... it's a girl. We don't do girl diapers." Everyone laughed.

Mike and Alex brought the boys home. When they walked in the house, they saw the baby and went right to her. Marguerite and Chase thought they had already known something was going on at the house, but didn't know how much they had felt.

"Can we hold her?" Zac asked. Chase handed the baby over to the boys and told them to be careful and support her head. They looked annoyed. "We know, Dad. We held Mark and Matt all the time."

They sat down with the baby, who didn't cry or fuss at all. She just looked at them all with her big, light brown eyes and laughed and smiled and giggled. The boys were pleased with themselves.

"This is Baby Sarah," Matt said.

"Baby Sarah?" Marguerite asked.

They all said, "Yes. We knew she was coming."

They all had to sit down then. "What do you mean, son?" Chase asked. "How did you know?"

"Baby Margaret told us," Mark said.

They all turned white, and tried to hold back tears. Chase asked if they wanted to tell them more about it.

"No, not yet," they said. "We're trying to figure it out. When it's clearer, we'll talk to you about it then." They all just looked at the boys and then back at each other. As Ed had said many times, it was just *spooky*.

The boys passed the baby around between the four of them. It was amazing how they knew how to take care of her. The baby took to them immediately. She just giggled and smiled every time a different one held her. Then Matt looked at his mom and dad and said, "We don't do girl diapers." All the boys were shaking their heads enthusiastically and everyone laughed again.

In the meantime, Ed arrived and saw everyone there. Chase had called him and filled him in. He went right to Marguerite and held his arms out to her. She walked right into them with tears in her eyes. He looked at Chase and the others and saw that they all looked worried. Next, he went to Chase and embraced his brother. The boys lit up when they saw him.

"Meet our new sister!" they said. Ed went over to them and saw how beautiful the baby was. "I know you'll be great big brothers." They all nodded their heads.

The pediatrician, Dr. Ward, arrived around seven that night. "Tell me what happened," he said.

Marguerite filled him in on everything, even the horrible child services woman. He knew her and knew that she was tough, but he assured them that her main interest really was the welfare of the baby. Marguerite took the baby from the boys and then led the doctor into the den, where he could examine her. Marguerite and Chase were pacing back and forth. Everyone else was too. The boys seemed to be the only ones who were calm.

"What do they know?" Marguerite asked Chase, looking at her sons. "They're so calm." Chase just shook his head and embraced her.

The doctor asked to see them in the den and they both went in. The boys got up to follow them, but the uncles asked them to stay out there with them. They looked at their father, who nodded his head. So they stayed, each clinging to an uncle as they waited for the verdict.

The doctor told Chase and Marguerite that she had done a good job with the diaper rash. He was going to prescribe something a little stronger though. He could see that the baby was malnourished and so he said he would write down the name of a formula they should buy that should help. Her vitals were good, and her heartbeat was strong, but he wanted to get some blood work. The baby could have something wrong with it that he couldn't see in an examination. He also thought that it might help them identify the mother. If the note was accurate, and the mother only had a few days left to live, they could possibly find her in a hospital in the area. He suggested they try hard to find the mother, because otherwise they would be looking over their shoulders for the child's whole life, wondering if someone was going to come and claim her. Marguerite and Chase had never thought of that. This had all happened so quickly. The only thing they really knew was that they couldn't let her go.

Dr. Ward said, "The baby looks to be about nine months old. She's tiny because of the conditions she most likely lived in." It broke Chase and Marguerite's heart. Then the doctor prepared to take the blood samples.

"This is going to pinch her a bit." He was right. The baby screamed, and the boys flew from their uncles' embraces and ran into the room.

"It's okay. It's okay," Chase said. "The doctor had to take a blood test to make sure the baby was healthy." That seemed to calm them down. Once the baby saw the boys, she calmed right down too. Chase and Marguerite just looked at each other.

Setting Up

Marguerite handed Drew a key and asked the brothers and sisters if they could please go to the attic playroom, open the locked door on the left, and bring down the crib and some other things they thought they could use. They had been Baby Margaret's. Marguerite had kept them all of these years. She had packed them up and covered everything to keep them preserved. Chase had always known they were around somewhere. He held his arms out to her and she took the embrace.

The sisters said, "Come on," to the guys and headed upstairs. They opened the door and found everything neatly packed away and covered to keep the dust off. They brought the crib down, cleaned it all up, and put it in Chase and Marguerite's bedroom at Chase's request. They thought that the mattress would be fine for the night but that they should really get a new one. The girls volunteered to go right out and get one. It was still early and the stores would still be open. Besides, they knew they needed more stuff. Sheets and a bumper for the crib, as well as more clothes and blankets. Marguerite sent Chase to the drugstore to pick up the prescription and formula. The guys said that they would go with him. Ed was going to go too but Chase said, "Please stay here with Marguerite and the boys." Ed nodded, and then went over and kissed her cheek. Chase had always loved the connection Marguerite shared with Ed, ever since he had taken her to the hospital when she'd gone into labor. It seemed like a century ago.

Everyone was gone and Ed was holding the baby and rocking her back and forth. It felt natural to him. After all, he had experience with four babies before. Marguerite told Ed what the boys had said about the baby and her name, and that they knew she was coming because baby Margaret had told them. Ed just looked at her with his eyes wide. She nodded. "And I used your term for that. SPOOKY!" He laughed.

He shook his head. "How do you think that happens?"

"I don't know. Who could I ask without someone wanting to commit me?"

"Chase said the same thing. When you were in the operating room in Italy and we were all waiting for news, the boys told us all about those dreams they had, that they shared with you and Chase. He was frantic thinking about it. He asked the exact same thing. Who do you tell about that sort of thing? And could you even tell someone without them wanting to commit you? He was afraid someone would take the boys away from you because they thought you were delusional."

"Chase told me about that. And about what Quinn and Jeanine said."

Ed remembered. "That's right. Quinn said that no one felt any of you were crazy. What you feel is real. What the boys feel is real."

Marguerite nodded and started to cry. Ed went to her. "What you two have is so amazing and precious. I can't begin to imagine how to feel the way you two feel each other." He gave her the baby so that he could hug her more effectively.

The guys came back with the formula and prescription. Marguerite changed the baby and the guys saw the condition of her for the first time. It shocked them. They were offended too, because they already loved her too and thought of her as their niece. Marguerite cleaned her up and put the new cream on her. She was a happy baby. It made everyone smile.

Chase took her as soon as she was changed. Marguerite thought he felt weird about changing her too, and knew that she would have to break him of that.

The girls arrived with about ten packages of stuff. Clothes, blankets, sheets, a new mattress, and a bumper guard. They were pleased with their purchases, and all fussed with the new clothes for a while before putting the crib together. The guys took the baby and went to sit in the family room with the boys.

The courier arrived with the paperwork around eight-thirty. Before they signed it, the brothers asked, "Do you really want to do this?" They both nodded. Like they always did, they all agreed, which made everyone laugh happily. Chase and Marguerite signed it and returned it to Judge Powell.

Chase's mom was traveling, and when they finally reached her to tell her what was happening, she was stunned. She didn't know what to say. Marguerite's parents, as well as her cousins Donna and Sue, were all told and were shocked by what had happened.

They asked her what she was going to do, and she said, "Chase and I agreed we could not give the baby away." She tried to explain to them how they felt, and they understood but were concerned that the mother, or someone posing as the mother, would come and try to take the baby away, which would hurt Marguerite and Chase. But Chase was going to hire someone to investigate and see if they could find the baby's birth mother.

Everyone stayed that first night at the house, including Ed. Of course, the boys were fighting over him, so to please everyone, the five of them slept in the play room. They pulled out the couches into beds and all slept there with him. He was thrilled that they loved him so much and always wondered why they clung to him in particular.

Chase sang to the baby and she fell right to sleep. He laid her in her crib and covered her. They had a bottle ready in case she got up. He was smiling from ear to ear.

Then he locked the door, and Marguerite knew what that meant. He got in bed and Chase just grabbed her and held her in his arms. Marguerite needed to feel him and he knew it. Her body was so stiff and stressed from the events of the day.

As soon as he felt her melt against him, he made love to her.

When they were done, he opened up the door and crawled back into bed. Marguerite held him, wrapping her arms around him, stroking his face and hair. He gave a contented sigh and said, "So, what do you think of Sarah as the baby's name?"

Marguerite considered it. "We certainly need to call her something other than 'the baby'."

She thought about it for a long moment, and felt a smile creep across her face. She loved the name Sarah. "What about Sarah Mary Jessica Amelia Martin."

They never knew how they could ever repay the Dooleys for what they had done for them in Italy when Marguerite was sick. This was how they could honor Mrs. Dooley and the other mothers. Chase loved it.

The baby had a name and was a Martin. Upstairs in the loft where the boys were, they all sat up suddenly.

"What is it?" Ed asked.

"Mom and Dad named the baby." The four boys just looked at each other and smiled. Then they all lay back down, hanging onto Ed, and falling quickly back to sleep.

Ed was awake for a while longer. *Spooky!*

71

Sarah

Chase hired a private investigator to try to find Sarah's birth mother. Dr. Ward called and said Sarah's blood work came back and she was in perfect health. A few levels were down but he felt that, with the new formula she was getting, they should be back up quickly. He also said to start feeding her baby food, but slowly. The formula would not be enough for her once she got her strength back up. Chase went to see Franco and Anna with the boys. He also wanted to tell them what was happening. They were so thrilled for them all, and the boys left with candy as usual. They said *grazie* and Franco and Anna smiled and waved goodbye.

"Dad," Zeke said, "didn't you say this baby food, chicken with peas, was your favorite? I remember you said that to Mom once when she was feeding Mark and Matt."

All he could do was burst out laughing. He remembered texting Marguerite and telling her how awful she was for feeding them that. He laughed again and the boys just looked at him. He didn't say anything after that. He just walked in the house smiling and laughing. Zeke repeated the story to Marguerite and she burst out laughing too and had to walk away. She remembered the text also.

Dr. Ward was a big help in his suggestions about finding the baby's birth mother. The investigator had the note that was left with Sarah. He had all the hospitals on alert, looking out for a woman who was devastatingly ill. After only a week, someone came in with a short time to live. They checked the woman's DNA against Sarah's and it was a ninety-nine percent match. Marguerite and Chase froze. They called their lawyer, Colin Baker, and Peter to figure out how they should go about approaching her. They couldn't call the hospital to see what exactly was wrong with her because of all the privacy laws, so Colin spoke to the judge and he suggested they just go visit her and see if she gave out any information herself. He didn't know what else they could do. For now, all they knew was that Sarah's birth mother was in the hospital. They still didn't know how ill she actually was.

Marguerite called the girls to tell them. She and Chase were shaking. The family came back over and they all discussed it with Colin and Peter.

"If she is that ill," Colin said, "we might want to have paperwork ready for her to sign, relinquishing her rights as Sarah's mother and turning her over to you." It sounded so cold. Relinquishing!

"If she were willing to sign them," Colin continued, "the child services woman would have to be present so she could confirm that you weren't trying to coerce the mother into giving up the child."

They all nearly dropped when they heard that. This wasn't good. Colin just looked at Peter, who explained, "Chase threw her out of the house when she tried to take the baby away."

"That was unfortunate, because now you're going into that room with a woman who already has it out for you."

The brothers understood but couldn't fault Chase for what had happened. "If he didn't throw her out, we all would have."

Colin shrugged. "Then let's hope for the best."

He suggested that they ask the judge if he could also be present, which could really help them. "Because he was the one who granted you temporary custody, his neck will be on the line if the mother is not that ill and wants her daughter back."

Marguerite and Chase got annoyed when he called Sarah that woman's daughter, but they knew it was true. Little Sarah wasn't their daughter yet, and wouldn't be until and unless the paperwork was signed.

Lastly, Colin suggested that a police officer accompany them, in case things started going bad. Marguerite sighed. They now would have a whole posse going into that poor woman's room. It was so frustrating, but she knew everything had to be done legally or they would lose Sarah.

"I will have the paperwork ready by morning," Colin said. "If the woman is as ill as she said in the note, you should just hope she's still alive by morning." It sent chills up everyone's spine when he said that. He didn't sugar coat anything.

The next morning, everyone was up and ready to go. No one got any sleep. The brothers and sisters would hold Sarah in a waiting room. Thank God the boys had to go to school. Colin had the paperwork ready. He contacted the police, and the patrolman who had responded to the initial call by Mike would meet them at the hospital. Colin also contacted child services and the woman who was at the house would also meet them there. The judge didn't have an issue being there either. They were all to meet in a conference room first so they could talk and decide how they were going to approach the situation. The birth mother's doctor would be present too.

So many people! Chase thought. They all met and were on time. Marguerite and Chase were visibly shaken by the whole experience. They were walking on egg shells and knew it. They knew they could not lose Sarah.

Colin spoke first. "These are my clients, Mr. and Mrs. Chase Martin." They all shook hands. "A week ago today someone left an approximately nine-month-old baby girl on the door steps of the Martins' house. They left a note." He produced it and showed it to the doctor and the judge. Everyone else had seen it.

The doctor interrupted. "There are two men standing outside this room. Does anyone know why?"

"The Martins travel everywhere with a bodyguard. So do their four sons. It is not an issue with any of them." It finally hit the doctor exactly who they were. He apologized profusely.

Colin continued, addressing the doctor. "Is the baby's mother coherent?" The doctor said, "Yes."

"Is she gravely ill, as the note stated?"

"Yes."

The judge intervened. "Can you elaborate? Does she have days, weeks, years?" He looked down at his hands. "I know it sounds cruel but I have to know."

Because he was the judge, the doctor decided to answer. "Hours."

Marguerite started to cry. Chase just put his arm around her and kissed her head.

"Based on the note she left," the judge continued, "her intent was for the Martins to take custody of the baby. We need to see her to confirm that is what was intended."

"How do you want to proceed?" the doctor asked.

"Let's let the Martins go in to talk to her."

The judge nodded to the doctor. "It might be best if you were present. The rest of us could wait outside."

The judge looked at Chase. "Mr. Martin, I recommend that you simply talk to her and tell her not to be upset that you've found her. It should give her solace to know her baby is well and will be taken care of."

Chase nodded.

He continued. "At that point, if you think she can handle it, ask about the baby's father. If he is not in the picture, find out if she would sign adoption papers, giving you the right to raise the baby." He turned to the doctor. "One more question. Is there any cure, or any way for her to survive the illness she has?"

"No," the doctor said, "none."

Marguerite and Chase were shaken. They felt so badly for the woman.

"And is it something that her daughter will have to watch out for genetically?"

The doctor shook his head. "It is not that sort of illness."

They all walked to her room and realized that they didn't even know her name. They composed themselves, quietly knocked on the door, and walked in.

The woman's eyes went wide when she saw them and she started crying. Marguerite went right over to her and took her hand and held it. "Please don't cry and worry yourself over our visit."

"How could I not after what I did with my baby?"

Chase stepped closer. "What you did was what every mother would do. You saved her."

The woman nodded her head, and felt that they understood why she'd done what she'd done.

"Why us?" Marguerite asked.

"I know your whole history, and after you lost your baby girl all those years ago, I thought that maybe you would welcome another girl."

Chase put his hand on the woman's shoulder. "Even if we didn't lose our daughter, we still would have taken your child in."

The woman smiled at them both. She could see the love between them and it warmed her dying heart.

"What's your name?" Chase asked.

"Sarah."

Marguerite tried not to hyperventilate at that moment. She just kept breathing in and out.

Chase's face went gray. "That's the name we were going to give the baby. Sarah Mary Jessica Amelia, after our mothers and someone who helped us out when we really needed help. Now she will be named after you as well."

Sarah cried tears of joy. They tried to calm her. Chase said, "Do you really want us to have her?"

"Yes."

"Can you tell us about Sarah's father?"

"He was killed in Afghanistan before my daughter was born. Neither of us have any family. That's why I brought her to you."

"We have papers for you to sign, making Sarah our daughter. Will you sign them?"

She cried. "Thank you. Yes. Thank you for taking her."

Marguerite was crying and so was Chase. "We already love her, and so do our boys. She has so many family members now. She will be taken care of forever."

They told Sarah that the judge who had approved temporary custody of the baby was there, and so was their lawyer, who had prepared the adoption paperwork, and the child services representative.

"Would it be all right for them to come in?"

She agreed.

Colin told her what the paper work entailed and the judge confirmed it, so she knew it was legal.

She was ready to sign, but the child services woman gave her one last chance to back out. "You understand what you are doing, correct?"

"Yes," she said loudly, so they could all hear her. After a long moment, the child services woman nodded. Sarah signed the papers.

Everyone breathed a sigh of relief.

Then Chase asked, "Would you like to see baby Sarah?"

"May I?"

Chase texted Quinn the room number and told him to bring her up.

The judge and Colin left with the paperwork to get it filed. The policeman shook everyone's hands and said he'd say a prayer for her. Peter just waited outside the door. The doctor stayed.

Quinn arrived holding Sarah. Everyone in the room was crying. Chase took baby Sarah and kissed her. Marguerite did too.

He said to baby Sarah, "This is your mother. Her name is Sarah too."

Everyone waiting in the hall turned white and started crying.

Sarah reached out to her daughter, who was smiling and giggling. "She's happy. She never smiled for me or giggled." She stared at her daughter with love and amazement in her eyes.

"Would you like to meet my brothers and sisters?" Chase asked. "They're already aunts and uncles to her and love her just like we do."

Sarah had tears in her eyes. "Yes please." She handed the baby back to Marguerite, and slumped back against her pillow. She seemed to be losing ground even as they watched.

Blake and Abbey came in first, kissed her, and said, "We will always make sure baby Sarah is happy and we'll always help take care of her."

"Thank you so much."

Drew and Cara came in next and did the same. They kissed her and said, "We're honored to be baby Sarah's aunt and uncle, and we already love her."

She just nodded, with tears rolling down her cheeks.

Quinn and Jeanine came in last and kissed her. "We love baby Sarah with all our hearts, and will remember her mother always in our prayers."

"Thank you." She seemed to be running out of strength. They had to lean close in order to hear her. "All of you, for the love my baby will have from now on."

Her eyes closed. They stood in silence as she became more and more still. Her doctor stepped forward, checking the monitors. "It's not going to be long now, I'm afraid."

They all gathered around her bed and reached out, touching her gently, reassuring her that she wasn't alone. In tears, they all thanked her for the gift she had given them, and stayed with her until she passed away.

The doctor, still stunned by their display of loyalty and love, pronounced the time of death, and solemnly, they all left the room.

Chase told Peter to make the arrangements to have her buried near Baby Margaret. After all, she was family now.

Chase and Marguerite called George and Amelia Dooley, and told them what had happened. They were stunned. Then they told them the full name they had in mind for their new daughter—Sarah Mary Jessica Amelia

Martin—and asked if they would be offended to have her name included. Before this opportunity had arisen, they hadn't known how they could ever repay them for the kindness they showed them when Marguerite was ill. The Dooleys were so happy, surprised, and incredibly moved by the kind gesture.

Time to Go

The brothers finally got to buy the battery-operated sports car they'd fought over twelve years ago. When Sarah turned 2, they arrived at the house with it. It was pink. There seemed to be a lot of pink going on at the Martins' now. They had turned one of the bedrooms into a pink girly-girl room. The aunts showered Sarah with all the latest styles. She was already a fashionista and the happiest baby ever, especially when her brothers were around.

They loved her and felt like her protectors. Every now and then, they even gave their parents a little attitude about what they should or shouldn't be doing with Sarah. Chase and Marguerite had to settle them down in those moments, and say, "Let's remember who the parents are in this house!" Then they knew they'd overstepped their boundaries.

As with all the boys, time flew by. Zac and Zeke were headed off to boarding school. Marguerite thought she was going to lose it when they'd told her they wanted to go to a boarding school. All their friends from school were continuing on there though, and they wanted to as well. Chase was beside himself and talked to his brothers about it. They were shaken but said that he had to let them go. The boys were so smart and Chase had to let them go their own way. He knew they were right but didn't have to like it.

They were leaving two brothers and a sister at home who were equally devastated that they were going. Zac and Zeke talked to Mark and Matt about leaving. "You know you're always with us, and you know we'll continue to feel each other no matter how far away we are."

Mark and Matt nodded, knowing they were right, and feeling better about letting them leave.

"Besides," Zac said, "someone has to be here to take care of Sarah and Mom and Dad." Sarah was 4 already. Mark and Matt agreed to step up to the plate and take over for the Z's.

When they were leaving, Zac and Zeke said to their parents, "Thank you for letting us go. We feel how much this is hurting you and we don't mean to hurt you. We just know that we have to do this."

With that, Marguerite and Chase remembered that their children could feel their pain. They felt horrible. Then they realized that, if the Z's felt them hurting, Mark and Matt were feeling it too.

Chase sighed. "Yes, we are hurting, but do you know why?"

They nodded. "We love you too," Zac said.

Zeke shrugged. "How could we not?" That meant more to them at that moment than anything. "You will come visit us whenever we have something going on though, right?" He sounded nervous and uncertain.

Chase smiled, remembering that they really were still quite young, regardless of their maturity in other ways. "Absolutely," Chase said. "And if you ever want us to come up to see you 'just because', you only have to ask and we'll be there."

The boys promised they would be home for all the holidays, even the American Thanksgiving holiday they celebrated every year. After hearing that, Marguerite and Chase were ready to let them go.

If that wasn't hard enough, the aunts and uncles (including Ed) were outside waiting to say goodbye. Everyone tried to put on a brave face until the car pulled away. Then they all lost it.

They openly wept in front of Sarah and the M&M's. They just couldn't control themselves. Mark and Matt took Sarah up to the playroom so that everyone could grieve over the Z's leaving. They didn't have to call them back down once they'd composed themselves. They already knew that everything was fine.

Father/Daughter

Matt and Mark were 19 and studying at the University of London, and Zac and Zeke were studying at Oxford, working towards doctorate degrees in math. Chase and all the brothers had just shaken their heads when they told them they were studying math by choice. They had told Chase that something had just clicked one day and all of a sudden they were able to grasp the field and they loved it. Whatever block they'd had in the past was just gone, like a switch being turned off. Chase and Marguerite were so proud of them. Their boys had all excelled in school and were good boys.

Sarah was now 13 and just full of surprises for Chase and Marguerite. She came home from school one day and was very worried.

"Do you want to tell me about it?" Marguerite asked.

"Yes, please. Will you make us some tea so we can sit and talk about it like two girls?"

Marguerite was smiling from ear to ear. She and her daughter were going to sit together and talk. Like two girls! After four sons, she absolutely loved the idea.

The tea was poured and scones were put on the table, and they sat and ate. Marguerite waited to hear about what she wanted to tell her.

"There is a father/daughter dance at the school next month."

"Really?"

Sarah nodded. "I want to ask Dad to take me."

Marguerite was confused. "Sarah, your dad would be happy and proud to take you. Do you think he wouldn't go?"

"Well, I was hoping he would, but I've always heard him telling Uncle Drew, Uncle Blake, and Uncle Quinn that he hated dancing."

Marguerite tried not to laugh. "Not that kind of dancing." She took a sip of her tea and explained. "When they'd perform in concert, sometimes Patrick the choreographer would want them to all do the same things on stage during a song. Like dance moves. Your father and all your uncles would say "Absolutely not. No way. We don't dance.""

Sarah thought back to the things she'd heard over the years and realized that her mom was right. This wasn't going to be that kind of dancing. She let out a sigh of relief and they both started to laugh.

Chase got home and heard them laughing in the kitchen. He came in and saw them sharing a nice moment. It warmed his heart to see it.

Marguerite looked at Sarah. "Should I leave you to speak to your father?" She nodded.

Marguerite got up, smiling from ear to ear. Chase looked at her questioningly. "Sarah would like to talk to you." Chase knew it wasn't bad, because no one was crying and both his girls were smiling.

"Dad, can I get you some tea?"

Marguerite was behind Sarah, nodding at Chase to say yes to the tea and he decided to go along.

"Yes, I would love some."

With that, Marguerite headed to the family room to wait until she was summoned back to the kitchen.

They were both drinking their tea. Sarah took a deep breath and let it out slow. "Dad? Next month there's a father/daughter dance at school. I was wondering if you would take me. I would be so happy if you would take me."

Tears welled up in his eyes, and in a quiet voice that was almost a whisper, he said, "I would be so honored to take you to the dance." Sarah started to cry and so did Chase. He couldn't hold it in any more. Marguerite was in the other room crying.

Sarah got up and ran to her father, who was waiting with open arms for her, and they just hugged and hugged.

"I love you, Sarah, with all my heart. I would do anything for you."

"I love you too, Dad." Then she yelled, "Mom, come back now! Dad said yes!"

Chase and Marguerite just laughed.

The preparations for the dance were elaborate. Marguerite called the school to see if there was anything she needed to know about the dance, like whether or not Chase should wear a suit and how dressed up the girls got. In the preparations, she discovered something else, which would be a surprise for Sarah.

All the aunts went with Marguerite and Sarah to help pick out a dress, shoes, and accessories. It was a big production. Sarah told them exactly how she wanted her hair and makeup done, in detail. The girl talk was so exciting after four boys. Then they all went to lunch at their favorite restaurant, overwhelming Rocco with their excited chatter, telling him they were celebrating a successful shopping trip.

Chase got a new suit too. He insisted on it, and all the brothers went with him to pick it out—like he was ten years old. Later, he admitted that it was fun.

Of course, the boys all webcammed them the night of the dance and saw their dad pacing back and forth in the kitchen, waiting for his daughter to come down so they could go. Everyone was waiting excitedly, and they said to him, "If you don't stop pacing, we are going to tie you down." They all laughed. Then she came down. She was beautiful! Chase looked at Marguerite. "She looks just like you!"

Nothing could have been a higher compliment, and Sarah knew it. Her long, light brown hair was pulled off her face and curls cascaded down the back of her beautiful pink dress, which had rhinestone flowers all around the skirt's hem. All their jaws dropped, looking back and forth between Marguerite and Sarah. They all said quietly, "She does look like you!" It was almost eerie, and they all tried not to look freaked out about it.

Chase told his daughter, "You look so beautiful, I don't know if I want to let you out of the house!"

All the brothers agreed. Sarah smiled and smiled. She was incredibly happy and excited.

"I have a surprise for you," Chase said.

Her eyebrows shot up, surprised. "You do? What is it, Dad?"

He pulled out a box from the florist and handed it to her. She opened it up and saw a wrist corsage of baby pink roses, with a bow in the center that was covered in rhinestones. Her eyes got wide. "It matches my dress! How did you know?"

Everyone was laughing as he took it and placed it on her wrist. She was beaming!

He took her hand and placed it on his arm, and together they went to the waiting car. Nick would drive them, and Mike and Alex would accompany them—staying in the background as always. They had huge smiles on their faces as they watched them approach the car, and complimented her on how beautiful she looked. On cloud nine, Sarah practically floated into the car. Then off they went.

Inside the house, the girls were just relieved the preparations were over. They had loved every minute of it, but it was emotionally exhausting. "We are never going to survive dressing her in her wedding gown." With that, they all started to cry and went into a group hug.

The uncles shook their heads. "Don't even think about it. She is never getting married, if we have anything to say about it."

Sarah's brothers chimed in over the webcam. "Right. That is never going to happen." That made everyone laugh.

Chase and Sarah arrived home safely. They'd had a wonderful time. Sarah hugged her dad tightly and thanked him again for taking her to the dance. She told him she loved him and then looked him in the eye. "Can I talk to Mom now?"

He laughed, knowing he was being dismissed so that they could have some girl talk. He nodded, kissed her cheek, and headed upstairs to change out of his suit.

Sarah was beaming. She grabbed her mom and gave her a quick squeeze before letting her go. "Everyone loved my dress and hair, and my flowers were the nicest ones there! And Dad and I danced so much we had to take a break!"

Marguerite just kept smiling. She was very happy for her. She pulled her daughter back into a warm hug.

"Thank you, Mom, for everything you do for me." Sarah pulled back and kissed her on the cheek. "I love you."

Marguerite could see happy tears welling up in her daughter's eyes as she pulled away, flew up the stairs, and went off to bed.

When Marguerite got to her bedroom, she closed the door and locked it. Chase started laughing and held out his arms to his wife. They settled down in bed, and he told her all about their evening and seemed very pleased with himself. Marguerite told him how happy Sarah was, and how blessed they were to have her.

Then she leaned closer and told him how handsome he had looked in his new suit.

"Really? You think I'm handsome?"

Grinning, he kissed her deeply and she responded with enthusiasm.

Much later, after unlocking the door, they went to sleep as they always did, with arms and legs wrapped around each other.

Date 74

Sarah was now 16. Zac and Zeke were 26 and Matt and Mark were 22. Both Z's were professors at Oxford. The M&M's had decided they were going to stay in school also. They had both decided that they wanted to be pediatricians. When they told their mother and father, they were stunned, having had no idea that was the field they would choose. They were so proud of them. Like their father, they loved children and that had prompted their choice. Everyone was so proud of all the boys.

Sarah was invited to a formal dance at school—*by a boy!* Chase started stuttering and stammering when he tried to respond to the news that his little girl had a *date!*

"B-but I-I... b-but... " He was walking in circles in the kitchen, and Marguerite was laughing at him.

Sarah was just looking at him with her head cocked to one side like a confused puppy. "Like, what is the problem, Dad?"

Just then, they heard a call coming in on the webcam TV on the counter, and Marguerite's phone was ringing off the hook. It was the M&M's on the phone and the Z's on webcam. They answered both calls, and put Mark and Matt on speaker.

"What do you all want?"

"Well," Matt said, "we felt something was wrong." Everyone just started laughing.

"What did you feel?"

"Is Dad all right?" Zeke asked. "We felt him."

Chase was sitting down now and shaking his head, smiling. He couldn't wait to see how they would react to Sarah's news. Marguerite knew what he was thinking and started to laugh.

"Your sister has a date!" Chase said.

All at once, they were all talking over each other. "No way!"

"She is not going out with anyone!"

The Z's immediately said, "We are coming right home!"

The M&M's said, "Yes! Us too! We will be there tomorrow!"

Chase and Marguerite couldn't stop laughing. Sarah just looked at everyone and was stunned. She hadn't thought twice about the date, but now, with their reactions, she didn't know what to make of it.

Marguerite said, "You can all come home. Your father and I miss you. Then we can all talk about this date." Everyone felt a little better.

Well, Marguerite thought, *if I had known they would all come home because their sister had a date, I would have told her to go out sooner.* She laughed to herself. Chase called his brothers immediately and told them that the boys were on their way home. When they found out what was going on, Sarah could hear her uncles freaking out, and her aunts laughing at them. Sarah went to her room and locked the door. It was like the end of the world out there. The women couldn't seem to stop laughing at the men.

About a half hour later, Marguerite and all the aunts went to Sarah's room and knocked on the door. "Let us in, my love," Marguerite said. Sarah opened the door. Then they all laughed together and Sarah felt better. They told her not to worry about it. Everything would be fine. The men just needed attitude adjustments.

The boys all came home and it was a great reunion, with everyone loving being together again. Marguerite sat the men down and got serious with them. "Sarah has a date to a holiday formal. We are not going to interfere. She wants to go. The boy is nice. We know his parents and that is the end of the story. You will all be home when this happens, because it's during our American Thanksgiving holiday weekend. So you will be right here, just in case she needs her brothers."

They did not like that at all. They were glad they would at least be home but were not happy that she was being allowed to go.

Marguerite rolled her eyes at them. "What do you want us to do? Put her in a nunnery and cloister her up?"

They all nodded their heads. They looked completely serious, and it was so obviously ridiculous that they all started laughing again.

Matt had a great idea. "We are home now, so one of us could take her out on a date and show her how she should be treated. That way, if her date doesn't measure up, she can kick him to the curb." The brothers all loved the idea. They called their sister to the kitchen.

"We will sanction this date, but only if you will allow us to take you out on a date first to show you how you should be treated and what to expect." She started laughing but saw that they were serious. She agreed.

Her cell phone rang and as she answered, she noticed that Zac had his phone in his hand as well.

"Hello?" she said.

"Sarah? This is Zac Martin. I was wondering if you are free tomorrow evening."

She said she was, and he continued. "Well then, would you like to go for pizza around six?"

"Yes, that would be nice."

"Okay, I will pick you up."

Feeling foolish, she said, "I look forward to it. Goodbye." They both hung up.

Chase was pleased with his sons. They had taken right over and let him completely off the hook. If Sarah didn't like what was going on, she'd be mad at them and not him. More importantly, he thought, the practice date would really help her to understand how well she deserved to be treated.

At 5:55 the next day, the doorbell rang. Chase opened the door and Zac was standing there, looking dapper. "Hello, I'm Zac Martin. I'm here to pick Sarah up." Chase let him in and shook his hand. All the uncles and aunts were there, trying not to laugh. Sarah was standing in the foyer, waiting for him.

Chase said, "Please come in and meet Sarah's mother."

Zac followed Chase into the kitchen where everyone was, with Sarah in tow.

"This is Sarah's mother, Marguerite."

Zac extended his hand to shake hers. "Hello, Mrs. Martin. I'm Zac Martin." Chase introduced him to all the aunts and uncles.

Sarah tried to be patient with the silliness that was going on. She really appreciated all the effort they were going to, but thought that this part was a bit much. Chase wasn't done yet, asking him a series of questions: Where will you be going? What time do you think you will be home? Blah blah blah...

Everyone had stupid grins on their faces. When they finally let them out of the house, Zac walked Sarah to the car and opened the door for her. She got in and he closed it behind her, and then went around to his side of the car, got in, and they drove off.

When they parked at the restaurant, he said, "I will get the door for you," and ran around to her side of the car and opened the door. He held out his hand and she took it, letting herself be helped out of the car. He opened the door to the restaurant too, allowing her to enter first, and then he followed. During dinner, he asked her questions about herself, and listened attentively to her answers. After they ate, he paid the bill and the same process started over again with him opening the doors for her.

When they got to the house, eleven sets of eyes were peeping out the front windows of the house.

Zac came around and opened her door again and helped her out. He walked her to the front door, where the light was on. "I had a really nice time tonight, Sarah. Thank you for coming out with me."

Sarah was incredibly happy. She was out with her brother. She adored all of her brothers. She knew what they were trying to do and really appreciated it.

He went to hug her and gave her a kiss on the cheek. Then Sarah went in the house... and cried.

Zac came right in after her, because the date was over. He saw her crying and watched as she ran to her father, who had his arms open for her.

"What's wrong?" Chase asked. "Did he try to take advantage of you?" Everyone started laughing, which settled her down.

Sarah looked at her four brothers. "I love you all so much. You've all taken care of me since I was a baby. I've missed you and am so overwhelmed right now. You all came home for me. For me! Because you all worry about me. I *feel* you worrying about me."

They all looked at her. "You feel us?"

"Yes! I know when you're upset or when you're worried about something."

Marguerite looked at Chase, and Chase just looked at the boys. The boys were looking at each other. They all knew they had to sit down and talk it out.

The aunts and uncles stood up. "We're going to get going." They hugged everyone, but when they came to Marguerite and Chase, they hugged them tightly and kissed them, and told them they loved them.

Chase said to Quinn, "Please wait for our call."

"I'll be ready."

The Final Answer

Everyone was in the kitchen sitting around the table, and Chase said to Sarah, "What did you mean when you said you feel them?"

"Dad, I don't want you to think I'm crazy."

"We don't think you are crazy, my love," Chase said. "Just tell us. It's okay. Just tell us."

"I always feel them."

Chase looked at the boys. "Do you feel your sister?"

They all put their heads down and couldn't look at their parents. "Yes."

Chase and Marguerite sat straight up in their seats, not believing what they were hearing. They had kept this a secret? This whole time? Marguerite got up and Chase followed her. He grabbed her and took her in his arms. They were both so angry and hurt.

Chase shook his head. "How long have you been feeling her?"

"Since the beginning. Since she first came to us."

"And you didn't say anything to us?" Chase couldn't believe it. "After all we've been through, with your mother and well, just everything, you didn't ever think to have that conversation with us? We talk about everything! This was just way too big for you to leave out!" He was angry!

Sarah was just looking back and forth between her parents and her brothers. Marguerite noticed her confusion. "Sarah, just give us one minute, and we'll get back to you, I promise. Then you'll understand."

Marguerite was just staring at Chase; all the color had drained from her face. Her legs went to jelly. She was suddenly holding onto the counter to keep herself up, and he wrapped his arms around her again, and caught her. He knew what she was feeling. He felt it too. They had been betrayed by their own sons.

The boys got up immediately and ran to the both of them, feeling the betrayal through their bond even without them saying anything.

"No, Mom!" Zeke said. "We weren't betraying you or Dad! We talked about it and felt that it was too much to tell you both. Sarah came to us." Sarah knew all about how she had come to be their daughter. *"She came to us!"*

Marguerite knew what he was trying to say, and that he was trying not to hurt Sarah's feelings. Marguerite hadn't given birth to Sarah. In tears now, they all sat back down.

"Dad," Mark said, "how could we tell you that we felt Sarah? Think about it." He was trying, and so was Marguerite. They calmed down and looked at Sarah.

"How are you feeling?" Chase asked her.

"I think I understand more now," she said. "I'm not scared about it."

Marguerite said, "Do you understand that what we feel is a connection we all have?"

She said that yes, she knew. "I understand how you didn't think I would have that same connection because I wasn't really—"

"No, don't say it," Chase interrupted. "You are our daughter. You always have been and always will be."

"I am not a blood relative though," Sarah said. "I know I'm your daughter, and I love being your daughter," she glanced at the boys, "and your sister. You never made me feel like I wasn't, and neither did any of my aunts or uncles. What's more important than anything else, Mom and Dad, is that I know I belong here with you. I know I belong to you. I know I belong here. I know it in here." She pointed to her heart.

Then she got up and went to Zac, placing her hand on his heart. "And in here." She did the same to each of her brothers in turn, touching their hearts and telling them that she belonged there. When she reached her parents, and did the same, it got to be too much for her, and she just collapsed in her mother's arms. Everyone at the table just cried. They couldn't hold it in any more.

Chase looked at all of his children. "Your mother and I always wanted a big family, and here you all are. I'm sorry for getting cross with you."

"We deserved it," Zac said. "Holding that back from you. But we were only trying to protect you both."

"I have been telling you since you were born to take care of your mother when I'm gone to work," Chase said. "Then when Mark and Matt were born, I told you to take care of your mother and brothers. The same when Sarah came to us. That is exactly what you were doing. I know that now."

"Do you want to call Uncle Quinn now?" Matt asked.

"Yes. Could you call him for us?"

Matt nodded and made the call. Quinn and Jeanine had been waiting to hear from them and came right over.

Chase explained to Quinn that Sarah had the same connection to all of them that they had to each other.

Quinn didn't seem surprised. "Don't you remember when Sarah came to you? Every time she saw the boys she calmed right down."

Marguerite and Chase looked at each other. "Now that you mention it, we do remember that."

"And how they knew Sarah's name?"

Mark nodded. "Baby Margaret told us." The boys all remembered saying that.

Marguerite asked the question that she had always wondered about. "How did baby Margaret tell you?"

"We just felt it," Mark said. "Somehow we knew. We still can't explain it. We all just felt that it was her telling us."

Quinn smiled at them. "You know that we've always told you the connection you all had to each other was a gift from God."

Marguerite and Chase nodded their heads.

"Well now you know."

Chase frowned. "Know what?"

"That there was one more gift. Your connections to each other and to all the boys were all gifts, and now you have one more." He looked at Sarah. "One more connection making that bond even larger and greater. One more gift!"

Quinn waited for that to sink in, and then continued. "When the boys fall in love and want to marry, who's to say they won't find someone just like them? Someone who feels them like you all feel each other. I'm guessing there are more people out there like you. This gift is not exclusive to just you." He looked at everyone around the room.

They had never thought about it before.

"Sarah was led to you because she is like you. Think about it. She was led right to you, and you knew she would be your daughter the minute you saw her. Didn't you?"

Marguerite and Chase nodded. He was starting to make sense.

"You all belong to one another. Sarah was yours the minute you saw her," he said. "She was her brothers' the minute they saw her. Even as a baby, she knew all of you were hers."

Everyone was crying, even Quinn and Jeanine, but they were happy tears. A lot of hugging was going on.

Quinn and Jeanine started getting ready to go.

"Don't you want to stay?" Chase asked, surprised.

Quinn looked around and at Jeanine and then said, "Not this time. I think you're done needing me now, and you'll all be just fine."

It had been a stressful night, but now they all felt a kind of peace surrounding them that they couldn't explain. They all hugged and kissed each other goodnight and said I love you to each other, with the boys and Sarah paying particular attention to their parents.

When they all retired, Chase closed the door to their bedroom and locked it. Marguerite laughed. She held her arms out to him and he undressed as he walked over to her.

She wrapped her arms around him. "I love you so much, Chase. You are the very air I breathe."

Chase looked up at his wife. "I love *you* so much, Marguerite. And you are the very air I breathe."

And they made love.

When they were done, Chase opened the door and there were five "children" sitting on the floor outside their room, waiting for them to open the door.

"If you didn't unlock that door in ten minutes we were going to pound on it," Zac said, with a playful grin on his face. Everyone laughed, remembering all the time that had passed, and the good times they'd all shared.

They all climbed to their feet, a little more slowly than they had when they were just young kids waiting in the hall for a final hug goodnight, but they all jumped in bed with their parents just like they always had. This time though, instead of the boys squeezing in between Mom and Dad, they put Sarah in the middle between them, and then sandwiched the three of them from the outside. Their arms were all wrapped around each other. Everything was exactly as it should be.

They were the Martins. The wife and children of Chase Martin of the Band 4.

Chase looked around at all of his children, and then smiled happily at his wife.

"Look what we did!"

Epilogue

All the doors on the penthouse floor of the hotel were open. Everyone was walking in and out of each other's rooms. Vita was doing her hair, which would be pulled back off her face and secured with a clip, where a pearl tiara would be placed, holding the ten-foot-long veil, which would also act as her train. Her hair was long, and Vita had placed curls all down her back and sprayed them so they would last the day. Her gown left her shoulders bare, and had a lace bodice with pearls all over it. Lace and pearls trimmed the bottom of the gown, which flowed when she walked. There were one hundred and twenty satin buttons that could only be buttoned up with the help of a knitting needle.

The photographers from *Citizens* magazine of the US and *Greetings* magazine of London were snapping pictures left and right.

Then a photographer said, "Mr. Martin, can we get a picture of you handing your daughter her bridal bouquet?"

That's when the whole room lost it. Marguerite was crying and so was Chase. The tears would not stop, and all the aunts and uncles were beside themselves. The Z's and M&M's and their wives all had to walk away. They couldn't believe this day was here. They felt like they were losing her, even though the marriage meant Chase and Marguerite were gaining another son, the boys were gaining another brother, and the aunts and uncles were gaining another nephew.

The flower girls all came in to take some pictures. The group was made up of 8-year-old Margaret, who was Zac's daughter, 8-year-old Mary, who was Zeke's daughter, Mark's daughter Jess, who was 6, and Matt's daughter Amelia, who was 5. They were all beautiful little girls.

They were also the apple of their grandfather's eyes, and called him Papa with great affection. Four girls!

Jeanine whispered to Marguerite, with the other sisters listening in, "I cannot believe how much she looks like you. It's not just because she chose to wear your wedding gown. She truly looks like you." All the sisters nodded in agreement, while trying to wipe away their tears without wrecking their makeup.

It was time to go to the hotel's chapel, where Father Cummings would be waiting to officiate the wedding of Sarah Martin, just as he had done with her brothers, Zac, Zeke, Mark, and Matt.

Security was tight but they made it to the chapel without being noticed. Everyone took their seats. The flowergirls did a fabulous job of walking down the aisle and throwing rose petals, and then the doors to the chapel closed, giving the bride some privacy to prepare for her grand entrance. Vita fixed her veil and gown so it would flow when she walked, just like she had done for her mother before her.

The doors opened, and Sarah and Chase started walking down the aisle. They could see everyone looking back to see them. Sarah was gripping her father's arm so tightly he didn't think he would have any circulation left in it by the time they arrived at the front of the chapel. He tilted his head to her and told her she was the most beautiful bride he had ever seen... except for her mother, which made her smile and calm down.

Tears streamed down Chase's face, and many people in the aisles (including Sarah's brothers and uncles) were crying along with him. Then he saw Josh, who would be his daughter's husband in a few minutes, and saw that he was crying too. He immediately felt better.

When they got to the front, Father Cummings asked, "Who gives this woman to be married to this man?"

"Her mother and I do," Chase announced, loudly. He turned to kiss her and then whispered in her ear, "Your mother and I will always be here for you. No matter what, no matter when, no matter where. You will always be our daughter. We love you." Chase silently thanked his father-in-law, Joe, who had helped him know what to say—he'd told Marguerite the same thing when he'd given her away to Chase.

It was such an emotional day for everyone. Chase and Marguerite got back to their room when everything was over and barricaded the door, because they didn't know if any of the boys were going to pull something.

Chase held his arms out to Marguerite and she gladly went to him. She needed his embrace. She cried but he didn't. "How come you're taking this so lightly?" she asked.

"For two reasons: First, when I was walking up the aisle with Sarah, I could see that Josh had tears streaming down his face. I knew at that moment that he was right for Sarah and would love her and take good care of her."

Marguerite kissed him just for saying that. "And the second reason?"

He pulled her down on the bed and started laughing. She just looked at him, puzzled.

"Because now that poor guy has to get her out of one hundred and twenty satin buttons, that take three minutes per button to unbutton."

Marguerite just laughed. "Chase, I gave Sarah the shears Vita gave me when we got married and told her what to do."

"Yes, and I took them out of her purse."

Marguerite's eyes got wide. "No! Tell me you didn't do that!" She was mortified. Sarah would be looking everywhere for those shears.

They couldn't help but laugh!

At the same time, the boys all felt what was happening. They knew their father had just told their mother what he had done. They all met in the hall and were laughing. They just thanked God it would be a while before they had to think of what to do when their own daughters got married.

"Margaret is never getting married," Zac said. "I will not allow it."

Zeke said, "Mary either. She is going to a nunnery."

"I'm not letting any boy in the house to see Jess," Mark said. "Ever!"

Matt nodded. "Right. Amelia's not going anywhere near boys. That will never happen!"

The four of them all laughed and hugged like they were in a huddle. Then all the little girls came out, took their fathers by the hand and said, "Come on, Dad! We're reading Cinderella before we go to bed." They all smiled as they went into Zac's room, where everyone was camped out to read Cinderella. All the girls had their dad's wrapped around their little fingers. All the dad's knew it, they just wouldn't admit it out loud.

Zac's wife, Anne, knew what Chase was planning because she always felt it when her husband couldn't control his emotions, and when he'd found out what his father had done, he'd been terribly thrilled and amused.

So she got together with the other sister-in-laws—Ari, who was Zeke's wife, Catherine, who was Mark's wife, and Cali, who was Matt's wife—to do something about it. They went to Sarah and gave her the only thing they could come up with at the last minute: a pair of the children's safety scissors. Sarah hid them under the mattress of her honeymoon bed. They all smiled at how sly they were. They laughed about it while hugging and kissing each other.

Of course, their husbands felt what they had done, and smiled mischievously, plotting their next move.

A LETTER FROM THE AUTHOR

I am so honored you have chosen to read my book. The story stemmed from a dream I had one night. Weeks later that dream was still on my mind, so I felt I had to finally sit down and write it out—even having never written a novel before.

Thoughts about Chase and Marguerite flooded my mind day and night. The one thing I want everyone to feel about them is—how much they loved each other—along with that special gift they had that banded them together. How precious they thought their life together was and how close they were to all of Chase's band mates and their wives whom they treated as brothers and sisters.

When I first read a book—I find I breeze through it because I just want to find out what happens in it. Then I go back and read it again catching everything I missed the first time. And it always surprises me on all I missed.

Go back and read this book again. There are so many things going on and I don't want you to miss one kiss between them. Don't overlook one time they express their love for each other with "You are the very air I breathe." It will be worth it. I guarantee it!

I hope you love this story as much as I loved writing it.

Pay attention to Ed their best friend.

Just maybe his story will be next!

Fondly

Marguerite

ABOUT THE AUTHOR

Inspired to write this story by a dream she simply couldn't get out of her head, Marguerite Nardone Gruen has enjoyed every step of this journey, laughing and crying along with her characters as they slowly took shape and came to life. While writing the final line was bittersweet, she is thrilled to share this dream, and its heart, with her readers.

Marguerite is an avid football fan, and loves March madness college basketball—almost as much as spending time with her ten nieces and nephews and their children. She lives with her husband of 35 years, in Pennsylvania.